£6.60

CW00925701

THE WITCHING STONE

HUGO McEWEN

THE WITCHING STONE

HAMISH HAMILTON · LONDON

HAMISH HAMILTON

Published by the Penguin Group
Penguin Books Ltd, 27 Wrights Lane, London w8 5TZ, England
Penguin Books USA Inc., 375 Hudson Street, New York, New York 10014, USA
Penguin Books Australia Ltd, Ringwood, Victoria, Australia
Penguin Books Canada Ltd, 10 Alcorn Avenue, Toronto, Ontario, Canada M4V 3B2
Penguin Books (NZ) Ltd, 182–190 Wairau Road, Auckland 10, New Zealand

Penguin Books Ltd, Registered Offices: Harmondsworth, Middlesex, England

First published 1992
1 3 5 7 9 10 8 6 4 2

Copyright © Hugo McEwen, 1992

The moral right of the author has been asserted

Filmset in 11/12 pt Monophoto Bembo

Printed in England by Clays Ltd, St Ives plc

A CIP catalogue record for this book is available from the British Library

ISBN 0-241-13036-0

To C.M. and The Wheeb

With heartfelt thanks to Poon, Tash, Peeps, Kate,
Gill, Colin Murray and Mr Adams, for their help
patience, perseverance, ideas and snippets of
inspiration

CONTENTS

BOOK ONE

I

CRAIGAIRIE

Places reminded him.

Places and smells.

The latter had a less immediate effect, on the whole; a gradual re-awakening of long-dormant memories associated with a particular odour, a particular moment. They would sneak through his sinuses before he knew what was happening and cut like cold knives into the tender part of his mind where she still held sway.

He had defences against the places; not fail-safe defences, admittedly, but enough to keep him sane. He simply did not go to some of the nightclubs and restaurants they had been wont to frequent together. And some pubs and some streets and some parks and some parts of the city.

The river was to be avoided at all costs.

When it came down to it he could barely move from his flat in Chelsea without returning in misery. His defences against any specific places only scratched the surface of his phobia for London at that moment. Five years he had been in love in this city. Over sixty-two months of his life had been spent indiscriminately plastering memories around it.

Now that they were coming home to roost they did so like rooks in autumn; black and raucous and in flocks. There were so many places to which he could pin a memory that they had ceased to be plural and had become one huge, all-encompassing singular.

London.

Music hurt as well.

For him it was yet another bitter irony of their parting that he did not even have the solace of music to fall back on, when all else failed. He had hundreds of records and tapes, but he could hardly touch any of them. She was there, all over them, behind every lyric and tune, talking, laughing, smiling, loving him.

He missed her terribly, agonizingly. He could close down his emotions, like a city struck by a power cut, and succumb to lethargic gloom. But if one light flickered on, if one spark awoke in him, he knew that the whole lot might follow suit, blinding him with his loss. He could lock himself up like a fortress and deny access to anyone or anything which would upset him; but there was a dragon at the gate, waiting for a chance to charge in and shatter his fragile equilibrium.

It haunted the city while he was awake and twisted his dreams when he slept. He was dazed by it, too numb to make any but the most mundane judgements or decisions. He was separated from the world, enveloped in a tiny little invisible aura of loneliness and depression which was entirely his own.

It had been so sudden, at least for him. She had fallen in love with someone else. She told him when he recovered from his jet-lag after arriving back from South America. She went over the past eighteen months of their affair with the detachment of a one-woman jury, tracing in intricate detail each little lurch towards its eventual demise.

He listened in silence.

He had known things had been rough, but he had made the mistake of thinking that because he was barely pulling through, she would be doing likewise. He had never for a second imagined that she would go all the way down the road to the point where she could see no choice but to leave him. They had problems, not least his incessant travelling, but there was never anything he considered to be insurmountable.

His travelling had summed up their fights; he had never wanted to do that job, but she had bullied him and cajoled him and flattered him, trying to realize a picture of him she had formed for herself, regardless of his feelings. He had gone to the interviews, done his apprenticeship and then, to everyone's amazement, had proved to be quite a good journalist. When he quit his job for some squalid ex-Fleet-Street rag he had sworn never to report again; he didn't need that kind of hassle. But television had been different; the jobs had been infinitely more interesting and, for a while, the excitement and adrenalin had kept him on the move almost constantly.

When things had been going well she was quite happy to take the credit for his success, but now she complained about it, in a ladylike way. She had said that she was no good at long-distance love affairs, that a voice on the telephone and a face on a television screen was no substitute for the real thing.

Her new beau lived in town, apparently.

He had wanted to argue with her grinding logic, but she killed any chance of a debate by adding that she had meant to leave him anyway, despite the new love interest.

'The practical side followed the urge, rather than vice versa,' she had said.

She was always big on aphorisms.

He could not fight this. His habitual attitude of laissez-faire optimism could not bring him through this. There would be no more 'one more times', no more attempts to work out what was going wrong.

4

It was over. She was gone.

The emptiness hit him in waves. She had become a habit, like a drug and he was simply not equipped for the scale of the withdrawal.

She had left him without having an idea of the totality of his addiction. She had torn the bottom out of his life in the space of one short lunch, cutting the umbilical cord which connected them with little more than a perfunctory apology. Even the setting for this cold-blooded assassination, a very expensive brasserie in Chelsea, was vintage Natasha. She knew he would not overreact there. She knew how easily manipulated he was on her home turf. There were few places Natasha was safer than in that brasserie, in any brasserie for that matter; knock 'spritzer' from her vocabulary and her social life would have been in tatters. Even at the moment she was formally relinquishing her grip on him, she still had him by the balls.

He had tried writing to her, but the letters invariably degenerated into a mush of hopeless entreaties. His bins were full of them. He wrote short, simple, wretched poems to her and scrawled half-articulated thoughts on random pages of his notebooks. He could not forgive her for giving up on him.

Months passed without the misery decreasing. The waves of emptiness came less often, but with no less intensity when they did come. In between there was an awful lot of lethargy, thinly disguised as a sabbatical from work. After three months in South America making eight documentaries, back-to-back, he was sufficiently drained to deserve a rest and to require one.

But the job was over for him; it had been over long before he left South America. The fact that Natasha had left him just served to steel his resolve. He had laid his work on the altar of his obsessive love for her and had lived for his homecomings. Without her to come home to, there was no longer any point in risking his life halfway across the world. His motives for doing what he did had been a mixture of compassion for his subjects and an increasing addiction to adrenalin, but Natasha had been the force which drove him, week by week, year by year.

He had been to Cuba, Azerbaijan, Botswana, Eritrea, Mozambique, South Africa, South America, Libya, Iran, Iraq, Beirut. On just his second job he had been the only western journalist covering the first week of the Tibetan revolution. The visas in his passport read like a blacklist of war and terrorism the world over, for the past five years.

David Armstrong was a good journalist, with a good camera crew, but it was his unnerving ability to be in the wrong place at the right time, coupled with an almost insane courage, in the eyes of his peers, which set him a little way clear of the pack. The basic difference between him and any other reporter was a question of distance; usually a question of about two hundred yards closer to the gunfire than anyone else doing the same sort of job, according to his long-suffering crew. He did not believe he was doing his job properly if he was not in at least as much danger as the subjects whose plight he was reporting. After a few months of vomiting out of sheer terror or wetting himself, or worse, he had come to the conclusion that if old women and kids could continue to live normally in a place like Beirut then he could live with a bit of gunfire. The first time he had witnessed a person being killed he had wept like a child for an entire night, but the last time, days before leaving South America, he had felt little more than a dull resentment. What had started as a virtual one-man crusade against inhumanity and injustice, anywhere on earth he could find it, had slowly, insidiously become a job. He reached a stage when he had been scared witless, or gripped by a powerless, bitter rage, in so many different 'trouble-spots' that he ceased to be able to distinguish between one war and the next. After a while they all looked the same.

The final straw had been six months earlier, on his last job before the South American series. He had been in the foyer of a hotel, on the first morning of a brief sojourn in Bahrain with two American journalists, when they were gunned down by masked terrorists in front of his eyes.

These people had names and characters. He knew their girlfriends. He had been stoned with them in two thirds of the countries in the Middle East, over a nine-month period. They were good friends. One minute they were alive, the next they were a mess.

Then came South America. It had taken three months, but there had always been a strong element of finality, of this being his swan-song. He had taken some idiotic risks and had produced eight documentaries which even his boss, Rachel Ifbak, had grudgingly admitted were 'straight As'. He had wanted to batter some of the horrors of the world into the living rooms of England, he wanted to make each documentary so shatteringly immediate that people back home had no choice but to feel as he did. After that he would try no more.

Whatever happened he had no intention of working for Channel Seven Cable News station again. After a couple of months moping in his flat he was not sure if he felt capable of holding down any job again, let alone one in which he was regularly shot at, arrested, beaten up and monitored by governments whose respect for the press was usually limited to a garotte after some heavy sole-battering with rubber pipes. He said as much to Rachel Ifbak, at least three times, when she rang to ask when he would be back. She did not appear to take him seriously.

As far as Rachel Ifbak and others at Channel Seven were concerned, David was due a sabbatical, but they were buggered, to quote one executive, if they were going to let him slip through their fingers without a fight. He had been threatening to produce something of the calibre of his South American reports for some time and had accrued something of a notoriety in the business as one of its most talented under-achievers. It made no sense for him to quit just when he seemed to be realizing his full potential.

Rachel's persistence prompted him, finally, to go around to Channel Seven and hand in his resignation formally, in person. It was an unsatisfactory meeting, just as theirs had been a thoroughly unsatisfactory relationship. He liked her enough, but she was so diametrically opposite to him in so many different ways that they rarely failed to annoy each other. This problem was compounded by the fact that she was frightened of him, or at least deeply disconcerted by his attitude to life, and he knew it. She could not comprehend his lack of ambition; he had turned down the chair in which she now sat twice before she finally came along. He had never participated in office politics, had never asked to be promoted, except to demand more important jobs by dint of being the only person around willing to do them well.

His sudden decision to quit was in keeping with the apparently arbitrary way he went about his career and his life. People considered him to be a loner, but that was too simplistic; he seemed to be performing his life as a one-man play, with himself as its only audience. Rachel had once heard someone remark that David was so good at being himself one tended to forget how much work went into it and, although the full implications of this insight eluded her, she remembered it whenever he was being inexplicable. It was comforting, somehow, to think he was posturing, rather than being gratuitously unpredictable, as often seemed to be the case.

The same person who had made the remark had added, almost in the same breath, that Rachel had an oddly lopsided view of David, because she made him defensive, which in turn made him uncharacteristically belligerent. She was the part of his job he suffered, rather than the part he enjoyed.

He had not meant to fight with her when he went to hand in his notice. He had intended to go in, drop it on her desk and leave, but she wanted to discuss it and the discussion inevitably turned sour.

'Why are you doing this, David?' she had asked. 'Is it Natasha, or what?'

'This has nothing to do with Natasha,' he replied, with an ominous flicker of anger. 'And even if it did, it would have nothing to do with you.'

'It's to do with me if I let you walk out of here without this.' She waved his letter of resignation at him. 'Besides, I know Natasha. I can understand it if you're hurt.'

'Don't patronize me,' he snapped. 'I quit. Read my lips, Rachel.'

She stared at him, as if trying to read his mind.

'I don't understand it, David,' she replied. 'Is it like someone's offered you something better? Is that what this is about?'

He stared back at her in genuine consternation for a few seconds, then shook his head.

'You don't get it, do you? You think this is reality?' He waved his hand around. 'A job, a career, a mortgage, a suitable marriage, maybe some kids, all built on peddling emotive pictures of wars and famines in places no one's ever heard of. You're so cushioned that you think all that stuff I've been sending you is just news, programme-fodder.' He shook his head slowly. 'Well it isn't. It's real and ugly and I'm sick of it. I have to go somewhere quiet where I can just lie back and forget all this shit.'

'Where, for instance?' she asked sarcastically.

He shrugged. 'I'll follow my nose,' he said. 'Maybe I'll go home.'

'Home to Scotland?' There was disbelief in her voice, as if she could think of nothing on earth more absurd and distasteful.

'Home to where I belong,' he replied defensively.

'Don't give me that bullshit, David,' Rachel said. 'You're running away, pure and simple. Don't make it sound any more romantic than that.'

It was not the perfect approach to take with David and he dealt with it perfunctorily.

'Fuck off, Rachel,' he replied, and left.

After that meeting he stormed around his flat for a couple of hours, remembering all the put-downs he had meant to use on Rachel Ifbak. He then sat down, consumed the best part of a bottle of whisky and began to think about leaving London.

The idea of going home to Scotland seemed, for about the first third of the bottle, to make perfect sense. He remembered the wide open spaces, the immediacy of nature, the wild beauty of the hills and the moors, and the emptiness. It was a long time since he had been back, since he had come south, fresh and callow, feeling like an innocent abroad and sounding like Sean Connery.

He remembered the geese coming in to the Solway in October, tens of thousands of them converging from all directions, each voice raised into a huge cacophony, like a paean to autumn. He remembered the hills of Nithsdale turning purple and dusty as the summer grew old, the pubs full of leather-faced farmers who filled your glass again and again and again – the only people David had ever met who could be funny about sheep and pheasants.

The idea of returning to that life appealed to him. He craved silence.

Then he remembered the reality.

Home to sunny Gretna, the wettest place in Britain, into the encircling arms of his mother; the prodigal son returneth. For a while he would be fêted, then seven long years would drop off his life and everything would return to the way it always had been. He would inevitably bicker with his father, who had never really forgiven himself, or David, for the metamorphosis of his only son from the budding manager of textile mills he was supposed to have been, into a city hooray with a funny accent and an even funnier set of values.

8

Then there were all the people he had left when he was eighteen, when he went off to university, still doing the same things, seeing the same people and exchanging the same sort of gossip nine years later. Every time he went home it depressed him how far apart he had grown from his childhood friends. It was almost as hard for him to describe a war in Botswana to them as it was for them to interest him in a new type of fertilizer.

Then there was Mama. She would do her mother hen impression once again – tuck him into bed every night, drag him to mass every second day, worry about his eating habits, his lifestyle, the state of his soul; suffocate him.

He didn't feel up to it.

But Scotland still held an attraction lacking in almost all the other alternatives. It was home, for a start. David had not exorcised his upbringing in Dumfriesshire so much that he had forgotten his Scottishness. There was a phrase that had been one of his mainstays when he was depressed and halfway across the world from home. It had come up in a conversation he once had with four friends, a Canadian, a Greek, an Australian and another Scot, about how and where they wanted to be buried. The Canadian wanted to be cremated and his ashes scattered across a lake in British Columbia; the Greek wanted to be buried at sea; the Australian said that he wanted his body to be left on top of an appropriate mountain and devoured by eagles. The Scot just said, 'Bury my heart at Hampden.'

One way or another David Armstrong wanted to get back to his roots. The decision, like the original impulse, was sudden. David got up one morning in October, prowled around his flat for a couple of hours, then went out to the nearest estate agent and put it on the market. He also described, to an increasingly disbelieving yuppie, the kind of house, somewhere in south-west Scotland, he wanted to buy.

Remote was the key word.

Three weeks later he took the shuttle to Glasgow, hired a car and drove down through Ayrshire into Galloway, to see a house his estate agent had described as 'your baby'. As he drove south the population seemed to spread itself more thinly over harder, wilder country. By the time he reached Barrhill, the town in which he was to meet his guide to the house, he found himself on the edge of a large expanse of wide, empty moors. This was Carrick, an untamed corner of southern Scotland bounded by the Merrick Hills on the east and the Clyde coast on the west. It was a part of Scotland David did not know, although he was born less than a hundred miles away, but it was rich in all the romantic history he had been taught as a child. Robert Bruce had been Earl of Carrick and had reputedly seen his spider on Rathlin Island, off the northern coast of Ulster, only fifty miles away across the North Channel, within sight of his earldom. Robert Burns was a local man; the last Pict, according to legend, had leapt off the cliffs of the Mull of Galloway rather than divulge the secret Pictish recipe for heather ale.

David was in love even before he reached the house. It was a beautiful, crystalline, autumn afternoon, with frost still lying on the southern slopes of the valleys, out of reach of the low sun. The trees still held on to the last vestiges of their autumnal regalia and the quick, dark rivers were patterned with red and copper and gold, carrying the fallen leaves out to the sea.

Barrhill was basically a one-horse town marking the point where the only road through the Merrick Hills crossed the river Duisk (pronounced disc which, David thought cheerfully, was typically Scottish) and left the more fertile coastal lowlands.

The person who met David was a phlegmatic young man in a suit and overcoat, driving a four-wheel-drive Japanese car, who seemed to find this sojourn in the sticks faintly distasteful. He shook David firmly by the hand and immediately advised him to change cars.

'The roads in aren't what they might be,' he said.

There were two roads in to the house, which was called Craigairie. The more direct was on a Forestry Commission track straight from Barrhill to within half a mile of the house, six miles away. The other was a round trip on a minor road which wound over the moors from Barrhill to Glenluce, down on the Solway coast. After about six miles out of Barrhill they swung left, on to a dirt track, which then found an uneven path through the forestry to Craigairie Valley.

The valley, after the dull monotony of regimented Christmas trees, was like a tiny pocket of the ancient landscape surviving in the middle of an eternity of man-made forests. It was about three miles long, bounded by low hills, with a long view back towards the Merrick Hills and the serried ranks of sitka spruces sitting on the far horizon, like a grim army waiting to plunge down into the valley.

The house itself sat in amongst a scrawny copse of Scots pines; a compact little two-storey cottage with a small square garden in front of it and a wide courtyard formed by low outbuildings protecting the back door.

'We should've come in the hired car,' David remarked as they pulled up with a muddy splash which made the estate agent wince.

'Mebbe,' he said, pulling on the handbrake and opening his door, 'if we'd both known it was a hired car.'

David climbed out, smiling slightly, and they stood on either side of the car for a minute, looking at the house.

'D'you mind if I go in alone?' David asked at last.

'Be my guest.'

When the door had been unlocked for him David went in and found himself in a long room, the length of the house, with an open fire and 'dining area' at one end, and an Aga and kitchen area at the other.

'Does that work?' he asked over his shoulder.

'What?' his taciturn companion asked from outside.

'The Aga.'

'On oil.'

'And how d'you get oil out here?'

'You don't need to very often,' came the reply. 'But when you do, you ask nicely.'

David nodded and went on through the house. There were two possible sitting rooms at the front, looking out across the valley. Apart from the dark fitted carpets there was no furniture or decoration, but the house seemed dry and not particularly cold. Upstairs there were four bedrooms and a bathroom – or perhaps three bedrooms, a large cupboard and a bathroom. There seemed to be more space inside the cottage than its external size allowed for. The bedrooms all had sloping ceilings, two of them had open fires with deep window recesses looking across the valley.

David stood in the master bedroom and gazed out over moors for fully five minutes, deep in thought, before he took in what he was looking at. A little river looped its way along the valley floor, through reed beds and around outcrops of rock and the steep hillsides, then dived suddenly into a series of pools between well-grown beeches, birches and oaks. Above the point where the river began to steepen and quicken, on the far hillside almost opposite the house, there was an unmistakable standing stone. Even as his mind registered the stone David experienced a dizzying attack of *déjà vu*.

It felt like home.

Four hours later he was back on the shuttle to London, a small file of bumf on Craigairie Cottage lying in front of him, wondering how quickly he could uproot himself from the south and install himself in a farmhouse in Scotland. Two months, he thought, to do the uprooting, then six months to a year to get used to it, once he was there.

As he contemplated this suddenly very immediate prospect he remembered something the estate agent had said as they parted in Barr-hill.

'I feel I ought tae warn you . . .' he began. He shrugged as if dismissing the warning in advance. 'I mean, it's just country gossip, but Craigairie's got a peculiar reputation locally. It's been rented out every summer for fifteen years, but no one's lived in it properly for a good twenty. They call it "Purgatory" round here; something to do with it once having been a leper colony, back in the Middle Ages. People say it's haunted.'

'But you don't?' David had asked.

'Ach, it's naething,' he said, his accent slipping right back into broad Gallowegian for a second. 'It's a long way from anywhere out here. I'm told the wind sounds like voices sometimes and things go bump in the night unexpectedly. You'd be amazed how spooked people can get by an owl in the loft, or the like.'

'No, I wouldn't,' David murmured. 'So what you're telling me is that no one around here would live up there, because it's haunted?'

The young estate agent looked at him for ten seconds, then nodded. 'Aye, that's what I'm saying.'

'Is that why the place is so cheap?'

For a moment David thought he might get a straight answer. The young man paused, just for a couple of seconds, then gave him a tight-lipped smile.

'Property's cheap around here, Mr Armstrong. It's what some might call a geographical cul-de-sac.'

On the whole David might have thought twice about buying himself a cottage which was reputed to be haunted, let alone one an estate agent had seen fit to warn him off – even if it had been rather a half-hearted attempt. But he knew before the plane touched down in London that Craigairie was meant to be his home. It was not so much love-at-first-sight as instant recognition. It was as if he had a trigger hidden in his sub-conscious, primed to go off only if he ever set eyes upon this one cottage.

There were more orthodox ways of coming to a decision, David realized, but he had always been a creature of instinct, when it came to how he ran his life. Besides, he had set his mind to the problem of getting out of London almost as if to prove to himself that he was still capable of making a decision and sticking by it. Now that Craigairie had stuck itself in his mind there was no going back.

Inevitably, word got round.

People began to call his answering machine, leaving messages which ranged from surprise to ridicule. Nobody seemed to believe that it was possible to live outside Greater London. The general gossip was that David had 'maybe had a bit of a breakdown' and needed to be dissuaded from making a commitment he might later regret.

He had anticipated this sort of reaction on the plane down from Scotland, which was why he left his answering machine on. It was not that he thought someone might be able to change his mind, simply that he had better things to do than explain himself to society.

He had thought that the business of uprooting himself after so long would carry with it all sorts of unexpected pitfalls. He expected it to be harder to break the emotional bonds he had with London and with the people who had helped him to like the place. But the moment he started to clear his flat he realized that he had quite enough problems there, without going out and looking for more.

It was a considerably more traumatic experience than he had anticipated. He uncovered the last six years of his life slowly, painfully; buried in layers like strata in bedrock. He found bundles of letters, from his earliest love affairs through to Natasha, from his friends, his parents – small, disembodied snippets of his past.

He found things he had forgotten ever buying, tapes he had no recollection of making; articles, poems and even parts of novels he had once attempted to write, only to discard them when the initial momentum had been spent. He found cheque cards in a wallet he had reported stolen four years earlier. It still had an old five pound note in it and a garbled note, written on the back of a paper napkin, which read, 'Pick it up on Tuesday. May God rot your soul if you forget.'

Slowly, gaps appeared in his flat as mountains of rubbish were undermined and pushed out from the walls, cupboards and shelves into the middle of each room, like mini-landslides. He sifted through it all with a mixture of fascination and horror, packing up about a third of it and consigning the rest to a series of bin bags. A small pile of borderline cases on the bed in the spare room grew until it spilled on to the floor as he progressed.

When he was not engrossed in this he was running up a large overdraft based on a rough mathematical calculation he made between the bloated price he would get for the flat and the comparatively minuscule cost of a house in Scotland. The difference was more money than David had ever had at a single time, even after he had sunk a sizeable part of it into his overdraft.

He bought tables, armchairs, beds, a couple of carpets, a new hi-fi, a job-lot of expensive tools, fire-guards, lamps, cutlery, some records he had always meant to buy, but had never got around to it. Everything, in fact, that caught his eye. As a foil for the clearing of the flat it was the perfect pastime.

He went up to Scotland three times, staying in a hotel outside Barrhill, partly to lead the transport of his life up north, partly to finalize the purchase of Craigairie and five acres around it and partly to reassure himself. Each time his initial attraction to the place was re-affirmed, growing until, on his third visit, it became almost uncanny. He kept having the same spasms of *déjà vu* he had on his first visit, not revealing where they came from but coming with the frequency of long-dormant memories. He knew he had never been there before, except perhaps in a previous life – which was a concept he was only willing to toy with. But he knew he was meant to be there.

He returned to London for the last time at the end of November and felt like a stranger. He spent a week saying goodbye, which was monotonous rather than actively unpleasant. Only one person, his long-term friend and cameraman, who came from Dundee, drank a lot of whisky and spoke more sense than anyone else David knew in London, bothered to ask him why he was doing this and then listened to his answer. He sat on the floor of an empty flat shortly before David was to leave, watching as the last scraps were tucked into the last packing cases.

'Have you really thought this thing out, Davie?' he asked.

'No,' David replied, his back to him. After a moment of contemplation he added, 'I've tried not to. I figured if I sat down and cold-bloodedly weighed up the pros and cons I'd end up thinking about it for six months, then forgetting it.' He paused in the act of stuffing a mug with newspapers. After a second he turned and said, 'It *feels* good, you know? I'm not sure I need anything more substantial than an instinctive feeling I'm doing the right thing. Besides, whatever I do, it couldn't possibly be worse than the last six months in this city.'

'Couldn't you just have rented a place? I mean it all sounds a bit . . . radical.'

David thought about this for a while before answering, his voice betraying his doubt.

'It *is* radical,' he replied. 'It's meant to be.'

Christina MacRuarie was bored; bored and restless. She prowled around the small sitting room like a caged animal, picking things up and then putting them down somewhere else, apparently unconscious of what they were or what she was doing.

She lit a cigarette, took a couple of drags and then placed it in an ashtray, where it lay unattended until its ash was like a tiny fallen pillar, two inches long, lying over the other stubs.

She lit another one.

Wandering to the window, she gazed out through the rain-spattered glass into the half darkness, where curtains of rain were sweeping up the valley from the sea.

Ever since she had come home from Paris the weather had been foul. It had taken her about a week before she remembered exactly why she had lived abroad since leaving school almost seven years earlier. Another fortnight had only served to prove the point.

After that she was into unknown territory.

Home was dull.

But home she was now, for better or for worse, and for the foreseeable future. It seemed unlikely that this virtual house-arrest would be lifted, at least before Christmas.

It was October now.

She had been unwell. She was the first to admit that her life had hit a rocky spell. But she felt much better now and if she spent much more time here she thought it more likely that she would have a relapse, if only out of sheer boredom.

The feeling of depression and lethargy was an extremely uncomfortable bedfellow with the unabated maelstrom which had been raging inside her head for the past six months.

She had come home; correction, she had been forced to come home when reports had begun to filter back to Scotland that her normal eccentricity was rapidly snowballing into near-madness. If she hadn't already suffered a breakdown, then she was very close to one. The people who went to see her confirmed this and advised her parents to get her back before someone got hurt.

It was a matter of general agreement that Erlend's death had brought this on. Erlend MacRuarie, her surrogate brother and part-time husband, had been killed in a motorcycle accident whilst driving back from a party outside Paris. This, in itself, would have been enough to seriously unhinge Christina: their effect on each other might never have seemed very wholesome, but it had been about living, even if the living in question had been frantically fast-moving.

The fact that she had been on the back of the motorcycle when Erlend crashed only served to rub salt into the wound. She had woken up in a field, shaken and concussed but otherwise uninjured, with a throbbing memory of blinding headlights, skidding tyres and a sickening crash.

She stood up and staggered to the wall they had hit. She found the place the bike had careered into, jack-knifing over the wall into the field. The bike itself, mangled and twisted now, lay about ten feet away in a trench caused by its own fall. Erlend lay to one side, face down in the mud, a broken huddle of humanity, still and cold. Among other things he had broken his neck.

The car which had caused this by failing to dip its headlights had not stopped.

Christina was barely scratched.

Erlend was dead.

Initially the shock of it so numbed her that she had been found about three miles from the accident, wandering down a dark country lane in a sort of stupefied daze.

Although the daze had modified itself in the days and weeks which followed, she never really shook it. It was as if doors had slammed shut all over her mind to protect her from reality. As this, to the eye of the untrained observer, was precisely how she lived her life anyway, the growing insanity of her behaviour had gone unnoticed for quite some time.

She still danced and spoke a lot, making unnervingly little sense in either. In her spare time, when some vestiges of normality punctured the afternoon haze of sinsemilla, she still painted bizarre and disturbing pictures. In these, a lurid mixture of colours swirled and rushed, occasionally congregating to do battle around what could only be described as the collages of a unique and perverse imagination.

Syringes, half-filled with red paint, dripped blood down the canvas, condoms of many shapes, sizes and colours hung in a bunch on a pin, like some nightmarish and long-dead plant. Faces, half-obscured by the violent colouring of the backdrop, peered blearily through as if from some private hell restricted to the canvas.

The paintings were good, in a crazed sort of way. Particularly if you happened to know the artist. Her agent liked them, which meant he thought he could sell them, but it was hard to tell what kind of person wanted such things in their sitting rooms, or worse, in their bedrooms. It would be somewhat like someone sitting on your mantelpiece having a nervous breakdown.

She did a lot of speed as well, which showed both on her face and on her canvases. She was like a bomb ticking noisily towards its inevitable explosion. She did not appear to be conscious of what she was doing, even when people were prompted to tell her.

It had to stop.

Her parents flew out, packed her bags and virtually manhandled her on to an aeroplane straight back to Glasgow. She was in a frighteningly fey mood, playing with death in the same way a baby reaches out towards a naked flame: curious, fascinated, serenely unaware of danger.

And so she was home in Ayrshire after a self-imposed exile of over six years.

After six weeks she was bored.

She had decided to write about how she felt. So far she had yet to get past the word Erlend; but she lived in hope. She sat for hours at a desk in her bedroom and gazed into space, paper blank and pen unused in front of her. Around her were the instruments which ensured her continued sanity, and her parallel buffers against reality; whisky, coffee mugs, cigarettes, dope, a little bit of speed a friend had sent.

She wept a lot. Not the self-indulgent shrieks of a petulant child deprived of its favourite toy, but sudden, unexpected ambushes of tears; without warning or solace. Again, on the whole, she did not really notice these attacks. They were spasms her body was making without permission or sympathy from her mind.

She had, however, noticed her last attack, which had been only minutes before she lit the cigarette and forgot to smoke it. She had been caught so much by the first lurching sob that she had developed violent hiccoughs. By the time she had got these under control she was weeping out of frustration. She gave up after a moment in confusion.

The subsequent joint had been the biggest one her shaking hands could roll. As a preventative this was usually quite effective, but it was a compromise all the same – pleasant but short-term.

It also helped her to cope with her mother, who was rapidly becoming the most tiresome person on earth.

Christina used every available opportunity to avoid her.

At the moment, thank God, she was charging around the country-side indulging in what her father was pleased to refer to as 'rampant squandermania': this meant that she was buying a lot of things she didn't need.

Compared to having her in the house all the time, ordering her family around, it was thought that this compulsive spending was a compromise everyone could learn to live with.

Meanwhile, Sir James embedded himself in his study and slowly, methodically sifted through five hundred and eighty years of family history which had, until recently, been gathering large quantities of dust in a makeshift overflow library in the attic. It was a gloriously fruitless task; the manuscripts and books were confused, jumbled and in poor condition, quite apart from being almost endless in number. Christina's elder sister, Georgina, had once referred to her father as a neurotic sisyphus. If this sort of classical simile was typical of her, it was almost unique in its accuracy.

So Christina was alone in the house. Daddy was in his study, which didn't really count, as it was about a quarter of a mile away and he was, to all intents and purposes, a quarter of a million.

She sighed and glanced at her watch and seemed to come to a decision. She turned and left the room for the first time in three hours. It was the sort of house wherein the small pockets of light and noise and life were separated by miles of dark corridors. Although Christina knew it was haunted and in some places this feeling was strong enough to quicken her pace, the darkness did not particularly bother her. She turned lights on regularly, one by one, as she walked, chasing the shadows into constant retreat in front of her.

She reached the main hall and paced across the acres of echoing stone. This was the oldest part of the house and was one of the places through which she usually ran. But she held on to herself on this occasion, determined not to succumb to anyone, man or spirit, who got their kicks by sneaking up on people in dark halls. At the far end she dived through a dark doorway and ran up a tight spiral staircase which led up to the Victorian extension of the house, a huge room on the second floor which housed the library, a billiard table and a small adjacent sitting room. It was a peculiar, hulking hybrid of a house; a medieval keep gentrified by Adam and then 'added' to by some maniac Victorian architect with a great eye for practicality and the aesthetic sense of a mad cow. He had slapped a wing on to the old keep in a space, he must have thought, left for him specifically by Adam. He only discovered the underground stream when he was laying the foundations and by then he was far too excited to stop. The ground floor had been intended as a drawing room until water started coming up through the floor, at which point it had been abandoned. Sir James had made the library his own, like his father before him, retreating from the over-inhabited west wing where his wife held sway.

Light slid under the door in a thin, yellow carpet when Christina

17

reached the otherwise dark landing, slightly breathless from the steep staircase. She stood for a moment, recovering her composure, then knocked.

'Come,' her father said from inside. She opened the door and went in. As she closed the door behind her a small smile flickered involuntarily across her lips. She always forgot how great this room was. A huge desk was strewn with papers, weighted down with a heavily ornate magnifying glass. A fire roared in the hearth, throwing a flickering red light into the armchairs and the leather sofa which surrounded it. The room smelled of old leather and fresh cigar smoke.

The sofa especially caught Christina's attention. It was large and deep and worn, so wide and long that it had easily accommodated Christina and her two siblings when they were children, playing such boisterous games as 'pushy-offy' and 'sinking ship', with room to spare.

In front of the fire, below the Raeburn painting of his great-great-grandfather, Sir James Graham, sometime politician and born again weird west-coast laird, stood and watched his daughter cross the room. He was an elegant man in his mid-sixties, not unlike Christina, who alone of her siblings took after him in both looks and temperament. They were both blond, they both had the grey eyes of his family and the pointed, Cleopatran nose Raeburn had captured four generations earlier. They were both tall. Sir James was a handsome, attractive man and Christina was a quietly lovely woman. They both shared the compulsive lethargy of his family.

They understood each other instinctively.

'You working?' she asked, sitting down on the sofa and sinking deep into it.

'No, not really,' he replied in the melodious voice which had done him so much good service on many a podium.

'D'you mind if I stay a while?' she asked.

Her father gazed at her for a while and shrugged slightly. 'Be my guest,' he said. He stifled a quick smile. 'So', he said, 'how's Countess Gertrude?' It was a favourite joke of his, likening Castle Graham and its inhabitants to Gormenghast. In many ways it was rather too close to the bone for comfort, when one started comparing in earnest, although Christina did not mind assuming the role of Fuchsia.

She jiggled her shoulders non-committally.

'Mummy's out,' she answered. 'All quiet on the western front.'

'Or the west wing, at least,' he replied. This time his faint smile hung around for long enough to exert some influence on the rest of his face. It was an attractive smile.

'Small mercies,' she said. 'Is she always this frantic?'

'Mostly,' came the laconic answer.

Christina moved, turning and straining her neck over the back of the sofa to see what was on his desk. He moved away from the fire, walking with bolster-straight legs because of the intense heat on the back of his trousers. He went to the drinks tray.

'Drink?' he asked.

'Is there any beer?'

'Beer?' His voice betrayed vague disgust. He ducked down to look at the lower shelf of the tray.

'McEwan's?' he inquired.

'That'll do just fine.'

He picked the can out, put it in a tumbler and handed it to her. He then watched with a slight frown as she cracked the ring-pull open and put her lips down to hoover up the froth as it emerged from the hole.

'You really do have some peculiar habits, Tina,' he said wonderingly.

She nodded. 'What're you reading?' She gesticulated towards the desk.

'Nothing much,' he said. 'Although . . .' he added, seeming to remember something interesting. He walked briskly over to the desk and began to sift eagerly through reams of paper. By what appeared to be a miracle, he unearthed the one he wanted almost immediately. He gave it to her with a small, unconscious flourish.

She looked at it for a moment, turned it over to make sure there was nothing on the back and gave it back to him.

'It's in Latin,' she said simply.

'They didn't teach you Latin at school?' he asked.

'They did but it never stretched to anything like this. It was more *Amo bellum*, that sort of thing.'

'I love war?' he persisted. 'All that money and they taught you to say I love war in Latin?'

'They would've taught us to say it in Swahili, given half a chance,' she said. 'What's in the document? It looks old.'

'Oh,' he said, regaining his thread. He looked at it for a moment, then pulled a pair of half-moon spectacles out of his inside pocket and put them on the end of his nose. He read it, then looked up at her, over the top of his lenses.

'It's very rare,' he said. 'It's very rare, *very* old, and I don't understand it.'

She waited for a bit and then realized he was not going to elaborate any further until she asked why he didn't understand it.

'What's odd about it?' she asked.

He made a dismissive gesture. 'Nothing really. It's just some undated letter from the Abbot of Crossraguel to the Bishop of Glasgow. I'd say probably in the late fifteenth century.'

'Should I know Crossraguel?' she asked.

'You know it,' he said. 'The ruined abbey outside Maybole, on the way to Glasgow.'

'Where they found the earliest laundry list in the world?' It was half a statement, half a question.

'In Scotland, I think,' he replied. 'And it was an inventory.'

'Not far off,' she said. 'Do go on.'

He continued. 'Anyway, it's fairly normal ecclesiastical stuff. Some bored abbot writing a report for his superiors on a cold winter night when he had nothing better to do.'

He thought for a moment.

'Terrible Latin,' he said. 'Bad spelling, illegible script, very clumsy; two out of ten. Typical backwoods stuff. Apart from a lot of stuff about the rapacious Kennedy family, there was an odd postscript concerning some Pagan, demonistic rituals going on up in the hills.' He stopped again, shaking his head slowly.

'Odd lot, the Gallowegians. An ancient and distinct race. You know, of course, that they spoke an entirely unique language until quite recently? Only a couple of hundred years ago, or so.'

Christina nodded, although it was news to her. To allow him off on one of his tangents at this point was to wander willingly into a completely different mire of local history.

'What kind of ritual?' she asked.

'Oh, the usual kind of things; virgin-sacrificing, dancing naked around standing stones, invoking Satan or something similar, that kind of thing. They were cannibalistic, of course.'

'Who were?' she asked. She regretted it even as the words left her lips. To her surprise and relief, however, he did not seem particularly disposed to elaborate any more than to say,

'The Gallowegians, of course ... Anyway, what struck me, strikes me, is the way he described it. He seemed so scared of one particular standing stone that he wanted a small crusade to go up into the hills, dig it up and stamp out its cult.' He looked down at the manuscript and translated instantaneously, '. . . so that the evil therein may be uprooted and dispersed for ever.'

Christina felt goose-pimples rise at the nape of her neck, spread to her arms and down her spine. She bit her lip.

'Isn't that standard stuff for medieval monks?' she asked, despite what some deeper instinct was telling her. 'I mean, anything they didn't understand was automatically assumed to be satanic.'

'In theory,' her father replied pensively. 'They were very superstitious. But even then they didn't usually refer to perfectly innocent standing stones in the middle of nowhere as dangerous, or foul, or . . .' He glanced down at the paper. '. . . Unclean.' He said the last word with a distaste which underlined it.

She thought for a few seconds. 'Strong stuff,' she said. 'Did they say where it was?'

'The stone? Somewhere down behind Barrhill.' He glanced at the manuscript again and read out 'Luce', pronouncing it in Latin: Luché. They both thought for a moment.

'Luce,' Christina said. 'L-U-C-E?'

'Glenluce,' her father said with a quick frown. 'You're right, of course. How silly of me.'

Somehow that conversation stuck in Christina's mind, appealing perhaps to the fey part of her emotions – the one which was on the ascendant at the moment. It was, however, the end of January before she did anything about it. She had meant to look into it before Christmas, but the complicated and lengthy planning for the festive season got in the way. Before she knew what was happening the house was suddenly packed with relatives, retired retainers and tinsel.

New Year came and went, a gloriously anarchic long weekend when any self-respecting Scot ought to have been indulging in an orgy of unabashed debauchery. If ever a Pagan ritual sneaked its way through to the present, Scottish New Year is the one that succeeded.

To Christina, who had good reason to turn her back on the previous year and draw a deep breath before the next one, it was a blessed relief. It was, however, over very soon, leaving the house confused by its own emptiness. It echoed more than normal, as if trying to compensate for the absence of noise which had suddenly descended.

After a while the emptiness began to get to her and she sank gradually, but inexorably, into a deep depression. She became more and more bound to her room, trying to paint and failing, trying to write and failing, trying to do anything which would take her mind off the dismal wailing of the wind in the chimneys and the incessant patter of rain on the windows.

After a fortnight of this she sank to her lowest ebb since the accident. All the impurities, the sickness of spirit she had thwarted for nine long months came out like some latent disease which had finally caught up with her. The countryside outside her bedroom window washed in and out of view, a bleary, grey landscape half-obscured by swathes of rains and wisps of mist which clung in cold tendrils around the black pine trees.

To Christina the weather reflected her mind. She allowed it to seep, like an insidious dampness, into her body, her bones, her soul. She welcomed it and wallowed in the way it coddled her misery. She felt herself caving in to the sense of hopelessness.

She would have been unbearable company, had she been strong enough to face her family at all. As it was, she gave them even more cause for concern by sitting in her room in a state of dazed exhaustion, chain smoking. In a matter of days she became grey and haggard, her eyes bruised with fatigue, her cheekbones standing out of her face, her hair lank and tangled. What was usually a finely moderated look of disinterested dishevelment now became the real thing. She didn't give a damn any more and it showed. All she could feel was the grey vacuum in her very core and the aching lethargy of her grief.

She had nightmares when she slept and lived a nightmare when she was awake. She would wake in the morning after an exhaustingly restless night with vague memories of the horrors her subconscious had shown her in her dreams. But waking did not so much disperse the night's mental torture as coagulate it into something with words.

Erlend was with her always, holding on to her, clawing at her back as if unwilling to let go of her even in death. And rather than trying to shake him she let him get a firmer grip.

However despairingly they tried, her family could not break through even the outer layers of her sorrow. On her side Christina ignored all attempts to communicate with her. When she spoke it was like a mechanical reflex action to any given question. It was as if all the circuits in her mind, apart from the ones which governed her immediate movements, were shut down until further notice.

And then, one morning she awoke from another private odyssey through the night with a clear image in her mind. She saw it as clearly as if she had just looked at it minutes before; a standing stone about fifteen feet high. She could see its shape and texture, even its colour, slate stained with dirty, green lichen. She could see the shallow hollow it stood in and the hillside in which the hollow nestled, a long escarpment, barren and treeless, overlooking a small, winding river. On the far side of the river the hillside climbed up again through thigh-deep bracken into coarse heather. Right on the horizon, stretching for miles in both directions, the opposite hillside was lined with serried rows of sitka spruce Christmas trees – the indelible rash on the landscape created by the Forestry Commission. But below these, slightly lower down than the stone, was a gaunt copse of wiry Scots pines standing alone on a shelf of level ground, with a white cottage in the middle.

Christina remembered all of this as she lay in bed. She remembered the feeling of tranquillity the place had exuded, even into her troubled sleep. She knew, somehow, it was the place her father had spoken of and she also knew that Erlend had found his way into her dream to show it to her. He wanted her there and she felt that, having waited so long for such a sign, she had no choice but to go.

For the first time in months she felt at peace.

She got out of bed and opened the curtains. It had snowed during the night, laying a soft, white blanket on the countryside. The sun was shining in a sapphire blue sky, the countryside was sparkling.

Again the weather appeared to have followed her mood.

She smiled.

She had a bath, washed her hair and then dressed in warm clothes. She even put on some eye make-up.

She then took a deep breath and went downstairs for breakfast. Her father was in the breakfast room alone, the debris of his repast all around him. He was reading a large newspaper, but he stopped and watched her over the rims of his spectacles as she came in. She poured herself a cup of coffee, took it to an unused place in front of the fire and sat down. She lit a cigarette.

'You smoke too much,' he said, folding his newspaper and finding a space on the table in front of him to discard it.

'I guess,' she replied. She nodded to the windows. 'Nice day.'

'Cold,' he said simply.

She shrugged. 'It's winter.'

Although her father raised his eyebrows he did not reply.

'I thought I might go and look for your standing stone,' she said.

He leant back in his chair and studied her for a moment before nodding.

'What a good idea,' he said. 'You don't happen to feel like taking your brother with you, by any chance?'

'Ed? No way.' She sounded emphatic. 'Why?'

'He tires me,' Sir James remarked.

'He's hyperactive, like Mummy. It's all that junk food he insists on eating.'

'I think it's public school,' her father said. 'If I'd wanted a human dynamo for a son I'd've plugged him into the mains and let him get on with it.' He said it deadpan, in a monotone.

After breakfast the two of them pored over a large map of the locality which hung in a downstairs cloakroom. Between them they narrowed the possibilities down to a moor at the head of a river called Tarf Water. It was near to a large Forestry Commission plantation on Craigairie Fell, behind the small town of Barrhill. It was less than twenty miles across country from Crossraguel Abbey. There were one or two other standing stones in the area, and a few neolithic sites, but all of them were already engulfed in new forestation. Christina was adamant that the stone was clear of any plantations and her father acquiesced without asking why she was so sure. The fact that she was going outside at all was reason enough to humour her.

David never expected Craigairie to give him the emotional roller-coaster ride which it gave him in his first three months there. When he had left London he breathed a huge sigh of relief, glad to have shaken himself free of the social and spiritual incarceration he had accepted for so long in that city. He felt free, unshackled. But Craigairie soon presented him with such a wide range of unexpected problems that any thought of its being relaxing soon evaporated, to be replaced with a hard will to cope.

For a start there were a host of mundane chores, on a day-to-day basis, which consumed his time and necessitated some fundamental altera-tions in his behaviour. For instance, he had forgotten how inclement

23

Scotland can be in the winter. In London, when it was cold or damp, he had twiddled the thermostat in the kitchen and put a match to the gas-burning imitation log fire in his sitting room. At Craigairie, however, heat and warmth were not so easy to come by. He never expected to spend so much of his time chopping logs, chopping kindling wood, fetching coal, building and lighting fires then cleaning out the ashes the following morning. The elements gave him a baptism of wind for his first couple of months, besieging the cottage with a continuous gale. It rained, sleeted, snowed, finding any chinks in Craigairie's armour and exploiting them, leaking through the tiniest holes, into the house. It was like being caught in a sea-tempest in a small but sturdy boat; there was never any danger that Craigairie would cave in under the pressure, but it sustained some minor structural damage and needed to be maintained constantly, otherwise it soon reverted to a kind of cool dampness, inhabitable but uncomfortable.

Then there was the matter of cleaning up after his own mess; cans, empty bottles, books, newspapers, cigarette packets, ashtrays, coffee mugs, unwashed plates, dust, teaspoons . . . always a plethora of teaspoons. Somehow it all contrived to look homely before he went to bed every night; there seemed to have been an order in the way that things were strewn about, according to their accessibility, relative to wherever he had chosen to spend the largest part of the evening. The next morning, however, any order he might have perceived had vanished, to be replaced by a mess. In London there had been a cleaning lady who periodically blitzed his chaos, leaving his flat pristine, like a clean blackboard to be scrawled upon all over again.

In Craigairie there was no cleaning lady, no feminine eye for dust and unsightliness. Failure to do the housework on a relatively regular basis, the washing up, dusting, hoovering, making of his bed, cleaning of the bath and a hundred other things, soon resulted in an accumulation of debris not even David could live with. For a man who had never considered his pathological untidiness to be a problem, it required a basic shift in his attitude to house-pride. If catching the mess before it became unmanageable meant climbing a mental Matterhorn every three days, that was preferable to scaling Everest every week.

There were countless other things which had once been unthinkingly simple in London and now became so time-consuming that they required advance planning and thought before they could be achieved. Shopping had to be done in bulk, rather than when whim or necessity forced him to buy what he needed or wanted. After six in the evening, for example, the nearest shop open late was eighteen miles from Craigairie. Even basics like cigarettes, newspapers, milk and booze, which had entailed a five-minute walk in London, now meant a twelve-mile round trip. Not even his post, such as it was, came to his door.

He was more isolated than he had ever been in his life before. Emotionally the experience of being alone and static was wholly new to David. Loneliness had never been a problem for him — as long as he had something time-consuming and comparatively constructive to occupy his mind, he was quite content with his own company. Sometimes it was frustrating not to have somebody with whom he could share a good mood, or admire a sunset, or wake up beside. But for five years of wandering around the world on his own he had considered these a quirk of his trade and he had learned to recognize the beginnings of boredom, depression and loneliness and scotch them before they had time to gather pace.

That was when he was on the move for up to eight months every year.

Craigairie was different. He had to be more flexible with himself, allowing himself enough room to let his moods fling themselves around more. There was no point in trying to obliterate any negativity which sneaked into his mind when and if it reared its head. Shoving it back down only meant it would pop up somewhere else, in a different form. He had to meet his moods head on, analyse them, dissect them and finally shelve them. He could not run anywhere to escape himself, except on to empty moors.

The winter dragged on. David occupied his spare time writing a series of reports on Third World governments he had rashly agreed to do for a human rights organization. He began to feel quite settled.

Then Delilah moved in.

When the estate agent who had shown the cottage to David back in the autumn had mentioned, as if in passing, that the locals considered Craigairie and its immediate environs to be 'peculiar', he made one of the world's great understatements. Craigairie was not just peculiar, or even positively bizarre. It was seriously haunted. At first he ignored the bumps and bangs, even the localized cold spots in the cottage, putting them down to a combination of the wild weather and unseen flaws in the structure of the house.

He flirted, for a while, with the idea that the inexplicable noises were a figment of his imagination. As he began to notice them and wonder about them, a little rational voice of reason would increasingly chastise him for being paranoid.

But they became gradually more frequent. Furniture and ornaments would move out of place during the night. Lights turned themselves on and off, doors opened by themselves, or slammed shut.

And if the cottage behaved strangely, it was no alternative to run out on to the hills. The locals called it Purgatory, with justification. There were times when, in broad daylight, he was so scared that he was petrified, rooted to the spot. There were times when it made his hair stand on end, the skin on his neck, shoulders and spine crawl and his heart stop. It was electrifying, like stepping on an invisible pressure pad and suddenly finding oneself drawing the pointed attention of a thousand invisible eyes. It was not so much a question of being watched as of being surrounded.

There were particular places around which the very air seemed to blur, as if they were not quite in the same world as everything else. For instance, there was a conical hill in a bend in the river at the top of Craigairie Valley, crowned with a ramshackle drystone dyke enclosing five gnarled rowan trees, like old women against the skyline, which never failed to freak him out. Then there was the shallow, rectangular quarry just below the summit of Artfield Fell; the cairn on top of Eldrig Fell; a big round boulder down in the valley, where the river cut a deep gash through the hills. Then, of course, there was the king of the valley, the standing stone. There seemed to be nowhere one could go to avoid it; from below it pierced every skyline, from any of the surrounding hills it stood black against the pale, coarse grass around it.

Looking outwards from the hollow in which the stone was set one could see from the highest of the Merrick Hills to the north and east through to a tiny blue triangle of sea way down at the bottom of the Tarf Valley. There was nowhere else inside the ring of hills which surrounded Craigairie which afforded that view. Walk ten yards in any direction and you lost the sea behind Artfield Fell or the whale-backed Merrick behind the steep mass of Craigairie Fell itself. It was as if even the hills paid homage, ducking down so that the stone could see past them.

The only place, oddly enough, which was in its blindspot was the cottage itself, because the dark heather behind the stone concealed it from view and it stood below the skyline. You could see it, but it was as if it lost some of its power to dominate. Somehow David found this reassuring. He did not dislike the stone in the same way that he disliked the hill with the rowans, but it disconcerted him more than anywhere else, even the cottage. The very air around it hummed with electricity, like standing underneath a big pylon. There was something about it which David knew he was not strong enough to withstand. Everything else could be ignored or avoided, but the stone was always there, sometimes a fang, sometimes a penis, sometimes an old man, but never just a chunk of granite.

There was something about it which drew David back to it again and again, despite a large part of him that wanted nothing to do with it. He would stand for hours and listen to that humming, so low it was almost subliminal, wondering what the hell was causing it.

By that time, around the first fortnight of January, the hauntings had increased dramatically and David was thus more inclined to be open-minded about humming hillsides than he might have been a month earlier.

It began late one night, when he was slumped in front of his television.

Beside him the fire was almost out. The log basket was empty, as was the coal bucket – there was nothing left to burn and David did not have the energy to do anything about it.

'Apathy has become a problem,' he murmured out loud. About ten seconds later a pipe band struck up in the kitchen. David leapt like a scalded cat.

The noise was deafening. David was so terrified that he could only crouch down like a foetus, his eyes tightly shut and his ears blocked, praying that it wouldn't find him, whatever it was. After about half a minute, however, it stopped as suddenly as it had started, mid-beat, and the silence crashed back in again. David did not even open his eyes for another ten minutes and did not move, except to shiver uncontrollably, for over twenty. He finally stood up and moved slowly back into the middle of the room.

'I'm going mad,' he said out loud. 'This is it.' As he said it the fire beside him roared back into life for a few seconds, then died down, leaving only a constellation of twinkling red embers in the soot at the back of the chimney. This time he stopped dead, still as stone, turned his head very slowly and stared straight at the fire.

'What is going on here?' he asked the silence.

About two seconds later the fire did its trick again, right under his eyes. It was as if an immensely powerful wind was dragging the flames up from the last heat left in the embers, not an explosion, as if some unseen hand had thrown petrol on it, but a controlled burst of flame which was turned on, then turned off again.

He looked at it for a very long time.

His first instinct was to cross himself. This was followed by an overpowering desire to run and not stop until he had put at least fifty miles between himself and Craigairie. Then he sat down, lit a cigarette, allowed a spasm of shivering to shudder through his body and dug down into his reserves of courage. If it happened again he would be ready for it.

It did not happen again that night, but David did not sleep or move until daylight filled the house. He contemplated leaving throughout that day, which happened to be the most beautiful since he had moved in, did not sleep much the next night and then began to come to a decision.

He was not running away, not from boredom, not from loneliness and certainly not from a ghost. It was partly his pride which kept him there; he had told too many people that he would not go mad in Scotland, that he would adapt to any circumstance it sprung on him. He could not leave just because he was scared.

There was also a rich vein of courage, or foolhardiness, in David which had been one of the main characteristics which distinguished him from his peers when he worked for Channel Seven. He was genuinely unafraid of dying. He was sure, for some reason, that he would be warned in advance when he was going to die and was therefore quite happy to take the most absurd risks, in the calm knowledge that he had not had any foreboding of death. It had never yet let him down.

For about a week he lived on his nerve-endings, exhausting himself by jumping at every unexpected noise, every breath of wind, the slightest irregularities in the cottage. But slowly, as the hours and days passed, he began to cope. He had a recurring image in his mind, of himself sometime in the future, laughing as he described the time when he nearly went bonkers in Scotland.

But here, now, David knew he was quite sane. He was also not in any imminent danger. He did not know exactly how he knew this, but it was a very strong feeling, strong enough to keep him in a house which had a resident poltergeist in it. He did not feel threatened; he felt scared, amazed, shocked, baffled, even, deep down, a bubbling exhilaration. The haunting did not seem directed at him in the malevolent, clichéd, Hollywood sense. It was not violent, flinging household objects around with random bloody-mindedness. Instead it liked to move anything heavier than a matchbox and lighter than a full whisky bottle from one place to another, at first behind his back but then in front of his eyes. It moved furniture a few inches out of place, turned the stereo on in the middle of the night, crashed around in the kitchen or the spare bedroom at the back of the house. It even did the washing up once.

'It', David decided, was a she. He called her Delilah and, as the weeks passed, amazed himself by building the beginnings of a rudimentary relationship with her. She was like having a noisy and boisterous child in the house, apt to take advantage of the leeway David gave her, but perverse rather than particularly malevolent. When she pushed her luck he took to shouting at her, which more often than not shut her up.

It occurred to him that he was projecting these paranormal disturbances on his surroundings as some sort of an extreme subconscious reaction to his isolation. 'You're never alone with your own poltergeist,' he thought. But Delilah was more complicated than that; she reacted to David, but she was not a mirror image of his mind. She would, for instance, stick to one room for long periods of time, usually the back bedroom, whether he went there or not. He would hear the floorboards creaking, or small noises like furniture shifting on a carpet, and when she decided to come out she would warn him with the same noise, metal clinking on metal, in the same sequence, like a private code. When he heard that, whatever he was doing, whatever his mood, he knew that she was coming out.

He got used to her. He was quite proud of himself for how he adapted.

No sooner had this come about and he had outmanoeuvred another pitfall Craigairie had created for him, a new and even more disconcerting one began. He began to have dreams so vivid that he remembered every tiny detail of them when he awoke. They were bizarre and surreal and often had an odd, detached feel to them as if they were being projected to his mind from the outside, like movies. They did odd things for him; for example, showing him the flat, table-like rock a few yards behind the standing stone which was under two feet of heather and peat until he unearthed it with a spade. It was six feet long and was covered with faint, flowing hieroglyphs, or runes. There were concentric circles and spirals, about a centimetre deep, with two cups, one at either end, as deep as halved tennis balls, cut into the rock. It was the first evidence of the Picts David found and he found it because of a dream.

At first they came at the rate of one every two or three nights, but they accelerated rapidly until, after ten days, they were coming thick and fast, four or five a night, back to back.

It was like a crash course in Craigairie Valley; its history, who had been there, how they lived, how they died, what they believed. There had been misery and unhappiness in this hidden valley, fear and madness, persecution and death. David saw fire in the night and heard the unmistakable sounds of men fighting. He saw a place, way out in the forestry, where huddles of frightened people had starved to death as they vainly waited for their persecutors down in the fertile lowlands to go away and leave them alone. He saw old, childless men up by the cairn on top of Eldrig Fell, the furthest hill one could see from Craigairie, watching, powerless to stop the interlopers from usurping the land. There was an immense sadness in these hills, of a people who had invited no war upon themselves but who had been hunted into extinction for it. Many other people had been through the valley over the centuries, but only one group, the very first, could claim any lasting bond. The stones and runes, burial mounds and ghosts were theirs. This was the last bolthole of the Picts.

At first David revelled in these dreams. They opened up his interest in the surrounding countryside, which had hitherto been little more than a blurred view for him. He bought maps of the area and circled all the tumuli and stones, as well as a few of his own discoveries and specific places where he felt presences. He discovered that the conical hill with the tumbled wall and the five rowan trees, which he avoided like the plague, was called Witches Hill. And the rectangular quarry on top of Glenkitten Fell was actually the remains of a tumulus, a burial mound.

On a whim he began to draw lines between different marks on his maps, graduating to larger and larger maps when he discovered a definite pattern. He had never been much into the idea of ley-lines, but there was no way of denying the startling revelation which unfolded the more he double-checked his findings. If he connected any two points to which he attached a significance they invariably formed one of two patterns. Either they crossed directly through his stone, making it seem that it radiated them outwards, or alternatively they connected, to form a near-perfect polygon, surrounding the stone, in a circle constructed from straight lines, at a distance of about five miles.

Fascinated by this, David picked other standing stones anywhere in Britain and tried to perform the same trick, with nowhere like the same results. Craigairie was like a vortex for these lines, putting it more on a par with neolithic sites like Stonehenge, Glastonbury, Avebury, Callanish on the Outer Hebridean island of Lewis, Brogar on Orkney. In fact it was slap on a sort of cosmic motorway running from Callanish to Glastonbury.

Meanwhile, Delilah the poltergeist, was becoming such a regular part of life that even she began to lose some of her initial sting. For the first dozen or so times the pipe band trick, or the splintering crashes in the back bedroom – the worst of her repertoire – were truly terrifying. But after that they were just irritating. Almost as if to rectify this situation she broadened her horizons from being a mere poltergeist and became what the dictionary confirmed to be a succubus. In other words she gave David the most mind-bending blow job, picking a moment when he was lying in bed, wide awake, thinking about Natasha. It was not one of the dreams; they were subtler. It had the unmistakable feeling of naughtiness, of childlike mischief, which was Delilah's trademark.

The following morning he got up, packed an overnight bag and drove to a salubrious and ridiculously expensive hotel down on the coast, in search of some peace and quiet. He booked himself in and stayed there for three nights, undisturbed by Delilah, dreams and everything else. He spent much of the time walking on the beach, or sitting on the dunes, watching the waves riding in, lost in thought.

He was not leaving Craigairie. It took a couple of days of rest before he thought he had the strength to go back, but there was hardly any doubt that he would do so, sooner or later. When it was not scaring the living daylights out of him, or sapping his energy, or simply bemusing him, Craigairie was a source of constant fascination to David. If he was not going completely mad, then he was sitting in a house which was haunted on an astonishing scale. Few people even believe that ghosts are anything more than a quaint myth, fewer still could claim to have had the slightest contact with the supernatural. And yet David, who had never committed himself either way, had bought himself a sort of paranormal Disneyland.

And if he was losing his mind and imagining it all, then the process was unexpectedly interesting.

Either way, it did not follow him when he left Craigairie. It was bound to that one place and was therefore quite easy to escape. He could take a break whenever it got on top of him, or quit if it became intolerable. It was his choice to go back; and as long as that choice remained, he still had the final, check-mate move.

He arrived back at the cottage late in the evening, feeling like a soldier returning to the trenches, or a battered and bloodied boxer picking himself off the canvas for one more round. There was a feeling of expectancy, as if the house had been saving up its energy for him. He took a deep breath and steadied himself for the inevitable resumption of hostilities.

That night he had a nightmare of epic proportions.

It ripped into his sleep with no warning and with a vicious ferocity which made him scream out in the silent bedroom. There were flames raging in his mind, not cosy, controlled hearth-flames but a wild, hungry fire which filled his skull. He was consumed by them, burned away until there was nothing left of him but a little, cowering entity, naked and vulnerable. After what seemed like an aeon fleeting images started to coagulate amongst the flames. As soon as he saw the first one, David knew, with sinking dread, that the deepest, darkest vault in his subconscious had been penetrated. There were memories stored in there, locked away from view, which he had hoped never to see again.

He saw the first person he had ever seen killed, a Palestinian kid shot in the act of slinging a stone at some soldiers, his whole body jack-knifing backwards with the force of the impact. He had relived that scene every night for three months, until he had finally been able to incarcerate it where it could not get at him. He saw the two American journalists murdered in a Bahrain hotel once again, gunned down right in front of him. He even saw himself, aged eighteen, sitting in a dark, impersonal hospital corridor, waiting to see a girl who had just aborted his child and felt again the cold shame he had felt then.

Then it was over and he was standing out on the hill, naked, an icy wind cutting into him. There were voices whispering and murmuring around him and eyes watching him, but it was pitch dark and he could see nothing. He looked around and realized that he was lost. He had no idea where he was, except that he had heather under his feet and the ground was crunchy with frost. He began to walk, to escape the voices. They followed him.

He broke into a run. He ran and ran, tripping and falling and picking himself up again, still running. He hit stones with his pounding feet, stubbing his toes and bruising his soles until he was hobbling, pain throbbing up inside his legs. He went across what appeared to be a peat-bog, pitching headlong into a mire but still running straight on, the moment he was on his feet. His lungs were wheezing and whining in his chest, his heart was pumping so fast that it sent little spasms of shooting agony against his ribcage. Still he ran.

He went down a hill, tripping again and rolling most of the way, into some trees, cannoning off them like a pinball, through unseen brambles which ripped at his skin and tore his feet to shreds and finally, at full sprint, into a bitterly cold river.

Only then did he begin to see things. He saw the dark trees looming over him and the ghost of a moon behind a screen of scudding clouds. He saw where he was; about a mile down the River Tarf from the cottage. He struggled through the water and out the other side, shivering uncontrollably. He could feel his pursuers on the other side, on the far bank, glaring at him. There seemed to be an uncertainty about them, something from some long-forgotten story leapt into his mind.

'Ha,' he yelled out, throwing his head back in triumph. His voice echoed straight back at him.

'You can't cross running water, can you?' He gloated over the gurgling river. 'Witches and ghoulies can't cross rivers. You can't get me here, you bastards.' With that, he turned and trotted up through the trees and then straight up the deep cutting made by the river, pulling himself up on roots and branches until he was out on the hill. It was beginning to snow, thick, fluffy flakes drifting down in the darkness. Undeterred, David marched straight back up the valley, straight to the stone.

'OK, shithead,' he said to it. 'Now that your minions are all stuck over there, I'm going to dig you out of the fucking ground.'

He knelt down and began to tear away the turf around one side of the stone. The ground was not yet frozen up here and he dug his fingers deep into the earth, pulling out handfuls of peat. About six inches down he hit a rock and had to dig around its edges until he could get enough purchase on it to prise it out. He went on with feverish determination, talking to himself as he worked. He was telling the stone how he was going to uproot it, break it into little pieces and make a rock garden out of it. He knew that he was hurting it with every inch of earth he dug: he had won a victory back at the river and for the first time in over three months he was not scared of this standing stone. It was not an advantage he was willing to forgo.

Not, at least, until the ground froze solid and he tore his fingernails to shreds trying to scrape out earth as hard as stone. He gave up finally, and huddled down with his back to the stone and his feet in the hole he had dug, guarding it from anyone or anything which might have wished to fill it in again.

That was how Christina MacRuarie found him six hours later, shortly after discovering, to her profound shock, that this was the same stone she had dreamt about the night before.

'Tell me, what were you digging for?' Having found a naked man at her standing stone, his feet and hands covered in blood, his body twinkling with frost, almost dead with cold, Christina MacRuarie had given him her coat and had all but carried him right over to the far side of the valley to the nearest house, which turned out to be his. She had washed his wounds in front of a fire she built and lit, had found him clothes and given him a mug of tomato soup, followed by some whisky. After all that she thought she probably deserved some kind of an explanation. He was beginning to come back to life again, at least enough to shake his head slowly and murmur, 'It's a long story.'

'You said something about having to dig the stone out when I found you. In fact you kept saying it.'

'Did I?' he asked dully. 'I don't remember.' He thought for a second and added with a faint shrug, 'Not such a bad idea though.'

'Why not?' She tried not to sound as if she was pouncing on the remark, but the attempted nonchalance did not ring true. He looked up at her, frowning, and she found herself staring into the most beautiful eyes she had ever seen. He was odd-looking, almost Arabian, like a white Tuareg. He had a hooked nose which dominated an angular face, or would have done so if it had not been for those emerald green eyes.

'Who *are* you?' he asked.

She looked back at him for a while, not knowing quite how to answer this. In her confusion she gave him the bare facts.

'My name's Christina MacRuarie. I live not far from here.'

'What're you doing *here*?'

Again she had to think before she replied. 'I came to look at that stone.'

'My stone?'

'Your stone?'

'I'd always assumed it was mine,' he mumbled. He looked at the floor for a while then turned another deep frown on her.

'What's wrong?' she asked, raising her hands as if in surrender.

He shook his head. 'Nothing,' he said. 'I've been having some kind of strange dreams lately and I was wondering whether this was one of them.'

'Pinch yourself,' she replied dryly. 'It's real.'

There was something in his voice which bothered her. It was almost as if he resented her. Admittedly, it was a little embarrassing to be found in the condition he was in, by a complete stranger. She could understand that, but she could not understand why he had not thanked her. If she hadn't come along he might have died.

'I feel I ought to thank you for saving my life,' he said, still levelling that unnerving gaze on her. His tone suggested that he weighed his thanks against his general dissatisfaction that she was there in the first place. Not ungrateful but not enthusiastic either.

'That's OK,' she replied, this time getting the studied nonchalance spot on. 'I couldn't've left you there.'

A brief silence fell.

'So, Christina MacRuarie, what *were* you doing up by the stone?' he asked.

She opened her mouth to answer but thought better of it and closed it again, looking embarrassed and confused.

'Don't tell me,' he said tiredly. 'You dreamt about it?'

Her surprise was pure, spontaneous theatre. It was the second time in five minutes he appeared to have read her mind and it was beginning to disconcert her.

'How d'you know that?' she demanded.

'Just a guess,' he murmured. For a second he rolled his eyes heavenwards and opened his hands in supplication, as if to say 'Why are you doing this to me?' He let out a small sigh.

'So is this the first time you've been here?' he asked.

She nodded. 'I'm not even sure whether this is the place I dreamt about. I mean, everything looks pretty much the same out here.'

'Believe me, this is the place,' he muttered.

She lit a cigarette and gathered her thoughts. Ever since the moment she had first laid eyes on the self-same standing stone she had seen in her dream the night before she had been engulfed in a mist of unreality. Everything that had happened seemed almost to have been contrived, like a play in which she was unwittingly playing a part. It was not artificial; it was very well staged and acted because it was, as she had assured this weird man, real. But she had to admit that it had a dreamlike quality no amount of hard-headedness on her part could entirely dispel.

Part of the problem was the man. Her initial reaction when she found him had been horror and surprise, closely followed by a sort of business-like protectiveness she sometimes felt when faced with people, or indeed animals, in distress. She had always rather despised it in herself, but when it took over she could do nothing about it. When the man was safe and warm, however, and obviously not as close to death as he had appeared at first, she began to wonder about him.

He was curiously incongruous, out of context. Judging by his accent he was no farmer, in fact he was not local. There might have been a hint of Scottish in his voice, but it was very faint. And the house was surprisingly opulent; not showy, but expensive; the hi-fi was good, the kitchen was well-equipped and well stocked, the carpets were good quality, his books ranged from history, politics and great literature through to well-chosen trash. In fact he was obviously intelligent, well-educated, which prompted the question, why was he living there? It also led her to wonder what he thought he had been doing up by the stone.

'So?' she asked. He jerked out of his glum reverie and looked up at her. '. . . What are *you* doing here?'

'Not much,' he said. 'Proving to myself that I'm not going mad . . .' He paused, sneezed, then gave her a peculiar, wry smile. 'And failing, for the most part.' He stopped and rubbed the end of his nose with the back of his hand. He had a nasty knack of saying the unexpected.

She decided to change tack. 'You lived here long?' she asked.

He looked at her for a moment, then smiled faintly to himself, as if he knew where she was trying to steer him. 'A few months.'

34

'And before that?'

'I worked in London . . . ish.'

'What did you do?' she asked.

The same slight smile returned to his eyes and she was afraid, for a moment, that he would advise her to mind her own business. Instead he shrugged one shoulder.

'I was a journalist.'

'Would I have read anything by you?'

'Not recently,' he said, still wary of all these questions but willing, for the moment, to answer them. 'I worked in television, Channel Seven News.'

'Oh,' she said, trying to recognize him. 'Really? What doing?'

'Being shot at, mostly.'

She narrowed her eyes at him involuntarily, as if warning him about the unexpected remarks. He saw the look and elaborated.

'I did a lot of work in places like Beirut,' he said, wondering whether this was the point where he should curtail this line of inquiry. 'I stopped.'

'Why?' she asked.

He shrugged. 'I got bored.' It didn't ring true but Christina was aware that she was on thin ice, so she backed off.

'And now you live here?' she said. There was a note of incredulity in her voice which Rachel Ifbak would have approved of.

He nodded but did not reply.

'It's kind of remote isn't it?' she remarked innocently.

'That's why I bought it.' He looked straight into her eyes for a moment and smiled. 'I know what you're thinking,' he said. 'You're thinking, no wonder you go mad and try to dig up standing stones, bollock naked, on the coldest night of the year, when you incarcerate yourself in a centrally-heated stone box in the middle of nowhere.' He paused, just to make sure that he was right, before continuing. 'But, strange as it may seem, I'm not a nutcase.'

'So what were you doing up at the stone?' She was pleased to see that he had to think before he answered.

'Trying to dig it out, I guess.'

'Why?'

'You ask a lot of questions,' he said, 'some of which I'm not inclined to answer right now.'

She blushed. His tone was so mild and well-mannered that she suddenly realized how hard she had been probing this complete stranger and she was embarrassed at herself.

'I'm sorry,' she said. 'I got carried away.' As she said this there was a loud 'clink' somewhere in the house, like a hammer being tapped on a metal pipe. David sat up, bolt upright, listening.

'What was that?' she asked.

He raised one hand to silence her.

'Clink clink.'

'Oh, shit,' he said very quietly.

'What is it?' A door slammed upstairs, followed by something that sounded like a fast-moving St Bernard thudding down the staircase.

'Was that a dog?' she asked unsurely.

'Not exactly,' he said.

Christina was about to ask him another question, but she half-caught a movement out of the corner of her eye and turned towards it, frowning. It had been in the corner of the room, somewhere behind the sofa, but there was only a table and a standard lamp over there. Hairs prickled on the back of her neck. David followed her gaze, craning his neck to see over the back of the sofa

'What's the matter?' he asked.

She shook her head in mild bemusement. 'Nothing . . . I thought I saw something move.'

'The ashtray?' he asked.

It might have been an innocent inquiry, but it jolted her. She had just convinced herself that a large marble ashtray could not have moved on its own. She turned and looked down at him. He was still staring at the ashtray on the table, an odd, avid look on his face. After a second he stood up and offered her his hand.

'Listen, can I buy you a drink in Barrhill?' he said.

She looked up at him, noticing an anxiety in his eyes as if he was suddenly in a big hurry.

'I figure I owe you a drink, at least,' he said, still offering her his hand.

She shrugged. 'OK.' She took his hand and pulled herself to her feet. He swept up her coat and helped her into it, then gave her bag and camera to her. She dawdled, doing up her buttons and looking for a non-existent lighter, intrigued by his sudden, secret hurry. When she could not locate her lighter he confirmed her suspicions by giving his to her.

'Part exchange,' he said. 'If I find it I'll send it to you.'

'What's the rush?' she asked.

He was jiggling around, moving towards the door. He glanced at his watch.

'The sun's over the yard-arm,' he replied. He went out into the hallway, heading towards the kitchen. After about half a minute she strolled out after him. At that moment pandemonium broke out in the kitchen. It sounded as if about ten people were in there, all holding a pan in either hand, each trying to make as much noise as possible.

Christina froze. David passed a tired hand over his eyes and lost all his sense of urgency. In amongst the racket a long drone began. David shook his head and put his palms together in front of his face, as if praying.

36

'Not the pipes, Delilah, please not the pipes.'

The drone burst into 'The Black Bear'. David sighed.

'What the hell *is* that?' Christina demanded, terror registering in her voice. 'Who's Delilah?'

'My pet poltergeist,' David said. He thought for a second and added, '. . . I say "pet", but she pretty much pleases herself.'

Christina was crouching down on the floor and, what with the racket going on only a wall away and the fists in her ears, she did not catch most of this.

'Poltergeist?' she asked, her teeth chattering. 'Jesus Christ, what is this place?'

'Haunted,' David said. 'It's very, very haunted.' He leant down and offered her his hand again. 'D'you want to shut it up?' he asked.

She nodded dumbly.

'D'you want to stay here on your own while I do it, or will you come with me?'

She grasped his hand, stood up and reluctantly allowed herself to be pulled to the kitchen door. The noise on the other side was deafening; a hellish cacophony backed up by an insanely competent rendition of a military march, played full blast, on bagpipes. As if that wasn't enough, something started trying to break down the wall, battering it so hard that books were falling off shelves on the other side, the side Christina was on. David, however, appeared unafraid, nonchalant even. He put his hand on the doorhandle, grasped it firmly and turned it very, very slowly. He released Christina's hand and, in one movement dived against the door, staggering through into the kitchen. As he crossed the threshold and the door banged open the noise stopped dead. He turned to her, where she was crouching outside in the dark hall and offered his hand once again. He had a faint, ironic smile on his lips.

'You'll be wanting that drink now?' he said.

Christina walked two steps before her legs buckled and she fainted.

Christina was ashamed to have passed out. She was ashamed to have stood shivering in the winter night while the man she had saved from hypothermia only hours earlier pulled on a jacket and boots so that he could accompany her to the pub in Barrhill, in her car. God only knew how, or even if, he got back.

She was particularly ashamed to have played childish games with him while he was trying, gently but firmly, to get her out of there before the mayhem started. She had spent all afternoon thinking that she had found an interesting variety of eccentric and treating him as such, only to find that what really made him odd was that he was a normal person trying to deal with a wildly abnormal situation. He had not seemed scared by the bedlam, in fact he had been quite calm about it.

For several hours her mind refused to settle on the events of the afternoon and allowed only brief glimpses of memory to flash past, leaving marching armies of goosebumps crawling all over her body in their wake.

After a while, however, the initial horror began to recede and she found herself wondering at the man she had left behind in Barrhill. His attitude had been amazing. Nothing on earth could have convinced Christina to stay in a house which had that going on in it, and yet he had not been at all disconcerted by it. In fact, if anything, he had been amused. He knew, somehow, that it would not hurt them, which deprived it of its power to frighten him. On reflection she could not help but admire the man's resilience.

Also, when she thought about her day and remembered it in detail she remembered the overpowering feeling of unreality which had pervaded it. From the moment she got up, went out and found the same stone she had dreamt about the night before, to the point when she had left the strange, green-eyed man in Barrhill, the whole day seemed to have been pre-ordained. She had been pointed towards that particular stone out of the blue, had found the naked man there, had saved his life, spoken to him, become fascinated by him without knowing why and then, the climax of the afternoon, had been given several very good reasons for thinking him extraordinary. Christina had always been a great believer in fate, in certain things happening in her life over which she had no control. This stone had first insinuated its way into her life, via her father, three months earlier. She had not invited it to be there; she had never been within twenty miles of it in her entire life. It had called her quite deliberately; she had felt that when she first saw it, from half a mile away across the moor and recognized it, that morning. She felt it even stronger now that she thought about it.

And, if she needed any confirmation for her suspicions, any proof that she was not just being silly, there was the letter, lying unfinished on the desk in the sitting room. She had read it before it occurred to her how rude she was being, but he had been comatose on the sofa and she had been looking for some idea of who he was. It was written on foolscap, scrawled across the page, but legible and lucid.

'Dear Kelv,' it began.

'Further news from Craigairie, the Borley Rectory of the north. Same rules as always apply – breathe a word of this to Meg and I'll disembowel you with a breadknife.

'This is what I think, while I'm still capable of it. There *is* something very bizarre going on here, perhaps not unique but certainly way out of the ordinary. It's all around, in the hills, the river, the boulders, the trees, my cottage and most of all in the standing stone. It hums, Kelvin. I can't explain what it feels like, but if you stand anywhere near the thing you can feel the vibrations in the ground. There's no electricity cable buried there, or pipeline or anything like that. It's coming from the stone.

'Living here in general is weird as hell. I've told you about Delilah, my poltergeist, but she's just a part of it. Everything is sort of shimmery, as if it can't quite decide whether it's real or not. The basic fabric of nature in the valley seems to have been disrupted, so that normal laws of time, space, science, gravity and nature itself are all suspended here. Nothing seems real because I can trust nothing to behave how I expect it to behave. It's like a constant, waking dream.

'I realize that this must sound nuts, from a distance, but bear with me. I'll never be more serious than I am about this. For me living here is like being in a kind of half-world, a limbo. This is not a human thing I am sitting on, it doesn't translate easily into words, or into any rationale. It works according to its own laws, defying me to explain it, which I can't do. All I know is that there is a power here, underneath me, all around me, which is like a vast oil-well. The only human thing is the stone itself, like an old, rusty, unused derrick, rattling and clanking and leaking with the enormous pressure building up beneath it.

'I think – and this is one of the trickier bits – that I am, to some degree, causing this. My presence here has woken it up. This power has been neglected and dormant for ages, but someone knew about it and understood it once, which is why the stone is here. Already, before I turned up, this power was getting close to exploding. The stone was put there to stop that from happening and perhaps needed only a relatively receptive human to reactivate it. At that point I walked in, wide-eyed and bushy-tailed . . .'

At this point he had stopped and scribbled, 'Conjecture, conjecture, conjecture' across the page. Then: 'Anyway, I don't think I can deal with it alone. At first I thought I could, but now I'm beginning to doubt that I have enough of what it seems to want from me.'

After that two sentences had been scored out, so that not a word was legible. Then finally he had written, 'I think', scored it out with three lines and had added, 'No I don't'.

When she read it, long before the poltergeist turned up, Christina had thought that, despite protestations to the contrary, the guy was going nuts. But in retrospect, taking into account both Delilah and his obvious reluctance to discuss Craigairie with her, she had to accept that the man wasn't just sane, he was remarkably level-headed.

As far as his claims about Craigairie were concerned, Delilah had put paid to any doubts Christina might have had. The poltergeist had scared the shit out of her, but once she got over the shock of it she did not find it hard to believe that such things existed. Ever since she was a small child, as long as she could remember, Christina had believed in ghosts, witches, magic and all the rest of the Hallowe'en rigmarole. She had been so regularly frightened by the unseen in large houses that she had come to accept her sensitivity as a part of life. Some of her earliest

39

memories were of being led around by her elder cousins and pushed into rooms, like a canary in a coalmine, to see how she would react. If she cringed and shivered they avoided the room thereafter. If she was unaffected, they used it.

What had happened in the cottage was the same theory, only much bigger. In an odd way, Christina suspected that she was better equipped to understand the phenomenon at Craigairie than the man who actually lived there. He had learned to cope with it, whereas she had lived with it all her life.

After several hours of hard thinking, Christina was more confused than when she had started. All she could think about, over and over, was the end of that letter, the bit about the stone needing a receptive human to reactivate it . . . 'At that point I walked in, wide-eyed and bushy-tailed.'

He did not think he could do it alone and yet he had made it quite clear that he did not want or need help from her. In fact, if anything, he resented and mistrusted her for stepping on to his territory at such an inopportune moment. She clearly remembered the look on his face and the note in his voice when he had asked: 'Who *are* you? . . . What are you doing *here*?' It had not been a polite, conversational inquiry; he had been asking why she was trespassing on his turf, by what right she thought she was there.

Her right, like his, was the stone.

She came to a snap decision at two o'clock in the morning and dialled the number she had written down earlier. It rang half a dozen times before he picked it up, still sounding wary.

'Yes?' he said.

'Hello?' she asked.

'Who's speaking, please?' he asked, trying to sound polite and for the most part failing.

'Did I wake you?'

'No, I was just farting around through the house . . . sorry, who is this?'

'Christina,' she said. 'MacRuarie. From this afternoon.'

There was a short, somewhat pregnant silence.

'Oh,' he said. 'Hello.'

The 'what do *you* want?' was unsaid but implicit. She almost chickened out at that point, but rallied and soldiered on.

'I was just calling to see if you got back OK,' she said. 'I was worried.'

'You shouldn't have been,' he said after a moment. 'I'm fine.'

'Oh, good,' she said. She paused. 'One thing?'

'Yes?' he asked.

She gave a quick laugh. 'I'm really embarrassed to ask, but I don't even know your name?'

'David,' he said. 'David Armstrong.'

'I was just wondering, maybe, if you're around and . . .'

'Yes?' he prompted.

'. . . And you're free and stuff, I just wondered if you'd like to come over and have dinner sometime. Maybe this weekend.'

'That's very kind, but I think I'll be in Orkney this weekend.'

'Oh?' she said, sounding disappointed. 'What happens there?'

'Standing stones, mostly,' he replied. 'Lots of standing stones.'

'Sounds great.' There was a brief silence. 'So how are you getting there?'

There was a small laugh from the other end. 'On my motorbike.' He sounded as if he did not relish the prospect.

'I have a car.' She blurted it out before she had time to think and regretted it instantly. On the other end David briefly contemplated a facetious rejoinder along the lines of 'That must be nice for you', but thought better of it and compromised with a cool, 'Really?'

'. . . If you want,' she said.

He was not sure whether she was offering her car, herself, or both. Judging by her tone she wasn't sure either.

'I mean, I've got nothing much to do and I'd like to see Orkney and . . . I could give you a lift . . . if that's all right.'

This confused David still further. Normally he would have been both flattered and dumbfounded to have a very good-looking blonde showing an interest in him, but now he just felt suspicious of her. He could not think what on earth she wanted from him.

'That'd be good,' he said.

Mistaking the confusion behind his voice for uninterest, she began quickly, 'Listen, sorry. You hardly know me and I'm already treating you like an old friend. I don't know what's got into me . . .' She paused. 'Besides, I wouldn't even know where to stay in Orkney.' She was honestly not trying to manipulate him, it was just coming out that way.

'Oh, that's not a problem . . .' He was on the verge of saying that there were hundreds of hotels, but on a split second decision he changed his mind. 'Kelv and Meg will put you up.'

'Kelv and Meg?' Christina asked, remembering the names from the letter.

'My friends up there. I'll call them and tell them we're one extra. They won't mind.'

It was only after they had both hung up that they had time to wonder at the way the conversation had gone. David thought about it for a few minutes, staring into his fireplace. As far as he was concerned this woman was as much a product of Craigairie as the poltergeist and the dreams. He was wary of her in the extreme.

After a while he shook his head, frowning slightly then got up and went to bed. He did not dream that night.

2

ORKNEY

Christina and David were already on the A9, north of Perth, well on the way to Orkney, when the thought suddenly struck her: 'What the hell am I doing?' She was going halfway to Iceland, a third of the way to the Arctic circle, with a man she had known for only a few days and had only spoken to properly once.

The car was a small, quick French number which Christina had driven until Perth very much as a French person would have driven it: flat out, with undisguised contempt for everyone else on the road and with music thumping from all sides.

It was not a style ideally suited to the A9 across the Grampian mountains, in the middle of the Highland winter, in a blizzard. It had been rain in Ayrshire, sleet north of Glasgow and was now fast, swirling, mesmerizing snow. David had taken over and was giving Christina an object lesson on how to drive in such conditions, which amounted to an unspoken criticism of her method. He was infinitely more patient and cool, willing to sit behind crawling lorries with dirty slush spattering his windscreen, awaiting his chance to hop past them.

She held on to the edges of her seat for a while, but he did not drive like a man liable to crash and she gradually relaxed. Once or twice she had cause to make exaggerated stabs at an imaginary brake, but he ignored them. He only scared her once, when a Volvo pulled out into his path as he was overtaking a line of slow-moving lorries. He would have crashed into it had it not been for the long lay-by on the far side of the road into which he swerved to double-overtake the Volvo. For about half a minute they were going at ninety, through deep slush, in a lay-by which might have ended at any moment.

All he said was 'Idiot'.

He listened to his own music as he drove, which was a mixture of country, blues and folk. Some of the songs made him smile slightly, as if some old secret was buried in the lyrics. He usually then stuck his foot down and drove faster for a few miles, as if to dispel the memory from his mind.

On one of these occasions she was embarrassed to find herself gazing at his profile. She turned her attention back to the road instantly, but his silhouette remained for a split second: the falconine nose, the sharp line of his jaw. It was a fascinating and unusual face, unmistakable after one had seen it once.

She had seen him on television the other night, quite by accident. It was a day or two after their first meeting and she was sitting with her parents, talking and half-watching the news on Channel Seven. A picture of David had come on to the screen, making Christina dive for the remote control to turn the volume up.

'. . . Most prestigious award in British television journalism and widely thought to be one of the highest accolades in the business.'

'That's him,' Christina said.

'That's who, darling?' her mother asked.

'David Armstrong. The man I met up by Barrhill, the other day.' She had not told them about her afternoon. All that she had said was that she had met rather an odd man.

'Really?' her mother asked, putting on her spectacles, and squinting at the television. 'Looks kind of Mediterranean.'

'I think he said his mother's Italian,' Christina said.

'Damned good journalist,' her father remarked unexpectedly.

Christina turned and stared at him.

'A bit on the pink side, perhaps,' he went on. 'But good all the same.'

'You know him?'

'Of him,' he replied, still gazing at the television. 'The PM used to listen to his reports on the World Service during the Tibetan revolution.' He thought for a moment. 'Brave man. "The only sane voice in Tibet" was the way Jack at the Foreign Office used to describe him.'

Christina thought about this as David drove through the snowstorm.

'I saw you on television the other night,' she remarked casually.

He raised his eyebrows but did not take his eyes off the tail-lights of the lorry in front.

'Yeah?'

'You're up for an award.' She said it almost as if she was peeved that he had not told her.

He nodded. 'I know.'

'That's great, isn't it?' she asked.

He shrugged. 'It's OK,' he said. 'I guess.'

At that point he decided to take the lorry. He changed down a gear, pulled out and eased past it unhurriedly.

Christina looked for an emotion which might have escaped his voice but could not avoid betraying itself in his driving. There was none. After a minute he realized she was looking at him.

'OK, it's nice to be given awards. It's always nice to be complimented. But if it gives Channel Seven a chance to give me a hard time for quitting, which it will, no doubt, then I'm not interested.'

'My father likes you,' Christina said after a short silence. 'Says you're damned good at your job. I quote.'

'*Was* good at my job,' he corrected quietly. 'Your dad's Sir James Graham, right?'

'How d'you know that?' she demanded.

'A guess.' He drove on for a while before adding, 'He's a damned good politician, your father; an honest one.'

'Was,' Christina said. 'You should get together. You could get off with each other on mutual admiration.'

They chatted for a while. Inverness passed by, an orange blur to their left just before crossing the neck of the Beauly Firth on to the Black Isle. It was about an hour later, north of Dingwall, before she managed to steer him back to the thing she had originally intended to ask him.

'I can see why your bosses are pissed off, though,' she said, out of the blue. 'I mean, just when you win a major award, you quit.'

'They're too stupid to understand my reasons,' he replied. 'If they did understand, they'd never try to stop me.' He delivered everything he said in the same low, calm voice, which made it almost impossible to work out how he really felt.

'What were your reasons, then?' she asked.

He fell into a frowning silence.

'If you don't want to talk about it . . .' she said.

'It's not that I don't want to talk about it,' he replied. He shrugged. 'It's just that I don't know how to. When I first started, when I first saw somebody killing somebody else, with my own eyes, I thought I'd never get over the horror of it.' He thought, chewing his lower lip. '*That* was quite healthy. It was when I got to the stage that I could watch someone getting their head blown off and not flinch that I knew I had to get out.' He paused and emitted a snort of dry mirth.

'Besides, I was getting close to a state of mind known as gun-happy, in the business.'

'What? You took risks, or what?'

'I took risks, with a bit of "or what" thrown in.'

'Like?'

'Like wandering around during gun-battles, taking cabs in Beirut, that sort of thing.' He laughed again. 'I once suggested a little too pointedly that there were American troops actively participating in a South American civil war, which they're apparently allowed to do so long as nobody's tactless enough to mention it. Thereafter, I had a constant tail of CIA heavies.' He laughed again, this time with genuine mirth.

'It must have been fun, some of it,' she said. 'I mean, getting to travel anywhere in the world for free.'

'Travelling's much over-rated,' he remarked. 'After a while you just crave a bit of stability, a nest you can hide away in and let the world flow over you.'

'Is that why you bought that cottage?' she asked.

'Craigairie?' he said with a faint, indecipherable smile. 'Yeah, I guess.'

He smiled to himself, then seemed to shake himself free of the train of thought.

'And you?' he asked. 'You don't seem like a country lass. What are you doing up here?'

'Hiding,' she said, after a few seconds' thought.

'From?' he asked.

She did not reply for a long while, then she breathed a quick laugh. 'Myself, I 'spose. I know that sounds melodramatic, but that's basically how it is.'

'What's there to escape?' he asked, his eyes on the road.

She shrugged, shook her head, then ran a hand through her flaxen hair.

He turned and gave her a quick look.

'Tricky one, huh?' he asked. He looked back at the road, smiling slightly. 'What with you hiding from yourself and me running away, we make a fine pair.'

She laughed. After a minute she frowned. 'Are you running away?' she asked. Considering what she knew or guessed about his life at Craigairie, running away seemed a bit harsh.

'That's what everyone said, and I'm not one to buck a majority.'

'What did they think you were running away from?' she demanded, annoyed on his behalf.

'Life?' he replied. 'I think. Haven't you ever wanted to get away from everything, shake everyone off and head for the hills?'

She thought for a second and shrugged. 'I'm not sure that I've ever been to the place everyone wants to get away from,' she replied.

David smiled. There was a disconcerting air of innocence about her, like a child. It occasionally crept into her voice, betraying a genuine and rare ingenuousness, which seemed to see no evil in the world and saw no reason to go looking for it. For David, who had been fighting a long rearguard action on behalf of his ideals, against a gathering tide of cynicism, Christina was an unnerving creature. He did not know whether to believe her, or to be wary of her, or to treat her as another figment of Craigairie's fertile imagination and steer a course well clear of her.

For her part Christina was aware of his confusion, but knew that she could not do anything about it. She dearly wanted to draw him into a discussion about Craigairie, but she sensed his reluctance to talk about it and held herself back.

'*I've* been there,' David said.

Christina turned and looked at him.

He snorted. 'There are only five people left there.'

Christina grinned and he smiled in answer, although he did not take his eyes off the road. He bit his lower lip.

'We're not going to make the Orkney ferry tonight,' he said. 'We'll have to find a hotel.'

Christina peered through the windscreen, which was now covered in snow except inside the arc of the clicking wipers. They were crawling along a dark, empty road, cutting through half a foot of virgin show.

'Where are we?' she asked, a little anxiously. 'I haven't seen a house in about half an hour.'

'That's because there wasn't one,' he replied. 'Don't worry, we'll make it to Bonar Bridge.'

They reached the small, one-horse town at ten o'clock in the evening, in a swirling blizzard. After checking in to the only hotel they could see, they showered, went down for a drink and David managed to shame the proprietor into cooking them some dinner. It was while they were waiting for this that David decided to broach a question which had been intriguing him.

'I can't help noticing your ring,' he said.

She put down her glass and inspected the wedding ring on her finger.

'I was married,' she said simply. 'That's where MacRuarie comes from.' She looked at him and correctly identified the speculative look on his face. 'I'm not as young as I look,' she said.

'How old do you think I think you are?'

'How old do you think I am?' she asked.

He studied her. 'Twenty-four?' he guessed. He thought she looked twenty-one but carried herself and behaved in general somewhere in the late twenties.

'Twenty-five,' she said.

He expressed appropriate surprise, missed the point of this sidetrack completely and asked, 'So are you separated? From your husband?'

'In a way,' she said, looking down towards the table, away from his eyes. 'He died nine months ago. In a motorbike accident.'

He was genuinely apologetic and luckily the scampi and chips arrived in time to save him from any clumsy attempts he might have made to rectify his error, but it threw him off balance for the rest of the evening. He had been thinking of Christina as a potential threat, out to ensnare him, and of himself as the put-upon subject of her undeniable charms. He had thought she had 'divorced' written all over her, whereas she was a widow at twenty-five.

He went to bed still rebuking himself.

The next morning dawned bright, sparkling, clear and bitterly cold. The snow had smothered Easter Ross during the night, from the peaks of the old, rounded mountains down through the laden pine forests, right to the shore of the Firth, where the steel-grey water lapped on to the white-washed mud-flats.

David looked out at it from his bedroom for all of twenty minutes, unmoving, allowing the ringing silence of new snow in the mountains to seep into him. Then, with a smile on his face, he went and woke Christina, doing his best to be gentle but firm. He agreed to meet her downstairs, in the breakfast room, when she was ready. He then went and played with a large, utterly unappetizing breakfast.

He was on his fourth cup of coffee and had pushed his plate to one side by the time Christina wandered in, looking like a young Julie Christie on a rough morning and dressed for the Antarctic. She sat down, murmured 'G'morning' and lit up her first fag. He poured her some coffee and lit a cigarette of his own.

'I like a person who smokes as early as I do,' she remarked. After that there was a reflective ten minute silence before Christina allowed her sluggish thoughts out into the open.

'Are they nice, your friends?'

He thought for a while, then nodded. 'Yeah. The guy, Kelvin, is my oldest friend on earth. I've known him since I was sent to prep school. We went through our entire education together, from nine to twenty-two.' He paused. 'He's funny, Kelv. He's a didakai, a half-gypsy, which makes for some weird hang-ups.'

'Like?' she inquired.

He shrugged. 'Nothing, really. He has problems relating to some people. He's a bit too fey for comfort, he finds it hard to settle down . . .' He smiled, as he thought. 'Which is where Meg comes in. Meg's terribly sensible and down-to-earth, but she cloaks it in a sort of dottiness which can be kind of deceptive.' He thought for a moment more before shaking himself out of it. 'They're good people. You'll like them. They'll certainly like you.'

'How d'you know?'

It was a peculiar question, catching him off guard. She had asked it to the table in front of her, but now she raised her grey eyes and looked into his face. He looked back for a couple of seconds, twitched his shoulder in a slight shrug and gave her one of his half-smiles.

'Because you're with me,' he said.

She held his gaze for a moment more then conceded the point with a single, slow nod.

When they took to the road again the snowploughs and gritters had done their work. David still drove, which suited Christina fine. She was not at her most conversational first thing in the morning and she was quite content to stare out of the window at the passing landscape, allowing her mind to embark on a languid, semi-conscious ramble. Besides, she trusted David's driving. It suited his general demeanour – cool, unruffled, intelligent.

As they passed from Sutherland into Caithness, first along the winding coast road and then inland, across the eastern rim of the Flow country, David started a quiet but informative running commentary which lasted until the ferry outside Thurso.

'I used to come up here with my father,' he said. 'We'd drive up in his Zephyr and sit in a bog for a week watching birds. I saw my first

47

eagle up here.' He smiled. 'Birds are the only thing Father and I ever had in common. Needless to say, my mother can't stand them.'

With that he dismissed his family and returned to his commentary, like a backdrop to the meandering road through Caithness. Away to the left the husks of old mountains squatted on the edge of a white desert which stretched for hundreds of square miles, away to the north and west. It made Christina shiver to look at it. It was like Siberia, like tundra without the trees, an undulating wilderness as big as a southern English county.

As they passed across it David began a slow, dreamy eulogy which was so loving and lyrical that Christina was swept away by it. It was like listening to a fairytale. He spoke of a magical island full of ruined castles and palaces, standing stone circles and sunken battleships. He told of how an entire German fleet had scuppered itself in Scapa Flow at the end of the First World War, rather than surrender, and how a single German U boat had repaid the debt in the Second War by sneaking into Scapa Flow and running amuck amongst the anchored British fleet, sinking a battleship before getting away.

And a thousand years earlier the Vikings had been up to roughly the same tricks, coming across the grey, wild sea in their sleek, low-slung ships; colonizing Orkney and using it as a springboard and base for three hundred years of systematic slaughter, pillage and mayhem further south. He told her of a burial mound the Vikings had broken into, to hide from a storm, and had carved graffiti on the walls with their axes as they waited for the storm to subside. It was still there, describing their systematic pillaging of the grave, declaring that Ingibiorg was the fairest lady in the world, they even chipped out little dogs and dragons.

Then further back still, there had been the ancient race who had come to Orkney over two thousand years before Christ, and had erected open temples of standing stones whilst burying their dead in chambers with entrances aligned directly to the setting sun on the winter solstice and other celestial events.

This was what he had come to see, along with his half-gypsy friend. He described it as his 'soul-home', where he wanted his heart to be buried. He was coming back here, to where he felt his safest, so that he could compare Craigairie and ascertain whether it was as real as he thought it was.

By the time they reached Thurso the slight trepidation Christina had felt first thing in the morning had largely evaporated, to be replaced by expectancy. Her first sight of Orkney did not diminish this. It rose out of the blue sea in a long, undulating line, climbing slowly from the east up to three high, green hills which fell away in sheer red cliffs, to the sea, chopped from the mainland, like a hand from an arm. If ever an island seemed proud of its isolation Orkney did, with its back turned on the mainland and its face staring west, into the wide Atlantic.

'It never fails to impress me,' David said. 'Every time I come here I think I'll be blasé about seeing it again and every time I see it again, I think, *SHIT*, it's good to be back.'

The ferry crossing was calm; the Pentland Firth had the glassy, smooth look, on top of considerable swell, which seemed to say 'Trust me if you dare'. For David, who knew this part of the world and was therefore acutely aware of the Pentland's wild reputation, the crossing felt somewhat like attacking a sleeping panther with a feather duster, but he kept this to himself. Christina came out on deck to admire the Old Man of Hoy, but she did not seem to be particularly enjoying the crossing. 'I hate boats,' she said with quiet feeling. 'I've always hated being on water.' She complained of a cramp in her stomach and a feeling of slight sickness.

'I used to get heartburn every time I came here,' David said. 'Something to do with electricity, I think. They stopped having resident curators at Stonehenge because they kept dying of heart attacks; same sort of thing.'

This gobbet of information failed to cheer Christina up, especially after they disembarked and the cramp and rising nausea were joined by the predicted heartburn.

She was in considerable discomfort during the comparatively short journey to David's friends' house. A searing, red-hot pain shot through her heart and clenched her chest in a talon-like grip. She doubled up, trying to breathe in a way which would not give her so much agony. She did not notice the road, nor the route they took, until the car stopped. He undid his safety belt.

'We're here,' he said.

She looked around in surprise. They were sitting in front of a small farmhouse which stood on the side of a low hill with a spectacular view spreading away in front of it. Straight ahead was the high, steep-sided Island of Hoy, with a line of smaller islands joined by a single straight causeway stretching out towards it. On the right, mainland Orkney curved in a long bay which came to a point about ten miles away, forming the narrow Sound of Hoy. Right below the house there was a small fishing village strung out along the shoreline.

David climbed out of the car, stretched his legs and took a long, deep breath. Christina got out carefully and slowly pulled herself erect, grimacing with pain.

'You OK?' he asked with genuine concern.

'It'll go,' she said. He looked at her for a couple of seconds and then shrugged as if to say 'suit yourself'.

At that moment the door of the house was wrenched open and even before David could turn properly, let alone defend himself, a man launched himself out and dived on to him with an inarticulate yell of joy. His momentum made David stagger, trip and half-fall to the gravel, with the man still on top of him.

He was a stick insect of a man; thin, with long legs which were the breadth of most men's arms. He was wearing torn jeans and a threadbare smoking jacket made of green velvet, the latter mercifully covering most of a tee-shirt with Christina had a nasty suspicion had once been white.

'Armstrong, ya bass-turd,' he shouted. 'Ye dinnae talk tae me fur four fucking years, then ye turn up wi-oot warning me.'

'I told you I was coming almost a week ago,' David gasped.

'A *week*?' the stick insect yelled derisively. 'There's three years' debris in there. It'd take a bulldozer just tae shift the dust.'

As he was talking Christina came out from behind the car and took him in at a glance.

The phrase 'speed casualty' leapt to mind.

He looked as if he had not slept in weeks, had not eaten in months and not washed in years. His hair was so tangled and unkempt that it had formed a good imitation of dreadlocks. His face was gaunt, grey and angular, with dark smudges under bloodshot eyes.

As she was looking he raised his head with a jerk.

'So,' he said, 'where's the b . . .?' His eyes lighted on her.

'The bird,' she said firmly, 'is here.'

'Ah,' he said. 'You must be . . .' He frowned and scratched his cheek.

'Christina,' she said. 'Christina MacRuarie.'

'Christina MacRuarie?' he said speculatively. 'Now there's a name to conjure with.' He stood up and offered her a slender, beautiful hand.

'Kelvin Ball,' he said. Somewhere in the deep recesses of her mind a bell rang. She ignored it.

'So are there still MacRuaries of Garmoran?' Kelvin asked. She was surprised and it must have showed because he grinned, revealing a gold tooth at the back of his mouth.

'Ah'm intae Scottish history,' he said in an exaggerated accent.

'Obscure Scottish history,' she replied. 'I'm only a MacRuarie by marriage. I thought they were the only people on earth who knew about their family.'

'Och no,' Kelvin replied. 'Christina MacRuarie's wan o' my heroines.' He turned to David, who was only just picking himself off the ground. 'Why did ye no tell me you were bringing wan o' my heroines?' He led her off, into the house, leaving David to tag along behind. He stopped in the hall and yelled up the staircase.

'Meg y'auld ratbag, get yer arse doon here. Wiv got company.'

There was a muffled thud, a curse and then the quick padding of hurrying feet. A white face enveloped by thick red hair looked over the banister, saw Kelvin and whispered hoarsely, 'Who is it?'

'It's me.' David walked into her line of vision. 'Davie.'

She peered at him through her hair and, after a moment, let out a piercing shriek and leapt down the stairs into David's arms.

'My favourite man,' she said, pushing him away to arm's length and inspecting him. 'Shite,' she said. 'I thought you were gonnae be the filth.' She smiled quickly. 'You're looking good, though,' she said. 'A wee bit peeky mebbe.'

'Meg. I'd like you to meet a friend of mine.' He steered her across to Christina.

'Christina MacRuarie, Meg Anderson. Meg Anderson, Christina MacRuarie.'

'Meg Ball,' she said.

'Sorry?' David asked.

'The name's Margaret *Ball*.'

It took a moment before it sank in. When it did, a huge, incredulous smile broke out on his face. 'Kidding me?'

She shook her head.

'You got married?' he said.

She nodded.

'I don't believe you.'

She showed him her ring. He laughed.

'Brilliant,' he said with feeling. 'When did that happen? Why wasn't I asked?'

'Last spring,' Kelvin said. 'You were in Libya, or was it Syria?'

'Something like that,' David said, dismissively.

They moved through to a sitting room, which lived up to its billing as the untidiest room Christina had seen in a very long time. Months of old newspapers and scores of records carpeted the floor, ashtrays perched precariously all over the room, overflowing with cigarette butts. Half-empty coffee mugs and glasses nestled amongst the debris. The only odd thing Christina noticed, when her eyes became accustomed to the murk, was that, as in Craigairie, there was an amazing collection of extremely expensive television, video and stereo equipment. The television on its own must have cost upwards of eight hundred pounds; with a screen which could have done respectable service in a small cinema. The stereo was large, spit new and ostentatious. Its speakers in the corner of the room were large enough to double as side-tables.

The two men knelt down by the fire and attempted to light it whilst bickering good-naturedly about who had the best method. Christina and Meg sat down on the sofa, the latter watching David with a slight smile. When the fire lighters went outside to get logs, she turned to Christina who was massaging her chest, wondering whether she might have had a minor stroke.

'How long've you known Davie?' Meg asked.

'A few days,' Christina replied. She saw Meg raise her eyebrows slightly, and added, 'We're not, er ... um ... going out, having an affair.' She told Meg how they had met and how they came to be in Orkney, until the two men staggered back in, laden with logs, still debating how the fire should be lit. Meg followed David with her eyes, frowning slightly. As he reached the fireplace she shook her head quickly, shaking herself free of whatever thoughts had been running through her mind. She turned to Christina, who was now massaging her temples.

'You OK?' she asked.

Christina gave a quick, forced smile. 'I've got the worst attack of heartburn I've ever had, and trying not to think about it is giving me a headache.' She thought she saw Kelvin and Meg exchange quick glances.

Meg stood up. 'Well then,' she said. 'Mebbe we oughtae go and take a look at the medicine cabinet.'

David and Kelvin lit the fire and then disappeared in search of a pub with a pool table. Christina, with two pills of indeterminate nature fizzing around in her stomach, lay down on the sofa while Meg put on some music.

'The class of eighty-whatever,' the latter remarked, looking at a dog-eared and faded photograph of youths in rugger kit in two neat rows, the front one sitting and the back one standing.

'Have you known David since he was at school?' Christina asked from her prostrate position on the sofa.

Meg nodded. 'We had a wee affair. He was sixteen and I was twenty-five.' She let out a breath of laughter. 'It didn't last long.'

Christina did a little mental calculation and came out with the surprising conclusion that Meg was at least thirty-six years old. She looked ten years younger – at least she looked like a somewhat raddled twenty-seven-year-old, rather than someone upon whom a fortieth birthday was closing in fast.

She sat down beside the smouldering fire and exhaled a lungful of cigarette smoke in a long sigh.

'I'd like to've had an affair with David when he was about twenty-four,' she said, speculatively.

'Why didn't you?'

'He was hitched.' She gave Christina a quick look. 'Far as I know he still is?'

'Is he?' Christina asked, conscious of the note of interrogation behind Meg's words. 'He never speaks about anyone.'

For a moment they fell silent, and then, simultaneously, had the same thought about Christina's last remark.

They looked at each other.

They both shook their heads, smiling.

'Naa,' Meg said. 'I know David. If he was still goan oot wi' the bird I'm thinking of he'd've told you about her.'

'Who was she?' Christina asked. 'Is she?'

'She was called Natasha something. He carried a bonfire for her for two years, then she noticed him . . .'

52

'And?'

'And you've never seen two less compatible people totally in love wi' each other,' she laughed quickly and then looked towards Christina. 'Aye well, if he's no talking about her my guess is she's chucked him. That'd mebbe explain what he's doing hiding in Ayrshire.'

'He told me he intends to stay in Scotland.'

Meg nodded. 'That'd figure,' she remarked dryly, took a deep breath and threw her cigarette into the fire.

'So?' she said, standing up and walking towards the stereo. 'What's all this about Davie and a standing stone?' She took the classical music which was playing off the turntable and clicked a tape into the machine. Christina waited for her to return to her chair before answering her question. She felt she could trust Meg, without having to think about it.

'I think if I told you, you wouldn't believe me.' As she said it she was conscious of the fact that she was about to attempt to explain something she not only did not understand, but also had little inclination even to think about.

'But I think I ought to tell you anyway, because I saw it happen, or at least part of it, and I think David came here to try and figure it out.'

'So what is "it"?' Meg asked.

In short sentences, to avoid subjecting herself to any more of the stabbing pains in her chest than she had already, Christina told Meg everything she knew or guessed.

Meg listened in silence, only occasionally interrupting Christina to ask her what she had seen, or heard, or felt. At one point when she did this Christina was evasive and they slid into a brief side-track. Christina had been describing David's condition when she found him by the stone.

'Why were you there?' Meg interrupted.

'Where?'

'By the standing stone. What were you doing there?'

'Oh, just walking,' Christina replied airily.

'And you just happened to stumble across David lying naked at the foot of a standing stone in the middle of nowhere. Why don't I believe you?'

Christina raised her head from the cushion it had been resting on and looked at Meg. They gazed at each other for a while before Christina shrugged and let her head fall back.

'It's kinda complicated to explain,' she said.

'I'm in no hurry.'

There was a brief silence.

'It called me,' Christina said. 'I guess.'

'You guess?'

'I dreamt about it. I had a conversation with my father before Christmas and he mentioned a stone up on the hills . . .' She paused to regulate her breath. 'Some fifteenth-century monk had tried to have it destroyed. He'd written to a bishop asking for permission to uproot

53

it . . . I forgot about it until I had this dream, when someone I loved very much, who died recently, told me to come to this stone . . . so I went.'

She did not look up, but she could feel Meg's eyes on her. She continued slowly.

'It's not bad, the stone,' she said. 'I mean, I don't think it's evil.'

'But there *is* something there?'

'Oh sure.' She tried to picture it in her mind, to remember how it had felt when she saw it for the first time and then when she first touched it. Hard as she tried she could only get a vague picture, as if through opaque glass. Something in her mind had instinctively closed the memory off in a dark corner where she could not get at it.

'You know . . .?' she began. She shook her head. 'Did I tell you the name David's got for his poltergeist?' she asked.

'No.'

'He calls it Delilah. He thinks of it as a woman; he treats it like a woman. In fact you could say they both seem to treat each other like . . . almost like lovers. He ignores her, she gets angry, he tolerates her bad temper, she burns out her mood and becomes coy. I think it's kind of the same with him and the stone.'

'Dé Doveleski,' Meg said.

Christina raised her head again. 'Sorry?'

'Dé Doveleski. It's the Romany name for Mother Earth. Ask Kelvin about it; he's the didakai.'

This time Christina sat up straight. She opened her mouth to speak but the words never came. She remembered something which had been nagging her since they had arrived.

'Kelvin Ball?' she said. 'Of course. The writer.'

'The very one.'

Once it had got a finger into a crack in the wall of her appalling memory it quickly pulled itself up to the dizzying ledge of her conscious mind. Kelvin Ball had written a cult book a couple of years back called something like didakai.

She thought for a moment.

Meg had said it only a moment ago and it had passed over her head without registering. Dé something. Dé Bov . . . Rov . . . Doveleski.

Dé Doveleski.

Everyone had been reading it, all through one summer. Someone had sent it to Erlend and he had read her bits of it he had liked.

She remembered how he had described it.

Cider With Rosie on acid.

It had been a long silence, but when Christina broke it it was only to say 'Shit'.

'What?' Meg asked.

'I should've remembered. That's terrible.'

'Listen, forget it. Kelvin disnae usually know what he was daeing last night. He's hardly likely tae hold it against a complete stranger if they don't remember what he was up to three years ago.' She paused. 'You were telling me about the stone?'

Talking about it helped Christina to deal with something she had shut off for two weeks. At times she had thought it was just another subtle mental torture she had created for herself.

But when she finally articulated it, attempted to explain it to someone, she knew that whatever it had been, it was real.

It was also feminine.

That occurred to her for the first time during that conversation. The more she thought about it the more obvious it seemed. Everything fitted; Delilah's antics, David's failure to understand it despite his amazingly calm perseverance, the feeling of womb-like safety she had felt when she had touched the stone.

Everything made sense.

Quite suddenly she ceased to be disconcerted by the thought of Craigairie.

Kelvin beat David three times running, twice on a black ball game.

David retaliated with seven victories in a row.

Some locals took them both on in a doubles game. On the first one Kelvin sank the black from the break, which won him the game in one shot. The locals doubled the stakes to a pint each for the winners.

Fired by a combination of unbelievable luck and the flashes of sheer brilliance which occasionally afflict seasoned pool-players, they took on and duly stuffed all opposition. Eight games and six free pints later they bowed out undefeated, aware that their winning streak was at the expense of the pride of the local talent, who did not take kindly to being humiliated on home ground.

They went to another pub, then another.

They called in the end from a pub in Finnstown, fourteen miles from where they had started. Christina took the call and then repeated the message to Meg, who was in the bath.

'They want us to meet them at a pub called the Croft, they said you'd know it.'

'Out by Maes Howe,' Meg said. 'Were they stotius?'

'I'd say very,' Christina replied. Meg appeared from the bathroom, wrapping a towel around herself.

'Well then,' she said, 'we're just gonnae have tae get ourselves stoned before we go.' She went into her bedroom, which was chaotic, picked her way across to the dressing table and picked up an Indian box. She lobbed it on to the unmade bed.

'D'you smoke?' she asked. Christina nodded.

'Can you roll them?' Meg inquired. Christina nodded again and got down to work as Meg dressed herself.

'Are they always like this?' Christina asked after a while. 'Kelvin and David?'

'They haven't even started yet,' Meg replied. 'When they really get going I've known them keep at it for months.'

'Does David come up here often?'

Meg was sitting at the dressing table, her back to Christina. But Christina saw the look on her face in the mirror as she replied.

'He used to.' She paused. 'Before I moved in with Kelv.'

David and Kelvin turned up at the Croft, holding on to each other, half an hour late and wove through a maze of tables to where Meg and Christina were waiting. Before they reached it they stopped, had a short discussion and diverted their course across to the bar. Five minutes later they returned, David holding two pints, Kelvin clutching four whiskies.

'I didn't know what you'd want,' the latter said, sitting down. 'So I got these.' He put them down and produced two bottles of soda water from his trouser pockets. He removed the lids with the butt of his lighter; quite a neat trick, Christina thought, considering his condition.

'Evening, ladies,' David said as he sat down. 'Sorry we were late. My friend here got into a row with a fisherman, which very nearly came to blows.' He said it deadpan, as if he had never been remotely concerned. Kelvin saw the look on Meg's face and raised his hands defensively.

'S'no me,' he said. He jerked his thumb towards his friend. 'It's him. He's a bad influence.'

Meg nodded. 'I ken. You should know better, though.' She could not conceal the affection in her voice. Kelvin saw it and grinned back at her.

Christina watched the three friends affectionately ribbing each other. David and Kelvin were in charge of the conversation, working together like a double-act. David played quietly laconic to Kelvin's manic good-humouredness.

Meg, meanwhile, ran interference, disapproving of Kelvin in an almost maternal way, and of David with something more akin to suspicion. She was occasionally a bit too sharp with him, sending out barbs tipped with perhaps a little more venom than she intended. David, in turn, lobbed one or two of his comments back at her with a sort of delayed fuse, so that they exploded only when you stopped to think about them. It was like a quick game of mental tennis, with Meg slicing a few tricky ones in his direction, and David chipping them back. Meg won every exchange, but only, one suspected, because David was not really trying.

They were over and forgotten in a couple of minutes, the two of them reverting to a more acceptable level of badinage. Kelvin ignored them, or treated it as all part of the general cut and thrust, grinning at them as they sparred. But there was something between them which was as private as it was faintly uncomfortable. Kelvin was not included in it.

On the whole, however, Christina enjoyed their company more than she could have dared hope that night. They were funny, gentle people, with relationships she could understand and like. If it had not been for the crippling heartburn which still clawed at her chest with iron talons, Christina would have had an unexpectedly pleasant evening. As it was she was distracted by the pain and had to drink too much in order to keep it at bay. By the end of the evening a combination of the pain and the whisky made it so hard to concentrate on what was happening that she missed the beginning of the sharpest disagreement, only managing to focus on it when Meg suddenly flared up at Kelvin.

The two men had been discussing what they were going to do when the pub closed. They had been exchanging names which meant nothing to Christina and it was only when David made some remark about there being a full moon that Christina saw Meg shifting irritably.

'Can we not just go back home?' she asked.

'You can, if you want,' he said. 'I'll take the other car.'

'You're too pissed tae drive and you're not insured either,' Meg argued.

'I'm staying,' Kelvin said. 'At least I'm insured.'

Meg looked from her husband to his friend, then back.

'What's goan on here?' she said.

'Nothing,' Kelvin said. 'Just a wee sightsee. It'll take ten minutes.'

'Ten minutes tonight is an hour tomorrow,' Meg replied cryptically.

David stood up, pushing his chair back. He seemed slightly exasperated with Meg.

'We're just going to Brogar,' he said. 'It's not as if we're joining the Foreign Legion.' He gazed down at Meg, his eyes softening.

'Come on, Meggie,' he said. 'Ten minutes round trip, just so Christina can see Brogar by the light of the full moon.'

'What's Brogar?' Christina asked.

'Come with me and I'll show you,' he said.

She followed him out, followed by Kelvin then, last and reluctant, Meg. Once out of the pub Christina pointed David over to where her car was parked, leaving Kelvin and Meg behind them. As she reached her car she turned and looked back towards the door of the pub. Kelvin and Meg were facing each other under the light, the latter gesticulating and talking very fast. Kelvin said something back, to which Meg shook her head. Kelvin shrugged and disappeared out of view behind a parked Volvo. A moment later a raw, hoarse engine revved into life, two car doors slammed and with a screech of tyres a battered Alfa-Romeo reversed across the car park, performed a slewing turn, spraying grit in all directions and took off down the road. Christina followed them at a more leisurely pace.

'What was all that about?' she asked.

'What? . . . Sorry?' David jerked his head around to look at her.

'All that angry driving.'

57

'Oh, that . . .' he said. After a while it became apparent that he was not going to say any more, so she persevered.

'They were fighting back there, weren't they?' She was not interested enough to continue for much longer, but having started she felt she should see her inquiry through.

'They were fighting all evening,' he said.

'Really?' she asked, thinking that the only fight she had detected had been between Meg and him. 'What about?'

'Take the next right,' he said. She indicated and turned on to a small road leading down to a glittering loch. 'Me, I guess,' he said.

'Oh? Why?'

He shrugged but did not answer. Christina was slightly irritated and more hurt than she cared to admit that he had shut down again the moment he was left on his own with her.

'Meg disapproves of me.'

'Goodness. Why?'

'She thinks I'm a bad influence. Whenever I turn up Kelv gets involved in all sorts of shiftless schemes.'

'Like?' At that moment her headlights fell on the Alfa, parked in a lay-by on the other side of the road. Behind it, in a field, Christina saw something which made her hit the brakes so hard that David almost went through the windscreen.

'Jesus,' she exclaimed. In the arc of her headlight she could see a big, dark slab of stone at least twenty feet high. Its sides were straight as rulers, one larger than the other so that it was not squared off on top, but instead rose to a sharp point. To its right there was another one, just as big but less symmetrical.

'What is that?' Christina asked, with awe.

'Stenness,' David said, picking himself off the dashboard. 'Drive on.'

'But Meg and Kelvin?'

'I know.'

She obeyed him and parked, as he instructed, about a hundred yards up the road.

'OK,' he said, climbing out of the car. 'Fun time.'

It was not a completely clear night; a thin, cold, easterly breeze was scudding small, dark clouds in front of the moon, silhouetting them with silver halos. Behind them the sky was black and ice-clear, with the major constellations of stars alone in the universe; the Plough, Orion's Belt and the closer planets.

They were standing in a wide, flat basin between a low circle of dark hills. On both sides of the road, about a quarter of a mile away, there was water; two rippling lochs whispering to each other across the wide causeway. Christina stood for a moment, breathing in the clear, cold air, savouring the faint tang of salt on the tip of her tongue. David walked around the car to her, removing his scarf.

'I'm going to give you a chance to do something I've always wished I did myself when *I* first came here,' he said. 'But if the idea freaks you out in any way, please say so and I'll spare you the ordeal.'

At that moment she had a spasm of heartburn which doubled her up, reducing her to a foetal huddle on the ground. He crouched down beside her.

'It'll go away here,' he said. 'Follow me and it'll be gone in ten minutes.'

She looked up into his face. 'How?'

'Trust me.'

She winced as a new spasm assaulted her.

He waited patiently as she regained her composure.

'D'you think it'll freak me out?' she asked. 'This idea of yours?'

He shrugged underneath his greatcoat.

'Maybe. There's no accounting for taste.'

After a few seconds' thought she nodded.

'OK. I'll do it. What is it?'

'It involves being blindfolded,' he said, a little guiltily.

She looked at him for a moment.

'OK.'

He blindfolded her with his scarf, tying it as tightly over her eyes as he could without causing her discomfort. He then led her on up the hill. In her pitch darkness Christina imagined the ground in front of her. Great chasms opened up at her feet and the path was strewn with hard, unyielding obstacles to trip over. But she met no such pitfalls and when the path did become remotely uneven David held her hand and guided her over them.

'Right,' he said, 'Um, when I take the blindfold off . . . um . . .' He laughed quickly. 'Just feast your eyes.' He untied the scarf and she opened her eyes.

She looked for a long, long time, with David beside her, watching her intently with an excited glint in his eyes.

She turned slowly through three hundred and sixty degrees, taking in the stone circle of Brogar as it should be taken; unhurriedly and from the inside.

It was stunning. They were smaller stones than the ones up the road, but there were a hell of a lot more of them. They were in a near-perfect circle on the gentle slope of a hillside. The light was deceptive, but Christina calculated the distance from herself to the stones to be more or less thirty yards. As she was standing in the middle this meant that the circle was sixty yards wide.

She had been to Glastonbury twice, both times to see a pop concert.

There was no comparison. There could never have been a concert here; it would have been desecration. Besides, the stones would not have allowed it. They had the calm, lazy power of a pride of lions taking their afternoon siesta. You could look at this place and admire it, but Christina knew that this was not a place you messed about in, or with.

As she completed her circle she laughed quietly and nodded.

'Nice, V-E-R-Y nice.'

'I envy you,' David said. She nodded again.

'I can see why.' She wandered away from him, across towards a sort of gate composed of two stones, like rough-hewn faces looking at each other, rather closer together than the others. She walked up to it and felt the stones. They were glittering with frost and their dim grey shadows lay on the sparkling ground.

She moved upwards, slowly walking towards the top end of the circle. Spotting one which looked particularly like a face – in fact rather like David's profile – she cut across the top corner, her tread scrunching in the frost-brittle grass. She touched the stone, her hand tingling, as if the hard granite was hot, rather than icy cold. She turned and looked down across the circle. The wind whipped her hair around her face and she shook it away, letting it stream behind her like a fraying golden banner.

David had moved away from the centre of the circle towards the gate, his pace slow but steady. She watched him, captivated by the effect of movement within the moonlit circle. She could see his face, white as marble with dark shadows around his eyes. He was looking towards her. For a moment he stopped and was dead still. Just as his movements had served to accentuate the feeling of age-long watchfulness in this place of vigilance and immense stillness, his motionlessness seemed, to Christina, to contrast with the slow turning of the aeons. Since two thousand years before Christ, when the Hebrews were writing the earliest chapters of the Bible, the Egyptians were constructing the first tombs in the Valley of the Kings, before the first traces of the civilizations in Greece which would later influence the west, men had been coming here to worship and wonder.

The movement of one man in such a place was like the beat of a mayfly's wing in a hundred years; tiny and insignificant.

David was obviously conscious of this, or of something similar. He began to walk up towards her, but twice on the way up he stopped and looked around with a slightly unnerved defiance; on both occasions it took a couple of minutes for him to reassure himself that nothing untoward was happening out of his line of vision.

As she watched him, Christina was surprised and shocked to find herself wondering whether he would come to her, would take her in his arms and kiss her. She did not know if she wanted it, but the fact that her subconscious had been contemplating the possibility without her conscious permission was a sort of seal of approval in itself. She braced herself as he drew near. He reached her, stopping a couple of yards in front of her. They looked at each other for fully half a minute, gazing steadily into each other's eyes, before he spoke.

'D'you like it?' he asked.

She began to nod her head, but it was ten seconds before the movement speeded up enough for him to notice it. He bit his lip pensively and for a moment, a second, she could feel how close he was to taking the step across the space between them, like a salmon turning over in the water around an enticing fly. Then he was away again, snapping back into himself like elastic.

'Good,' he said. 'I thought, maybe, you wouldn't see the point and you'd be furious with me.' There was something in his voice which told her that this was a deliberate, if subtle, double entendre; that they were back to the silent conversation they had when they were gazing at each other.

'I'm not furious,' she said.

Not furious, just slightly disappointed.

They had intended to stay in Orkney for a week at the outside. Instead they arrived in the depths of winter and left, six weeks later, in the spring. In Orkney, time was measured in days and seasons, with nothing of importance in between. Weeks would sneak by unnoticed; nothing seemed to happen on a regular enough basis to merit the days having names of their own. This timelessness had a lot to do with Kelvin and Meg's meandering lifestyle, but it was also something to do with Orkney itself. It was as if the small archipelago had seen too many changes, in thousands of years, to be much affected by the day-to-day goings-on in the world over the water. It was like an old, venerable, wise woman, sitting on her rocking chair in the shadiest corner of the room, dozing peacefully, with a smile on her face. Time did not quite stand still, but it kept itself to a bare minimum.

Christina and Meg found that they liked each other, which was lucky, considering the amount of time they were left on their own by the two men. There was a bond between Kelvin and David which made it impossible for anyone else to be anything more than bit-parts in their friendship.

It was not hard to see why Meg disapproved of David. It was not so much that he was a bad influence on Kelvin; Kelvin was perfectly capable of leading himself astray, without David's assistance. But there was something aimless and purposeless about Kelvin, which acted as a built-in regulator for his otherwise all-consuming desire to have a good time, at any cost. When David was not around, even for a short time, Kelvin quickly became idle and apathetic, as if reverting to type. David motivated him, feeding ideas into him, appealing directly to his hedonistic nature and bypassing his lethargic side.

Long ago, Meg told Christina, Kelvin had done his earliest experiments with drugs on David's instigation. But whereas David had long since lost interest in any but the most occasional use, Kelvin had flung himself into years of debilitating habit. It had been David, also, who persuaded Kelvin to leave university, so that he could rediscover his Romany roots, his birthright. He had taken the advice, left university and had written one beautiful book, blowing any chance he might have had of obtaining credible qualifications from twelve years of education.

The list went on. There was even a strong irony in Kelvin and Meg's relationship, in that David had met her first, when he came to Orkney on his own, as a teenager, and had introduced both her and Orkney to Kelvin. When she split up with David, Kelvin stepped in. It always appeared to work that way, which was why Meg was so uneasy about David. He had been nudging Kelvin's life off course for as long as they had known each other, but no one, not even Kelvin, had ever budged David from the private furrow he ploughed for himself. Kelvin always ended up living his friend's whims.

It had been the cause of the argument Christina had seen on the first night. Meg did not mind if they were off getting slaughtered in a smoky pool-room – it was par for the course, as far as she was concerned, and she could live with it. But then they had dragged her off to Brogar in the middle of the night and warning bells started to jangle in Meg's mind. She had seen them like that before; Kelvin like a flushed schoolboy, ready for anything and David smiling to himself as he prodded his friend on. She recognized the symptoms and knew she could not do anything to stop it, which angered her. She could only sit back and watch glumly as Kelvin went flying off on another tangent, like a high-powered motorboat roaring off into the sunset with David water-skiing in his wake.

The odd thing about them was that they found Meg's behaviour genuinely inexplicable. They did not go out of their way to annoy her, in fact David made a point of lighting fires, taking out the rubbish, helping with the washing up and sucking up to Meg in general, or at least keeping her sweet. He made no pretence of the fact that he did not want to fight with her and, up to a point, this defused her anger. But behind all of this he was working on the assumption that Meg, not he, was being unreasonable. He could not understand what it was about himself that she so feared; as far as he was concerned, he was seeing his best friend and perhaps being a little selfish and secretive about their new obsession. But he knew how Meg would react if he told her about Craigairie and admitted why he had come to Orkney. She would freak out, think that it was some fiendish plot to lead Kelv from the path of righteousness once again, whereas he was just bouncing an idea off the only person he knew who would take him seriously. And he had his reasons for not telling Christina.

So they went off together, quite happy to take the women – if they wanted to go out and stand around looking at standing stones, often in driving rain. After a couple of afternoons of sitting in a steamed-up car while David and Kelvin wandered around barren hillsides, looking at, listening to, feeling and measuring any old standing stone they could find, Meg quit. Christina would have liked to stay with them, but she could sense David's unease with her and she knew when to back off. As long as she kept a safe distance from him he was gentle, courteous and kind to her. But if she stepped across some invisible line he drew around himself she could almost hear the portcullis clanging down in front of him.

Ambivalence was too small a word for the way he thought about Christina, or tried not to think about her, as the case might be. He liked her as a person, at face value; there was very little about her on to which he could hook any dislike. She was intelligent and intuitive enough to be able to steer a comfortable course through a potentially uncomfortable situation, without ever appearing to be fazed. She was an easy and sensitive guest, never an encumbrance or a problem. There seemed to be no malice or ill-will in her, no affectation or insincerity; what you saw in her was what you got.

What David saw was a woman who got more beautiful every time he looked at her, who had come from nowhere at the very point when his private war with Craigairie had reached a climax and had then insinuated her way into his life with careless ease. She knew something about him that not even Kelvin would have thought possible, and David could certainly not describe, even if he had wished to. When she visited Craigairie she had left with a little bit of its secret, like a small infection, which might some day become a raging fever. She knew more about what David had found at Craigairie than Kelvin could possibly guess, because she had been there.

And now, somehow, she was here with him in Orkney. She had found her way into his inner sanctum and the only thing he knew for sure was that he did not want her there.

For her part Christina was as confused as he was. She had just gone for a walk one morning, after having an unusually vivid dream, and had ended up on an island four hundred miles away, with three complete strangers. One day she was wading through a mire of self-pity and boredom and despair, the next she was somehow snagged on to the coat-tails of a strange man. The fact that he did not seem to want her there was hardly relevant, given that she did not know quite how she had got there in the first place.

At first she was just embarrassed by her own presence – though not enough to make her turn around and go home. Then she began to settle into the formless life in St Mary's, wandering about with Meg and spending the evenings, the four of them together, listening and talking and laughing. It was fun, on the whole – and when, because of the friction underlying these friendships, it wasn't fun, Christina backed off tactfully and pretended not to notice.

But apart from it being an amusing holiday, she found herself drawn, unwillingly, to David. He fascinated her. She had never seen anyone so self-contained, so at ease with themselves. He was like an impregnable fortress, so expansively fortified that something of great worth had to be lurking inside; dungeons or treasure-troves, or both. Meg saw a part of him he would have preferred to have kept hidden and ran up against his armour trying to get at it. Kelvin was let in on the understanding that he could come and go as he pleased, but he only saw what he was shown. His ex-girlfriend, Natasha, who had shared a bed with him for five years, must have been there as well and it must have hurt him terribly when she left, taking his secrets with her. But other than these there cannot have been many people who ever pierced David's bubble.

Ninety-nine times out of a hundred Christina would not have been remotely interested in anyone who made such a point of locking the world out. He did not, after all, seem to need anyone else but himself. But there was something about him which made him the rare exception. For a start, he hid behind the most beautiful manners, not just when he was eating, but in everything he did. He was considerate and generous, never failing to pick up the bill in a restaurant, or a shop, or pub. Christina hardly opened her purse in all the time she was in Orkney. He went and picked up the newspapers in the mornings, disappeared on solitary shopping trips, returning with boxes of goodies. At the same time, he was not doing it to be liked. He freely admitted that he was willing to buy himself a quiet life, but even that was part of his fortification. In truth, Christina suspected that he used this gentlemanliness just as he used his habitual irony, to deflect attention from himself.

She found herself watching him and having the same feeling she occasionally got when she was watching a movie, slightly stoned; marvelling at the skill of the actors instead of following the story. He was good at it, so good that Christina could only sit back and admire such a complex and sophisticated defensive system.

But she had seen through it once and she could not stop seeing through it thereafter. By accident, or fate, or coincidence she had stumbled upon him at the very moment when all of his defences were down, naked and vulnerable, half-dead with cold at the base of a standing stone. She had found him when he was in such bad need of help that he could not even refuse it. With his fortress intact and his defences at hand he was an interesting enough person to merit keeping in touch with, but without them, from where Christina was looking, he was somehow deeply attractive. There was not anything awful or ugly underneath, he just had some very ingenious and clever ways of making shyness look like strength.

'Does anyone ever get through to David?' she asked Meg at one point. 'I mean, does he ever really *let* anyone through?'

Meg stopped chopping carrots in the kitchen sink, and stared thoughtfully out of the window in front of her for a few moments.

'No,' she said finally, shaking her head. 'He thought that Natasha got through, but that was because he was so flattered that she even bothered to look at him.'

'Why?' Christina asked. 'Was she very beautiful?'

'She was the sort of woman that intelligent men go silly over.' She paused, then added, 'Which is ironic, really, because David's the sort of man some women go silly over. It's his eyes, I think.'

'But she did get under his skin?' Christina asked. 'I mean, nothing seems to bother him. It's like he's impregnable.'

'Aye, she got under his skin,' Meg replied, after brief contemplation. 'I think mebbe he was in love with her.' She paused and added, 'As much as he's capable of it.'

'What d'you mean by that?'

'I mean . . . I think, mebbe, Natasha only ever got David in his "lover-mode", just like Kelv only gets him on the "let's-be-eighteen again" kick. I'm not sure I've ever seen Davie be completely honest about himself, except mebbe when he was in front of a camera, with bombs going off all around him.'

'That's interesting,' Christina murmured.

Meg put down the carrot she was holding and turned, giving Christina a long, steady look.

'It's scary, if you ask me,' Meg said finally. 'This is a man who's only ever really happy when he's too feart tae think.'

As if to prove Meg's thesis, including her aside about David being the sort of man some women go silly over, the Linnhe Thurston affair kicked into life around that time.

Linnhe Thurston was the niece of Dorothy Thurston, who was one of the unofficial but influential matriarchs of Orkney, a select band of middle-aged women who seemed to have fingers in every available pie. She lived in a beautiful, ancient house set back from a side street in the middle of Kirkwall, which had once been the convent attached to St Magnus Cathedral. She was a very clever and shrewd woman of sixty-five, well-known both for her championing of environmental issues in the area and for her eccentric religious convictions. She would not go to church, for instance, because she said that if there ever had been a Christ, he would disapprove violently of all the bullshit that went on in his name (her very words).

She had a niece, Linnhe, who was reputedly the prettiest girl in Orkney and who lived in the Nunnery when she was not at university down south. Her parents had emigrated to Australia the previous year and she had gone with them, only to return a couple of months later, complaining that she was homesick and bored. Considering the fun she had in Orkney it was hardly surprising that her new home failed to live up to it. At twenty Linnhe Thurston was just the right mixture of wild, youthful exuberance, raw sex appeal and coquetry. She was slender and lissom, with a mane of Pre-Raphaelite bronze hair and a pale, oval face with wide brown eyes, a retroussé nose and bee-stung lips. Kelvin was obsessed by her, along with half the other men in Orkney. But like them he did not dare go near her for fear of running up against her aunt, from whom she seemed inseparable. There were endless stories about hopeful young men going to the Nunnery for tea, to woo the fair Linnhe, only to stagger out, shredded with embarrassment and humiliation after suffering at the taloned hands and whiplash tongue of Aunt Dorothy.

There was some consternation, therefore, when David turned up one afternoon, about three weeks into his stay in Orkney, and announced that he had been to tea with 'this wonderful old witch and her stunning niece'. By that point even Kelvin had ducked out of David's endless, pointless interest in standing stones. For a while it had been fun, but the novelty soon wore off and he left David to it. He was, therefore, not with David when he met Dorothy Thurston, by a burial chamber outside the little town of Finstown.

David had been sitting outside the chamber, which was high up on a hill above the bay of Firth, staring over the water towards the island of Shapinsay, a grey blur in the light drizzle. He did not see anyone coming up the hill and assumed he was alone until a voice right beside him jerked him out of his reverie.

'You're David Armstrong and I claim my five pounds.'

He jumped with surprise and the old woman, who had appeared from nowhere and was standing within three feet of him, stepped back, raising her hands in apology.

'I'm sorry, I didn't mean to surprise you.'

He stood up and looked at her. She was in her mid-sixties with grey hair, still flecked with black escaping from beneath a headscarf. She had a strong, wise face, with many laugh-lines around her eyes and mouth. She had an air of businesslike efficiency about her, as if she was used to getting her way.

'Do I know you?' he asked, still confused by her presence.

She smiled and extended her hand.

'Probably not,' she said, giving him a firm handshake. 'Dorothy Thurston.' The name rang a bell in his mind and he frowned momentarily.

'You live in Kirkwall, don't you?' he asked.

She assented with a nod and a knowing smile. 'With my niece, Linnhe.'

'Ah,' David said, returning the smile. 'I knew I'd heard the name.'

'Dear Linnhe,' she said. 'A sweet child, but perhaps a touch *too* aware of her effect on men.' She paused, then went on, 'And you *are* David Armstrong, or am I getting senile?'

'I am indeed,' he replied. 'How . . .?'

She answered his question before he had time to ask it.

'I admire your work, Mr Armstrong.'

'David, please,' he said. She inclined her head in a small bow.

'Then I admire your work, David.'

'Thank you,' he said.

'I was quite upset when I heard you had given up, but then I think I can understand your reasons.'

'Really?' he asked. 'You're in a minority.'

'People are so insensitive, when it comes to making money out of the vocations of others.' She hit it so squarely on the head in one sentence that David laughed out loud. She smiled at him, then glanced up at the sky.

'Terrible day,' she said. 'Would you like to have the best cup of tea in Orkney?'

He thought for a couple of seconds.

'I'd love to.'

'Then come with me and we'll get Linnhe to concoct one of her demon brews. The poor dear's a witch, but she doesn't know what to do with it, except confuse men and make uncannily delicious tea.'

Half an hour later David was sitting in a big, old-fashioned kitchen in the Nunnery in Kirkwall, drying off in front of the Aga and sipping a mug of tea which tasted of cardamom, among other things. Linnhe had been 'coaxed out of her lair' by her aunt and had appeared in a long skirt and a baggy shirt. She hardly spoke in all the time David was there, but hardly took her eyes off him either.

'So what brings you to Orkney?' Dorothy had asked, when they had settled down.

David contemplated this.

'It's a long story,' he replied.

'I like long stories,' she said.

So he told her.

Dorothy Thurston understood everything he said, listened in silence until he had finished and then started to ask a stream of pertinent questions, which David answered as well as he was able. The only facts he held back from her were the existence of Christina and where his stone actually was. She found her way to them both, identifying them by their absence and broaching them tactfully, at the end of her interrogation.

'There's a woman in this, somewhere?' she said. It was half a question, half a statement. 'I can feel her.'

David gazed at her for a few moments. He nodded.

'But you don't want to discuss her?' she said.

'Not much,' he admitted.

'You may not want to think about it now, but you may have to before too long. It's all very well being supremely cerebral about

67

something like this, but there'll come a time when you'll need a more oblique approach, if you're going to crack it. Also ...' She smiled slightly. 'I notice that you don't tell me where this is all happening and although I can understand why you don't want me to know, I think, maybe, you'll have to learn to be less possessive about this thing. As you said yourself, you can't take it on alone.'

A brief silence fell. David lit a cigarette and glanced at Linnhe, who took her eyes off him as his met them. He turned back to Dorothy.

'You don't seem surprised by this,' he said.

'Don't I?' she inquired. 'Believe me, I am. I'm not surprised that it *can* happen, but I'm flabbergasted that it *is* happening.'

'And you don't doubt anything I've told you?'

'No,' she said. 'Why should you lie? Besides,' she added, 'I know the truth when I see it.'

He left soon afterwards and returned to St Mary's. After he had gone, Dorothy Thurston sat, deep in thought, while her niece cleared up around her.

When David next went to see Dorothy he took Kelvin and Christina along with him. Unlike his previous visit the proceedings were complicated by a series of treacherous undercurrents which rendered conversation all but impossible. Kelvin was glued to the beautiful Linnhe throughout and could not help but notice that she watched David with an admiration which already had his clothes off and was moving swiftly towards the nearest bed. It was not the first time David had unwittingly done this to him with women but he felt no better about it now than he had in the past.

Christina also saw the look in Linnhe's eyes and was both shocked and annoyed at herself for the instinctive reaction it inspired in her. She had been assuming that David was her own personal conundrum, only to find that she had competition in the form of a twenty-year-old sexpot who lived ten miles down the road. She was jealous.

Only David seemed unaware of the complications going on around him, or unconcerned by them. He chatted away with Dorothy while she surveyed the scene from an armchair, smiling to herself. When, finally, Kelvin and Christina became restless and started making body-signals about leaving, it was Dorothy, not David, who noticed and brought the proceedings to a close. Christina and Kelvin took the opportunity gratefully, but David lingered for a moment and Dorothy took him aside.

'I've been thinking,' she said. 'And I think you ought to see Callanish.'

'Callanish?' he asked, thinking about the distance. She misunderstood him and explained.

'On the island of Lewis. It's the most important neolithic moonsight in Europe. If you're going to find what you've been looking for, you're more likely to find it there than here.'

While he was pulling on his coat, Dorothy followed Christina out into the dark courtyard, catching her as she reached the gate out into the street.

'You'll come back again, my dear?' she said.

Christina stopped and turned. She seemed confused.

'I'll make a deal with you,' Dorothy Thurston said. 'Come back for tea some afternoon, alone. I'll send Linnhe off on a good, long errand.'

'That'd be nice,' she said. At that moment David came out of the door behind them, closely followed by Linnhe, calling to him. He stopped and she trotted up to him, gave him something and then laughed out loud at some quietly laconic remark he gave her in return. Christina watched them, biting her lip. Dorothy turned and saw David kiss her niece on both cheeks, then watched her return into the house, his back to them. Dorothy glanced at Christina and saw the look in her eyes.

'I wouldn't worry about that,' she said dismissively.

Christina looked at her, frowning slightly.

'That's a man who's flattered, not in love.'

It was, Christina thought, a presumptuous remark, but on reflection it was rather reassuring.

There was an odd, uneasy atmosphere in the house in St Mary's that evening. Meg had no idea what had happened in the afternoon and was frustrated in her attempts to find out, but it was obvious that David had somehow got under both Christina's and Kelvin's skin. Christina was quiet and pensive, as if she was engrossed in some private debate with herself and was avoiding conversation for fear of betraying what was on her mind to the others. Kelvin was also quiet, but in his case it was a sullen silence; he made no great effort to hide the fact that he was in a huff with David. For his part, David was in quite a cheerful mood, but was obliged to keep it to himself for fear of rubbing up against one or both of the others the wrong way.

Linnhe Thurston had unwittingly hit a collective raw nerve. For Kelvin it was not that he had ever seriously contemplated chancing his luck with the girl, or even that it seemed remotely likely that David would do so. What annoyed Kelvin was that his friend had two very good-looking women indeed fluttering around him like moths around a light-bulb, and he could afford to be disinterested about both. After four weeks of Christina, Linnhe Thurston's obvious crush on David was adding insult to injury.

Kelvin could not work out what it was that Christina had on David, but he knew his friend well enough to know that he was scared of her. She had somehow found her way inside him, to places not even Kelvin had access to, or any other woman in the past had been allowed anywhere near. Natasha had known how to make him happy and how to hurt him, but she had never made any real effort to break his code. To her he had been an interesting scalp, to tuck under her belt, or dangle in front of her bored friends. Christina was different; not just another in the long line of women who had been through David's life. She was more than that; she knew what David was and she was still in love with him. That gave her a power over him that not even Kelvin could match, and he was jealous. Linnhe Thurston just made that envy keener.

For Christina, who had always despised jealousy in others, it was a somewhat uncomfortable experience having to admit it in herself. But then Linnhe Thurston had exposed something quite different in Christina, which was almost infinitely more uncomfortable than the knowledge that she was capable of an irrational fit of jealousy. It took a few days for her to fully realize what was going on in her heart, by which time David had disappeared off to Callanish, saying that he would be gone for three nights. In fact he was away for ten days, in which time Christina underwent a long and disturbing roller-coaster ride through her emotions, ending up with the unwelcome admission that she was falling in love with the man.

Of all the things she had expected a couple of months earlier, this had been furthest from her mind. And yet the signs were all there, if she cared to look. She missed him when he was away; wondering what he was doing, where he was, when he would be back and meanwhile killing time until his return. She found herself behaving like a shy child when he was around, running herself aground on the reefs of wry courtesy with which he protected himself from her. She kept worrying that she was making the most dreadful fool of herself with him and that every gaffe she assumed she made was driving him further away. She thought about him constantly.

There was still a substantial, nagging twinge of something approximating to shame, an unease that she was betraying Erlend's memory. She knew, in days, how long it had been since Erlend died, since she had buried the man she loved more than anyone else on earth. Yet here she was, falling in love again, less than a year later. But from the first moment she had clapped eyes on David she had known that she wanted him.

The fact that he did not appear to want her was a problem she dearly wanted to discuss with somebody.

Of all the people she could have told, only one person struck her as a suitable choice – an old, sharp woman Christina had only met once, but who had immediately sized up and assimilated all the complicated intricacies of the situation in St Mary's. Dorothy Thurston.

Christina rang her about a week after David went away to Callanish, almost thought better of it with the receiver in her hand and the phone ringing at the other end and was on the point of hanging up when it was picked up. To her surprise and relief Dorothy Thurston not only knew exactly who she was but also seemed almost excited at the prospect of seeing her. She told Christina to come straight over, if she wanted, adding that Linnhe was 'down south' for a couple of nights. Christina drove to Kirkwall before she had time to get cold feet.

It was early evening when she arrived, in time to be bustled into a small, warm sitting room and plied with sherry. She allowed herself to be steered into a big armchair while the old woman bustled around, sweeping papers and files out of sight and keeping up an unbroken stream of chatter about some power station which was leaking radio-activity. Then she sat down, levelled a steely, shrewd gaze on her young guest and said, 'So?'

Christina met her gaze for a few moments, than ran her hand through her hair and shook it, so that her fringe fell forwards, covering her eyes. It was a habit of hers when she was embarrassed.

'I'm not really sure why I'm here,' she said.

Dorothy smiled. 'An existential question?' she inquired. 'Or a statement of fact?'

Christina smiled and pointed between her legs, at the chair she was sitting on.

'Here in Kirkwall, now, talking to you.'

'Don't think of me as a stranger,' Dorothy Thurston said. 'I may not know you, but I've had long experience of life. I know, for instance, that you're only here, talking to me, for want of a more . . .' She picked the right word. 'Appropriate person?' She phrased it as a question, although they both knew she was right. Christina contemplated it for a moment, still hiding behind her fringe.

'What else do you know?' she asked.

Dorothy thought for a minute, gazing at her.

'All right,' she said finally. 'I know that you want to talk to me about David Armstrong. I know why and I think I can help you.'

Christina appeared to swallow this, so Dorothy continued.

'The first thing I ought to reassure you about is my dear niece.' She shook her head emphatically. 'She's not a problem. Not your problem, at least.'

'Why not?' Christina asked.

'David Armstrong is out of her league and both of them know it. She's got a crush on him and he's pleased with himself about it. It's good for his pride, nothing more.'

'Why aren't I good for his pride?' Christina asked. She realized as she said it that this was a deeper admission that she had planned to make so early in the proceedings. She had been lured into it, but now that it was out in the open she was glad to be shot of it.

'Because you're a threat?' Dorothy suggested.

'To what?'

'Oh, all sorts of things. For a man who leans on himself as heavily as David Armstrong does, the last six months have been a trying time. He's weaker and more confused than he's probably ever been in his adult life.

You couldn't have picked a worse moment for him to have to cope with you; I mean,' she said, keeping her flow despite Christina's obvious desire to discuss these points in more detail, 'you have to see it from his side. If what he told me about his cottage is even half of the truth, then he's been living in a place where fantasy and reality are virtually indistinguishable. As far as he's concerned you're as much a part of that as his poltergeist.'

'He told you about Craigairie?' Christina asked, surprised and hurt. 'That's more than he gives me,' she added in a mutter.

'Don't be offended,' Dorothy replied. 'You have to see his behaviour towards you as a sort of back-handed compliment. He knows he needs help there and he knows that you can give him that help; which is why he's so suspicious of you. This is a man who's used to fighting his own battles, even fighting everyone else's battles for them, on his own. It doesn't come easily to admit that he's beaten.'

'I understand that,' Christina replied. 'But I'm not trying to usurp it from him. I just want to . . .' She stopped.

'Help him?' Dorothy inquired.

Christina shrugged. 'I s'pose. I know I could, but I don't know why I want to.'

Dorothy Thurston frowned, as if confused.

'That's the easy part, I would have thought.'

'Easy?' Christina asked.

'Well, you're in love with him, aren't you?' Dorothy said.

Christina managed not to blush, but she took refuge behind her fringe again.

'I'm not even sure I like him,' she said after a moment. 'Besides, there was . . . someone else.'

'I noticed your ring,' Dorothy remarked. 'Did he die?' It could have been a brutal question, but Christina found her directness infinitely preferable to a hundred clumsy attempts at verbal gymnastics, designed to spare her feelings. She nodded, then frowned.

'Did David . . .?'

'Nobody told me,' Dorothy said. 'You carry it with you . . .'

She gazed at Christina, shook her head and sighed.

'I'm sorry,' she said. 'I'm sorry that I can't tell you it won't continue to be a problem for you. It's an unkind trick for fate to have played on you, but if I may resort to an ancient cliché, Cupid has a famously inopportune sense of timing.' She let her smile return, filling the creases in her face like water into a network of irrigation canals. 'And as for not knowing whether you like him, I don't think that's . . .' she picked the word, 'germane.'

Christina contemplated this, absorbed it and finally conceded it.

'So what do I do?' she asked.

Dorothy laughed. 'Oh, come now, my dear girl,' she replied. 'You're not a child, like my niece. If you want something, I'm sure you know how to get it and if you don't, I'm sure you know how to extricate yourself before things get too messy.'

'I want your opinion,' Christina said. 'That's why I came here.'

Dorothy gazed into space for a minute, biting her lower lip.

'In my opinion, for what it's worth,' she began finally, 'I don't think you could avoid each other, even if you wanted to. These things don't happen by accident; even if it may not be immediately apparent why your two fates happened to get tangled with each other, tangled they are.' As she was speaking Dorothy Thurston was thinking about a standing stone in the middle of an empty moor four hundred miles away, pulling these two children to it like iron filings to a magnet, meshing their destinies together. It was a frightening, but somehow beautiful, thought.

'So you're saying that I should forget Erlend, ignore David's qualms and go for it?' Christina asked.

'If Erlend was your husband, you'll never forget him, which is how it should be. But you should never think of the dead as sitting on a cloud somewhere, watching your every move and pointing an accusing finger whenever you step on their memory. If they can see us at all, back here, I don't doubt for a moment that they pity us terribly and wish us all the love and luck we can find.' She paused and a big smile broke on to her face. 'But yes, ignore David's qualms.'

Christina fell silent for a long time and Dorothy let her think, staring into the fire and wondering how she had come to be involved with these two. Christina was more than she had expected, and she had anticipated a person strong enough to punch a hole in the armour of a man like David Armstrong. For a start Christina was the most beautiful young woman Dorothy had seen in many, many years. She was not the kind of conspicuous, explicit beauty typified by Hollywood actresses, but instead fine and subtle and unflawed. A gardenia rather than a rose. She had the grace and serenity of a swan, without needing make-up, either on her face or on her character.

There was also a strength in her, an instinct for survival which had clearly carried her through appalling crises in the past and would continue to do so in the future. She was a very special creature indeed and part of her charm was that she didn't know it. She was not remotely self-aware.

There was also something else about her which was curiously old-fashioned, as if she had been born out of her time and was really meant to be more like one of those pure, unblemished women of medieval court poems. She did not belong in an age or a place where innocence was considered to be a defect.

She moved, finally, and looked across at Dorothy Thurston with her clear grey eyes.

'May I ask what part you play in all of this?' she asked. 'You've had both sides of this now, which makes you doubly unique.'

Dorothy smiled with her eyes.

'I would like to think I'm playing the part of the well-intentioned old matchmaker, about to pull off the match of a lifetime,' she replied.

'But?'

'But I think you may find more and more people, with whom you come into contact, becoming instruments of your fate. Call it the garbled prophecy of an old witch, to a young one.'

'Are you calling me a witch?' Christina inquired, amused at the idea.

'Oh yes,' Dorothy Thurston replied.

When David left Orkney he went straight to Ullapool, to catch the ferry to Stornoway on Lewis. He stayed in Ullapool that night and caught the ferry the next morning, reaching Stornoway by lunch. He had a couple of pints and some food then moved on towards Callanish, fifteen miles away. It had been drizzling in the Minch that morning, but now the clouds began to break up and the sun broke through, so he elected to hitch, rather than waste a tenner on a taxi. He was dropped three miles short of Callanish at four o'clock in the afternoon and walked the rest of the way, with the setting sun in his eyes. For this reason he did not see Callanish until he was almost underneath the hill upon which the stones stood. When he did finally see it he stopped short in amazement, then ran the last half mile.

He had expected it to be neglected and empty, a distant, ruined cathedral on the last dry land short of the sunset. Instead he found something shocking in its serenity, surrounded by an aching silence so intense that it was deafening. It was not a simple circle, like Brogar, but a small, tight central circle with lines of stones radiating from it; one south, one pointing east and west and two parallel lines, like a passage-way, or a nave, pointing north. At the very centre there was the most beautiful standing stone he had ever seen, a tall, narrow masterpiece of sculptured rock. It was flat on the face and back, about a foot thick, five feet wide and twenty-five feet high, with a curve on both its horizontal and vertical planes, giving it the impression of being warped with age. David leant his back on the western face and looked down the short lines of stones in front of him towards the setting sun. As it set and shadow crept up the hill, up the line of stones, up over his head and up the stone behind him, he looked back, to the north and east. When everything else was plunged into shadow, red sunlight still reflected on the tip of the central stone.

This was not like Orkney, or like anything in Wiltshire, Dorset and Somerset. It was as magical and powerful as any of its peers, but had a femininity in it quite unlike anything David had ever felt before. Standing inside the central circle was like being in a womb; safe, protected, soft.

He stayed in Callanish for three days, unable to drag himself away from it and, when he finally pulled himself together and left, David was not remotely ready for Orkney and all it entailed for him. In three days a great deal had settled in his mind, like dirt in a river pool in which someone had been splashing around. The water was beginning to clear for the first time in months, but he did not want to dive back into it quite yet.

He meandered south, through Skye and Argyll and ended up in Glasgow. From there he took a train down the coast to Barrhill, arriving in the deserted station at nine o'clock on his eighth day out from Orkney. With little chance of a taxi and even less of hitching a lift, he took a deep breath and struck out up the single track road back into the hills. In the dark, with an unerring sense of direction which amazed him, he turned off the road after three or four miles and cut across the moors to Craigairie. At no point did he think for a moment that he was lost and he duly found his way home like a lost dog returning to its master.

The moment he came over the brow of the last hill and looked down on the back of the cottage from half a mile away, he saw that the lights were on. He ran down the hill, wove his way through the trees behind the house, ducked around the corner of the barn and sprinted across the yard to the back door, which was slightly ajar. Praying that he had not been burgled he pushed the door open and was hit by a wall of unexpectedly warm air. Frowning to himself he tiptoed on through the house, looking in the cupboard under the stairs for his valuables; his television and video, his stereo and some artefacts he had hidden away. They were all gone. He went on, to the sitting room, hearing a crack from inside as he reached the door. He braced himself then barged the door open with his shoulder.

The first thing he saw, as he entered the room, was his television, in the corner where it should have been, had he not locked it away somewhere else. Then he saw the roaring fire in the grate, then the wall above it. He stopped and stared. The big, heavy mirror which normally hung above the mantelpiece had been removed and placed carefully on the floor in front of the fire and in its place, in letters two feet high, was scrawled the message:

'Welcome home, honey.'

He looked at it for a very long time, feeling that same crawling, tingling on the back of his neck he had almost forgotten in his five-week absence from Craigairie.

'Shit, Delilah,' he said at last. 'I didn't know you could write.'

The writing on the sitting room wall appeared to have been written with coal-dust, which made it easy to wash off. A cursory inspection of the house, however, revealed that she had been at work in the back bedroom, one of her favourite spots, and in this case only paint would suffice. When David opened the door and turned on the light he was again afflicted by the crawling skin which was like a sensual aftertaste of

Delilah's presence. She had been in here in a big way. She had amassed every conceivable writing implement in the house, from pencils to thick silver marker pens, and had used them to cover the big room with writing. It was on the ceiling, the walls, the back of the door, the window recess, the window itself; big, small, neat, scrawled, vertical, horizontal, backwards, upside-down.

It was the spookiest thing Delilah had yet done to David. The room had been full of her and her repertoire had been harnessed into this one, determined assault on it. David did not have to look long to see that the same word, or collection of letters, reappeared so frequently that it had to constitute an intelligent message of some sort. There was some Latin and something that resembled Gaelic, most of it meaningless gibberish, but the letters NYMATILI dominated the room. It came in a hundred different forms: NY matili, Nym Atili, even scrambled into anagrams like 'Inmiltay' or 'Yimanilt'. There was an insistence to it which unnerved David even more than Delilah's incarnation as a succubus. He did not know the word, he could find it in no dictionary, no thesaurus, no encyclopedia. He spent all that night, until long after dawn, searching through all of his large collection of reference books and even reading the indexes of any other books he thought might be relevant. He went to bed, slept for most of the day, waking in the late afternoon and immediately went at the spare bedroom with a can of emulsion and a paint-roller. By the time he had finished the painting, at four o'clock the following morning, he had covered over all of Delilah's work. He left a yard of wall in one corner, by the window; for posterity and because it had a lucidity to it which was largely lacking elsewhere in the room. There were five different inscriptions, all in different colours, sizes and styles, in a column.

The first, in large black letters, had the two words: 'Lacrimae Mundi'.

Then, in small red italics: 'Nymatili'.

Then, below this, there was a single, long line of Greek characters. It took David some time to decipher this; it had been ten years since he last had to translate Greek. He recognized the words 'Petra' and 'Cephos' amongst the jumble of letters, meaning 'rock' and 'stone'. He took this to be some reference to the standing stone, but could not understand the rest until, with a flash of inspiration, like seeing through an optical illusion, he recognized the sequence of letters. It was from Matthew, Chapter sixteen, Verse eighteen.

'Thou art Peter and up on this rock I will build my church.'

That shook him. He was not overflowing with pleasure at the thought of Delilah speaking, or writing, English, but to have her showing a working knowledge of biblical Greek, along with the intelligence to apply this knowledge, was a whole different ballgame.

Below this there were another two 'Nymatili', in blue, then finally, five words, all with small, rough shapes drawn underneath.

'Tejas', with a red triangle beneath it; 'Vayu', with a bluish circle; 'Prithivi', with a yellow circle; 'Apas', with a silver moon lying on its back; and 'Akasa', with a dark purple oval underneath. David did not know what these meant, but they unnerved him.

The next day, he removed his motorbike from its long hibernation in one of the barns and drove it all the way back to Orkney.

Nothing had changed in St Mary's when he arrived back, late that evening. Meg was in bed with a blow heater on the table beside her head, which partially deafened her and made her conversation with Christina, who was in the bath next door, both loud and almost entirely unintelligible. Kelvin was downstairs, lying on the sofa in front of a smouldering, heatless fire, listening to a Bob Marley record at full volume and watching snooker on the television. He did not hear David arriving outside and was not aware of him coming into the room until the volume of the stereo was turned down. Kelvin looked over the back of the sofa.

'Oh, it's you,' he said.

David closed the door and walked over to the fireplace, carrying a clinking knapsack.

'Where're Meg and Christina?' he asked quietly.

'Upstairs,' Kelvin said, sitting upright, with his eyes on the bag in David's hand. His friend knelt down on the floor and began to empty his bag, pulling out a bottle of whisky, a bottle of tequila, some champagne, several cans of beer and a carton of cigarettes.

'Yo!' Kelvin said with quiet wonder. 'You read my mind!'

'It doesn't take a mind reader to know you'd be out of booze here,' David replied dryly. Kelvin leant forward and peered inside the rucksack. David closed it and pulled it away from him, slipping the champagne back inside.

'Are we celebrating something?' Kelvin inquired. He looked at David and grinned. 'Or launching a boat, maybe?'

'Witty,' David murmured.

'The girls would love a wee drink,' Kelvin remarked, still giving his friend a long, shrewd look. 'Shall I call them?' He drew his breath.

'Don't you dare,' David said.

'Why not?' Kelvin asked innocently, knowing that he was touching a nerve. 'D'you not want to see Lady Christina? She's been pining for you, while you were off on your travels.'

David frowned at him, surprised by the gratuitous and unnecessary use of Christina's title. But he let it go, in order to deal with the second half of his remark.

'No, I don't want to see her just yet,' he murmured.

'She's hardly gonnae miss you, now you're back.'

'Drop it, OK?' David said.

Kelvin raised his hands in mock surrender. 'OK, fair enough, keep your hair on.'

As it was, neither Christina nor Meg came downstairs until much later. As far as they knew Kelvin was alone and probably wanted to be left that way. Christina wandered down to the kitchen around midnight in search of something to eat. She picked her way through the mess and opened the fridge, trying not to upset a stack of plates balanced on top, like some squalid pagoda of crockery, each layer on top of the cutlery and remains of food on the one below.

Inside the fridge there was a half pint of milk, a pat of butter smeared with Marmite, a half-empty bottle of diet Coke, which was flat, and a festering hunk of supermarket Cheddar. Christina grimaced, closed the door, one eye still on the precarious edifice on top, and walked back out into the hall. As she passed the closed door of the sitting room she stopped and listened for a minute, thinking she heard hushed voices. After a moment she realized it was the television and she continued to the front door.

She had been outside in the bitingly cold night, looking for shooting stars and satellites in the clear sky, before she stumbled into a large motorbike. It was big, laden with bags and panniers strapped on to the back and sides. She touched the ends of her fingers to the engine. It was icy cold.

She frowned.

Turning on her heel, she went back inside the house and returned to the sitting room door. Without realizing it she became stealthy, turning the handle slowly and slipping in. The television was on, a blaze of colour in the otherwise stygian gloom.

Kelvin was slumped in a chair, his head lolling, a bottle of tequila cradled in his lap, the burnt-out butt of a cigarette still clutched between the index and next finger of his dangling right hand.

David was on the sofa, his back to the door. He was commentating on the snooker he was watching, being funny for his own amusement.

'Will he pot it?' he asked. 'No. Again, Steven misses the pressure shot.' He paused. 'Is this, I wonder, the dullest frame of snooker in history, or was the last one worse?' David glanced towards Kelvin and sighed sadly.

'Aye, well,' he murmured. He went to the television. 'Power surge in Orkney,' he said. 'As another evening of snooker watching ends in St Mary's.' He put his finger on the on–off button and then swore under his breath.

'Lights,' he said. He turned and looked straight at Christina. For a moment he contemplated asking her whether she habitually skulked into rooms without announcing her presence, then he remembered what thin ice he was on.

'Hi,' she said. 'Welcome home?' She said it as a question and he took it with an ironic smile and a quick glance around the cheerless room.

An awkward silence fell.

'What're you looking at?' Christina asked.

He shrugged. 'You,' he replied. 'It's good to see you.'

She thought she picked up an odd note in his voice, as if he hadn't expected it to be a pleasant experience at all. He looked at her for a second more, then went in search of a light.

'I brought you some presents,' he said. He switched on a small lamp and looked around the room with theatrical distaste.

'*Some* presents?' she asked.

'Just some stuff,' he said vaguely. He bent down and took the bottle of champagne from the rucksack. He handed it to her. Christina thought she ought to say something, but she knew that a sea-change was in the process of happening and she did not want her tongue to betray her.

'Thank you,' she said, taking the bottle.

'The rest's on the bike.'

She trailed out after him and waited while he unloaded the panniers. They returned to the hall and David dumped his luggage, opening a battered canvas bag and rummaging through it. Christina climbed the first two stairs and waited.

'Um,' she said. He looked up at her. 'D'you want to do that upstairs?'

He gazed at her, his eyebrows drawn together. His room was downstairs, beside the sitting room. There was nothing upstairs but Meg and Kelvin's room, and Christina's bedroom.

'It'll be warmer up there,' she said. 'It's like a mausoleum down here. I've got the gas-bomb and the electric blanket and things.' She tried to slip the latter in nonchalantly and immediately regretted it. She had no idea what she would do next, if he refused her veiled invitation.

'You stole my electric blanket?' he asked.

She smiled, with relief as much as anything else. 'I got bored of hot water bottles,' she explained. 'They go cold.' She looked down at him and saw the confusion in his eyes.

'This invitation self-destructs in thirty seconds,' she said. She stepped back, up one more stair. 'Probably never to be repeated.'

He thought for a moment, then picked up his bag.

She led him up the staircase, to her bedroom, smiling to herself. Among his presents, once he had emptied his bag on to the floor, was a various tape entitled, cryptically, 'The Tears of the World'.

'What's it mean?' she asked him.

'Just something I read somewhere,' he said, without looking at her. '*Lacrimae Mundi*, in Latin. I can't get it out of my mind.' He handed her a lump of uncut amethyst and a wilted crocus. She took them, put them on to her pillow and disappeared through to the bathroom, returning five minutes later wearing a long tee-shirt and her hair in a loose, golden pony-tail. She climbed into bed and inspected the crocus and the amethyst, wanting to say all sorts of things but unable to decide what, if anything, was appropriate.

'There was a sort of a theme,' he said, sitting down on the other side of the bed.

Christina frowned. 'What was it?'

'Well, the tape's my music, the crocus is from the lawn at Craigairie and the amethyst . . .'

'Yes?'

'It's lucky.' He said embarrassedly. 'Or at least, I've always assumed it's lucky. It got me through my A-levels.'

Christina bit her lip, still gazing at the object in her hand, smiling to herself. She turned to him, pushing her fringe back from her eyes. She had been dreading this moment, but now it was here she felt a hot rush of courage. She wanted to laugh out loud, but she suppressed it.

'So what was the theme?' she inquired.

'They're supposed to be little parts of me,' he said.

'But not the whole thing?' she murmured. She placed the stone and the flower carefully on the table beside her, then looked back at him, savouring the moment.

'Thank you,' she said simply. She leant across to him and cupped his cheek in her hand, drawing him to her.

They kissed.

3

CRAIGAIRIE TOGETHER

There was a storm that night, a wild, shrieking hurricane which came roaring in from the Atlantic and raged around the house in St Mary's, clattering in the roof and whining in the windows, rising in a new crescendo with each new gust.

David lay in bed, wide awake, staring up into the darkness. Christina's head was resting on his shoulder and one arm was flung out across his chest. Despite the deafening racket thundering against the house she was sound asleep, her body completely relaxed, her breathing regular. David was comfortable and warm, not thinking but listening. A vicious squall of rain clattered against the window as it swept past.

'*Lacrimae Mundi*,' David murmured. He sighed. 'What is it, Delilah? What should I know?' Christina moved, murmuring something incomprehensible in her sleep. He removed one of his hands from behind his head and gently stroked the soft hairs behind her ear. She made a contented noise. He continued to run the tips of his fingers through her hair, wondering at its smooth silkiness. After a while he stopped, taking his hand away.

'Whazzamatter?' she murmured, still three-quarters asleep. She raised her face off his chest. 'Why've you stopped?'

A blast of wind smashed against the side of the house and a door slammed somewhere downstairs. David could feel Christina groping her way into consciousness. She nuzzled into his neck and the smell of her filled his sinuses. She smelled of coconuts, for some reason.

'Shh,' he whispered. 'Go back to sleep.' He thought this had worked until, five minutes later, she said, 'Why are you awake?' She sounded sleepy but conscious.

'Can't sleep,' he said. 'The storm.'

'Oh,' she said. She listened, which was hardly necessary considering the din going on outside. She took his face in one hand and raised her head so that she could brush her lips across his.

'I've always found something unbearably sexy about storms,' she said. He laughed quietly.

'Same here,' he replied. 'Funny that.'

'You see?' she said, manoeuvring herself on top of him, kneeling astride his prostrate form. Her hair brushed across his face as she lowered her lips to his again. 'We do have something in common after all.'

The storm was still raging when they fell asleep, which seemed like poor timing on its part. It was still blowing a full gale when David awoke late the following morning, finding himself alone in a strange bed, in a strange room. He lay for a while, staring at the ceiling, then dressed and wandered downstairs. Meg was in the kitchen, reading a newspaper and smoking a roll-up. She looked up as he came in, and smiled.

'Hello,' she said.

He nodded as he walked over to the kettle.

'You missed the storm?' she asked. 'I mean, d'you get back before it started?'

'Just.'

'Lucky. Apparently the ferry isnae running.'

'Really?' He stopped what he was doing, ladling spoonfuls of instant coffee into a mug. 'Damn.'

'What's the problem?'

'I meant to leave today.'

'Today?' Meg asked. 'You just got back.'

'Or tomorrow,' he said. 'Soon.'

'Why the hurry?'

He shrugged, with his back to her, but did not reply. After a couple of minutes he left the kettle to boil, unwatched, and sat down opposite Meg.

'Where're the others?' he asked.

'You mean Christina and Kelvin?' she inquired.

He looked up at her and frowned. 'Who else?'

Meg shrugged. 'They went down to the village. Seven boats tore their moorings last night,' she snorted. 'Matchwood.'

'Really?' He stood up and returned to the kettle. 'Gosh.' He brought his coffee back to the table, stirring it listlessly. Meg pushed a packet of tobacco across the table. He grimaced.

'Why're you smoking that shit,' he said, producing a packet of real cigarettes from his pocket. 'Have one of these.'

She stubbed out her roll-up and took one from him. They lit up and puffed away in silence for a while.

'So why d'you come all the way back, if you're just going back south again?' Meg asked finally.

'Loose ends to tie up,' he said.

'Like Christina, for instance?'

He took a pull on his cigarette and exhaled a series of smoke rings, studying Meg's face, as if looking for something behind it. He let out a tiny breath of mirthless laughter and shook his head. Undeterred by this wordless put-down Meg continued.

'I hope you know what you're doing with that woman, Davie, because I certainly don't.'

'Is there any reason why you should?' he asked. 'I mean, whatever's between Christina and me is our business, I would have thought.'

'I like her,' Meg said. 'I like her a lot. I don't want to see her hurt; that makes it my business.'

'Oh, give me a break, Meg,' David said tiredly. 'Much as it may surprise you, I'm not the sort of guy who gets pleasure out of hurting people.'

'I didn't say you were,' she replied. She left it at that, but there was an obvious 'but' in her voice. David gave her a sharp look, then relaxed.

'I'm sure Christina would appreciate your concern and I'm sure she'd tell you that she can look after herself.'

'Like Kelv?' Meg asked.

'No, no, no,' David said. 'I don't want to be having this conversation. I just got up and I'm really not in the mood.'

'Oh, and he's reached his short-circuit point,' Meg said, as if commentating on a spectator sport. He frowned at her.

'What's with you this morning? Why're you so belligerent?'

'Was I being belligerent?' she inquired. 'I thought I was just trying to get you to discuss your behaviour.'

They stared at each other across the table for half a minute.

'What behaviour?' he asked.

She shrugged and stubbed out her half-smoked cigarette.

'So?' she asked, as if changing the subject. 'Where did *you* sleep last night?'

'That's none of your fucking business,' he replied. He shook his head in disbelief. 'Christ Almighty, Meg, who d'you think you are? God? If you think you can turn Christina into another moral battleground between you and me, think again honey, because I'm not playing.'

At that point a door slammed through the house and voices drifted through to the kitchen. They both looked at the doorway. David took a deep breath and let his anger out in a long sigh.

'Listen,' he said quietly. 'I don't pretend to understand what's going on with Christina . . .' He glanced at the door again. 'I don't even pretend that I know I'm doing the right thing. But I'd appreciate it if you refrained from sticking your oar in before I've even tried.' He paused. 'OK?'

She waited until Christina and Kelvin were almost into the kitchen before she replied.

'OK,' she said. She too glanced at the door and delivered the last word with immaculate timing, just out of earshot of Christina and Kelvin as they came down the passage from the hall.

'But keep your libido in check while you're in my house.'

The next three days, until David and Christina finally left Orkney, were the most fraught yet. David was torn between continuing with the course of action upon which he had embarked with Christina, knowing that the only way he could face her at all was as a lover, of sorts; and on the other hand trying to appease Meg, whose mistrust of him had reached an all time low in his absence and his subsequent return. Meg, in turn, watched him like a schoolmistress keeping an errant child in check.

Christina had the sense and intuition to know that there had been a row between Meg and David and to make an intelligent guess as to what it had been about. She was therefore willing to forgive David for the distance he put between himself and her. She could see him wrestling with the dilemma; and her peculiar, growing affection for him was in no way diminished for knowing he was trying as hard as he possibly could to defuse the tension. The fact that he was patently failing was hardly his fault. Meg, however, felt betrayed by Christina; especially when she attempted to warn her off David, and was told, in no uncertain terms, to mind her own business, for the second time in one day.

If this was not bad enough, Kelvin sidled up to David the evening after he returned and proudly announced that he had made more than a passing acquaintance with Linnhe Thurston, of the pouting lips and the dangerous aunt, in David's absence.

If the ferries had been running, both Christina and David would have been glad to have left earlier, but as it was they finally extricated themselves four days before Easter, six weeks to the day after they had arrived in Orkney. They crossed the Pentland, on the ferry, together; with Christina being violently sick from Scapa Flow to Scrabster; they then drove in convoy as far as Bonar Bridge, where they had stopped for the night on the way north. For Christina, watching the brake light of David's indecently large motorbike in front of her, it was as if she was returning to the real world after an age in a sort of waking dream. The night in Bonar Bridge had not been a month and a half earlier, it had been a lifetime ago; a whole range of emotions and experiences had invaded her life at a moment when she had thought that life held no more surprises for her, good, bad or indifferent.

It was appropriate, somehow, that he chose to pull over in Bonar Bridge, of all places. In hindsight it had been there, after the blizzard and before the drive through Caithness to the ferry, that Orkney had begun for her. She was glad that it ended there as well, giving the whole experience a roundness it did not have while it was happening.

He dismounted and walked over to her car, shaking out his stiff legs. She wound down her window.

'Listen,' he said, bending down to look through the window. 'I'm going to outrun you on these roads.'

'Don't wait for me,' she said.

He smiled wryly. 'I wasn't going to.' He glanced down the road. 'D'you know the way? Just . . .'

'Point myself south, until I reach Galloway,' she said.

He grinned. 'That should do it.'

'So when'll I see you?' she asked.

'I'll call after Easter,' he said.

'OK,' she said.

He leant in and planted a quick kiss on her lips.

'Drive safely,' he said.

'You too.'

After she had gone he went to a tea-shop and had a cup of coffee. Then he climbed back on to his bike and pretended he was doing the Isle of Man T.T. race. He overtook her, without knowing it, on a stretch of dual carriageway south of Inverness. She was travelling at a steady ninety and he left her standing, cruising at a good hundred and ten, head down, his bike making a noise which announced its presence half a mile in advance and remained half a mile behind it, about half a minute later.

If nothing else, he drove a bike like Erlend.

From the moment David arrived back at Craigairie, he was restless and irritable. He had come back from Orkney relieved to be out of the situation at St Mary's and glad to be back where his mind had been all along. He had gone to Orkney to get some sort of a perspective on Craigairie, to see whether it was possible for a standing stone to emanate and generate a power of its own. There had been times, during those six weeks, when he had thought he was being absurd and ridiculous; when the immediacy of Craigairie had so faded that he seriously considered the possibility that it had all been in his imagination. But then he had talked to Dorothy Thurston and she had not only accepted what he said as the truth, but had also understood the phenomenon he described. Or he had found some standing stone site, most particularly Callanish, which had re-affirmed his belief that his suspicions about Craigairie were well-founded, were not some idiotic obsession he had concocted for himself in the long, dark months of the winter.

Then he had returned to Craigairie, after Callanish, and had found that Delilah was still there, as weird and hyperactive as she had ever been in the winter. This was not his imagination and it was not a random haunting. It was directed at him, for his benefit alone. Delilah had known he was coming home that night and had been ready for him, lighting the fire in the sitting room and scrawling the mind-bendingly banal message for him above the fireplace. And then there was the extraordinary energy she had put into the spare bedroom, repeating the same word over and over again and suffixing it with Greek and Latin quotations, as if trying to point him towards something.

He did not know what he expected when he returned for the second time: a blast of supernatural energy; a wild, explosive welcome home;

something suitably bizarre and Gothic from Craigairie's repertoire – dreams, perhaps, or a new trick from Delilah or maybe even something entirely new and unexpected. Instead he was subjected to silence.

For the first time since he had moved into the cottage it behaved like a normal house. No pipe bands struck up in the kitchen, no dreams afflicted his sleep, no furniture moved out of position. Nothing untoward happened.

It depressed him. He became suddenly prey to loneliness and frustration. Of all the tricks Craigairie had played on him, this was the meanest. He spent half of the time on tenterhooks, expecting it all to spark back into life at any moment, and the rest of the time prowling around the cottage, filling it with music and light and himself as if to compensate for the sudden lack of any other activity and excitement. The silence was like a sullen rebuke, as if Craigairie had expected some favour from him and he had refused it.

It had something to do with the writing in the back bedroom. Delilah had given him a message, but he had painted over it and left without trying to understand what she had meant. He should not have gone back to Orkney that day, before he had time to decipher whatever code was behind the word 'Nymatili' and all of the classical quotations he had destroyed in one afternoon of painting. He felt that he had come within an ace of uncovering what he had been searching for, only to let it slip out of his grasp at the critical moment.

He tried to bring it back, imprisoning himself in the valley so that he could be receptive to the faintest twinge of anything abnormal if and when it happened. He refused to answer the telephone, reverting to his hitherto obsolete habit of leaving the answering machine on, even when he was in the room, and allowing the callers to run themselves dry on the tape. Christina called four times in the week after they left Orkney, each call betraying increasing desperation in her voice. In the last one she said that her family were forcing her to go to a party down south and behind every word there had been a plea for him to give her an excuse not to go. He listened, understood and, in a fit of surly bloody-mindedness, had not called back.

He felt guilty about Christina. He had never wanted to have to think about her, but she had forced him, which she had every right to do. He still did not want to think about her, but now he had a responsibility to do so. In deliberately shirking this responsibility he aroused his own guilt, which fitted neatly into his overall mood of self-indulgent depression. She wanted to break into his domain at yet another moment when it was beating him, when his defences were at their weakest. But he had got this far without her help and he was damned if he was going to let her sneak in now.

Other people called him. His ex-boss, Rachel Ifbak, rang to say that he was odds-on to lift an award for his South American documentaries and 'it might be courteous' for him to turn up to the ceremony. She added that when he had finished pissing his talent against a wall in Scotland she had some offers for him that not even he could refuse.

'Wanna bet?' he said to his answering machine.

Various friends called, sounding concerned and worried, wondering where he was, why he never answered their messages and when he was coming home. He ignored them.

He contracted flu and it lasted for ten days. It was the first time in fifteen years he had been so unwell, but it made sense that it should happen now. Even the weather turned gloomy and grey, neither cold nor hot. It drizzled for days on end, keeping him shut inside the cottage. Most days he felt too lackadaisical even to light a fire and the house became damply cold. He was dour and lonely and morose and perversely content to remain that way.

April blurred into May and nothing changed in the cottage, or in the valley, or in David. Delilah did not return and he could think of no way to bring her back. His negativity and lethargy spiralled into depression and from there progressed close to the edge of an abyss of despair. It was only at the very last moment, when he had dug himself into his deepest trough and was reaching the point when even suicide seemed preferable to the empty world he had created for himself, that some last safety mechanism clicked in his mind and he pulled back from himself far enough to see what had been happening to him.

He had been sitting in his kitchen all through an endless night. His flu was raging, now well into its second week; his limbs were heavy as lead, aching dully, his head felt as if it was full of wool, his breathing came as if through an invisible pillow which was slowly smothering him.

'How do you feel?' he asked himself out loud. For a long time there was silence as he considered the question.

'Cold,' he said finally. 'Cold and tired and lonely.' It was then that something clicked. He sighed. 'But most of all lonely.'

He hauled himself to his feet and looked around the kitchen, seeing it with the eyes of a newcomer for the first time in weeks. He then went from room to room through the house, inspecting each one with increasingly disgusted detachment.

He ran a bath and got in, washing himself assiduously; his face, feet, arms, hair, everything. He shaved and brushed his teeth. Returning to his bedroom he uncovered his ghetto-blaster, put on the most violent music he could find and began, with grim determination, to tidy the room.

Finding this curiously therapeutic, he moved on to the spare bedroom, in which the writing had been and which was David's unofficial playroom. He swept the cigarette ends from the floor, emptied and washed the ashtrays and began to remove the dirty mugs and glasses. He jabbed at the punchball hanging from one of the roof-beams, swung a weak right and gave up. Clearing up was one thing, but he was not yet ready for exercise.

By the time he had exhausted himself it was mid-morning and he had cleaned every room apart from the kitchen, which had got worse as a result of being the final dumping-point for all the dirty cups, mugs, plates, glasses, clothes, towels, cutlery and rubbish he had collected elsewhere in the house. He then lit the fire in the sitting room, the wood-burning stove in the hall and collapsed in front of the former, still feeling grotty but now, at least, grotty and clean.

Over the next couple of hours he attempted to re-map the blurred contours of his mind. It took a while, against an apathetic disinclination to think, which oozed all the way up from deep in his subconscious. He sat on a low stool, staring out of the window at the far side of the valley.

As he thought, his eyes came to rest on the stone and stayed there. It was still there, a small dark finger pointing accusingly at the sluggish clouds as they lumbered overhead.

It had not changed. It still stood on the side of the hill, as it had for three thousand years, let alone a paltry six months. Whatever it had wanted from David since he first came into contact with it, it still wanted the same thing now. If it had some innate power, then that power was still there. Still filling the valley and still working on David. With the blinding clarity of a person pulling clear of a dense fog and looking back at it over their shoulder, he saw his depression in hindsight and knew that it had not come from within himself. While he had been excited and positive, so too had the power of the stone been wild and anarchic, leap-frogging him with terrifying ease every time he thought he had exhausted it of all its tricks. By the same token, when he had been negative and depressed, it pushed him right to the point of destruc-tion. But all the time it was telling him the same thing, over and over again; drumming the same simple message against his stubbornness and pride.

He could not cope with it alone.

It would tear him apart, as it had been doing since he left Orkney. He had been treating it as a game, a complicated knot he wanted to unravel. But it was too big a thing to be played with, too big even for the mighty David Armstrong. He needed help.

He picked up the telephone, still gazing out of the window, and dialled Christina's number. After a long time a man's voice answered.

'Hello?'

'Is Christina there?' David asked.

'I'm sorry, she's gone out. Can I take a message?'

'Yes,' David said. 'Please could you tell her to call David. She knows my number.' As he was talking his eyes lighted on the rowan tree on the lawn. He had meant to get rid of it months ago, but had never got around to it. There was nothing much wrong with it, except that it had occasionally given him the creeps, sent an icy little shiver down his spine. Now that he looked at it he grimaced involuntarily and resolved to cut it down. It offended him – he felt a sudden, inexplicable urge to be shot of it, to hack it down and burn it. The defiant, feverish energy he had employed to clean the house earlier on returned with a vengeance and as soon as he had hung up the telephone he went in search of an axe.

Ten minutes later he had inspected the tree, cutting away some of the lower branches so that he could get a clear swing at the trunk. It was a big, healthy tree; twenty feet high and at least as wide around its girth. It was about to flower.

'Nasty little blossoms, too,' he muttered and took his first, vicious swing. The effect was pleasing. Swinging with the whole of his torso he hacked away until he had made a deep wound in the trunk. He stopped for a smoke, inspected his handiwork and started again, with renewed vigour. He was swinging the axe for the fifth blow of his second assault when a voice spoke behind him.

'What on earth are you doing?'

He swung around, the axe still hovering over his shoulder. Christina was standing at the corner of the cottage, her head cocked to one side, her brow creased with a frown. He stared at her for a few seconds, then unleashed a swift, sideways kick at the tree. It creaked sadly for a moment, then keeled over on to the lawn with a crunch.

'It deterred witches,' he explained embarrassedly. He bit his lip and laughed. 'A happy coincidence, wouldn't you say? . . . Welcome back.'

'I thought about you.'

'Oh?' She was silent for a couple of seconds. 'You didn't answer my calls.'

'I didn't answer any calls.'

Somehow they had contrived to be together for the best part of a day without managing either communication or physical contact. They had been for a long, silent walk on the moors and were now back at the cottage, sitting side-by-side on the wall at the foot of the garden, looking out over the valley. As the afternoon had progressed the clouds had dispersed, allowing the sun to sink towards the hills unimpeded. Somewhere beyond the stone the rich, bubbling whistle of a curlew rose into the still evening air. A couple of snipe were drumming over their heads, the eerie whirring seeming to come from nowhere in the fading light.

'I was worried about you,' she said, sounding matter-of-fact.

He nodded. 'So was I.' There was no tone in his voice, no clue as to what was going on inside. He let out a long, tired sigh.

'I haven't been well,' he said.

'It shows,' she replied. 'You look like shit.'

He snorted. Christina turned and gazed at him and a voice inside her mind began to nag again, as it had been for most of the afternoon. She was not going to be messed around by this man. If he wanted her, she wanted to hear it from him. On the other hand she could feel his need and it was hard to restrain herself from attending to it without asking for any reciprocation.

'What's been happening here?' she asked. It was only a last second decision not to say 'What's happened to you', an altogether more specific indication of her concern.

'Nothing,' he said flatly. 'Nothing at all has happened.' There was a confusion and bitterness in his voice which he could not conceal. She left a silence for him to fill.

'I've been so stupid,' he said at last, from a long way away, as if talking to himself, rather than to her. 'I thought Craigairie was going to reveal some astonishing secret to me. I thought I was on the verge of discovering something fascinating and unique, something which I've been looking for all my life. I thought . . .' He shook his head. 'Ach,' he exclaimed disgustedly. 'I dunno.'

'What?' she asked.

'I don't know,' he said. 'I thought I'd found "the Reason".' He turned and gave her a wry smile. 'You know? "The Great Secret", the answer to all those questions like "why am I here" and all that stuff.' He cupped his hands in front of him. 'It was *there*, you know? It was like all I had to do was say "open sesame" and the treasure was all mine.' He stopped.

'But?' she asked softly. He shook his head and breathed a quiet laugh.

'But I got back from Orkney and I found that I didn't know the password; or at least I knew part of it, but not enough. I came back thinking that all I had to do was flick the right switch and this blinding truth would reveal itself to me, but when it didn't happen, everything just seemed to be even darker and more confusing than it had been before.' He fell silent again, staring out across the hazy valley to the stone. She turned and looked at his falconine profile. Reaching out her hand tentatively she nearly touched his neck, withdrew it a fraction, then reached out again, touching her forefinger on to his ear. She traced a gentle line from behind his ear around to the soft hairs at the nape of his neck. When he did not shy away she ran all of her fingers through his thick, dark hair. He closed his eyes and nestled his head against her hand.

'I can help you here,' she said quietly. 'I think I can help you find that switch.'

He nodded. 'I know.' He opened his eyes and turned to face her. He gazed at her for a very long time.

'I know the traditional cliché is for me to say "I don't deserve you",' he said finally. He paused, took a deep breath and let it out slowly. 'But the truth of it is, you don't deserve someone like me in your life. I'm selfish. I'm secretive, I'm arrogant, I hurt people.'

She sighed. 'D'you think I haven't weighed up the pros and cons of having an affair with you, David?' she asked. 'What d'you think I was doing for six weeks back in Orkney? Let me decide what I deserve and what I don't deserve. Maybe I'm stronger than I seem.' She paused and took a deep breath.

'Besides, I want you. Don't ask me why, because I really don't know, but I want you and I'm willing to take a few risks to have you. Or take any little amethyst, crocus and various tape you're willing to give me.' She stopped and held him in a steady gaze. His eyes were smiling and a little quizzical, as if he did not know what he had got for himself in her.

'In that case I don't deserve you,' he said. 'Meg was right.'

'What? Because I'm in love with you and you aren't ready to reciprocate it quite yet?' It came out easily. It had been lurking close underneath the surface of the conversation, and their relationship, all along and now, when it showed itself, they were both ready for it.

'Meg's full of shit,' she said. She slid off the wall, stepping in front of him and looking up into his face.

'Would you kiss me, or am I going to have to go through Orkney again?'

He looked back down at her for a few moments and smiled.

'I'm infected.'

'Then infect me,' she replied.

He slipped down off the wall into her waiting arms.

Without Christina, David could not have survived at Craigairie. She nursed his body and his mind back to health with infinite patience and, in return, he gave both to her on her terms, not just his own. His enthusiasm returned; slowly at first, like rain on to sun-baked earth, then quicker when it began to take hold again. She allowed him the room he needed, to be selfish, or silent, or to avoid her, if the mood took him, and he repaid this generosity by rarely succumbing to such moods. Just as he had always known with Christina, almost grudgingly, that she was extremely hard to dislike, he now discovered that the flip-side to this was that she was wonderfully easy to like. She was funny and sharp and wise, proud but without pride.

And she brought Craigairie back. Delilah returned after her long absence with a joyous gusto, as if she had not so much been away as been locked up in a cupboard somewhere. When she first exploded into life in the kitchen, the night after Christina arrived, with a full-blooded rendition of 'Flower of Scotland', David threw back his head and let out a wild whoop of joy.

'God, I've missed you,' he yelled.

It took Christina a while to get used to cohabiting with a wild and somewhat spoilt poltergeist, but David's utter lack of concern was infectious. She soon realized that Delilah was not malevolent so much as naughty and mischievous. She hid things, she flung objects around when one's back was turned, she scrawled things on the walls, especially in David's playroom and she made a terrible din, but otherwise she was not harmful and she usually shut up when she was told.

Her worst trick was to rip the covers from the bed when they were making love, which was irritating in the extreme, but an act of childlike jealousy rather than anything more vicious.

And, apart from reviving the supernatural part of Craigairie, Christina and David, never the most active people when left to their own devices, enthused each other into doing things together. May turned into a beautiful, hot month, after its shaky beginning, encouraging them outside. They sunbathed down by the river and swam in the deep, dark pools below the cottage. They went for long, meandering walks across the moors, discovering more standing stones and burial chambers and generally reconnoitring the whole area.

When they were not walking, or swimming, or simply lying around bronzing themselves, they began the long, leisurely process of converting one of the barns into what they optimistically called 'the banqueting hall'. It had a high roof, with cross-beams, like a church. It was in two parts; the main space at floor-level and a gallery at one end, six feet above the floor, on which they hoped some day to put a table, some comfortable chairs and an old Wurlitzer juke-box Christina had stored in her parents' house. David had made these plans for the barn when he first moved in, but had been daunted by the huge quantities of cow-shit on the floor and by the volume of work necessary if he was going to make it look like anything other than a barn. Christina, however, saw it and immediately recognized its potential, carrying David along with her excited enthusiasm. They broke up the rock-hard dung and shovelled it out, painted the walls, polished the flag-stoned floors and performed rudimentary D.I.Y. around the windows and the door. Then Christina went home and haggled with her mother for various bits and pieces in the cavernous store rooms of Castle Graham; a sofa, an old pine table, a threadbare carpet for the floor of the 'minstrels' gallery', a few chairs and stools and some lamps. David, meanwhile, went out and blew three hundred quid on an old pool table, for the main floor space.

It was also in that barn that they had their first strange experience with the fauna of Craigairie Valley. There was a barn owl which lived in there, or at least colonized a particular beam at one end, above the gallery. At first, when they began their work in the barn, it would disappear out through the skylight right above its favoured beam. But then, as time passed, it got used to their presence and remained where it was, watching them with a mixture of disapproval and interest, undisturbed however much noise they made. Christina called it 'The Don' because, for some reason, it reminded her of Marlon Brando in *The Godfather* – something to do with the way it looked down at them.

They avoided it at first, knowing how vicious even a barn owl can be if roused to self-defence. But they too got used to it and were able to work within feet of it without a second thought.

Then one day David was doing something in the gallery and The Don glided down off his rafter on to the floor right in front of where David was kneeling and watched him with big round eyes, head cocked to one side, from a distance of no more than a couple of feet. David stopped what he was doing and called out.

'Iz?' (Her name had been shortened from three syllables to one, because she said that the only time anybody ever called her Christina was when they were telling her off.)

'Yeah?' she said.

'Look at this.'

'What?' She glanced over at him, looked away again and then took a slow double-take.

'Marlon, what *are* you doing?' she said.

David reached out carefully until his fingers were only inches from the owl. It blinked slowly, opened its beak into what appeared to be a bored yawn, then hopped on to his hand and from there back up to the beam.

After that The Don regularly left his perch to inspect what they were up to, like a foreman watching his workers. He seemed to favour David, often landing on his shoulder or his head; it became such a regular occurrence that David took to wearing an armless leather jacket and an old fedora whenever he went into the barn, to protect himself from The Don's sharp, curved talons. It was a wonderful, comical sight, worthy of many a photograph, to see David at work in the barn, wearing only shorts, a leather jerkin, and a felt hat, with an owl perched on top, like a living ornament.

Then there was Shuduch, the fox. He had been found, with a broken hind leg, beside the road from Barrhill to Newton Stewart. Someone had been talking about what should be done with him, one night in the pub in Barrhill. The general consensus was that there was very little one could do with a full-grown fox, except feed him until he was healthy enough to release, or kill him. The majority opinion of the farmers and gamekeepers, who constituted a large part of the clientèle in the pub, was that one fox less was no great loss, particularly as he was too wild to tame and would not let anyone close to him. Christina heard this and asked if she could see him and, after some discussion, was shown out to a garden on the edge of the town, where the fox was incarcerated in an old chicken coop. A small group traipsed out of the pub to offer advice.

'Can I go in?' she asked, when she saw the fox. He looked half-dead with hunger and pain and watched the world outside his prison with frightened brown eyes.

'I wouldn't if I were you,' someone said. 'Vicious wee buggers, they things. They'll tak' awa' yer fingers soon as look at you.'

Christina shook her head. 'No, he won't,' she murmured. She opened the latch of the door and went in, closing the door behind her. 'Will you, little one?' She crouched down a yard from the fox, whispering to him. He watched her, then crawled over to her on his belly, dragging his hurt leg behind him. To the amazement of the watchers outside he licked her outstretched hand, then allowed her to probe around his leg, rolling over on to his side to make it easier for her.

After that, Shuduch – which is Gaelic for fox – lived in one of the old cowsheds while Christina nursed him back to health. She did not lock him in, leaving the door open so that he could come and go as he pleased, which he duly did as his leg began to heal. He would sometimes disappear for days on end, but he always returned sooner or later, as tame with them as he was completely wild otherwise. With The Don, Shuduch the fox was the first of a menagerie of wild birds and animals which came to accept their presence in the valley and became so used to them that they would allow David and Christina close enough to watch them at close quarters, even to touch them and play with them. It was a phenomenon which grew so gradually and naturally and was so much a part of Craigairie that neither of them ever stopped to think how peculiar it was.

That first month after Christina joined David in the cottage was idyllic. May in western Scotland is the prettiest, kindest and the most clement month of the year. It is like a secret gift from nature to the long-suffering Scots; a month which is for them alone. From April back through to the middle of November the weather is unpredictable; sometimes clear and bitterly cold; sometimes wild, wet and windy, but mostly just dour and grey. From June to September the clarity and abundance of spring gives way to the hazy light and the dusty colours of summer. Autumn is beautiful, with its coppers and reds and the precise, frosty light of the ageing year; a time of majestic, glorious death. But nothing else is quite like May, when the whole of nature seems to come out of hiding and rejoice.

Craigairie Valley was a little, private paradise. The surrounding hills and moors suddenly ceased to be dark and forbidding, as new life returned to them. They resounded now to a chorus of birdsong; the long, rising, orgasmic calls of the curlews; the urgent 'peep-peep' of oystercatchers, always seeming to be in a hurry to get from one place to the next; the drumming snipe; redshanks, greenshanks and grouse, all against a ceaseless backdrop of twittering larks.

Down in the valley, below the bright yellow gorse, where the hills dived down in sharp, tree-filled ravines into the steep-sided gorge, where the Tarf river cut its way through the moors to the lowlands beyond, there was a welter of hidden colour and life. The ground was carpeted with bluebells, with yellow splashes of primroses under the dappled light of beeches and oaks. In the evenings a cuckoo broadcast its presence;

its voice echoing like a chorister's hymn in a green cathedral, carrying far out across the hills.

To look out from the cottage at dusk, or dawn, was to feel peace. There were no machines out there, no man-made noises or smells; just empty, unadulterated nature. Even the miles of regular forestry along the horizon, behind the stone, had a brief moment of glory, as new shoots on ten thousand young conifers sprouted in an absurd blaze of bright, dayglow green.

There were days and weeks on end when David and Christina might have been the last and only people left on earth; a solitary breeding pair of humanity in amongst a wild, private paradise created for them alone. Nothing disturbed them; from Craigairie to the end of any horizon, they were the only living people. The hills rose and fell away from their hidden valley, with nothing between them and the blue sky but miles of emptiness. They could wander for miles and look back at Craigairie; a solitary white square against a huge backdrop of green hills and moors; a minuscule box of light and life in an endless wilderness, stretching as far as the eye could see.

Despite Delilah; despite the constant, humming blur of the standing stone behind everything that happened in the valley; despite even their uncanny relationship with the birds and animals which shared the valley with them, it took an unavoidable, undeniably direct supra-normal experience before they began to realize how far they could push the boundaries of possibility.

It was Christina who inadvertently stumbled upon it, just as she had unintentionally brought Craigairie back to life when she arrived there.

It was wonderfully simple, when it came to her. She was in the sitting room one Saturday morning, slumped on the sofa drinking a cup of coffee and watching children's television. David was through in the kitchen, making them breakfast.

She was comfortable in her seat, cocooned amongst the cushions, with the warmth of the fire lulling her into a state of blissful lethargy. The only niggling irritation in her otherwise serene repose was the fact that she had left her cigarettes on the mantelpiece. She contemplated calling David through to get them for her, but immediately thought better of it. She stared at them hopelessly, wishing that she could move them without moving herself.

They lifted off the mantelpiece so slowly that she did not realize they had moved until she suddenly saw the bottom of the candlestick which stood behind them, between the packet and the shelf. She frowned, thinking that her eyes were playing tricks on her, but she did not look away or break her puzzled concentration. After about half a minute she blinked hard to correct her faulty vision. As she closed her eyes she distinctly heard a small, hollow clunk.

She opened her eyes again, her brows now knitted in a deep frown.

'Now wait a minute,' she murmured. She stared at the packet again, willing it into the air. Slowly, almost imperceptibly, it began to rise off the mantelpiece again. When it was fully six inches into the air she called out to David, keeping her eyes fixed on the packet.

'What's up?' he asked from behind her.

'The mantelpiece,' she said. 'Look at it.'

'Yes?' he asked, obviously seeing nothing of interest to him.

'What d'you see?'

'Um,' he said, 'some invitations, a box, a couple of candlesticks, a packet of cigarettes, a . . .'

'The fags,' she cut in. 'What are they doing?'

'Floating?' he suggested. 'So?' He was so used to Delilah's antics that a packet of cigarettes defying gravity did not seem very exciting to him.

'Watch,' she said. She concentrated hard on the packet, willing it higher into the air. She had to make the cigarettes the sole object of her attention, excluding everything else her senses and the rational half of her brain was telling her.

'See that?'

'It lifted,' he said. He sounded confused. Her eyes began to sting and she blinked quickly; the packet sank a couple of inches, wobbled and then held steady again.

'Davie, I'm doing that,' she said.

'Doing what?'

'I'm lifting that packet.'

He walked around the sofa and turned off the television.

'Um . . .' he said, giving himself time to think of something more astute to say. 'How?'

'I don't know,' she admitted. 'But I *am* doing it . . . Tell me to put them somewhere.'

'OK,' he said slowly. 'Put it . . . um . . . bring them to you.'

There was a long silence. He watched her as she frowned intently and drew her head back in a series of quick jerking movements. The packet wobbled, sank a few inches and edged out from the mantelpiece.

'Tricky,' she said finally. 'It doesn't appear to work in 3-D.'

'OK,' he said accommodatingly. 'Put it over by the television.'

This was easier, as it was a lateral movement between her, the cigarettes and the television. The trick was to hold her concentration and not to allow herself to run ahead of the floating packet, and certainly not allow herself to think about it. She found that it was easiest to slide the packet downwards, rather than making right-angled horizontal or vertical movements. It was the most extraordinary feeling; a tingling all across the back of her brain, inside her skull, which focused her entire being forward upon the object of her attention in an invisible vortex. It took massive concentration just to keep her mind tunnelled on to the packet, but to slide it down towards the television as well, without letting it slip, was almost impossible. It was not unlike trying to keep a balloon in the air by lying on one's back and blowing at it. The moment she began to tire it sank lower and she could not raise it again. It took about two minutes to get it within a foot of the television, then, with a last gasp of mental effort she willed it to flick up so that its own momentum could carry it the rest of the way. It bounced off the screen and landed on the floor.

She closed her eyes tightly and sank back into the sofa. David leant down and picked up the pack of cigarettes, gingerly, as if he thought it might give him an electric shock. It was fuzzy with static, but otherwise perfectly normal. He turned it over in his hand.

'You did that?' he asked.

She opened one eye and looked at him blearily. She nodded.

'How?' he asked, still bemused. She twitched her shoulder in a shrug.

'I'm not sure. I was sitting here thinking how nice it would be if I was able to get them down from there without moving and they just sort of, kind of . . . complied.'

He licked his lips, still looking down at the packet in his hands.

'Goodness,' he said. He thought for a second. 'Could you do it again?'

'I could try.'

It was a rare grey, cold day outside and they settled down after they had eaten their brunch, hoping to repeat the trick. David found a small table and placed it in front of the fire, between the sofa and the television. On top of it, in a line, he placed a packet of cigarettes, a tennis ball, a large box of matches and a can of beer. Christina sat cross-legged on the sofa and stared at them, her brow furrowed with concentration.

After half an hour nothing had moved so much as a millimetre and she gave up, remarking that thinking about it made it more difficult. For David, who had driven himself to the point of despair, back in the month between leaving Orkney and Christina's arrival, by trying to rationalize Craigairie, this sounded depressingly familiar. But he concealed his disappointment and restrained himself from pushing her further.

She tried again a couple of times that afternoon, but still had no success. They watched a film and then drove into Barrhill for a drink. When they got back to the cottage much later on they settled down in front of the television again and David fell asleep, snoring gently beside her on a sofa. Christina returned her attention to the table, with its line of objects waiting for her to move them. She gazed at them for twenty minutes; nothing happened.

'Come on,' she murmured. 'Give me a break. Abracadabra, double, double, toil and trouble, *Lacrimae Mundi*, Nymatili.'

She sighed and looked up at the television. Even as her eyes passed over it the beer can tilted on its rim, fell over on to its side and trundled to the edge of the table. Her eyes jerked back on to it just in time to catch it as it reached the edge. It began to fall and then slowed, still sinking towards the ground but in slow motion, like something floating in an emptying bath.

It felt heavy, much more so than the cigarettes. She tried to arrest its downward motion and succeeded for about ten seconds before it began to sink again. She was barely breathing and she began to feel dizzy and faint, but she held on, so bemused by what was going on inside her that for almost a minute she forgot that she was holding a beer can in mid-air, by the power of her mind. Her breathing began to return, but it was not controlled by her lungs. Instead it was as if her diaphragm was shivering with gradually increasing violence, making her pant quickly, like a dog. Her whole body began to shudder and her panting began to register in her voice box in small, whimpering moans.

Still she held on to the can, now only a couple of inches from the floor. Her concentration was now so intense that every nerve-ending in her body seemed to be screaming. Her face was shivering and the tendons in her neck were standing out, hard as thin iron bars. She was no longer aware of the whining sound she was making, or of the frenzied trembling which gripped her body, or even of the fact that David had woken and was watching her with wide, horrified eyes, unable to speak or move. The beer can was the only thing she could see, the only thing in the world for her. There was a roaring sound inside her head and a crimson film behind her eyes as she strove to keep the can off the floor.

She did not feel the orgasm coming until it was on to her, and then it was too late. It exploded through her with a ferocity which threw her back into the sofa, spasms lurching through her body. She had never before experienced anything even close to it. It was agonizing in its intensity, fading and returning again and again, until exhaustion finally slowed it to a halt.

It took over five minutes before she had recovered sufficiently to stand up and stumble out of the room. She was away for about five minutes and when she returned, her face and hair dripping with cold water, wearing a towelling dressing gown, her teeth were still chattering too much for her to articulate anything more lucid than the occasional 'Shhhit'.

When she finally recovered, she picked up the beer can from the floor, opened it and emptied most of it down her throat.

She burped and then looked at David, who was still flabbergasted. She shook her head.

'Davie,' she succumbed to another quick shiver. 'Shit, Davie. I got to teach you how to do that. It's AWESOME.'

★

98

It was hot.

It was absurdly hot.

David had been tampering with the weather and, like everything he did when he drew upon the power of Craigairie, he had gone a bit too far. This was not Scottish weather, it was not even freak, greenhouse-effect weather. It was still, harsh, arid, searing heat one might have expected in Greece or southern Italy. This part of the world was not used to the sort of relentless beating it was taking from the sun; it was a bit like feeding rocket fuel into a tractor. The valley shimmered and scorched under an endless blue sky, with no breath of a breeze to take the edge off the heat. Apart from the Scots pines behind the cottage and the barns which clustered around it, there was precious little shelter between the river and the hilltops. The barns, although musty and airless, built to withstand wind and rain not sub-tropical temperatures, had become shelter for an unlikely aviary of birds. The barn owl shared his beam with swallows and wagtails; kestrels and sparrowhawks sat alongside blackbirds and thrushes. Down on the ground Shuduch the fox sprawled in a dark corner, too hot to care that a family of hares had moved in with him.

At night, when the moon and stars turned the valley glistening silver, Christina could muster up a good dew, which kept the thin soil from turning to rock, but she could not break the spell David had put on the days. Neither of them had realized he was doing it until it was much too late to be reversed. He just got up every morning for a couple of weeks wishing that it would be blisteringly hot again, and the weather had complied. It simply did not occur to him that there was a connection between his fervent prayers for a heatwave and the heatwave itself.

It took a while, the best part of a month, before they fully grasped the awesome implications of the Pandora's box Christina had opened when she first moved a cigarette packet by telekinesis. The mere fact that it was possible at all blinded them to the sheer magnitude of the power they had unearthed. They failed to see what it really was and where it was coming from until, like David's heatwave, it was irreversible.

For Christina, control over this new power had come with astonishing ease and rapidity, after her first experience of it. It was as if a door had opened in her mind, unlocking a latent sixth sense which, if used to its fullest capacity, could do almost anything. Moving cigarette packets by willpower alone was just a tiny part of it, the tip of a huge iceberg. But it was the key which opened up Craigairie for them. And Christina found it.

It would have been easy for David to have been jealous of the way she walked into his domain and claimed it for herself; he had always known, somewhere deep inside, that she was capable of it, which was why he had put up such bloody-minded resistance to her back in Orkney. But he realized now that she possessed the missing ingredient he had lacked when he was alone there. It was as if he had laid all the painstaking groundwork, by coming to terms with the bizarre and often frightening nature of the place, when anyone else would have run. But it was Christina's unquestioning, childlike understanding of the power which completed the recipe.

It was much more difficult for David. For a start, the power, the magic, was a feminine thing. It was hard to explain why, but it came much more easily to Christina, as if it was built into her instinct to understand it and accept it. It was not something which one bent to one's will, a thing to be dominated and subjugated, like an ore waiting to be mined. Instead, in Christina's words, 'you just opened yourself up and let it flow through you'. David wanted it and was frustrated when he could not lay his hands on it, whereas Christina just put herself into neutral and let it come, when and how it wished.

Secondly, David could not suppress a niggling twinge of rationalism which could not bear to see basic laws of science, nature and possibility broken so flagrantly. When he saw, for instance, a beer can floating in thin air, held up merely by his own will for it to be there, he could not help but doubt his own eyes, at which point the can would immediately disobey his less than wholehearted willpower and renew its acquaintance with gravity. The trick was to clear one's mind of all preconceptions of how the world was supposed to work and unquestioningly accept what appeared to be happening as the truth. For a man who had built his entire existence around a towering edifice of rationality and causality, it was far from easy to accept that there were things which happened in the world which did not stand up to, or indeed need, explanation.

His other great problem was that when the power came to him, he had precious little control over it. When he moved something by telekinesis he flung it around; he reduced half of the ornaments, knick-knacks, ashtrays and other breakables in the house to smithereens by rocketing them against the walls. Christina could hold a normal conversation whilst juggling several objects in the air around her, which was a control David would never learn. He, on the other hand, could blow a drystone dyke apart from two hundred yards away, which was something she would not have done, even if she could have.

When he lit a fire, pyrokinesis in American, it was with an explosive power which could reduce a full-grown tree to ashes, or send a sheet of searing blue flame across the surface of a pond, whereas Christina could light a single candle from the far side of a room without so much as singeing anything else.

When he was frustrated or angry he was at his most dangerous. He could crack boulders with a look, or start a fire half a mile away, or ransack a previously tidy room in a matter of seconds.

Or he could induce a scorching heatwave just by wishing it would be hot when he got out of bed in the morning.

There was more, much more. As the weeks passed, that first levitation of a cigarette packet receded into their past – the difference between the two-times table and quantum physics. Christina's control was breath-taking and her originality seemingly limitless, as she learned to apply the power, rather than just play with it. She could, for instance, induce smells. She surrounded herself with a haze of the waxen, romantic scent of gardenias, her favourite flower. She could also make herself emanate pheromones, so subtle that only animals could pick them up. She could fill the air with an aura of such aching calmness and peace that the shyest of the animals which passed through the valley would come to her hand; foxes, badgers, even the big, proud red stag which roamed around the moors, striking dramatic poses wherever he knew he could be seen.

And she could predict the near future, if she put her mind to it.

With no one against whom they could compare themselves they floated together into a sort of waking dream-world. The contours of reality became so blurred for them that they ceased to be surprised by what they were able to do. When they went out from Craigairie, to go to the pub in Barrhill, or to do their shopping, they knew how odd their life was, but they saw it as odd in the eyes of others, not in their own. For them Craigairie was normal, a secret which was best kept to themselves, a knowledge they were happy to have and which the rest of the world was to be pitied for lacking.

Even so, they could not entirely conceal their extraordinary gifts from the locals. They were considered foolish and misguided, foreigners to the area, who risked more than they could possibly understand by remaining at Craigairie. But as time passed and they appeared no less secure and happy there, in fact more radiant and settled every time anyone saw them, the speculation turned to quiet wonder. Craigairie had a reputation, generations old, for driving people mad, or spooking its residents into hasty and ignominious retreat, but these two had somehow overcome it. Jim and Ellen Rutherford, who owned Kilreuchal Farm, just three miles from Craigairie, were quizzed repeatedly about what they saw, or suspected, or knew about what went on up the hill. But Jim Rutherford was not the sort of man who bandied idle gossip in the pubs and shops of Barrhill and whatever he knew, or guessed, he kept to himself. And Ellen Rutherford was of good gypsy stock and knew fine well what sort of a place Craigairie was. She was aware of David long before Christina appeared on the scene and went out of her way to cultivate Ellen Rutherford. She knew what he must have gone through back in the winter and respected him for sticking it out. And then, when Christina wandered down off the moors one June afternoon and charmed the socks off Ellen, a friendship was struck which not even the most insatiable curiosity down in the town could break through.

The general consensus was that something weird was going on up there; an opinion which was in no way lessened by the suspicious silence of the Rutherfords. Small, remote towns thrive on idle gossip and relish anything even slightly abnormal or new. As that scorching, unnatural summer took hold, David and Christina were the flavour of the month in Barrhill.

They were blissfully unaware of most of this. They knew that people gave them funny looks and could tell by the way that people treated them that they were the object of speculation in the locality. But they shrugged it off and got on with their idyll, knowing that no one would believe the truth even if they were presented with it for all to see. They got browner and happier and weirder and let time flow past them without caring a damn about the outside world until, with a bang, it found its way into Craigairie and they suddenly realized how far adrift they had floated from reality.

It came in the form of Christina's cousin, Rosie Graham. Rosie was Christina's oldest friend on earth, more of a sister than her own sister. They had gone to school together and had shared a flat in Paris for two years; they even spoke similarly.

She called Craigairie, catching her cousin in a rare moment when the telephone was on the hook, the answering machine was turned off and Christina was inclined to answer it, one evening in late June. Christina picked up the receiver but did not say anything.

'Hello?'

'Hello,' she replied in a low voice.

'Tina?' Rosie asked. 'Enough with the silly voice, it's me, Rose.' Christina was silent for a few seconds.

'How did you get the number, you bitch?' she asked.

'Dahhhling,' Rosie said, '*God*, it's good to hear you. You are just impossible to get hold of.' She paused, then continued in the same effusive tone. 'So what the fuck's going on, sweetness?' she demanded. 'Word on the street is you're shacked up in the back of nowhere with an ace-journo who talks like Sean Connery.'

Christina looked at David, who was busy sticking photographs into an album. She smiled.

'Which street?'

'Just about any you care to mention. So is it true?'

Christina nodded. 'Yeah, it's true.'

'I'd like to meet him. Apart from anything else, I'd like to meet the man who can keep you in Scotland for six months. I hear interesting things about him, about both of you, in fact.'

'Really? Like?'

'Just gossip,' Rosie said vaguely. 'Someone said they thought you were in love with him.'

'Who said that?' Christina demanded, agog.

'Your father, I think. I spoke to him a few weeks ago when he was down here, on his way through to America. He was concerned about you; kept muttering something weird about you being in over your head.'

'Did he?' Christina said. She thought for a few seconds. Something told her that her father had not been talking about David, which meant that he had an inkling of an idea about Craigairie, which was both surprising and strangely unnerving.

'So is it true?' Rosie asked.

'What?'

'That you're in love with him and that you're in over your head?'

'Yes to the first no to the second and don't be nosy.'

'I'd like to meet the man,' Rosie said again.

'You could always come and stay.'

'Well, actually,' Rosie said, 'I was just coming to that. I've got to drive someone up to Baldarnock next weekend and I thought I'd stop off with your parents, but since they're not there I wondered if *you* might put us up for a night.'

'We'd love to,' Christina said immediately, without hesitation. 'Of course. Who're you driving?'

'A strange old bat Mummy picked up in L.A. She's a seventy-year-old Cherokee Indian called Clara Bow, who's made a mint in movieland by telling the fortunes of the rich and famous. She's apparently nicknamed the witch-to-the-rich, over there. Typical of Mummy to unearth someone like that.'

A slow smile grew on Christina's face.

'I'd like to meet her,' she said.

And so Rosie Graham and Clara Bow, witch-to-the-rich, were the first outsiders to stay at Craigairie. They arrived on another scorching afternoon, after a hellish drive north from London, bumping down the long forestry track from Barrhill and leaving a plume of red dust hanging in the air behind them. Rosie did not know quite what she had expected, but the sheer remoteness of Craigairie caught her by surprise. To drive there on this, the more direct route from Barrhill, one had to climb up out of the Duisk Valley, on to the barren, heat-scorched moors, across a wide wilderness one could only guess at from below, then through four miles of endless, regimented forestry, out the other side and finally down into an unexpected, hidden valley like a fertile, green gash in the hills. The little, square white cottage sitting on the hillside, surrounded by a cluster of outhouses and barns and sheltered by a small wood of tall Scots pines, was the very end of the road.

As they drove the last half mile, from the edge of the forestry to the cottage, Rosie shook her head in wonder. It was beautiful, with the blue river winding along the bottom of the valley and the still silence of the summer afternoon, but it was not Christina's natural habitat. She had always been a wild, gregarious creature, not suited to this sort of loneliness.

As for Clara Bow, the moment they entered the valley she sat up bolt upright in her seat and drew in a quick shuddering breath.

'*Mia dia,*' she murmured. 'What is this place?' Taking this to be an inexact translation of a slightly different question, Rosie shrugged.

'It's called Craigairie. It's where they live.'

'It's . . .' the old Indian began. 'It has an odd feeling.'

'No kidding,' Rosie replied. She swung the car around the barn and into a dusty courtyard, parking it in front of the open back door. She climbed out, stretching her legs, and walked around the front of the car to help her ageing passenger out. She was thus looking at Clara Bow, rather than at the door into the cottage behind her, when the old lady froze. She looked past Rosie with an expression of sudden, undisguised shock and recoiled a step backwards. Rosie swung around, expecting to see something which would elicit a similar reaction in herself, but instead saw her cousin.

Christina was standing in the doorway, wearing a slightly tatty summer dress, faded blue with red flowers, which stopped short of her bare knees and left her arms and upper chest uncovered. She looked wonderful; dark brown, lithe and healthy, with her flag of hair bleached the colour of straw and her entire demeanour seeming to say 'Look at me, see how whole I am'. When Rosie had last seen her, back at New Year, the question in everyone's minds had been whether Christina could pull herself clear of Erlend without sustaining considerable psychological damage along the way. To see her now, even at first glance, the change was astounding. She looked better than she had for years, even before Erlend had died.

She took them into the cottage, which was pleasantly cluttered, untidy but not shambolic, and gave them tea. David, she said, had gone down the hill to scrounge some provisions from nice Mrs Rutherford and would be back later. They drank their tea in the sitting room, until Clara Bow politely asked if she could take a nap. Christina showed her to the big spare bedroom at the front of the house, which had been made up for her. Rosie was to be put in their own bedroom, so that they could sleep in the long spare bedroom at the back of the house where Delilah held sway. After Christina had made sure that the old Indian lady was happy and comfortable, she went back downstairs and took Rosie out down the hill to the big pool in the river where she and David liked to swim.

As they wandered down to the river Rosie asked, 'So what do you *do* here?'

'Not a lot,' she said. 'We just sort of hang out.'

'Don't you ever get bored?' Rosie inquired carefully.

'Bored?' Christina asked. 'No. Should I be?'

'Well, no. But it's not . . .' She cast her eyes around. 'Montmartre, is it?' She paused, then went on. 'I mean, it's very pretty, but it's not exactly the hub of the universe.'

'You'd be surprised,' Christina replied with a small, private smile. She shook her head, almost as if confused. 'I really love it here. I've rediscovered myself. I've learned stuff about the world and about me, myself, which I haven't known for years, if I ever knew it at all.'

'And Erlend?' Rosie asked. She was the only person on earth who could have asked this question of Christina. She was startled by the frankness of the reply.

'Erlend's dead,' Christina answered. She walked on a few yards, then shrugged. 'I couldn't go back to Paris, or to being the person I was when I was there. When I was with Erlend it was as if we were living our lives against the clock and, with the crash, it was like time had finally caught up with us. We were both moving much too fast to think and when I woke up one night in a field and he was gone, the only thing I could think was "Why the hell am I still alive?".' She paused and frowned. 'I didn't want to die, but for months afterwards I kept thinking that it was a sort of weird, cruel accident that I was still alive and Erl wasn't. The deal always seemed to be that if one of us went, both did.' She snorted. 'Stupid, really.'

'So what's changed?' Rosie asked quietly.

'I have,' her cousin replied. She bit her lip and turned to look at Rosie for the first time since she had started to speak about Erlend. 'When Erl died, that frantic, live-fast, die-young bit I had died with him. With Davie it's not like a race; we have a good time together without having to go out to look for it.'

'Is *he* in love with *you*?' Rosie asked.

They had reached the river and they stopped, looking down at the deep dark pool. It looked cool and inviting, so thick with peat that it seemed to have no bottom; nameless monsters could have been lurking in those dim depths, waiting for a big, clumsy human to bite. Christina undid a couple of buttons on her dress and rolled her hips, letting it drop to the ground. She stood there stark naked, brown from her forehead to her toes.

'I really don't know,' she said. She laughed; a wonderful, joyful sound. 'If he isn't already, he will be sooner or later.' With that she dived into the river.

When they returned to the cottage David was coming over the top of the hill half a mile down the valley, carrying a big basket in one hand and two laden plastic bags in the other. They watched him from the wall at the front of the garden as he wandered lazily across the hillside with the red sun setting behind him. He saw them when he was about a hundred yards from the barns and changed course, to come round the front of the barn which was to be his pool room, to where they were sitting. He reached them and put his basket and bags on the ground.

'Fresh eggs, fresh milk, still warm from the udder, a bag of tatties.' He looked down, as if to remind himself what else he had brought.

'Some carrots, some radishes, and some strawbs. Ellen Rutherford did us proud.' He extended his hand to Rosie, levelling his piercing green eyes on her face. 'You must be Rosie.'

She was just as Christina had described her; a long, tall, elegant woman, nearing the six foot mark, with a figure like an adolescent boy's dream. She had thick, oriental-black hair framing a face which did not seem to belong in all of this raw sex appeal; thoughtful and gentle, given to laughter. In an odd way she did not look unlike Christina; they had the same grey-blue eyes and the same pointed, Cleopatran nose, which was like a hallmark of their family. But she was more city, more modern, than her cousin.

As for Rosie's first impression of David, he was not at all what she had expected. She had thought he would be a beautiful, ephemeral creature like Erlend. Instead he was dark and craggy, with almost Arabic features and a low, mellow, laconic voice. He was no Adonis, but he had a strange magnetism, like some flawed, fallen creation from the imagination of a nineteenth-century Romantic novelist. Rosie found herself instantly wrong-footed by him. It was not that there was anything nasty or unpleasant about him, but he was such a totally unexpected man for Christina to have fallen in love with that her cousin was stunned by him.

And, if Rosie's instantaneous reaction to him was a long way short of love-at-first-sight, Clara Bow's disquiet on seeing him for the first time bordered on panic and blotted out any vestiges of politesse she might have been able to muster. Rosie remembered the look of horrified shock on the old Indian's face when she had first set eyes on Christina and it was the same with David, only a bit worse. She came out on to the lawn a few minutes later, dressed in a simple black dress with a Navajo shawl around her shoulders, and a string of baroque pearls around her neck which would not have disgraced a duchess. She came across to them with a graceful, soft-footed poise which belied her age, began to say 'I simply love your ...' and saw David. She stopped dead, the words dying on her lips. She passed a hand over her brow and blinked, then finally, with obvious difficulty, managed a thin smile. He stepped towards her, disconcerted by her reaction, extending his hand to her. She did not take it.

'Nice to meet you,' she lied.

It was not just David who saw the look on her face, either. All three of them could feel her acute unease and, for a horrible moment, there was blank silence. Then, without knowing what she was doing or even knowing she was doing it, Christina let rip a blast of empathetic gentleness which came straight from her soul and burst into the air around her. She did not say anything, it was just an instinctive reaction to the situation, backed by enormous, if untutored, psychic power. It broke over them in a wave, bringing an involuntary grin to Rosie's face and making both David and Clara Bow turn to her, slack-jawed. A huge blush exploded on to Christina's face and she turned away in shame. David recovered first.

'I think I'd better go and make some dinner,' he said. 'Anyone know how to make a soufflé?'

It was the beginning of a long and tricky evening.

To begin with everything went quite well. They set the table, sitting Clara Bow down at one end, with a glass of wine, while they bickered about the cooking. Christina and Rosie made a soufflé while David threw every available vegetable into a large bowl and called it a salad, then spent a quarter of an hour making a perfect French dressing. Christina and Rosie did their best to engage Clara Bow in conversation, but she would not be drawn. She sat and watched them in much the same way that the family of hares in the barn looked at Shuduch the fox.

When they all sat down to eat, the two cousins began condensing six lost months into an evening, mostly talking and laughing about people and events only they knew. David joined in periodically and spent most of the first twenty minutes trying to be polite to the old woman on his right. She answered him in monosyllables.

As dinner progressed, however, he began to be aware of Clara Bow staring at him, taking her eyes off him the moment he looked towards her, then resuming her scrutiny the moment he turned away again. He slowly began to realize that she was trying to read his thoughts, trying to get herself inside his head. Far from being disconcerted by this he found himself succumbing to a growing irritation. Christina was completely unaware of this duel until she suddenly heard David say, 'Get out of my mind, old woman.' It was so savage that she swung on him in shocked amazement. He was polishing off the last of his soufflé, looking at Rosie, listening to what she was saying. Christina looked at Clara Bow, who was gazing innocently out of the window at the fading summer evening.

'Telepathy?' Christina thought. 'Shit. I didn't know he could do that.'

'Neither did he,' David's voice said, somewhere in her inner ear. 'Funny old world, innit?' She looked at him, her jaw dropping open. He put down his fork, took a sip of wine and smiled at her.

After that things deteriorated rapidly. David cleared away the plates and returned with the strawberries he had been given by Ellen Rutherford. The moment he sat down Clara Bow started her tricks again. He put up with it for a couple of minutes, then pushed his strawberries away and turned to her, shaking his head.

'I asked you not to do that,' he said.

They stared at each other for a moment.

'If you want to know something about me, all you have to do is ask.'

Christina and Rosie, particularly the latter, turned to him, shocked into silence. Clara Bow seemed unfazed. She nodded slowly.

'So,' she said. 'Shall we talk about witchcraft?' She looked towards Christina. 'Or whatever you please to call what you did out there on the lawn, earlier on.' She turned back to David, her eyebrows arched.

He shrugged. 'I s'pose witchcraft's as good a word as any,' he said.

Rosie was looking around the table in complete bemusement. Whatever was happening here, she was the only one who was not in on it. The old Indian nodded again. She turned back to Christina and studied her.

'What d'you want?' Christina asked, opening her arms, palms facing outwards.

'What can you give?' Clara Bow replied. 'What you did on the lawn was no accident. There must be more.'

'There's no such thing as an accident,' Christina said. 'You should know that: you're the witch.'

'Ah,' Clara Bow laughed dryly. 'That's very modest of you.' She continued to gaze at Christina. 'So what can you do?' she asked.

There was a note of provocation in her voice which irked Christina. She shrugged slightly, bit her lip thoughtfully, then turned to Rosie, who was now pinning her growing resentment on the old woman, who seemed to be behind this weird discussion.

'Hold on to your hat, sweetness,' her cousin said quietly. 'This could seem a wee bit peculiar.' She looked down at the table in front of her, touched the fingertips of her left hand to her left temple and levitated the salt cellar. It rose a foot into the air, tipped upside down, pouring salt on to the table and began to form the letters 'C.M.'. When she had finished the second letter, she tipped it back a couple of inches, stopping the flow of salt, then forward again just enough to make a full-stop, then lowered it back on to the table. Rosie goggled. She tried to say something, but nothing came out when she opened her mouth. Clara Bow sat back in her seat and ran her tongue around her lips.

She raised her thin, painted eyebrows and turned her attention to David, who was quietly rolling a joint. When Rosie saw what he was doing, her heart sank. She glanced at the old woman, expecting a shocked reaction, but Clara Bow did not appear remotely bothered.

'So?' the old woman asked. 'You must be a Snake in the Chinese horoscope, unless I'm much mistaken?' He glanced up at her and flashed her a quick smile before returning to the job in hand. Clara Bow continued, 'Snakes are supposed to have the wisdom of the ages and the keys to the mysteries of life?' She paused. 'Is marijuana the key?'

'No,' David replied, without looking up. 'But it makes it easier to forget there's a lock.' He rolled it together, licked the paper and stuck it together. 'What about peyote?'

'I know some shamans who swear by it,' Clara Bow replied.

For some reason Christina found this funny, laughed and then stifled it when she realized she was alone in her mirth. David glanced across at her, his eyes smiling.

'So do you do anything like that?' the old woman inquired, nodding at Christina's salt-initials. 'Or do you just roll the reefers?'

'And read the minds,' he remarked, without looking at her. He put the finishing touches on the spliff and stuck it in his mouth. Then, quite naturally, as if it was the most normal thing in the world, he opened his right hand, fingers splayed, below the tip of the joint. A blue flame, six inches high, sprang from the middle of his palm. He lit his joint, puffing until it was properly alight, then turned his hand over so that the flame licked up around the sides, then snapped his fingers shut, into a fist, extinguishing the flame.

'Who needs a lighter,' he remarked with superb nonchalance.

For a moment there was absolute silence, then Christina burst out laughing. Rosie rounded on her, a hard, angry look on her face, prodded her arm and nodded viciously at the door. Christina bit back her mirth and stood up, pushing her chair back. She led her cousin out of the room, still grinning.

Clara Bow continued to stare at David for a long time after they had gone.

'Where are you getting this from?' she asked finally, unable to keep the awe out of her voice.

'Where d'you think?' he replied. He took a deep breath and began to recite in a monotone, like a chant.

> 'The great sea
> Has sent me adrift
> It moves me
> As the weeds in a great river.
> Earth and the great weather
> Move me.
> Have carried me away.
> And move my inward parts with joy.'

He smiled. 'As your people say.'

'That's Cherokee,' she said, truly amazed. 'You got this from a shaman?'

David shook his head. 'No, I just read the right books.'

She continued to stare at him. 'You will not tell me where you got this from?'

'If you don't know, I'm certainly not telling you.'

'Why not?' she demanded.

He shrugged. 'Because it belongs to us.'

She contemplated this for a while, watching him as he hooped a series of smoke rings around the neck of the wine bottle.

'Are you aware of how dangerous this thing is?' she inquired.

'Dangerous for whom?' he asked, without looking at her.

'For you, for Christina, for anyone around you.'

He blew a couple more smoke rings and shrugged.

'You're unconcerned?' Clara Bow asked. 'Or you just have no idea what you're meddling with.'

'Who's meddling?' he remarked. He looked at her and flashed her a quick smile. She stared at him for a long, long while, still unable to read him.

'I just don't like to see a child with a loaded gun,' she said at last.

Meanwhile, through in the sitting room, Rosie was receiving a more forthright explanation from her cousin. Christina was quite happy to leave David with the old witch, knowing that he could deal with her. His passion for mindgames was too cerebral for Christina; he enjoyed playing intellectual chess with people, which she found incomprehensible. But it meant that he could run circles around Clara Bow while she dealt with Rosie in her own, inimitable, candid way. She set her cousin down, gave her a drink, shifted from foot to foot, biting her lip and frowning hard as she picked her words.

'I'm a witch,' she said. Rosie stared at her.

'You're a what?'

'No,' Christina said. 'A witch.' She grinned. 'Joke?'

Rosie didn't find it funny. She continued to stare blankly at her cousin. Christina spread her arms out wide.

'I'm a witch,' she repeated. 'I have become a witch, I have realized my latent witch-hood. I'm the sort of woman they used to duck and burn . . . I'm a witch.'

Still Rosie stared at her. 'What does that mean?' she asked.

'It means . . .' She frowned. 'Um. It means I can do things like what I did through there. I can work magic.'

'Not like Paul Daniels?' Rosie asked.

Christina laughed quickly and shook her head.

'No, no. This isn't like sleight-of-hand. It isn't card from the sleeve stuff. It's real.'

Rosie thought about this. A lot of questions sprang to mind, but she kept it simple.

'How?'

'Ah,' her cousin said. 'Tricky one. We think it's to do with the standing stone over the valley.'

'We?' Rosie asked. 'So David's one too?'

'Yeah.'

Rosie digested this for a couple of minutes, then asked,

'You're not having me on about this? I mean, this isn't some elaborate practical joke?'

'Would I do that to you?' Christina replied. 'Besides, you saw what happened in there.'

'I know what I think I saw,' Rosie said. 'I can't think of any good reason why I should believe it, though.'

'Believe it,' Christina replied emphatically.

Rosie looked back down at her and knew that she was not lying. She had always been a useless liar, in Rosie's opinion; you could see it in her eyes when she was trying to fib. Her eyes were honest now, pleading Rosie to believe her.

'Is it open to anyone?' Rosie asked quietly. 'I mean, can anyone be a . . . witch?'

'Not anyone,' Christina said. She could not suppress the smile which flooded on to her face. She knew she had got through. 'But I think you might be. Give me your hand.'

Rosie extended her right hand and Christina gave it a cursory inspection. She grinned.

'You're a witch, honey.'

'How d'you know?'

Christina let go of her hand. 'It's a trick an old woman taught me in Orkney. It's to do with the colouring; something to do with oestrogen. It only works with women.'

Rosie looked at her for a long time. She shook her head slowly.

'I don't know why, but I believe you. Can you teach me how to be a witch?'

'I'd love to,' Christina replied, with feeling.

David and Christina waved them off when they drove away the next morning, his arm draped around her shoulders, hers around his waist. They watched the red dust from the track receding up into the forestry.

'All things considered,' Christina said, 'I'd say we came out of that encounter bruised but undamaged.'

'D'you think?' David said, still gazing up the track. 'I'd say we cocked it up, pretty much.' He paused and laughed. 'We're going to have to be careful about how we communicate with people.'

'Telepathically,' she thought. They turned to each other grinning. He steered her around and they began to wander back to the cottage.

'Did I ever tell you I love you?' he asked conversationally.

She shook her head. 'Not out loud.'

'Well, I think now could be the moment,' he said. He stopped and turned her around, so that they were facing each other.

'I love you,' he said. 'I am in love with you. I can't remember a better thing ever happening to me than you.'

She looked up into his eyes, biting her lip thoughtfully, with a faint smile.

'My love, my heart,' she said with quiet joy. 'You make me so happy I want to cry.'

After the brief visit Craigairie was never quite the same again. The change was not immediately noticeable and not necessarily a change for the worse, but after their private idyll had been breached once, David and Christina had to share it, to a greater or lesser degree, thereafter.

When Rosie left she went to her parents' home, Baldarnock, in Perthshire, where she stayed for a long weekend before driving south again, with Clara Bow. Craigairie was not mentioned by either of them in all that time, but it formed an omnipresent undercurrent between them. Rosie could not stop thinking about it, even after she returned to London. She went back to the art gallery in Kensington where she worked and attempted to do her job without letting her mind wander back to the hidden valley in Galloway. But she could not erase it from her thoughts; she found herself wondering what they were doing, how they spent their time, what part their witchery played in their lives. She even dreamt about Craigairie. London suddenly became hot and dirty and claustrophobic, full of mediocre people doing pointless things and trying to disguise their mediocrity and pointlessness by accelerating their lives to the point of oblivion. The thing that most struck her about Christina and David's attitude to life, in retrospect, was their enormous patience and contentment, as if there were nothing that could dent their peace of mind. When she compared this with the impatience and petty aggravations she allowed herself to suffer in London; the traffic, the pollution, the bloody-minded selfishness of ten million people climbing over each other for a tiny fragment of tranquillity, she missed Craigairie and envied Christina for it.

At the end of a long, miserable week she took the two weeks' holiday she had put aside for Corfu in August, packed a bag, climbed on to a plane and went back to Craigairie. She never returned to her job.

Kelvin and Meg were the next to arrive, two weeks into July, after a four-week hike down from Orkney in a horsedrawn 'vardo', a traditional Romany caravan Kelvin had inherited from an uncle. It was pulled by a lugubrious and reluctant carthorse called Pegasus, with the gloomiest expression in the world and a habit of standing still for hours on end, immune to any efforts to cajole it into movement. The vardo itself was romance on wheels, with a wooden frame painted yellow, red and green, a rounded canvas roof, like a pioneer waggon, and heavy, spoked iron wheels with solid rubber tyres.

They arrived, unannounced, the same day Rosie had wandered off home to Perthshire, after a week at Craigairie, to find some clothes. There had been a thunderstorm earlier on, which had cleared the old, sultry air away, replacing it with the odour of pine-resin and wet grass, rich and fresh. It had rolled on eastwards, sticking on to the Merrick Hills in a huge, dark anvil of cloud, from where it sent distant, echoing grumbles back down across the moors of Carrick. A few white clouds still flecked the aquamarine sky, but the sun had broken through again to get the last word on the day.

The river, starved of water for weeks, was glutted with a quick, brown spate which had flushed all of the dead water from the still pools, pouring down through the steep valleys to the sea with the relish of a parched man downing a long, cold lager. The very air was drunk with new life, clean and fresh, with a light, soft breeze which stirred the wet grass.

When Kelvin and Meg arrived and pulled into the backyard, there was no sign of life in the cottage and no immediate clues as to whether this was indeed Craigairie. Kelvin climbed down from the vardo, walked across to the open back door of the cottage and looked into the kitchen.

'Hello?' he called. He waited, shifting from foot to foot and hand-drumming on his thighs. Meg wandered to a window and peered in.

'Hello?' she called. 'Anyone home?' Nobody answered. She went on through the house, with Kelvin trailing behind, past the open front door and into a sitting room. There was a beautiful smell in the cottage, waxy and subtle; gardenia or tuberose, or something similar.

In the sitting room there were signs of life; a few empty beer cans, a newspaper from the previous day, a half-eaten apple, still relatively fresh. To Meg's eye it could only have been a room inhabited by David and Christina. It had a feel to it which no farmer's living room would have had, not expensive, but sophisticated. The sofa was old and worn, but comfortable; the ornaments and lamps were junk-shop chic. The general effect was young, well-off, underplayed, slightly chaotic; David and Christina. Meg walked to the mantelpiece, noticing, on the way, an ashtray with a couple of spliff-butts in it. She looked at the invitations and postcards propped up on the mantelpiece.

Behind her Kelvin had taken in the television, the video, the stereo and finally the record collection. He knelt down and, after a moment, laughed.

'We're here,' he said. 'Who else but Davie would have Donna Summer, Simple Minds, four Stones records, Nina Simone and Shostakovich under "S"?'

Meg walked to the big window overlooking the valley.

'There they are,' she said. Two figures were walking up the hill from the river, caught in a ray of sunshine which had contrived to break past the corner of a small cloud and spotlight them. Beside them a red dog trotted through the heather, stopping frequently to sniff at nothing in particular, before running to catch them up again. They were hand in hand, stark naked.

'Earth children,' Kelvin murmured. 'Doveleskira.' He watched them for a minute then turned to Meg. 'What do we do? We can't very well . . .'

'Aye, we can,' she cut in, at her most businesslike. She walked out of the room, through the front door and on to the lawn to meet them.

David and Christina were engrossed in conversation, the former making the latter laugh, and they did not realize they were being watched until they were climbing over the wall. Christina saw them first and stopped dead on the top of the wall, bringing David up short beside with a hoarse 'Oh, shit.'

'Act natural,' he whispered back. They jumped down on to the lawn and walked to the house, bypassing Meg and Kelvin.

'Back in a second,' David said. They broke into a run and disappeared into the house. Even their bottoms were brown.

When they reappeared five minutes later they were only slightly more dressed than they had been when they went in. Looking at them Kelvin felt grey and unhealthy. They were like a pair of cats, healthy and sleek and quietly pleased with themselves. He went to meet them and they hugged each other, then all together in a huddle. David broke away first and walked over to Meg. She looked him up and down.

He was very brown indeed; they both were, but with David it was accentuated by scars on his arms and legs which were not normally so visible. Meg could not remember him ever having looked so well, but she was damned if she was going to say so. She inspected him un-hurriedly.

'I saw they gave you that award,' she said.

He shrugged and nodded.

'Saw it on the telly,' she went on. 'You weren't there.'

'I was busy,' he said.

'Too busy to pick up the biggest award of your life?'

'A nasty little slab of perspex on a chunk of marble,' he replied.

He held on to his unshakeable good humour, but her coldness was beginning to wear him down. He knew without having to resort to telepathy that Kelvin had brought her here against her will and that she had only come because she liked Christina. Her mistrust of him was becoming habitual.

Then, finally, she relented and allowed him to hug her.

When Kelvin and Meg arrived they both had an image of how Craigairie would be, which had more to do with the six weeks David and Christina had spent with them in Orkney than with how things worked at Craigairie. Kelvin expected it to be wild and fun, with him monopolizing David, leaving the women to fend for themselves, while the two old friends drank and mucked around and generally lived their own lives.

Meg, on the other hand, came expecting to be irritated by something reckless and irresponsible and instead had to readjust her preconceptions to allow not only for David's new-found benevolence, but also for the extraordinary magic – for want of a better word – which underpinned everything that happened there.

They had come a hell of a long way since Orkney, when their affair had been little more than a twinkle in Christina's eye and the magic had

been David's private obsession. They had barely been capable of addressing each other back in Orkney without getting tangled in each other's
inadequacies and it had seemed that only a miracle, or a serious
compromise on David's part, could break down their communication
problem and bring them together.

It was hard to imagine what had happened between them, but they
were whole now, intertwined in something intensely private; happy,
confident and in love with each other. When there were other people
around them they behaved as if there was nothing on earth they had
wanted more, that company had been the one thing their lives had
hitherto lacked. But there was a constant, silent communication between
them into which nobody else was invited, not Kelvin, not Rosie, and
certainly not Meg.

In different ways Kelvin and Meg were both stranded by the situation
at Craigairie. Meg found that she could not disapprove of David, on
Kelvin's behalf, without also necessarily disapproving of Christina and
her cousin as well. They did not flaunt their witchdom, but it was there.
When they wanted to light the fire, but could not find any matches,
they did without, just aiming a look at the fireplace and igniting the
wood by pyrokinesis. When they could not be bothered to fetch
something, it came to them of its own accord. When the mood in the
cottage was anything less than happy and peaceful, a sudden euphoria
would come from nowhere, picking them up and hurling them into a
good mood. At first Meg did not notice them doing this and pooh-
poohed Kelvin when he pointed it out. But after a while she realized
that he was right, and once she had overcome her initial dubiety she
realized how often they did it and it annoyed her. Nothing was real or
as it appeared at first glance; their whole existence was distorted by their
terrifying powers. Rosie Graham, as another outsider, might have been
a natural ally, but she was in on it as well. She did not have their
dismissive control of the magic, which gave them the ability to put it to
practical use without really stopping to think about it, but she understood
it, accepted it, and, like them, found it amusing.

For Kelvin the witchery was a source of immense frustration and
gathering resentment. He wanted to understand it and to have it at his
fingertips as they did, but he simply did not have it in him. However hard
David tried to explain to him that he had only come by these powers by
default and that it was not somehow an indication of weakness on Kelvin's
part that he could not be a witch as well, he still felt bitter and aggrieved
to be left out of the fun and games. He was half-Romany, after all; he had
been brought up on stories and a culture in which magic played an
integral role and was taken for granted. He felt he had as much right to
this thing, if not more, than David, whose background was middle-class
Catholic from Gretna, or indeed a couple of blue-blooded women who
had hitherto channelled most of their energy into being beautiful people.

It depressed him when he saw them play with earth-power as if it was no more than just an interesting new drug they had stumbled upon. And it depressed him even more when they deliberately restrained themselves in his presence, as if to spare him from his own envy. If there was one thing worse than feeling sorry for himself it was knowing that David and Christina felt sorry for him as well.

As time passed, this bitterness did not decrease. He did his best to conceal it, but it rankled and festered like a hidden sore. Everything that happened around him seemed to have been designed to undermine his self-confidence.

Then, Kelvin went into Barrhill one evening and discovered that Craigairie was far beyond a mere pretence of normality.

He was bored. David, Christina and Rosie had gone for a walk, their euphemism for going somewhere quiet and out-of-the-way to teach Rosie witchery. Meg was watching the television, in no mood to be disturbed, which left Kelvin with nothing to do. He took Christina's car and drove into Barrhill for a drink. It was nine o'clock when he arrived and the pub was crowded with locals; weathered farmers and game-keepers, drinking pints of heavy with whisky chasers. Kelvin pushed his way through to the bar and ordered a pint, then insinuated his way into a group of men conversing around him, listening to their lazy discussion about politics. After a while one of them, a wiry, dark man of about sixty, noticed Kelvin and decided to talk to him.

'Would you be a Romany, then?' he inquired.

This caught Kelvin completely off his guard. He had not expected to be addressed at all, let alone recognized as a gypsy.

'What makes you say that?' he asked defensively.

'Och, just wondering. You're no frae these parts and I thocht you micht be with they Romanies up on Wullie McClellan's farm.' It was an odd, lilting accent, with few hard consonants, more like Meg's Orcadian than Kelvin's own hard Glaswegian.

'No,' he said. 'I'm staying down by New Luce. Place called Craigairie.'

A few glances were exchanged around him.

'Craigairie?' the man asked. 'Whit? Wi' Christina Graham and thon Davie Armstrong?'

'You know them?'

'Know *of* them,' he replied. He gave his friends a peculiar look.

'We know of them, richt enough,' one of them murmured.

'She's a wee brammer, thon Graham lassie, so she is,' a younger one remarked. 'Richt bonnie.'

There was a brief, somewhat loaded silence before the younger one began, 'So is it true that . . .'

Kelvin saw the foot that kicked his shin, stopping him in mid-sentence.

'Naething,' he said, giving the man who had kicked him a sulky look.

'Is what true?' Kelvin asked him.

'Naething,' the young man replied. He looked around his older companions and a defiant look came into his eyes. 'I was just wondering if it's . . .'

'Dae listen tae him,' the original one cut in dismissively. 'Awa' wi' the fairies, Tam, so you are. A heid full o' shite about witches and ghosts and standing stones.'

'Well, you explain the lambing we had, then?' he demanded.

They all gave him sharp looks. One of them murmured, 'Wheesht, Tam.'

'Dinnae mind me,' Kelvin said, raising his hands as if denying any responsibility for Craigairie. 'I'm just passing through.'

'It was a good year, richt enough,' one of them admitted. 'Nivver seen the like, and I've farmed in the Duisk sixty year.'

'It was the best ever,' Tam said. 'And the harvest's gonnae be the best ever, too. Then there's auld Jim Rutherford's fairm. I was up there a week back and I've nivver seen anything like it. He's having tae hire an extra hand just tae bring his tatties in.'

'Get on,' one of them said in obvious disbelief.

'And you explain the Romanies,' one of them said.

'What Romanies?' Kelvin asked. They all looked at him, then at each other.

'They've been coming since the middle o' June. Hundreds o' them,' Tam said. 'Wullie McClellan's gi'en them yin o' his fields tae camp on, up the Luce road. You must've seen it; hundreds o' caravans and lorries up on the moor, past the station. A richt mess, so it is.'

Kelvin shook his head. 'I didn't use that road,' he said. 'We came out through the forestry.'

'Well, if you didnae see them there, ye'd see them in the Crown up the road.'

'The Crown?' Kelvin asked.

'Aye, up past the wee bridge.'

Kelvin finished his pint and extricated himself a few minutes later, walking straight along the main street to the pub past the bridge where the gypsies were supposed to hang out. His head was buzzing with amazement and wonder. He knew Scottish pubs well enough to know that gossip such as he had just heard was not entirely idle.

Kelvin walked into the Crown and the first thing he saw, apart from the throng of Romanies in the pub, was a group of people around the door he knew. There were four of them, Irish Romanies from Donegal, drinking Guinness and smoking roll-ups. As he came in, one of them, a man called Danny Duggan, turned, recognized him and called out in Romany:

'Kelvin Ball. What in the name of Jaizus are you doing here?'

'I might ask the same of you,' he replied, coming over to the group. They greeted him with much back-slapping and bone-grinding handshakes. One of them went off through the crowd to buy Kelvin a drink. The rest inquired about his mother, aunts, uncles and told him that some of his cousins were 'around somewhere'.

'Here?' Kelvin asked, looking around.

'Up at the Atchin-tan,' they said.

'What are you all doing here?' he asked. 'Are you on your way back from Appleby?'

'We were at Appleby, aye,' Danny Duggan said. 'But we won't be going home quite yet. What're you doing here?'

'I'm staying with friends down the road,' he said.

They all nodded into their pints. He knew that sudden silence from long and bitter experience. As a didakai, a half-gypsy, he was able to do what he had just done and walk into a pub full of Romanies without fear of being knifed, but if they had a secret, they would not trust him with it. They would clam up, or change the subject, or simply refuse to let him in on it. They knew something now that he did not and they were not about to tell him what it was. He allowed them to steer him away from the subject and had a pleasant, if frustrating, time from then on, trying to get it out of them while they drank him into the ground. When he left, around midnight, he was none the wiser but a lot drunker. The only thing that stuck in his mind as he drove back to Craigairie was a snippet of some obscure Romany verse which he could not quite place. He thought about it the whole way home, but his Guinness-fuddled brain refused to locate the correct context.

When he arrived back he found Christina and Rosie in the kitchen, sitting on two high stools, drinking herbal tea. As he staggered through the door his eyes fell on Christina and he stopped to take her in, swaying like a larch in a gale. He grinned at her.

'Ah, the fair Christina.' He paused and translated the only intelligible thought in his mind into words. 'Thine is the beauty of the innocent and the wisdom of the ages. Thou alone can stem the tears of the world.' He stopped, rather pleased with himself for his instantaneous translation. After a moment he realized that Rosie was gawping at him and Christina had stopped, in the act of raising her mug to her mouth and was staring at him.

'What did you just say?' she said.

'Nothing,' he replied. He rolled his shoulders in a shrug. 'Just a compliment.'

She continued to stare at him. He began to feel faintly uncomfortable and took a step back, falling against the wall. Only then did he see David, at the other end of the room, sitting at the dinner table. He too was staring at Kelvin.

'Evenin', Davie,' Kelvin said hopefully.

'What does that mean, Kelv? What you just said?' David asked quietly.

Kelvin licked his lips, smiled inanely and shrugged again.

'I cannae mind.' He shook his head. 'S'just something a Romany said tae me.' He was slurring his words and his accent was about ten times broader than normal. He tried to push himself off the wall, succeeded for a few precarious seconds then slumped back again. 'D'ye ken Barrhill's full o' Romanies? Thousands o' them. What're they daeing there, that's what I'd like tae know.'

They ignored this sidetrack. Christina looked at David, then back to Kelvin.

'Tears of the world,' she said, trying to jog his memory. '*Lacrimae Mundi.*' She paused and thought for a few seconds. 'Does the word Nymatili mean anything to you?'

As she said it a look of astonishment broke on to his face and his hand shot out, pointing at her almost accusingly.

'Thas it,' he said. 'That's exactly it, shite, aye; "The Song o' the Nymatil".' He paused. 'How the fuck d'you know that?'

'It's written in the back bedroom,' she said. 'What does it mean?'

'Och, it's just a . . .' He frowned. 'It's just like a Romany myth. The chosen one of Dé Doveleski, the blessed one. There's a great long poem that goes with it . . .' He thought for a moment, then began to recite.

> 'For you is the earth
> And the earth will move for you.
> For you is the water
> And the rivers will cleanse you.
> For you is the air
> Which will sing with sweet scents.
> For you is the fire
> Which will rain from the sky.
> For you are the Blessèd
> The chosen of chosen.
> Yours is the beauty of the innocent
> And the wisdom of the ages
> You alone can stem the tears of the world.'

He stopped and shook his head. 'I cannae mind the rest. There's a lot more. It's all thee and thine, but it doesnae sound the same in English.'

'It said Nymatil*i*,' David said from the far end of the room. 'With an "i" on the end.'

'That just means more than one of them,' Kelvin said. He yawned cavernously and slid a little further down the wall. 'Doesnae really work, though. S'like putting an "s" on the end of Christ. Doesnae happen.'

When he dragged himself from his bed the morning after his binge in

Barrhill, Kelvin had no recollection of how he had got himself home the previous evening, let alone of the conversation he had with Christina, David and Rosie in the kitchen. It was not discussed thereafter and the only tacit acknowledgement that it had happened at all was that David went up to the spare bedroom, first thing the next morning, and painted over the last of Delilah's scrawlings, left there since the spring. If he and Christina had learned anything from Craigairie it was that there was no such thing as an accident. Nothing that had ever happened there was blind coincidence, everything was connected to something else and to an all-encompassing whole, however obscure. Not even the magic and witchery was an end in itself, it was a component part of something which was constantly growing into an overall picture. The fact that David and Christina did not know what this picture meant and were more inclined to ignore it, or paint over it, than to guess, did not alter the fact that it was beginning to reveal itself with a momentum outside their control.

The presence of a growing number of Romanies in the Duisk valley by the beginning of August, like the extraordinary year the local farmers were having, might have had no direct connection with Craigairie, but it was another oddity looking for an explanation. As Rosie remarked to Meg, when the latter asked her how much of the apparently unrelated abnormalities in the vicinity were, in fact, connected to Craigairie, 'If enough people make the connection for long enough it becomes the truth, whatever the truth actually is.'

'I don't think I get it,' Meg had said.

'It's the basis of Craigairie,' Rosie replied. 'In fact it's the basis of almost any religion I can think of. Truth and reality aren't absolutes, they're a matter of what you perceive them to be. A matter of faith, if you like.'

'I don't think I do like,' Meg said. 'So you're telling me that Craigairie's a religion?'

'In a way,' Rosie said. 'Religion's just an acceptance of some power bigger than ourselves, or at least that's what the nuns taught me at school. Craigairie's just the same.'

The local weekly newspaper could not help but notice that half of its stories, since way back in May, had been coming from an area previously notable only for its anonymity. It had started with the astonishing lambing season, not just remarkable for the number of lambs born in the hillfarms of Carrick, but also for at least three verified reports of lambs with extra limbs or even, in one case, an extra head. Then there was the weather; eight weeks of almost continuous sunshine between the end of May and the beginning of August, including four days in the middle of June when temperatures of 94°, 92°, 97° and 90° were recorded in Barrhill, of all places; hotter than anywhere in Europe north of Provence.

In July there were a couple of minor earth tremors up in the hills, contributing to the general atmosphere of oddness and keeping the rumours on the boil. Then, after the ancient annual Romany fair at Appleby in Westmorland, the gypsies began to arrive. They came in caravans, cars, mobile homes, lorries and the occasional painted vardo, found themselves a friendly farmer and formed an encampment, known as the Atchin-tan, on the edge of the moors behind Barrhill. This grew steadily into a sprawling, ragged township, attracting swarms of police, health-inspectors and social workers, like flies to a pot of jam.

It also began to attract the attention of national newspapers up in Glasgow and Edinburgh. The gypsies refused to be moved. They exercised their ponies, lent relatively willing hands to local farmers, coursed hares and systematically poached the Forestry Commission, but they appeared to be making a point of not antagonizing the locals. They did not poach private land or rivers, they stayed out of trouble in Barrhill, did not go where they were not invited and kept themselves to themselves. They refused to be policed by gorgios, non-Romanies, but they dealt with their own troublemakers with quiet but summary efficiency.

There was something faintly unnerving about the way they had just turned up from nowhere, plonked themselves on a hill in the middle of Carrick, dug themselves in and refused to be moved. It seemed almost that they were waiting for something, but no one dared get close enough to ask what.

And if their refusal to conform to their own stereotype was peculiar, then the attitude of the locals to their presence was bizarre in the extreme. Instead of the antipathy, revilement and hatred traditionally accorded to Romanies, the people of the Duisk just affected to ignore them, treating them with a studied unconcern which bemused outsiders and infuriated councillors and police alike, who were itching for an excuse to get rid of the Atchin-tan. It was as if some sort of tacit truce had been struck between the locals and the Romanies so that the latter could remain there unmolested, as long as they behaved themselves.

More intriguing still were the rumours one heard further afield, where people were not bound by the oath of silence which permeated the Duisk. There was talk of witches and covens up in the hills, of 'witching stones' way out on the moors, where the covens met and where people left little offerings, in return for which they were granted their wishes. And there was hushed talk of a Mother Coven somewhere way back behind Barrhill, secretive and hidden, from where everything that was weird in the Duisk originated.

It did not take long for some bright young journalist to come up with the names of David Armstrong and Christina MacRuarie, née Graham.

At the end of August, Christina's brother Ed came to stay at Craigairie with his girlfriend Emily. They were both at university in Edinburgh and arrived at Craigairie straight from the Festival, bringing a large article they had cut out of a Saturday newspaper. It was entitled: 'WHAT'S GOING ON IN PURGATORY?'

There was a great deal of gossip, rumour and speculation, jumbled together with all the facts and figures from the Duisk's extraordinary year; the lambing, the harvest, the heatwave, the earth tremors, the lot. There were pictures of David Armstrong, some-time award-winning tele-journalist, and Christina MacRuarie, beautiful daughter of an ex-cabinet minister and major local landowner. The editor of the paper had been careful not to open himself to a libel suit, but the clear implication was that these two were heavily involved in all the witchcraft rumoured to be thriving in the hills of Carrick.

At first, when they saw the article, Christina and David just laughed. They stuck it up on the kitchen wall, above the kettle, and grinned whenever they made a cup of coffee and saw it. As far as they were concerned their secret was not especially compromised for having someone distilling a lot of pub gossip into an article for a newspaper published and mostly read two hundred miles away. Besides, they had both been the subject of media gossip before, although in very different ways. Neither of them was someone anonymous for whom this sort of thing was a new and horrifying experience; they knew how to shrug it off.

They did not expect, however, to have half of what used to be Fleet Street, including a posse of some of the grubbier tabloids, picking up on the story and rushing north, armed with cameras like bazookas, to get a piece of the action. The hills were soon crawling with paparazzi and it was only a matter of time before one of them got a picture worth a headline and a few sub-literate words. The photograph, when it appeared on the front page of a tabloid, under the headline 'WHAT A MAGIC SUMMER!', was blurred and airbrushed almost beyond recognition, of two naked people beside a river, a man standing next to a lying woman.

It was of Kelvin and Meg.

Of all the things Sir James Graham expected on his return from a very pleasant two-month holiday in America and Canada, finding Christina in the middle of a media storm on his doorstep was a shocking surprise.

He had known about Craigairie before he went away in June, in fact he had known about it since the winter and had meant to talk to his daughter about it. But she had been up in Orkney for the best part of two months, then was closeted in Craigairie with David Armstrong, who had an irritating habit of leaving his telephone off the hook. Sir James had intended to drive up there one fine day, but had put it off, partly because he could not really see what damage Christina could be doing to herself on a moor in the empty hinterland of Galloway and partly because he could not be bothered. Then he had gone away to America and it all seemed a terribly long way away, a winter obsession which evaporated under the summer sun.

It had been an obsession for him, all the same. He was not normally a superstitious man, but the more he thought about Craigairie and the more long-hidden references to it in his papers and his library that he unearthed, the more uneasy he became. As a rule he considered most superstition to be the preserve of the unsophisticated; charming, baroque but nevertheless spurious ornamentation on the structure of real life.

But Craigairie was different. It was not even the same thing as the rich panoply of fairytales – witches and ghosts and magic – which permeated west-coast, Celtic culture. There was nothing quaint or poetic about a medieval abbot writing a letter to his bishop in which he referred to a 'foul, unclean, standing stone'. Those were the words of a frightened monk describing a direct threat to his own ministry and begging for help to have it 'uprooted' and destroyed. And he was by no means alone in having singled out Craigairie and its immediate environs for particular attention. Christ had been brought to this part of the world only four centuries after he was nailed to a cross on Golgotha, and his messengers and ministers had been complaining about the hills around New Luce ever since. From St Patrick complaining about the 'apostate Picts' right through to the Presbyterian minister of Barrhill in 1872 writing a letter railing against 'cults of witchery and blasphemy' in his parish, Christianity had consistently seen this area as a problem and a threat.

It had been on the pilgrim road between the ancient kingdom of Strathclyde and St Ninians Kirk at Whithorn, down on the Solway coast, but despite this it had remained stubbornly pagan until deep into the Christian era. In the twelfth century the Cistercians, the theological storm-troopers of the middle ages, established a monastery at Glenluce and, with the Cluniac monks of Crossraguel, spent the following four hundred years, until the Reformation, waging what amounted to a long-running private crusade against 'heathenish' beliefs. They plundered and destroyed any Pictish burial mounds they could find, dug up and smashed the standing stones, including a circle of thirty-six stones, each one 'as tall as two men and carved all over with strange heathen runes', according to the monk who recorded its destruction for posterity. When they could not uproot or break the stones they carved crosses upon them, or even built them into small chapels, like holy sentry-boxes, guarding the sites for Christ. Failing that they turned Craigairie into a leper colony.

When witch-hunts were almost unheard of, in pre-Reformation Scotland, Craigairie was drawing an inordinate amount of attention, year after year, generation after generation, century after century. Then, in the sixteenth and seventeenth centuries, after the Reformation, when four thousand people were murdered as witches all over Scotland, hardly any were brought to trial in Galloway. It seemed almost that in the absence of the organized monastic persecution of the previous centuries, the locals closed ranks and protected each other from the mayhem which was happening elsewhere. It was only in the eighteenth century, when the danger was past, that local ministers began to complain about witches again.

One could disregard the idle tittle-tattle of newspapers looking for a story, just as one could discount west-coast superstition and dismiss the paranoia of medieval monks obsessed with supposed demon-worship, but a recurring pattern stretching back fifteen hundred years into history was harder to ignore.

Quite apart from which, he was far from amused to find several Fleet Street hacks doorstepping Castle Graham when he arrived home – or at least front-gating it. At first he thought that some forgotten mis-demeanour from his political past had come home to roost, and he had that feeling of sick panic in the pit of his stomach. He was therefore almost as relieved as he was annoyed when he discovered the truth.

It took a couple of days for him to overcome his jet-lag and the culture shock of being in Scotland again, then a couple more before he felt that he had put the Craigairie situation into perspective enough to approach his daughter about it. Luckily his wife, her mother, was still down south in London, which gave him a short breathing space before he was obliged to talk to Christina. He flicked through his papers, refreshing his memory about the history of the place, read the newspapers and talked to his housekeeper, Mrs Roberts, whose knowledge of local gossip had earned her the nickname 'Radar' Roberts in the family. She was typically circuitous with him, but he did learn from her that people had been talking about Craigairie for at least a month before the press began to take an interest. He also discovered that both his son and niece, Rosie, had been staying with Christina for several weeks.

He considered his options, then opted for one of his 'Far be it for me to interfere, but . . .' letters, recognized and established code in his family for him being annoyed about something. In it he described, in some detail, all the things he had found out about Craigairie before he left for America, then informed her, also in detail, exactly how he had felt on his return. He was not normally given to expletives, but after two months amongst Americans the phrase 'shitting on one's own doorstep' leapt to mind and he used it in the letter, correctly surmising that Christina would recognize this uncharacteristic strength of vocabulary as anger.

She rang him three days later and gave him a practical lesson in why he had always found it so hard to scold her over the telephone. She asked how America had been, got him talking, laughed at his descriptions and very nearly succeeded in sidetracking him. It was only at the last minute that he recovered the initiative enough to suggest that he should go over to Craigairie.

'I'm not sure that'd be wise, Papa,' she said. 'The place is crawling with paparazzi.'

'Then you come here,' he said. After a short silence she demurred, obviously not relishing the prospect of meeting him on his home ground. She suggested that they met in Ballantrae, near enough halfway between Craigairie and Castle Graham. He agreed.

When he arrived in Ballantrae, the following afternoon, he half-expected to find that she had brought her boyfriend, Rosie and perhaps even Edward as well, just to be sure that he would behave himself and not make life uncomfortable for her. He was surprised, therefore, to find her waiting for him alone in the agreed pub.

They exchanged pleasantries, asked after each other's health and then he got down to business.

'So what's all this about?' he asked.

'Gossip,' she replied, with a shrug.

'Just gossip?' he inquired. 'Nothing else?'

'What else could it be?' she asked innocently, making a knife-edge judgement that he would not dare ask her if she was a witch so soon.

'You read my letter?' he asked.

She nodded. 'It was interesting.'

'You don't think that maybe Craigairie might have done something to deserve that reputation?' he asked. 'What I mean is that when I got home and found all these stories waiting for me, my immediate reaction was that they seemed to fit into the general pattern of the place.'

She thought for a second then turned down the corners of her mouth, as if it had not occurred to her until now, but now she thought about it she could see why he could make such a mistake.

'Which is one of the reasons why I wasn't best pleased.'

'I'm sorry,' she said. 'But what did you expect me to do? Ring you up in Vancouver, or wherever, and tell you that the gossip in Barrhill is that Davie and me are . . . whatever.'

'It's not just in Barrhill, Christina. This is national news.'

'Where d'you think they got it from? They're just picking up on a country rumour and regurgitating it as news. You know newspapers.'

'I know that there's very rarely smoke without fire, particularly in a place with a reputation like Craigairie.' Heat was beginning to creep into his voice and she met it head on.

'Oh, come on, Papa, I've hardly been able to fart for the last twenty-six years without it making Dempster, just because I'm your daughter. Those people don't need fire to make smoke. It's their job.'

'So they made up this gossip for nothing?'

'No, I told you; they just happened to focus on Barrhill and we just happened to be there.'

'But people *are* talking about you in Barrhill?'

'Maybe. I . . . we can't be responsible for what people want to think. A few oddish things have happened in the Duisk this summer and we're strangers, so maybe they think we're responsible. Added to that, if all that stuff you said in your letter is true, then it's hardly surprising that they all start pointing at Craigairie the moment anything remotely out of the ordinary happens. It's like a collective subconscious.'

'I'm serious about this, Tina. I'm not playing games with you. I think there might be something dangerous about that place.'

'I can look after myself,' she said.

'Maybe. But your mother and I are worried about you.'

'Oh?' she said. 'Of course. Mummy put you up to this?'

'I'm quite capable of making my own mind up,' he replied stiffly. 'And no, she didn't.'

'Well, so am I capable of making my own mind up,' she said. 'And Craigairie isn't dangerous.'

'I'd still feel safer if you weren't there,' he said.

'Maybe,' she replied. 'But I am there and I will continue to be there, so it's fairly academic.'

'You do realize what an unenviable position that puts us in,' he said. 'What are we supposed to say to our friends, let alone to all of these gutter-hacks?'

'The same thing I learned to say when people asked me about you,' she said. She stood up. 'No comment.'

She drove back to Craigairie in a mood split halfway between anger and shame. She could not remember ever having fought with her father before, in her entire life. Theirs had always been a solid, unshakeable allegiance, a counterbalance to her mother and elder sister, Georgina. He had always defended her wildness and feyness from criticism and had always understood when she pursued the erratic courses upon which her heart led her. It depressed her that he objected to Craigairie. She could deflect her mother with the ease of long experience, but her father was a different matter – he was a good and loyal friend and she hated having to tell him, basically, to fuck off.

If it hadn't been for all of this ridiculous media attention the situation would never have arisen. It had all seemed too absurd to worry about when it first started, even when Kelvin and Meg had been photographed nude down by the river. But it was spreading like a slow, insidious rot into the heart of the Craigairie idyll, destroying the privacy which was the oxygen it needed to survive.

Tensions were creeping in, where before there had just been peace and tranquillity and magic. There were too many people in the cottage most of the time, with too little room for manoeuvre. Kelvin had allowed himself to slip into a morbid melancholia which seemed to see every new development at Craigairie as a part of an overall conspiracy designed specifically to upset and depress him. He had slipped a notch from being David's best friend and confidant to being a sort of gloomy observer, armed with a pen and a camera and a sullen expression. David had not wanted this to happen, he had tried to include his friend in Craigairie and spent almost more time being attentive to Kelvin than he spent with Christina. Kelvin, in turn, soaked up David's friendship greedily, but gave little or nothing back, apart from a constant, debilitating negativity. It was as if he felt he deserved to be cosseted by David without any obligation to thank him for it.

Admittedly he was in an invidious position, unable to match even the most trifling act of magic, but acutely aware of how it worked. There had been an incident with some photographs which had summed up Kelvin's position in Craigairie and, after the arrival of the Romanies in the Duisk, had been the final straw which set him on his present morosity. He had taken some wonderful pictures of life at Craigairie, but nearly all of them had some surreal, bizarre element which underlined the abnormality of their existence there. His best, for instance, was of David and Christina in front of the standing stone, taken with a zoom lens from the other side of the valley, so they could have had no idea they were being observed. David had obviously said something funny because he was looking on with quiet amusement as Christina threw back her head in laughter, her hair sweeping back in an arc of gold, which caught the sunlight and shone against the green hillside behind. Beside her the fox was sitting on the ground, looking up at her as if mesmerized with adoration at this wild, beautiful creature. Then, the surreal touch which really rounded the shot off. A large, somewhat bedraggled buzzard was perching, precarious but defiant, on David's shoulder, also watching her, with round, yellow eyes, its head cocked to one side.

But by far the most disturbing photograph was of David. When Kelvin took the picture David had been standing on a cairn on top of a hill, his arms outstretched, hands splayed and his head lolling to one side, facing the ground below him. There was something uncomfortably close to the image of the crucifixion about it, even before the picture returned with a terrifying new slant to it. In the photograph David was engulfed in fire, as if he had been doused in petrol and set alight. It was an awful parody of a sacrosanct image which appalled Kelvin. He was even more horrified when he took it to David, expecting him to be at least a bit shocked and instead found him amused and even rather proud of it.

It was the same with everything for Kelvin, and Christina, for one, was beginning to tire of his incessant moaning. Besides, Kelvin was jealous of her, which complicated life enormously.

Meg was not much easier. Her mistrust of David had grown into a paranoia which was only equalled by her vituperative hatred of Craigairie as a whole. She considered the powers at work there to be the forces of evil and had 'got God', after an absence from His flock of a good twenty years. A long-dormant Presbyterianism had come flooding back, as if to compensate for the bunch of 'heathen Fenians' who were practising their forbidden, satanic arts at Craigairie. She did not share Kelvin's belief that this somehow came from the earth, or from a standing stone – although the stone did seem to emanate whatever it was that controlled the valley and their lives, like a petty despot tyrannizing a bunch of ignorant peasants. In Meg's mind it became a symbol of all that was evil and wrong in the valley.

As for the others, Rosie had wandered off home to Baldarnock, remarking that she would come back 'only when the situation chills out', in other words, when Meg and Kelvin had gone. She was shrewd enough to know that it was not worth falling out with David over these two; they were his problem and it would not do anything but complicate matters even more if she allowed herself to be dragged into the feuding. Also, she was capable of pulling herself away from the vice-like grip Craigairie exerted upon all of them, even Meg. When one was there it seemed that everything outside its narrow confines was trivial and unimportant, which made it an enormous wrench of willpower to break clear of it into the normal, real world. Of all of them, Rosie was the only one who had both the character and the inclination to come and go at will.

The last two components in this fragile situation, Christina's brother and his girlfriend, were a law unto themselves. They were by far the youngest, twenty and nineteen, respectively, about to begin their second year at university and as fresh as Kelvin was jaded. They had invited themselves to stay, on their first holiday together as a couple, utterly unaware of the nature of the place into which they were walking. Christina had not wanted them to come, fearing that her little brother and an unknown girl would not be able to cope with Craigairie. She need not have worried. They were both entranced.

They became the battleground over which the moral struggle of their elders was fought. David surprised even Christina by taking Edward under his wing, protecting him from Kelvin's sarcasm. There was something about Ed which attracted David, a simplicity and a lack of hidden complexities which he had never had himself. Ed had all of his sister's innocence and a substantial dose of her charm, without the fey grandeur which made her unique. He was not insecure or unhappy about not being able to emulate the others in their magic; it never occurred to him for a moment that he was capable, so it did not bother him to know that he was not. Just to have David whistle a wild falcon out of the sky and hand it to him was enough to enrapture Ed for days. He admired David to the point of hero-worship, adored Christina and was completely in love with Craigairie. He was touchingly proud of his girlfriend, Emily, when she proved that she too could work magic.

Emily was Christina's favourite. She was a pretty little thing, with wide blue eyes, a blonde bob, a mouth that was never entirely closed and dimples on her cheeks when she smiled. She was the daughter of an Anglican vicar in Wiltshire, which perhaps contributed to the overpowering Englishness of her character and looks. She was sweet-natured, unsophisticated and shy; so much so that she hardly dared speak when she first came to Craigairie and only overcame her awe of them all when Christina and Rosie took her under their wings.

Both Edward and Emily aroused Meg's righteous fury and Kelvin's embittered cynicism. Meg saw them as children who did not know any better and were being wantonly perverted by their elders.

Christina had hoped that if she avoided thinking about the situation it would go away. She did not want to make a scene any more than David did, but something had to be done, sooner or later. The idyll was being poisoned, from the inside as well as the outside. In between steering a course clear of all the potential hazards amongst the group in the cottage and retaining some semblance of privacy in the face of scores of paparazzi and all of the inquisitive people the media had pointed towards Craigairie, there was almost no room left for magic.

And now Christina had the added worry of her father.

As she drove back from Ballantrae she contemplated what had happened to their beautiful dream and a slow-burning anger began to bubble deep inside her. She drove up into the Duisk valley and on through Barrhill, noticing for the first time just how many people there were hanging around.

The final straw for Christina, on her drive home, was the sight of a bunch of hippies walking straight down the track towards the cottage, only a mile from the inner sanctum of the valley. They did not get out of the way when she drove up behind and she had to beep to remove them.

'Sod this,' she said out loud, as she left them in a cloud of red dust. 'Enough's enough.'

When she got back no one was to be found. It was a sultry, leaden afternoon, in tune with her mood. The clouds were bruised and angry, pressing down on the earth, threatening to explode into a thunderstorm at any moment. She walked out on to the lawn and stood, listening to the sullen silence, occasionally broken by distant, restive growls of thunder, like the noise a dog makes when it is about to attack. The power in the valley was coming to one of its peaks, as if unable to escape upwards into the sky. She could feel it, if she closed her eyes; a low, continuous humming which filled the air, adding to the violent silence which filled the valley.

After a while she sensed David, feeling him with a sensory tentacle, sent out by her mind, as sure as if she was touching him with her fingertips. He was in the woods around the side of the cottage. She went to him and found him sitting on a stump amongst the pine trees, deep in thought. She did not talk to him and he did not immediately acknowledge her presence, so she sat down a couple of yards from him and waited until, a couple of minutes later, he turned and looked at her.

'Have you noticed how all the birds have gone?' he asked. He looked up into the trees above his head and frowned. 'Perhaps we should follow their example,' he murmured. He looked back down at her. 'You probably don't want me to ask how your father was. You look like a volcano's going to erupt inside you.'

'I think one is,' she said. There was a short silence.

'If we leave, it'll soon quieten down,' he remarked distantly. 'No one can have this place but us. It'd tear anyone else apart inside a week.'

'I'm not leaving,' she replied. 'Not for Meg, not for Papa and certainly not because of a bunch of sodding newspapers. This is the only place I've ever felt safe. I'm not giving that up for anything.'

'Not even for the gypsies?' he asked, without looking towards her. 'They scare me, Iz. They scare me more than anything else.' He shook his head and fell silent for a while. He sighed and shook his head again. 'I wish they'd go away.'

'I wish they'd all go away,' she replied. He glanced at her and smiled quickly.

'It has been kind of fraught here lately,' he remarked. There was a note of wry humour in his voice, as if he was not quite as concerned as she was. He glanced upwards again and a sudden, unexpected grin came on to his face.

'Your storm?' he asked.

'Who knows?' she replied. 'There are so many vibes flying around here at the moment it's hard to tell what's ours and what isn't.'

She waited for a while, then stood up and began to wander back to the cottage. He called after her.

'Iz?'

She stopped and turned back to him.

'It's OK. We'll sort it out.'

'How?' she asked.

'We'll think of something.'

He listened to her as she returned to the house, his mind half-tuned to hers. He could feel her rage, could feel it spreading to other people. He could not see what was going on around the front of the cottage, but he knew that she had gathered Meg, Kelvin, Ed and Em together and was infecting them with her anger and frustration. He sat on his tree-stump amongst the pines and listened to the dead silence between growls of thunder and to the distant murmur of voices. He lit a cigarette and smoked it pensively, drawing his thoughts into a bunch, clenching his mind like a fist. When his cigarette was finished he flicked it away, and wandered around the corner of the cottage to the lawn. He found them sitting in a circle around five flickering candles.

'. . . I don't know what we can do,' Christina was saying as he came into earshot, obviously in answer to an inquiry. 'But we have to do something.'

'Who's we?' Meg muttered.

'Couldn't we just deny them access?' Emily asked. She still sounded shy and nervous, frightened of being seen to be stupid amongst the others.

'There's no trespass law in Scotland,' Kelvin said, as if it was something any fool knew. Christina shot him a cold look.

'And we don't own the land anyway,' David said, coming up behind Christina.

They all looked up. He knelt down behind Christina, placing his hands on her shoulders. She twisted around and looked up into his face.

'What I don't understand,' Edward said, 'is why the locals aren't more pissed off with us. You'd've thought with all this going on, they'd blame us for it.'

Christina was still looking at David as her brother spoke and so she saw the faintly quizzical, affectionate smile he gave Ed.

'I don't think the locals are a problem,' he said, with quiet certainty.

'What makes you so sure?' Meg demanded. 'If I was them, I'd be pissed off with you.'

David left a short silence before replying, just enough to convey a silent but clear 'you would, wouldn't you?' to her.

'They respect privacy,' he said. 'And they owe us.'

A long, uneasy silence fell on the group, broken only by the rumbles of thunder, closer now as the storm heaved itself inland. There was a feeling of oppression which lay on them like a warm, heavy blanket, on all of them but David. When Christina searched through the airwaves for his mind, expecting to find convoluted knots of anger and betrayal after his brief confrontation with Meg, she found instead laughter and calmness. She turned to look at him and he flashed her a smile, then stood up, waiting as she got to her feet. He wandered off to the other end of the lawn and climbed on to the wall. She followed him, climbing up beside him. It was utterly dark now, the view stopped a foot from their faces. The very air was sweating, still as death. David yawned.

'What was all that about?' she asked, nodding over her shoulder back towards the group around the candles.

'Nothing,' he said. He put his arm around her shoulders.

'I'm finding it hard to think,' Christina said, after a minute, by way of opening a discussion.

He looked at her and his teeth were white in the darkness as he drew his lips back in a smile.

'What's funny?' she demanded.

He did not reply for a moment, then took his arm away from her shoulder and raised both hands high over his head.

'Can't you feel it?' he asked.

'Feel what?'

'The power,' he said. 'It's like when I was alone, just before you came.'

'After Orkney?' she asked.

He nodded. 'Listen to it,' he said. She could feel his elation, like a bubbling geyser beside her. 'Listen to this place. Feel it. It's incredible.' He let her listen and feel for a couple of minutes, until he was sure she knew what he meant.

'We can do anything here,' he said. 'Anything.' He glanced over his shoulder, back towards the others. 'I don't think even we realize how stunningly powerful we could be, if we wanted. I think maybe only those bloody gypsies know, which is why they're here.' He paused, then went on, 'You get so used to being anchored down to earth, by Meg and Kelv and everything else, that you begin to forget how it is to fly.' He took her around the shoulders again and planted a kiss on her head, pulling her tightly to him.

'It's time to stop fuckin' about,' he said. 'It's time to go to the stone and ask it for a real favour, not just a neat trick which keeps us amused when we're bored and there's nothing on telly.' He nuzzled into her neck, much as Shuduch the fox did to her when he wanted something from her.

From the other side of the lawn their conversation was just a murmur, lost in the thick silence. They need not have left the sitting group; it was a matter of politeness rather than anything else which stopped them from conducting all of their private conversations mind to mind, without recourse to such clumsy raw materials of communication as words.

'What d'you think they're talking about?' Emily asked after a while.

Kelvin shook his head, Meg shrugged, and Edward said, 'Who knows?'

'Not me, for one,' Meg said. 'And I don't want to, either.'

'They're fired up by all this,' Kelvin remarked. 'Least, Christina is.'

'I think David is too,' Edward said. 'He's just a quieter thinker than Iz.'

Kelvin looked up, across the candles at Christina's brother. He was always caught out when Ed came out with one of his unthinkingly astute remarks and he always remembered what David had said, soon after Ed and Em had first arrived, when Kelvin had complained about them both being simple-minded.

'Never underestimate simplicity.'

Kelvin was beginning to hate how right David always was. This time, however, he was distracted before his anger could crank itself into gear.

As he looked up at Edward the sky to the south was torn by a flawless, jagged branch of lightning. For a moment it poked its skeleton fingers down on to Eldrig Fell and caressed the hilltop and the landscape flashed into stark, crystal clear silhouette. Kelvin saw David and Christina jerk upright before the brilliant light snapped off and darkness leapt in again.

Meg began snatching things off the ground around her, already planning for the inevitable rush back to the house when they were caught in a sudden downpour.

Christina loomed up behind Edward and Emily. Christina squatted down and spoke, while David remained silent, standing over her, the shadows of his face accentuated by the light of the candle almost below it.

'Listen,' Christina said. 'Davie and I're going to do something we're not very sure about. I have a feeling it might be a little dangerous and mebbe a bit weird too.' She paused and bit her lip. Kelvin found himself thinking, irrelevantly, that he had not noticed how much Scottish had slipped into her previously pure accent.

'The thing is,' she said, 'we both think it might be a good idea if you lot aren't around when we're doing it.'

Their reactions followed a predictable pattern: Kelvin objected, Meg shook her head, Edward looked thoughtful and Emily looked attentive but lost.

Then a lot of questions were asked at once, of which Christina chose to ignore all but one, the most immediately important.

'Why's it dangerous, Iz?' her brother asked.

'I don't know it will be. It's just . . .'

'It's just it might be and we don't really want anyone unnecessarily risking themselves,' David said. 'It's no big deal,' he added.

'If it's no big deal, why all the precautions?' Meg asked.

Sudden resolve flooded into Christina. 'Listen, there really isn't time to argue about this. If we are going to do it at all, it has to be soon. If it works, we'll tell you about it in the morning.'

They were halfway down to the river when they heard the muffled thudding of someone running up behind them. They stopped and turned as Kelvin ground to a halt, panting.

'I thought you'd be needing a hand.' It was a question, although it was said as a statement.

David sagged slightly. Christina thought for a moment, then shrugged.

'Fair enough,' she said. She took David's hand and turned away from Kelvin. 'Just don't say you weren't warned.'

Kelvin was taken aback by this. He had expected a fight and was somewhat deflated by their reaction. He wavered for fully half a minute before bounding off down the hill after them.

They swam first, not for the fun of it but silently, sedately, purely to refresh themselves. Kelvin began to get his first pangs of regret at that point. There was no wild, anarchic fun in either of them; on the contrary, they were grimly serious.

They left their clothes by the river and walked up the hill on the far side of the valley, towards the stone. Kelvin lagged a few yards behind, conscious of his nakedness and conscious of the acute empathy between Christina and David. On the way up he counted the seconds between three different shards of lightning and the thunder which followed them. It went from three miles to somewhat less than one.

By the time they reached the stone David and Christina were in a sort of trance, hand in hand, treading slowly but purposefully through the heather. Kelvin, however, was in the grips of an irrational but growing terror, a feeling of appalling menace. He did not follow them to the stone, but stopped on the lip of the hollow in which it stood and sat down to watch.

They walked around it a couple of times, stroking its surface in a way which was both tender and erotic; slowly, with wondering, sensitive hands. After a while David sank to his knees and allowed his face to rest against the stone, as if he were kissing it. Christina did another revolution and then slowed to a halt on the opposite side to David. Stretching out her arms and opening her knees she sank against the cold stone in a full bodily embrace. She sank slowly down, then pushed herself up again, then down, then up . . .

At first Kelvin refused to believe that his instincts about what he was looking at were right. This doubt, however, was short-lived. She flashed in and out of sight to the almost strobe-like effect of the ever-increasing flashes of lightning and the violent, ripping crashes of thunder, her ecstasy unmistakable as it quickened.

A fork of lightning searched its way to the hillside only a hundred or so yards away from the stone. Kelvin lay down on his belly, suddenly convinced that he would be struck if he offered himself as a target, even if only a sitting one.

As Kelvin wriggled himself into something approximating to a comfortable position, David stood up, hugging the stone. His hands brushed across Christina's, found them again and locked on to them. Her writhings became slightly less pronounced, but no less indecent. It was as if he had entered her, despite the stone which separated them; while he began to heave back and forwards she gripped on to the stone so hard that her feet left the ground and she clung, writhing, like some obscenely erotic spider.

The next bolt of lighting was simultaneous to the crash of thunder, flickering across the ground not more than thirty yards along the hillside. Their movements became more frenzied, two shadowy figures moving with fierce rhythm in the inky darkness. Despite the continuing growling of the last thunderclap Kelvin could hear their moans of ecstasy; David low, rising towards a deep-throated shout, Christina high, piercing.

The next finger of lightning found the top edge of the hollow. Kelvin hardly had time to be terrified before a second one crackled out of the sky directly above them and, to a deafening crash, zig-zagged straight down on to the point of the stone. It lasted for perhaps five seconds, but Kelvin lay, transfixed with horror, for an eternity, watching the mind-numbing scene below him.

As the lightning struck the stone David and Christina, still locked in an embrace around it, stiffened momentarily and then began to shudder horribly. The scene was so terrible, so unreal and yet so clear, that Kelvin did not notice that the stone was shuddering too, as was the ground it stood upon.

Then the lightning stopped and Kelvin briefly glimpsed them both stagger backwards, away from the stone, before darkness leapt in again. Thinking his friends to be dead he leapt up and ran down into the hollow. It was like diving into a large bowl of electrical force. His skin crawled, his hair stood on end; in fact every part of him but his conscience and his body were already halfway back to the cottage.

He reached the bottom and found David sitting on the ground, breathing in long, ragged gasps. Kelvin was so amazed to find him alive at all that he just stood and gaped down at him. David looked up, past him and smiled.

'Did the earth move for you too, my love?' he asked. With an animal growl Christina dived past Kelvin and flung herself down on to David.

As Kelvin reached the river the sky finally gave way under the immense weight of water and, with sudden, startling ferocity, rain began to lash down.

Kelvin did not look back. He hared down the hill with baying hounds of terror on his heels, falling headlong as he reached level ground. The earth beneath him was shuddering, a dull rumbling coming up through the ground. Kelvin stood up and ran through the reeds to the river. He attempted to hop across the stones at the foot of the pool they usually swam in, but was shaken off by a violent tremor in the ground. He floundered desperately through the water and emerged on the far bank, covered with malodorous, slimy mud. Without stopping to retrieve his clothes he took off up the far hill, halting only once to vomit before sprinting to the garden wall, vaulting it and stumbling across the lawn to the front door of the cottage. Only then did he look back.

Across the valley lightning caressed the hillside around the stone with forks of white fire. Kelvin could not see David and Christina, but the stone flashed in and out of view, a small, bent phallus pointing upwards at the epicentre of the storm.

Kelvin succumbed to another cruel spasm and vomit spurted from his mouth in a jet. He then staggered inside the house and locked the door behind him.

The storm sat over Craigairie Fell all through the night. It kindled hungry flames in the forest a couple of miles behind the house, sent the first big spate in months roaring down the river and kept the four people in the cottage huddled together in one room, cowering from the shattering barrage of noise and light. It was as if they were being besieged by a maelstrom of some immense, primitive force. They locked the doors, bolted down the windows, shut the curtains and even attempted to block the chimneys. Even so Delilah returned, splintering the kitchen door like a bull through a makeshift gate and colonizing the kitchen with a gusto unequalled in any of her previous visits. They pushed a chest of drawers against the door through to the hall and then added chairs, two tables and a sofa, when the initial barricade seemed inadequate.

It was a long night for them.

For David and Christina the night was both short-lived and endless. For a long, long time they danced around the stone in slow, weaving circles, intricate and graceful. Neither remembered much about that dance, although it went on for over two hours without so much as a pause; in fact neither of them remembered much about their actions throughout that night. All they both recalled about their dance was that there seemed to have been considerably more than just two people involved in it.

They remembered that their senses had been at such an acute pitch that everything, every step, every movement, everything they touched, or saw, or smelled, had a quality of such staggering sensual pleasure that they could not have stopped their dance prematurely, even if they had wanted to.

The stone sang to them throughout. When interrogated they could not explain what they meant by this and their descriptions of the 'song' were both hazy and wildly different. David described it as like having your favourite tune played inside you. Christina said it was something like listening to love.

The dance came to a long conclusion, reaching a climax some time around two o'clock in the morning. Then, having made love again, they wandered out over the hill and began a long, slow walk which took them about three miles across the moor, out to the east, then in a wide circle, centred on the stone. The next day David traced it on the large wall map in the upstairs loo. Beginning from a small river called Dargoal Burn their path went north-west, around the far side of Benbrake Hill, turned south-west, down past Glenkitten Fell, close to the Barrhill–Stranraer railway line. From there it curved eastwards, over Dirniemow Fell, over Artfield Fell and, finally, it turned back north-eastwards over Eldrig Fell and back to Dargoal Burn. In the middle of the night, stark naked, in bare feet, they had walked seventeen miles through bogs, marshes, rivers, hills and forests, ending up on the exact spot where they had begun. As they walked they had brushed their hands over any prominent objects; rocks, trees, river banks, hillocks and so on. Every now and again they stopped and urinated, or defecated, or even rubbed themselves in the ground as Christina had done with the stone; leaving their scents like wild animals, marking out their sovereign territory.

The storm had long gone when they finished and returned to the stone. Light was beginning to stain the sky to the east with yellow and the grey dawn yawned across the clear sky. A low mist lay in the valley between the stone and the cottage, like a shallow reservoir of cloud caught in the low-lying land during the night and left there when the storm had moved on.

There was a freshness in the air; a sweet cleanliness which made every breath taste of wild flowers and pine resin and earth.

Christina reeked of gardenias.

They thanked the standing stone for its help, caressing it and murmuring to it, as one might do with a workhorse after a long day's hauling.

The first crow of the new day cawed raucously as it flew across the lightening sky. From across the valley, somewhere close to the cottage, a blackbird broke into song, its low, richly intricate warbling carrying far on the still, cool dawn air.

They swam, washing the excesses of the night into the cold peat-darkened water. Unlike their swim the night before there was a languid joy in what they were doing. They played, more like otters than humans, diving deep down into the rain-filled pools, white flashes in the murk, hiding and chasing among the rushes and rocks. They gave up when they saw Shuduch trotting down the hill from the cottage, his head up, an arrogant assurance in his slightly tip-toed steps. When he saw Christina emerging from the reeds he quickened to meet her, finally breaking into a run when she knelt down on the ground, opening her arms wide in greeting. The fox reached her and leapt up, placing his front feet on her shoulders and nuzzling his face into her neck.

'You smell of blood,' she murmured, smiling. She took his forelegs in her hands and lifted them so she could look into his brown eyes.

'What've *you* been up to, you foul animal?' she said. He wriggled out of her grasp and ran over to David, who had located his rain-soaked jeans and was trying to coax some life into a cigarette which had survived the worst of the dampness which permeated the packet. He grinned as the fox ran over to him.

'He's been hunting,' Christina called over to him.

David rolled Shuduch on to his back as he reached him, tickling the soft hairs on his chest. The fox stretched out his legs in pleasure.

David pulled on his drenched jeans and then laced up the leather thong he wore on his wrist. Putting the thumb and forefinger of the same hand in his mouth he blew a piercing whistle and then waited, listening. After about a minute he did it again. He turned a slow circle, looking into the air. Christina came up beside him.

137

'No peregrines, yet,' he said. She looked up into the pale blue sky, biting her upper lip pensively.

'They'll come,' she said. 'When they realize the net's down they'll come back.'

David whistled a couple more times as they walked back up the hill to the cottage. Shortly after the second there was a whoosh-whoosh-whoosh of violently displaced air and a full-grown male peregrine falcon flashed down out of the sky, braking hard with its long wings. David raised his arm at the last moment, but the falcon could not land and pulled out of its dive with a shrill shriek. It banked sharply and returned, hitting the thong on the second attempt. It looked at David with shrewd, calculating eyes and then changed its footing to look at Christina.

'Put those talons on me and I'll eat you for breakfast,' she said. David laughed quietly and stroked the bird's neck with the tips of his fingers.

'Beautiful bird,' he murmured. 'And you know it.' He flicked his wrist up and launched the bird back into the air. It climbed into the sky and, with another shriek, banked into a long, gliding dive down the valley.

The others were still barricaded inside the house and, despite the terrors of the night, were all asleep. Christina tried the front door, swore under her breath and then trotted around the back, to the kitchen door. She returned, looking amused but faintly irritated.

'Delilah's been on the rampage in the kitchen,' she said. 'And they appear to've piled furniture against the inside door.'

'D'you think they're OK?' David said.

Christina appeared to listen for a few seconds. She nodded.

'Yes,' she said. 'If you listen you can hear them.' He went silent for about half a minute before nodding.

'Asleep,' he said.

'Seems a shame to wake them,' she replied. She put her finger to the lock of the door and closed her eyes. There was a faint click. She turned the handle and pushed the door open.

'I feel I could do just about anything,' she said. 'Don't you?' She headed for the staircase, still talking in a low voice. 'I feel so *good*,' she said. 'I feel I could fly, if I wanted.'

'There's a spell for that. I saw it in some weird book I read back in the spring. It's quite simple.' He stopped and laughed quickly. 'I mean, I don't think it'd be too much of a problem.'

They were sitting in the garden, having changed into fresh clothes, discussing the night's work, when Edward came out, followed by Emily. Both of them stopped dead in the doorway and stared at David and Christina with wide eyes.

'You . . .' Edward said. 'You're glowing.'

Christina looked at her arms and frowned.

Edward went across to them, leaving Emily standing on the doorstep. He reached down and touched his sister's arm.

'What did you do last night?' he asked quietly. 'You feel like satin.'

'Didn't Kelvin tell you?' she asked.

He smiled slowly. 'Kelvin wasn't terribly coherent when he came back last night.' He looked around, at the blue sky and the morning sun. Larks were twittering in the breeze which sighed across the moor. The low, rising whistle of a curlew echoed across the valley and was answered from behind the cottage. Edward stretched out his arms and turned to Emily.

'What a fantastic morning,' he said. 'It's so great I think I'd like to fuck.' He said it so naturally that Emily just smiled back at him and nodded. They disappeared into the house, hand in hand.

Christina and David looked at each other, grinning.

'OK,' Christina said. 'Tell me how to fly.'

4

AUTUMN

Summer waned slowly in the tiny sovereign realm of Craigairie. After the night when they marked out their 'exclusion zone', setting a wide perimeter around their domain through which only the chosen few could pass, the valley sank back into a watchful peace, quieter than it had been since before June.

Meg returned to Orkney two days after that wild night, without addressing another word to David. She had been there for two months against her will; partly to look after Kelvin and partly because she could not bring herself to leave. It was only when she was back in St Mary's, home in Orkney, that she began to understand the terrifying, staggering magnetism of Craigairie. It was like an addiction, it was an addiction.

Kelvin did not leave with her. Even after that night when he witnessed just how wild the magic could be, up by the stone, he still could not drag himself away. He was like a rabbit caught in car headlights, terrified by Craigairie but even more terrified of leaving. He knew as well as any of them what the implications of Craigairie were; he had understood as well what the migration of Romanies to Barrhill was about. Long before he plucked up the courage to actually visit the Atchin-tan he knew why they were there, although the knowledge was far too appalling to contemplate.

The gypsies were there because this phenomenon was theirs. They expected no favours from Craigairie, no preferential treatment, they just wanted it to be known that they were aware of David and Christina and that if these two belonged to anybody, they belonged to the Romanies. As for David and Christina's obvious reluctance to go to the Atchin-tan, it seemed at first to Kelvin that this was a welcome admission of fallibility on their part, as if their unwillingness was proof that they could not stand up to close scrutiny from the only people who could really tell if they were what they seemed to be. But when he suggested this to an old kyle-yak, a wise woman who had found her way to Barrhill all the way from Andalusia, she replied with a smile and a shake of her head. And when he demanded that she explain why she was so nonchalant she gave him a typical Romany answer.

'A great oak does not grow overnight,' she said.

'What does that *mean*?' Kelvin asked irritably, tired of being fobbed off with cryptic aphorisms by the gypsies.

'It means we must be patient and wait until your friends tire of playing. They will come to us when they are ready.'

They were waiting for a Nymatil, perhaps even for the twin Nymatili; the chosen ones, the Blessed. They did not admit it to him, but he knew Romanies well enough to figure it out for himself. They were waiting for an ancient, extinct messianic myth to come alive and the only people in the vicinity who remotely fitted the bill were David and Christina. Kelvin was stubborn and obstinate enough to think that the Romanies had gone collectively soft in the head, but whether he liked it or not the word had been hung on the gypsy grapevine and they, at least, took it seriously.

He hung on at Craigairie for another fortnight after Meg left and it was Rosie, in the end, who talked him into leaving.

'Pull back from this,' she had said to him. 'Get away from here and look at it from a long, long way off. You can't begin to understand how incredibly dangerous this place is, until you get clear of it.'

'What d'you mean by dangerous?' he had asked.

Rosie had thought for a moment. 'I mean it's like taking coke and ecstasy at once, times about a thousand. It accentuates every emotion to infinity. If you're in love, like Izzy and Davie, you're in heaven. If you're depressed or pissed off, you're in hell.'

So he left.

Edward and Emily went back to university soon afterwards, carrying with them a love affair consummated on the dubious altar of Craigairie. To them the summer had been a wild, fun holiday and the magic they had seen, or in Emily's case learned, was no more or less extraordinary than if they had instead spent two months experimenting with hard drugs, just marginally less destructive.

Christina called them 'our little Pagans' and found the idea of them entertaining student dinner parties with their newfound knowledge irresistibly funny. David, ever the quiet voice of down-to-earth practicality, murmured, 'There goes our secrecy' as they drove away up the track.

By then, however, Craigairie had done more than enough to deserve its notoriety. Their solution to the problem of their privacy was two-pronged. Firstly they set down the boundary around Craigairie which became known as the 'Carrick triangle'. Anyone who strayed too close to Craigairie found that they soon became hopelessly lost, and a torpid lethargy reduced their limbs to jelly and their minds to glue. Compasses went berserk, watches stopped, everything looked the same. Nobody was immune, except those who went in by invitation.

The second trick David and Christina let loose was as extraordinary and as effective as the first. In the middle of September a sudden and virulent illness swept through the Duisk and Luce valleys. Its symptoms were manifold and uniformly unpleasant; acute nausea, diarrhoea, vicious stomach cramps, migrainous headaches, depression, nightmares. If it had not been such a cruel ailment to suffer, the sheer breadth of its symptoms would have been almost funny. Doctors were baffled by it, not only because no cause or cure could be found for it, but also because it had two inexplicable attributes. It did not affect anybody who lived in the area, including the gypsies, and secondly its effects wore off outside a radius of about twenty-five miles of Barrhill. In effect it cleared every non-resident out of the area in under two weeks.

As far as the locals were concerned explanations were unnecessary. The general opinion was that Craigairie should have done it at least two months earlier. It did not matter how or why these things happened nearly so much as it mattered to know who was behind it. When one came to accept that David and Christina were responsible the really important question became, what can be done to avoid antagonizing them. To which the simple answer was, let them be.

Besides, the Rutherfords at Kilreuchal were living proof that amicable relations with the witches of Craigairie were not to be sniffed at. In return for the friendship Ellen and Jim had shown them, the inhabitants of Craigairie had blessed Kilreuchal farm with a period of profit and plenty which was the envy of the neigbourhood and had their bank manager bug-eyed with astonishment. And Ellen's garden was so beautiful that people came from miles around to admire it.

At the beginning of the summer David and Christina had been the subjects of a lot of somewhat nervous speculation. Then, when the mayhem of the high summer had started, with the media and the curious and the loonies all streaming in to Barrhill, a certain amount of anger and resentment had crept in. Why, after all, should everyone else suffer for the weird happenings up on Purgatory? The spectacular lambing was forgotten, along with the bumper harvest and everything else. The locals sank quickly into the archetypal Scottish habit of fleecing the tourists with a great deal of muttering and scowling.

Then, with the sudden appearance of the Carrick triangle and the illness known as the curse of Craigairie, their attitude changed again. David and Christina were suddenly back in favour and could show their faces in public without being shunned by the locals. The only sour-grapes still in evidence came from the young Presbyterian minister of Barrhill: there was nothing he wanted less than to see his entire flock defect to ways far older than those he preached; and disappear out on to the moors to worship at witching stones, rather than come to his kirk. Every Sunday he stood up on his pulpit and railed against heathenism, even going so far as to name Christina and David as the enemies of God. And every Sunday he looked out on fewer and fewer people in his congregation. The young went first, followed by the farmers and anyone else who profited directly from Craigairie. There were quite a few people around who had Romany blood in their veins, and many others who did not but found witches and magic easier to believe than an angry God who asked a great deal and gave very little in return.

He could not compete with Craigairie. He could invoke the wrath of his God, but Craigairie offered good harvests and clement weather. Hell seemed a long way away when Purgatory was just down the road and was giving far more than his God was wont to give, despite His infinite love.

On a clear night one could stand in the main street of Barrhill and see half a dozen different bonfires up on the moors, just out of reach of civilization, marking all the witching stones in the immediate vicinity, to which people went to offer thanks or to ask for more.

David and Christina were careful not to associate themselves directly with all of this Paganism. They participated in nothing, denied nothing when accused, explained nothing if asked, spoke to no one about what they did. In refusing to submit themselves to public scrutiny throughout the summer and in going to extreme lengths to protect their privacy, they had succeeded in exacerbating their near-mythical status.

As far as they were concerned, back in their impenetrable bolthole, the paradise had been recovered, if only for a short while, and the opinions of those outside the confines of Craigairie were unimportant. Their new peace had been won at a price; somewhere along the line they had lost half of the summer and the year was beginning to grow tired. At first, way back in May, each day had been as wonderful as the last and it had seemed that it would never end. The summer had stretched away in front of them, not so much a matter of days, weeks, even months as much as an endless, timeless bliss.

Then the others had come, slowly pulling them back down to earth; not just Meg and Kelvin, but all of them, Edward, Emily and Rosie as well. Self-consciousness had infiltrated their hitherto unthinking existence and had removed some of the joy which had dominated that first couple of months. As David had remarked, the evening before they drew the mantle of the exclusion zone around Craigairie, they had been so busy anchoring themselves to a norm everyone could accept that they had forgotten how it felt to fly, to be free of responsibilities and worries.

They regained some of that freedom that night and in the weeks that followed, but the timelessness had gone, never to return. Now, when they looked out from Craigairie it was as if they had woken from a long sleep and they found that the valley had changed. The curlews had stopped calling months ago; and the snipe did not drum in the dusk; and the grass was no longer so green and fresh, but was dry and brittle, burned by the ceaseless heat. When the sun set in the evenings it no longer sank through the horizon almost unnoticed, the evening continuing long after it had gone, as if unwilling to give up on so much beauty and life. It went down now in a blaze of red and orange and night descended behind it, chilly and black. The stars were clearer now, the Milky Way splashed across the sky like a thin cloud, each pinprick of light exact and precise through the clear, cold atmosphere. The swallows and martins were congregating along the telephone lines which ran from the house across to the barn, awaiting the moment when the temperature would dip below the point when it was fun to be in the north any longer.

There was no new life, begging to be noticed and admired in each tiny detail, but instead the first inkling of the urgency of autumn, as nature looked up from the months of ease and saw for the first time the lean months ahead. It was the same for David and Christina. They were alone again – Rosie having made one of her tactful exits – free to behave exactly as they pleased without worrying who they might be offending. They could go to the pub in Barrhill again, or to an isolated and less crowded hotel bar on the road down to the coast, where it forked to Girvan and Ballantrae. They could use the magic without restraint and without Meg giving them disapproving looks. They could make love in the sitting room, the kitchen, down by the river, up by the stone.

It was fun, for a while, but it was on a finite timescale. Each day was a handful of minutes shorter, a step further from summer and closer to winter. There had been times in the summer when each day had been so much like the last and the next that time seemed to have ground to a halt. It was different now. There was a new transience and urgency in the air, as if nature was making the point that all good things have to come to an end and now was the moment to start contemplating the hard times ahead.

For David and Christina this new awareness of time spurred them into experimenting with the magic again. They tired of the simple tricks and began to ask things of Craigairie they would not have dared even contemplate earlier in the summer. They were far stronger now than they had been then; better able to control the power, more discerning and imaginative in its use and with fewer qualms about the moral and theological implications behind it. If they had learned anything from the experience of weaving the spells which had laid the exclusion zone around Craigairie and had cleared the Duisk of all strangers, it was that they had not yet asked anything more complicated of their stone than child's play. They had been constrained by the belief that there were some things which were beyond them; that although there were no limitations to the power, there were definite limitations on the extent to which they could use it.

As the autumn drew in, they laid these constraints aside and started to test the limits of their strength, not for the fun of it, but to find exactly where, if at all, their limitations lay. They taught themselves to shape-shift, to assume the forms of animals or birds. To their surprise this was rather easier than it seemed when they first set their minds to it. It took a week of contemplation and meditation, purging themselves of all extraneous distractions, until they could think themselves out of their own forms and into others; most often ravens, foxes or wolves. Thereafter it could be achieved at will, but had some side-effects which made them wary of using it unless they needed to. It was, for instance, an enormous drain on their strength and stamina; hard to achieve, harder to maintain and harder still to revert back into their human forms. The longer one remained in animal or bird form the more one became that animal or bird and, proportionally, the less one wished to revert.

Flying was fun, though. Or swimming in the river as otters, diving and playing in the deep pools, smooth, sleek bodies slicing through the dark water with glorious ease. Eagles were seen soaring over Glenluce, where no eagles had been seen for centuries. And it was noticed how the inhabitants of Craigairie could get in and out without being seen, moving around the countryside with astonishing speed. And the Barrhill minister, driving back across the moors from New Luce late one night – a spooky road at the best of times – clearly saw two wolves cross the road in front of him, loping through the arc of his headlights.

They continued to hold the weather at bay, long after it had broken elsewhere, holding on to the last vestiges of summer until it clung to the valley like tattered clothing, playing Canute with the winter. Even on the thirtieth of October, Christina's twenty-sixth birthday, it was still clement enough to allow them out on one last barefoot ramble across the moors.

There had been a cold, blustery west wind that morning, the tail-end of a clumsy gale which had been blundering around the cottage during the night. They stayed in bed until midday, although David had been awake since dawn and had woken Christina a while later, submerging beneath the covers and kissing his way down her body until she could no longer sleep. They knew the wind would die around lunchtime and they were in no hurry to be up and about. When the wind duly dropped, on cue, leaving the day momentarily startled by its own clemency, they went out on to the hills and pretended that it was still May.

They walked in a wide semi-circle, from the cottage down the valley, into the steep part which was crowded with old oaks, ashes and beeches, interspersed with smaller rowans, silver birches and yews; the last remnants of the old forests which had once filled the coastal lowlands and now survived only here, out of sight and out of reach in the hidden valleys amongst the moors. The trees had turned copper and bronze, their ceaseless whispering mingling with the murmuring, gurgling river.

They waded the river, climbed out of the valley, back on to the moors and into the forestry and finally back round to the standing stone.

By the time they reached it the day was starting to fade, the sun sinking through a band of magenta-tinged clouds, towards the hills to the west.

They sat down on the altar rock behind the stone, which David had unearthed after one of his more vivid dreams back in the spring. It was surrounded with small offerings; the feet of rabbits and hares killed by David's birds, a roe-deer antler with locks of golden and black hair tied around it, some eagle-feathers Christina had left there, a few small posies of wild flowers. The cup-marks at either end of the slab of rock were stained reddish brown with dried blood, Christina's at one end, David's at the other.

They sat for a long time in silence, listening to the sounds of the evening. A long-eared owl was hooting down the valley, arousing The Don, the barn owl over at Craigairie, to one of his more spirited fits of territorial shrieking. The rich, 'back-back' burr of roosting grouse carried far across the quiet hills.

As the sun began to dissect the horizon, Christina sighed and turned to David. He was gazing at her and his eyes smiled faintly as she looked into them. She had meant to say something, but she allowed herself instead to be transfixed by those electric green eyes, which no one but herself could meet for long without shrinking away guiltily. They seemed to look into your soul, which was an odd and not entirely pleasant feeling, for anyone but Christina. Only she was not afraid of them, because only she had nothing to hide from them.

His smile flickered around the corners of his mouth and he drew in his penetrating gaze, looking away from her for a second before returning to her face, his smile broadening. She was so beautiful he could have stared into her face, grinning foolishly, for an eternity.

'I love you,' he said, reaching over and stroking her hair. He began to recite dreamily:

'Is thy hair not a flag of golden thread, and thy skin not like to the finest Cathay silk, and thy beauty not like a sickle moon in a velvet-black sky, or the morning star glittering above the dawn. Thou art the last blizzard of winter, the first crocus of spring. Thou art a distant beacon fire in the night.'

'What's that?' she asked, returning his smile.

'Something I read a long time ago, but never had the opportunity to say, until I met you.'

She held his gaze and stretched her hand over to him, touching his cheek with her forefinger and tracing a little heart.

'You know, Davie, you never cease to surprise me,' she murmured. 'I always feel so honoured that you fell in love with me.'

'Honoured?' he said. 'Surely not.'

She moved her finger to his lips and let it rest there, keeping him quiet.

'I never thought when I fell in love with you that I'd get as much back as I was willing to give. You didn't strike me as the sort to give yourself lock, stock and barrel.'

He began to pull away to say something but she shushed him. He shook his head and evaded her finger.

'I have something else to give you,' he said. He smiled almost shyly. 'A birthday present.' He fumbled in his pocket and produced a matchbox.

'With all my love.'

'All?' she asked, smiling to herself. She slid the box open and gazed at the small object inside for fully two minutes before removing it and holding it up to the last rays of the sun, turning it over slowly. It was a gold ring, narrow at the back, widening around the front to house a perfect ruby supported by the legs of two tiny lions which rose out of the band.

It felt very heavy and cold, the gold so soft that only minimal pressure could bend it out of shape. It was very ancient.

She let the sun glint through the ruby for a few moments before the last ray flashed across the miles from the horizon, as if directed solely on the blood-red stone, then suddenly flicked off. Christina looked down at David and shook her head with a sigh.

'It's a long time since Flavia gave this to Julianus with *her* love,' she said. 'Where d'you find it?'

'A cairn over by Eldrig Fell,' he replied.

She looked at it for a second more, then handed it back to him, stretching out the fingers of her right hand for him to slip it on to whichever one he chose.

The thrill of its cold weight sent goosepimples up her forearm. She closed her eyes and after a few seconds winced, drawing a sharp breath over her teeth.

'Poor Flavia,' she said. 'She waited for him, but he never came back.'

'Poor Julianus,' David replied.

She gazed at him, shaking her head and smiling.

'Doesn't this place ever scare you?' she asked.

He drew his eyebrows together in a quizzical frown.

'Not really, no.'

'Don't you ever feel we're maybe out of our depth?'

'Often,' he replied. 'But then I remember what Craigairie's given me and I think: "What the hell." As far as I know I'm only alive once, so I'll take whatever's on offer and damn the consequences . . . You?'

She thought, biting her lower lip, shrugged and yawned.

'Will you marry me?' she said through the tail-end of her yawn.

'How?' he asked.

'How? What kind of a question's that?'

'How do witches marry?' he explained. 'Churches are out and registry offices are kind of unromantic.'

'Ah,' she said. 'I do see . . . Maybe we just plight our troth on the stone.'

'I'm game,' he said.

They went to the stone and solemnly plighted their troth, palms on the cold granite, fingers interlocked.

For Christina's father, Sir James, his first encounter with the infamous David Armstrong was as much of a revelation as it was long overdue. For a start, he had not expected his wife to succeed in her mission to Craigairie the previous afternoon. She had gone to invite Christina and 'that man' to a birthday dinner at Castle Graham, on the face of it an olive branch after months of mutual silence, but she had gone there in a mood not tailor-made to inspire rapprochement – half-way between antagonistic curiosity and unforgiving disapproval. Even when she returned with the news that they had accepted, Sir James still thought it unlikely that David Armstrong would turn up. The list of guests who had been invited to celebrate Christina's birthday read like a long and unsubtle hint to her about the power of local gossip, a lion's den specifically designed to put the couple in their place. It would have been just like Christina to realize this and outmanoeuvre her mother by making sure that David Armstrong stayed well clear.

As it turned out, they proved to be quite capable of outmanoeuvring Lady Jane without recourse to anything so clumsy as failing to appear.

Before they arrived all the talk had been about this mysterious man. What kind of a person was he? What hold did he have over Christina? Would he live up to the rumours? What did warlocks look like? The underlying assumption was that he was behind whatever it was that happened at Craigairie and Christina, dear, foolish Tina, was back to her old ways again: caught somewhere between hopeless naïvity and wild hedonism; in love with another maniac. Only this time the maniac in question was quite possibly rather more dangerous than any who had come before.

But David Armstrong had confounded them all, even Sir James. He was so unlike any of Christina's previous lovers, including and especially Erlend MacRuarie, that comparison was not just unwarranted, it was all but impossible. Erlend had been a sweet-natured golden-child, full of beauty and easy, effervescent, throwaway charm. David was cleverer, harder, sharper and much quieter, with a restrained intensity to him which was more than a little disconcerting. If it had been Erlend up at Craigairie with Christina, Sir James would have been inclined to dismiss the rumours as a storm in a teacup. His effect on Christina had always been to bring out her hoydenish, experimental, out-of-control side, more given to mischief than to anything more overtly dangerous. They had been like children together: extroverted, theatrical, performing their lives to a rapt audience.

But David Armstrong was no child and Christina was not behaving like a tomboy for him. On the contrary, in fact. She had turned up to the dinner party with her femininity underlined in red ink, exuding a self-confidence which did not need the bolster of someone else's glamour to support it. David, it seemed, had touched upon the inherent strength in her character, the glittering diamond at her very core. The old naïvity had gone, leaving a creature of fire and air, hypnotic and ethereal.

Sir James had not known what to expect from Christina when his wife returned from Craigairie the previous evening; defensiveness, perhaps, was most likely. Christina had always had a cunning way of issuing silent but effective reproval, when she was backed into a corner, reflecting any anger or over-concern straight back in the form of a rebuke. She could be wary, cussed, difficult, using her feyness like a shield and her inherent mildness as a weapon. It was pointless trying to bully or cajole her, because she absorbed it until her attacker was so annoyed that they either gave up or exploded with frustration.

The way to deal with her was to be as mild as she was, to advise rather than dictate. Her father had made the mistake of trying to lay down the law with her for the first and last time when he returned from America, and had regretted it for two months afterwards. He was not about to make the same mistake again.

But Christina had not been defensive when she turned up for her birthday dinner. She had not been difficult, or cussed, or hoydenish. The transformation in her was astonishing, from a crippled, emotional wreck, trying to avoid facing a suddenly shattered future only eight months earlier, to this elegant, regal woman. They had both walked into Castle Graham and into that drawing room as if they knew that there could be no one in there who would disconcert them half as much as they would surely disconcert everyone there. If David had given her that confidence, then he was worth talking to.

And as for Craigairie, Sir James was beginning to find it just too complicated to be either rational or objective when he thought about it. He knew what he should have been thinking; his wife and her pet priest were vociferous enough on the subject. But he also knew Christina. If she was a witch, if she truly was responsible for all the extraordinary things being attributed to her, then it was in character. It had always been a source of enormous pride and happiness to Sir James that he knew Christina and that she trusted him, because to almost anybody else she was more like a myth than a real person. The world adored her because she lived people's dreams for them. There was nothing mundane about her, nothing ordinary or pallid or prosaic. There was no niche for her in life, just a pedestal or a stage, on which she could play out her existence in all of her ethereal, ephemeral glory, wonderful in her stunning unselfconsciousness.

149

Craigairie was a stage worthy of her and however bizarre, frightening or disturbing he found its implications, Sir James could not be the one who attempted to remove her from it. He had known that before he saw her and seeing her only made it clearer in his mind. It was too easy to say that in his eyes she could do no wrong, as his wife often accused him; she could do wrong and frequently did, but on her own terms and by her own definitions. She alone had to live her mistakes, just as she alone experienced her triumphs. And by the same token it was too easy to climb up behind the pulpit of Christianity and deplore Craigairie for what it implied, because it, like Christina, conformed to an apparently unique set of rules. As David Armstrong had eloquently pointed out during a conversation at dinner, the injunction against witches in Deuteronomy only applied if you happened to believe in the god of the Christians, the Jews or the Moslems.

'When you talk about witches and pagans in the same breath as black magic, devil worship, and all that stuff, you confuse your beliefs with wholly separate ones. If I'm neither a Christian, nor a Jew, nor a Moslem, how could I possibly worship the antithesis of your God?'

He had done that frequently during dinner; disarming inquisitors by meeting them head-on, on their own ground. Of all the people there, only Sir James knew his religion well enough to debate with David on his own level, and Christina's father was about the only person there who was not inclined to do so. For him it did not matter, in the end, if Craigairie was even half of what it was rumoured to be, or double. What was important was that Christina and David Armstrong clearly believed that it was extraordinary; the former on an emotional level, the latter on a cerebral basis. Before he dismissed or condemned Craigairie, Sir James had to know why they believed this. He had to talk to them.

So he followed them up to Craigairie the afternoon after the dinner, giving them fair warning that he was on his way, and talked to his daughter for two and a half hours, alone. David wandered around outside, meanwhile, trying to arrange his thoughts into some sort of order. He knew that Sir James had come to ask them both what was happening there and he knew that he did not have it in him to lie. The time had come to admit the truth about Craigairie and the stone, which they had both been avoiding, one way or another, for months. The time for games was over.

He knew what Christina was likely to say, if asked. He knew that she would not discuss the one worry they both had about what they were becoming. She would evade it, even if pressed, as she had been doing with him for weeks.

But he was too troubled to avoid it any more. It had been nagging at him, dull but incessant, ever since the gypsies had arrived in the Duisk. This was not a wild game they had invented for themselves. The magic, the power to be, effectively, gods inside themselves, capable of realizing the bizarrest whims of their imagination, was little more than an exciting, fun side-effect. It was an object lesson in just how great a gift it is to be a human being, able to tamper with the laws of creation itself. But it was not the be-all and end-all of Craigairie, it was just a by-product.

At first, until his return from Orkney and Christina's arrival, David's fascination had been almost academic. He had been drawn by his need to rationalize the irrational, to put Delilah and Craigairie into a neat box along with every other dilemma he had overcome in his life. But he had been ensnared by his curiosity and his pride and held there, almost against his will, until Christina came along and made real what had hitherto been only theory to him. Then, for months, Craigairie had poured out a shower of gifts upon them both, including each other, and they had been so blinded by the joy of their discoveries that they had hardly noticed what an immense power was needed to make it all possible. It had seemed that it was coming from inside them, whereas they were merely willing ciphers through which it was escaping.

Craigairie was a last remnant of an ancient worship, which was there precisely because the power, the life-force of the living earth, was so strong there, so close to the surface. The stone was stuck into a huge artesian well which had not been tapped properly for hundreds of years and had probably not been so active in two and a half millennia. It was using them to re-activate itself, removing them so far from normality that they were already too far gone to return.

It was not a thing one could shrug off. David had gone through life knowing exactly where he was going and holding himself alone account-able for what he did and how he did it. There had been moments when he had been frustrated, or unsatisfied, but he had never been out of his depth. Not until now. He had asked a question of Craigairie and had been given an answer of such magnitude that he could not avoid it. He could not get up one morning and walk away from it, because it had taken control of his life. This did not frighten him. What frightened him was that there seemed to be no end to Craigairie and he therefore had no idea where he was being taken.

The only thing he knew was that the time was coming when the confines of their exclusion zone would no longer hold them. They would have to find the courage to take what they knew out into the world, or else find a great deal more courage to stay put and be slowly torn apart, driven mad by the power of the place. At this point he and Christina disagreed and she reached her short-circuit point.

She would not think about it. She wanted to stay put, safe from those who would ridicule her, or worse, mob her like a soap star. She did not want to accrue a sort of spurious celebrity status merely because she was a photogenic witch. She was horrified at the thought of becoming a freak, dangled in front of a public which could only see the outward manifestations of her witchdom; the magic and the weird powers, all dressed up in a beautiful, gift-wrapped package. She knew that as long as she could continue to hide herself beyond the gloating eyes of the media and the public, safe behind the invisible wall which protected Craigairie, she could continue to consider herself normal. But the moment she went out into the world outside she was so extraordinary that the world could not help but notice her.

The answer, David knew, was to pluck up their courage, take a deep breath and come out of their closet. If the world was so eager to know about them, which the events of the summer would appear to have proved beyond doubt, then at least it should be on their terms. The Romanies had known they would have to make this decision, sooner or later, which was why they had been hanging around in Barrhill, waiting for them to do it. How they knew was a mystery to David, but they did and he just had to accept it.

He sat on the wall at the bottom of the garden in the dying autumn evening, gazing across the blue dusk in the valley, towards the grey finger of stone on the opposite hillside and knew what he had to do.

He was deep in thought when a shrill screech high up in the air disturbed him, jerking him out of his reverie. He looked up, a smile softening his frown. Raising his right hand over his head he let out a piercing whistle. At first the buzzard, high up in a thermal, spiralling lazily over the valley where the sun still was, pretended not to hear. David watched it intently.

'What to do?' he murmured. *'Qu'est-ce qu'on fait?'* He waved his clenched fist above his head.

'Come on, Doveleski, give me a sign.'

The buzzard glided out of its thermal, turned a couple of slow, banking circles then aligned itself on David. It missed by a good ten feet on the first pass, coming in over the hillside like a World War Two fighter to an aircraft carrier, undercarriage down, balanced on the wind. It aborted the attempt, lifting over the corner of the cottage and settling on one of the Scots pines. It wobbled uneasily for a while on a branch too narrow to hold its weight, then spread its wide wings again and glided down on to David's upraised wrist. Despite its weight he took it with practised ease and brought it down to face height. It clawed around on the talon-battered leather thong, consolidating its footing and blinking at him with round, yellow eyes.

'Hello, buzzard,' he said quietly. 'Are you a sign from heaven or just a fat bird?' It looked at him, its head cocked to one side and then opened its beak and shrieked at him. He laughed through his nose.

'Just a fat bird, huh?'

He transferred it to his shoulder and stroked the thick feathers underneath its neck, staring across the valley in the failing light. The clouds in the velvet-blue sky were tinged with pink across the rippling contours of their bellies. He was so engrossed by the brittle beauty of the frost-sharp evening that he did not hear Christina and Sir James come out of the house on to the lawn behind him. They did not disturb him, stopping halfway between the door and David and watching the day die in reverential silence. It went on for ten minutes, the sunlight streaking across the sky, receding gradually into the west, the colours fading away until nothing was left and twilight suddenly closed in.

David moved, glancing at his watch.

'Come on, come on,' he said quietly. *'Vitesse.'* He turned and saw the two figures behind him, silhouetted against the open front door. He looked at them for a moment, his face in shadow, then climbed down from the wall, carefully transferring the dozing buzzard back on to his wrist.

'You done?' he asked. He sounded a thousand miles away.

'Papa would like a quick word with you,' Christina said.

David looked through her eyes into her mind, just a glance, to see how she had fared with her father. There were thoughts washing around, new thoughts, as yet unprocessed, but there was also a calmness he had not seen for a while. Her father, it seemed, had helped her to massage out some of her knots of worries. She smiled faintly and David nodded once, handed her the buzzard and walked past her, into the cottage. Sir James followed him into the cottage and through to the kitchen. He settled in the chair closest to the fire and watched David as he removed a can of beer from the fridge, cracked it open and downed about half of it.

'I felt I should have a word with you . . .' Sir James began. He waited for a reaction, got none and continued. 'I meant to talk to you both this morning, but the opportunity didn't arise.'

David pulled out a chair on the opposite side of the table, deftly twisted it around and sat down, straddling it with his long legs, leaning his forearms along the back-rest and lowering his chin on to this custom-made cushion. He kept his silence, watching Sir James with an unfathomable expression on his face. Christina's father shifted uncomfortably in front of David's steady, green-eyed gaze.

He had that hawk-like look to him, now, as he sized up Sir James. He took his time, then said, 'You want to know whether my intentions towards your daughter are honourable?' There was a hint of irony in his voice. 'What did she say?'

'She invited me to use my eyes,' Sir James replied. He smiled wryly. 'Not such bad advice. It doesn't take a genius to see you're good for her.'

'It works both ways,' David remarked calmly. He paused momentarily, then said, 'So what's the problem?'

Sir James took a moment to pick his words.

'The problem, as I see it, is that I'm worried for both of you.' He saw the faintest flicker of a frown twitch the muscles around David's eyes and knew that the deliberate choice of words he had used had been recognized. There was a subtle difference between being 'worried for' and 'worried about'.

'In what way?'

'Would you say that what you are doing here is safe?' he asked carefully. David scratched his cheek thoughtfully. He shook his head.

'No, not particularly. It's no more or less safe than the sea, or the wind, or the seasons. It's elemental, natural.'

'Do you think you can control it?'

'I've never tried,' David replied. 'It'd be a bit like staying inside on a sunny day.'

'And when it ceases to be sunny?'

'I'll cross that bridge when I come to it,' he said. 'I guess.'

'And when will that be?'

'Good question,' David replied, after a moment's hesitation. He took a deep breath, letting it out in a long sigh. He shrugged. 'I don't honestly know. I know it's one of the great cries of youth, but I look into the future and I really can't see this ever ending. I mean, everything ends, obviously; even me and Christina might conceivably part company some day – both of us have thought that we'd found our life-long partners before, only to be proved wrong by time, or fate, or a combination of both. But this thing isn't affected by time in human terms. It's as old as the earth and it'll be here long after mankind's gone. And it can't be affected by fate; it is fate.' He paused and shrugged again.

'We're part of it; we're the fleas on its skin. Once you understand what that means you already know something you can't possibly forget. It's like discovering the one religion you've ever come across which gives you answers, not questions.'

'What about Christianity?' Sir James asked, thinking about Father Piers. 'Just out of interest?'

'I could be controversial,' David replied slowly, restraining his initial urge to repeat Sir James's question back at him, with slightly different inflections. 'But I won't. Christianity's a great moral code; a great way of running your life without doing unnecessary damage to everyone around you. If everybody who professes to be a Christian actually behaved like one the world would be a much nicer place. But when it comes to the big, ultimate "whys", like why any God could have been perverse enough to create flies and famines and psychopaths, it resorts to telling you, basically, to mind your own business. "Have faith" it tells you. "If there's no earthly reason for something, then it's all part of the Divine plan and who are you, mere mortal, to question God." But what Izzy and I have found here gives you simple answers, as long as you know how to ask the questions.' He frowned and breathed a quick, dry laugh.

'It's funny; both of us discovered a while back that we can't meet a priest of any denomination without instantly losing our tempers. I've been thinking about it today, thinking maybe this was some weird reaction to "good" because what we're doing is basically "evil".' He paused and shook his head slowly. 'It's just occurred to me why it happens.'

'Why?' Sir James prompted. Against all expectations he was getting what he came for, described with calm lucidity and not a hint of subterfuge.

'Because it's unbelievably aggravating to be patronized by a person who doesn't know as much as you do.'

Sir James laughed.

'Aye, but you're young and in love,' he said. 'It's easy to know all the answers when you have those on your side.'

David shook his head.

'When I found this place it was the last thing on earth I was looking for. It helped when Izzy came along, but it was here before me.' He yawned.

Sir James stood up and wandered to an unsteady column of paper about four feet high, in the corner of the room. A typewriter was perched on top with a piece of paper still in it. Sir James stooped down and read out loud.

'It was pulled by a reluctant and lugubrious carthorse called Pegasus, with the gloomiest expression in the world . . .'

He straightened and turned back to David.

'You write?'

David shook his head. 'That'll have been Kelvin or Meg. Kelvin, by the sound of it.'

'Oh,' Sir James said. 'Your acolytes?' He said it so naturally that it took a couple of seconds before David placed the word.

'I like to think of them as my friends. I hope they're not acolytes.'

'I'm sorry. I was testing you. I tried the same thing with Christina and she gave me a long lecture about my cynicism.'

'Did I pass?' David asked.

'You both did. You're honest, which is always refreshing and you're neither of you fools, which is a relief. I think we all expected you to be another Erlend and Christina to be back to her old, wild self. I think it's almost harder to comprehend you both when you're both so very plausible.'

For the second time in the conversation David failed to stifle a yawn. Sir James immediately stood up.

'I'm sorry, I'm boring you.'

David leapt to his feet. 'No, no, no. Please sit down. I yawn all the time, regardless of whether I'm tired or not.'

Sir James smiled. 'No, I won't keep you. I have to report back to base.'

'What will you say?' David asked.

Christina's father made a small shrug with the corners of his mouth.

'What I feel. I don't know what you've discovered here and I think I probably don't want to. You've maybe found something immensely important and I'm too much of a libertarian at heart to attempt to drag you away from that, even if it's only the remotest possibility. Besides, you're both adults and you're obviously in love; it'd be a stupid person who tried to get in your way.' He walked towards the back door, which David opened for him.

'Also,' he said, crossing the backyard to his car. He opened the door and climbed in. 'I can't help really rather liking you.' He closed the door and the window came down with a quiet whirr.

'Tell Christina to keep in touch.'

David nodded.

'Look after her, David,' he said. 'And look after yourself.'

'I will,' David replied.

The window began to slide up. It stopped.

'Oh,' said Sir James, 'there's a small present for you both. I left it on the hall mantelpiece. It's just something I thought of on the spur of the moment.' He smiled slightly. 'Call it a wedding present, if you like.' The window went up all the way and he started the car but, before it began to move, the window came down again.

'I'd just like to know one thing,' he said.

David nodded.

'How come, if the rumours are true about there being an invisible barrier around Craigairie, I can get in and out without being affected?'

David smiled quickly, bit his lip, drew in a long, speculative breath, held it for a few seconds and then said, 'Tricky.' He twitched one shoulder in the merest suggestion of a shrug. 'It's kind of hard to explain.'

'Try me.'

'We-ll,' David said slowly. 'There are two ways. Either you come in with one of us . . .'

Sir James nodded.

'Or?' he prompted.

'Or in your case, you know what Christina's soul looks like.'

Sir James contemplated this, gazing past David into space.

'Does that make sense?' David inquired.

Sir James thought about it for a second more and nodded ruminatively.

'Yes,' he said. 'Yes, the amazing thing is, it does.'

After he had gone, David went immediately to the hall. He found a thick, heavy envelope on the mantelpiece inscribed with flowing italics and sealed with red wax, impressed with the Graham emblem, a swan.

'To Tina and David,' it said. 'May it bring you all the happiness in the world.'

Intrigued, David began to open it, thought better of it and put it in the back pocket of his jeans. He glanced at his watch then took it off and placed it on the mantelpiece. He looked out through the window into the darkness, thought for a moment then looked around him, as if not entirely sure what he was looking for. His eyes stopped on the log basket and he went over to it, stooped down and began to rummage around amongst the logs. He pulled out a long larch branch about the width and length of a baseball bat, weighed it in his hands and nodded. He peered through the window again.

'Twas the Eve of the Samhain,' he murmured. 'And the witching hour was nigh.' He wandered to the foot of the staircase, a slight smile lingering around the corners of his mouth.

'Come, Delilah,' he called up the stairs. 'Time to show yourself.'

A moment later there was an almighty crash from somewhere upstairs, shaking the house to its foundations. David winced. A great rush of cold air swept past him, knocking him back a couple of steps and bursting the front door open. He braced himself against it, legs apart and continued to squint up the stairs, into the unnatural gale. After a second a huge dog, black as night, came to the top of the staircase and looked down at him.

'And Jesus asked him, saying, "What is thy name?"' David said. 'And he sayeth Legion, for many devils were entered into him.' With that he turned his back on the hell-hound and went out on to the lawn. It followed him, thudding down the staircase like a small landslide, and fell into step beside him and half a yard back, like a pet. As he crossed the lawn David raised the larch branch into the air and commanded it with a single, short word: 'Yog', the Romany word for fire. It burst into flames. A few seconds later, across the valley, a circle of fire exploded into the night, filling the bowl around the stone, showering sparks into the black sky. David snorted.

'Let there be fire.'

As he crossed the valley he became aware of a dull, red glow, thrown upwards against the bellies of the low clouds; an angry, sullen light from scores of bonfires bursting into life all over the moors. That was what Craigairie had done, the influence it had had upon the surrounding countryside. This was Hallowe'en, the eve of the Pagan New Year and the whole population of Carrick seemed to have come out on to the empty hills to celebrate. Those fires were not for fun, or not at least for fireworks and sparklers, roasting potatoes and shrieking, laughing children. They were not to commemorate a distant memory of an ancient, sacred festival, but to draw and guide the faithful, the covens of the Duisk Valley and Glenluce; Barjarg, Miltonise, Killantringan, Cammock Burn, Pindonan Craigs, Arecleoch, Kilmoray, Balmurrie, White Cairn, Corly Craig, Cairn Kenny, Loch Quie, Kilfeddar, Cairnscarrow, Meikle Eldrig, Glenour and many others. They surrounded Craigairie like a wide girdle, each one marking a full coven. There must have been upwards of two thousand people out there. A Pagan congregation to make the Barrhill minister weep.

As David neared the stone he waved the hound at his heels past him and it bounded forwards, leaping into the roaring fire, which roared out to meet it. His presence at Craigairie had punched a hole through which Delilah had escaped into his world. It had closed behind her, trapping her on the wrong side, but now it was open again, just for this one night. It was her choice which side she ended up upon come the dawn.

He tossed the burning torch after her, in a curving arc right into the heart of the fire, then undressed, shedding his clothes like an unwanted skin, and calmly walked down into the hollow, through the roaring fire to the stone. The flames massaged his skin and burned through his core, hot but not unbearable.

He rested his head and the palms of his hands on the cold stone and let them roar around him, licking around his body as they swirled in a vortex, about the stone. It was a delicious sensation, tingling and cleansing, like being licked by a thousand flickering tongues, which found their way into every crevice, every nook and cranny. He opened his mouth wide and breathed slow, deep breaths, drawing it into his lungs, allowing them inside him. Finally, after some five minutes, he pushed himself away from the stone and walked up the far side of the hollow, emerging from the raging fire with a huge erection and a contented smile.

Christina was sitting in the heather, waiting for him. She was wearing a red cloak, nothing else, held at the waist with her Orcadian belt. It had fallen from her shoulders, leaving her torso and breasts uncovered, alabaster, caressed with flickering red. Her hair cascaded down over her shoulders like molten gold. She looked like some fallen angel by Botticelli.

She watched him come out of the fire, expressionless apart from perhaps a hint of sadness in her eyes. Despite her unconcerned déshabillé it was bitterly cold away from the intense heat of the fire, which seemed hotter on the outside than in its centre. A thin, cold, east wind was bringing frost down off the top of the Merrick Hills and David shivered violently as it wisped past him. He sat down beside her, his teeth chattering.

'You get used to it,' she murmured.

He reached across and laid his hand on her forearm, which was lying over her thighs. It was ice-cold, but there was a burning, feverish heat coursing through the core of her body. She placed her other hand over his and left it there, without moving or speaking for several minutes. Finally she shook her head and looked away at the distant fires. She sighed. 'I love this place,' she said. 'I love its days and its nights and its sun and its rain and its silence.' She paused, then continued in the same dreamy, distant voice. 'When I sit up here, where the air's clear of words and thoughts and noise and all the clutter people surround themselves with, I know my place in it all and it makes me feel' – she thought for a second – 'terribly, terribly humble. There's no gift that mankind has which is more wonderful than the consciousness to know what a beautiful world this is. No other creature has ever had that; nothing else on earth has the capacity just to sit still and wonder at how extraordinary life is.' She paused again, this time for a long while, lost in her thoughts. It was several minutes before another shred of her contemplation broke the surface.

'I sometimes wish that my only achievement in life would be to leave behind just a tiny scrap of my love for this place after I've gone, like a bit of sheep's wool snagged on a fence.' She thought for a moment more, then breathed a quiet laugh, as if dismissing the idea. 'But I guess I'll just be' – she turned to him and smiled in his eyes – 'the flash of a firefly in the night, a falling leaf in autumn. Those are your metaphors, aren't they?'

'The breath of a buffalo in winter,' he said. 'The little shadow that runs across the prairie and loses itself in the sunset.'

'Indian?' she asked.

He nodded.

She nodded once and looked away again, back towards the flames. After a while she sighed again.

'That's what you've been trying to tell me, isn't it? In a roundabout sort of a way. That we're not important, but what we've found here is? That the price we pay for all of this peace is that we lose it so that other people out there get to know about it.'

'Nothing's free,' he said quietly. 'We weren't given all this so we could hide it away and keep it to ourselves.'

'What were we given it for, then?' she asked.

He shrugged. 'I dunno,' he replied. 'I really don't . . . But what I *do* know is that there's an ugly, messy, fucked-up world out there, full of people taking what they can while there's still something left to take and other people looking for some cosmic reason for it all. And we're in here, meanwhile, with more answers than we can think of questions to ask.' He stopped and they fell silent again. He moved his hand around her leg to the satin-soft skin of her inner thigh. It was not a sexual caress, but there was a gentle intimacy to it which made her turn to him with a soft smile.

'When I fell in love with you, I didn't realize I was embracing a whole new creed,' she said wryly. 'I thought maybe I'd end up changing my surname again.' She paused and breathed a quiet laugh through her nose.

'But not the world.' She turned back to the fire, closing her eyes and drawing a deep breath.

'What did your father say?' David asked.

She twitched her shoulder in a shrug. 'Some stuff which hadn't occurred to me, needless to say.'

'Like?'

'Like we should perhaps think in terms of having a responsibility to our family and friends and what he is pleased to call our acolytes. He said we have a duty to be honest about what we are and we should either put up or give up – his words, not mine.'

David nodded but did not reply. She turned and looked at his profile in the red firelight.

'You'd thought about that as well, hadn't you?'

He nodded. 'A bit.'

'You think *so much*!' she said wonderingly. There was admiration and puzzlement and gentle mockery in this statement. 'And never tell me what conclusions you come to.'

'You reach your own conclusions, in your own way, in your own time. I'm not going to nudge you,' he said.

She gazed at him for a few seconds and shook her head, laughing quietly.

'Nudge me, just once,' she remarked. 'What does the future hold for us?'

'You're the soothsayer,' he said, then added immediately, 'Oh, I forgot, you can't predict your own future. The curse of the fortune teller.'

'No need to be sarky,' she retorted. 'So tell me, wise ass.'

'What the future holds for us? Excitement,' he said. 'Wild times, witchery.' He laughed quickly. 'And rapidly diminishing resources.'

'Financially?' she asked, surprised but amused. 'Damn, I should've stung Papa.' As she said it he seemed to remember something. He jumped to his feet.

'Back in a moment,' he said, trotting down around the edge of the fire.

'What is it?' she called after him. 'Where're you going?'

He did not answer and disappeared around the back of the fire. He returned a minute later, carrying his jeans and rummaging around in his pockets. As he reached her he pulled out an envelope and dropped it into her lap. She pulled her cloak back around her shoulders and picked up the envelope, inspecting it with a frown.

'What is it?' she asked, holding it up to the firelight and squinting at it. Her cloak slipped back from her shoulders again.

'It's from your father,' he said.

She tore it open and pulled out a sheaf of papers, turning her back on the fire so that she could hold them up and read them. She leafed slowly through them, found a sheet of headed letter paper and stopped.

'Dear Tina and David,' she read out loud.

'I cannot advise you on what I do not understand, except to remind you of the old adage that power corrupts, etcetera. I give you my blessing, wish you well and ask you to be careful in anything you choose to do.

'I enclose the deeds of purchase for two thousand acres of utterly useless land, which Jamie Hamilton could not wait to be shot of, including Craigairie Fell, Craigmoddie Fell and, of course, your beloved standing stone, to do with as you wish. Possession, after all, is nine tenths of the law and I would sleep sounder at night if I knew that any indiscretions you might commit were at least done on land you own.'

She glanced at David, who was staring at her with his mouth open, theatrically aghast. She looked back at the letter, picked up her thread and continued.

'Da dum da dum da dum da dum ... broken the trust on your birthday ... the sum ... da dee da dum da ... Wo!'

'What?'

'Money. A lot of money.' She gave him the letter, pointing to the correct place. He read for a moment.

'Shite,' he said with quiet amazement. 'That *is* a lot of money.'

'We can forget the problem of resources, at least,' she said with quiet jubilation. 'Good old Papa.'

David laughed. 'Talk about keeping it in the family,' he muttered. He sat down again and put his arm around her shoulders. She leant into him, resting her head on his collarbone. They remained for a long time, staring into the fire and thinking their own thoughts. After a good twenty minutes Christina moved and glanced at her left wrist, as if hoping to find a watch there.

'How long to midnight?' she asked.

'An hour?'

'An hour to the witching hour,' she murmured. She sat up, stretched and yawned. 'We should go,' she said.

'Go where?'

'Out,' she replied shortly. She looked into his frowning eyes and smiled. 'If now isn't the moment to present ourselves to the faithful, what is?' She paused and her eyes seemed to twinkle in the firelight.

'It's time to meet the gyppos, Davie.'

He gazed back. 'You sure?' he asked. 'When we do this, we won't be able to come back from it.'

She laughed quickly and nodded. 'I know.' She stood up.

'There's a pall that's hanging in the air,' she said.

> 'And a plume of smoke back over there
> And an acrid taste that's in men's throats,
> From the fires of all my burning boats ...

... Erlend, after Dorothy Parker.'

David laughed and stood up beside her.

> 'Drink and dance and laugh and lie,
> Love the reeling midnight through,
> For tomorrow we shall die.
> (But alas, we never do)'

he replied. 'Also Dorothy Parker. She called it "The Flaw in Paganism".'

'Oh, how very appropriate,' Christina said.

Half an hour later David Armstrong and Christina MacRuarie made their long-awaited appearance for the Romanies. They walked into the Crown pub in Barrhill, where about two hundred gypsies had gathered prior to going out to a standing stone above the Atchin-tan, where all of their people were heading, in order to celebrate the turn of the Pagan year. They were on the point of leaving, throwing back their drinks and beginning to crowd around the door, when it opened and two young people walked in. The whole bar fell dead silent and shuffled clear of them, leaving them in a space. The woman, Christina MacRuarie, was as beautiful as all the rumours had claimed, with a dark red cloak wrapped around herself and her hair tumbling down over her shoulders. She, like her dark, falconine companion, was barefoot, despite the freezing cold night outside. He was wearing black jeans and a black tee-shirt, nothing else. They complemented each other like light and shadow.

They stood and allowed themselves to be sized up by the Romanies for a couple of silent minutes.

'You'll've been waiting for us?' David asked at last.

The silence continued for a moment more.

'Aye,' a voice replied. 'You're the ones.'

BOOK TWO

5

DAWN

Day leaked into the sky to the east, barely discernible at first; a softening in the velvet-blue sky, turning it half a shade paler, fading the weaker of the stars into oblivion. High above the first inkling of the dawn a thin, elegant, crescent moon began to merge into the lightening sky and a single, lone cloud had its brief moment of glory as the earth slowly turned over, allowing the still-hidden sun to explode a silent blast of burning crimson on to the drab underbelly of the cloud. For a while it basked in anticipation of the coming sun, a herald for the emerging god.

As the sun broke over the hills, edging its way clear of them with slow, majestic grandeur, orange-red light poured out from it, flooding across the empty moors, filling the valleys and glens, kindling cold fire across miles of dark forests. It struck Craigairie valley from almost behind the cottage, brushing over the tops of the pine trees on its way to do homage to the standing stone. The stone basked in the incandescent light, casting a long, narrow shadow back across the hillside, as if pointing the way towards night.

Twenty miles away two swifts lifted up over the steep, snow-capped back of Craigenreach Hill, at the northern end of the Merrick chain, and altered direction fractionally, so that they were heading for that tiny splinter of shadow on a distant hillside. Although they were in the wrong place by six months and several thousand miles, the swifts knew exactly where they were going and sped there with all the homing instinct of their kind. They came down off the face of the Galloway Hills, travelling as if in the downward dive of a roller-coaster, riding the cold down-draught coming off the summit behind them far off into the moors beyond.

They finally came over the valley, banking steeply from high in the azure sky, sliding into one last dizzying dive, from two thousand feet to ground level in a matter of seconds. The earth roared up to them, tilting at the very last moment as the two birds plummeted out of their dives, cushioned from the ground by a layer of still, cool air as buoyant as an invisible safety net. They came up the hillside to the cottage like winged bullets, flashed over the garden wall and whipped up over the gable of the house, leaving behind them a trailing chorus of urgent, shrieking cries, as if overjoyed to be back at their nest.

David took Christina down to the Rutherfords at Kilreuchal the afternoon after they arrived back at Craigairie. They had been in Orkney for a month, since New Year, and therefore needed to catch up on the gossip which had accumulated in their absence. Christina went along willingly, although she was tired after her journey, partly because she liked Ellen and Jim Rutherford, but mostly because she wanted some clue as to why David had brought her back to Craigairie in such a hurry. Behind them, in Orkney, they had left the only place where they were accepted openly in all their extraordinary power, without question and without fear.

The reason David had given her for their sudden departure was that there had been some trouble with the gypsies in the Barrhill Atchin-tan. At the time it had made sense to Christina, but in the heat of their haste to leave she had not really stopped to think about it. Now that she did, it did not quite ring true. David had never before showed any marked inclination to involve himself with the goings-on in the Atchin-tan and seemed to have forgotten all about the gypsies until Ellen Rutherford broached the subject in the course of her conversation. Even then he appeared to be more amused than perturbed when Ellen described the feud between the Atchin-tan and the local village of Pinwherry, which had culminated in the gypsies putting a hex on the whole village. The Rutherfords gave the impression that they felt much the same about it.

'There's some as'll say you get what you ask for,' Jim Rutherford had commented. 'Ye go pulling bulls by the tail and like as not ye'll get yersell kicked.'

'What about the Minister?' Christina asked, probing for something more sinister than the misbehaviour of the gypsies. It was a constant, nagging worry for her that there would be a Christian backlash against Craigairie sooner or later. However, Ellen Rutherford dismissed this fear with a snort.

'Aye, there micht be some muttering doon at the Kirk,' she replied smirking, 'the Minister's a wee bit flighty. But then he disnae have a lambing season coming on, so he can afford tae be.'

After this Christina gave up trying to second-guess David. Whatever he had brought them back for, it was not to pick up the pieces of some untoward occurrence that had happened in their absence. He was scheming and she was too tired to attempt to unravel his complicated mind. It was a habit of his, which was at once both thoughtful and annoying, to let her catch up with him in her own time.

She settled down and allowed herself to be charmed by the Rutherfords for the rest of their visit, listening to tales from this little, hidden microcosm and prompting them when they flagged. It was only after she and David were out on the dark moors, walking back to Craigairie, that she decided to ask David what he was up to.

'So what gives, Davie?' she asked. 'You get me all excited back in

Orkney about some terrible curse the Romanies laid on Pinwherry, then the moment we get back here you take me to the Rutherfords specifically to prove that no one gives a toss about it. Am I missing something here?'

'Not specifically,' he said.

'Not specifically what?' she asked tiredly.

'It wasn't the only reason we went to see the Rutherfords.'

'Why then?' she demanded. She stopped, but he continued to tramp on through the heather for a good half-minute before he too stopped, turning back to her in the dark. Although he was only a shadow against the black sky, she knew the expression on his face.

'What?' she said irritably. 'You want me to think, so I'm thinking.'

He retraced his steps to her, gazed at her for a minute, then took her hand and began to lead her on towards the cottage. After a while he said, 'I did it so it'd get around that we're back.'

She continued for a few more paces, then stopped again. He gave her hand a gentle tug, but she slipped it free and crossed it over her chest with the other one. 'I'm too tired for this shit, Davie,' she said. 'What are you up to? What's so important that we have to rush back at a moment's notice?'

'I don't know,' he admitted, with unexpected feeling. 'I was called, I guess. It's something Craigairie does to me when it has something important to tell me.'

'Like what?' she inquired, trying to be reasonable.

'How should I know?' he replied, shrugging. 'All I do know is that when it calls, I drop everything and come running. And now we're back, I can feel I was right.'

'Oh?'

'Can't *you* feel it?' he asked. He had asked the same question of her once before, the night they had laid the exclusion zone, and he had been right then. 'It feels' – he paused – 'expectant, as if something's going to happen, something important.'

She did the same thing she had done the last time he had asked this question: she made herself stop thinking, opened her mind and listened. After a while she sighed. 'Yeah, I feel it.' she conceded. 'It feels like a long tunnel stretching away in front of us.'

Kelvin left his home in St Mary's, after telling Meg that he was leaving her, in a state of dumb shock. He had no idea where he was going to go, he did not even have a clear idea why he had just left his wife. He had left seven years behind him in that house and all he could feel was a dazed emptiness, as if all the sap had been drained out of him. His alimony to her was the part of his soul she kept as he walked out on her.

He drove around for a couple of hours, alternately arguing with Meg, as if looking for a way to mitigate his behaviour, weeping miserably and feeling drained. He did not know what he had expected from her; her anger and bitterness had been predictable, but no easier for him to handle, all the same. Her mistrust of David, whom she blamed for this and many more of Kelvin's worst insensitivities, was an old grudge. Her hatred of Craigairie was a new one. But they had both been getting more virulent of late, ever since David and Christina had hit Orkney, four weeks earlier.

All in all, it had been much as Kelvin had expected, after weeks of psyching himself up to it. But somehow it had still managed to be ten times worse than he had ever thought it would be. Never for a moment did it occur to him that he was doing the wrong thing; he had what David called a 'moral short-circuit point', which meant, basically, that he could, on occasions, mistake his own self-interest for the general happiness and well-being of those around him. He hurt people, including himself, and excused himself on grounds of diminished responsibility: he was a gypsy, or a drunk, or a sometime junkie, or an artist, or a weak fool, but he was never responsible for himself.

He drove right across the Churchill Barriers, right down to the end of South Ronaldsay, where the road ended at the jetty for the John o' Groat's ferry. Then he turned around, drove all the way back, through St Mary's, past Kirkwall, to the Ring of Brogar, in the middle of mainland Orkney. Then he returned to Kirkwall.

When he arrived and parked the car, he was still shuddering so badly with fright and horror and emotional exhaustion that he dropped his keys and had to grope around in a muddy gutter to retrieve them. It was pelting; hard, cold Atlantic rain driven through the narrow streets of the town as if through a maze of conflicting wind tunnels. There was no one out as Kelvin ran to the centre of town, driven up from the harbour by the gale. He cut through tiny back-streets and alleys, which just seemed like the gaps between buildings to the untrained eye, emerging in the main square directly in front of the cathedral. He stood for a moment, watching the rain lashing past, plotting a course up past the cathedral to the street where Dorothy Thurston and, more importantly, her niece Linnhe lived. After about five minutes he took a deep breath, hunched himself deep into his coat and sprinted. As he broke cover the rain seemed to sense him and concentrated all of its power on to him. It ricocheted off the cobbles and stung his exposed face as he ran, and it was a relief to dive again back into the rabbit warren of old houses crowded over narrow streets. The Nunnery, Linnhe's home, was hidden behind a big gate which concealed a small, cobbled quadrangle with an old yew tree in the middle.

It was a while since Kelvin had been there. It was bad enough being eaten alive by Aunt Dorothy, a sort of Agatha Christie figure, with a beguiling homeliness which belied a mind like a stiletto. But David and Christina had been there for the past three weeks, along with Rosie Graham, Ed Graham, his girlfriend Emily and a stream of others who passed through to pay their respects to the so-called Mother Coven.

Witchery was big in Orkney this winter. Dorothy Thurston was loving it, playing the part of the wise old granny with relish. Kelvin had made a point of avoiding that scene and had met Linnhe elsewhere. But now he was desperate, so he went to the Nunnery, hoping to find her there. He rang the bell hanging beside the heavy oak gates and waited, hearing it clang miles away inside the house. He counted to a hundred very slowly, drumming his feet in the puddle in the street. He had reached seventy-seven when a small door opened in the middle of the gate and Dorothy Thurston peered out. She took Kelvin in, nodded and said, 'Oh, it's you.' She swung the door open, revealing the dark courtyard.

Kelvin looked over her shoulder. 'Is Linnhe here?' he asked.

'She went out,' Dorothy replied. 'They all went out.'

'Where?' he asked.

She shrugged.

'When?'

'This morning.'

'D'you know when they'll be back?' he asked.

She shrugged again. 'When they've finished what they went to do.'

'And what might that be?' he inquired, reacting to her studied uninterest with sarcasm. He relented almost instantaneously, adding in a more ingratiating tone, 'I mean, have Iz and David got something on tonight?'

Dorothy Thurston frowned at him. She shook her head. 'They've gone south to Craigairie. They went last night. Haven't you heard?'

'No, I haven't.' He sounded hurt.

'You must be the last person in Orkney to know, then,' she said. Amazingly, she sounded bitter. Kelvin stared at her for a moment too long, all of his worries evaporating for a moment as he marvelled at Dorothy Thurston's transparent annoyance. She had been vain enough to imagine herself to be their mentor and guardian, when in fact she was just another acolyte. It was a joy to behold her discomfiture. One way or another, you had to admire David and Christina's ability to rattle anyone, given a week or two to get their sights in.

'Listen,' she said, aware that she had allowed him to see her mood, 'it's not getting any drier out here. D'you want to come in, or will you be going away?'

'I'm going,' he said. 'I just don't know where to go.'

'Try Skaill. Linnhe mentioned something about having to go to Skaill.'

'Which Skaill?' Kelvin asked. 'There are two.'

'Why don't you try both?' she suggested, knowing full well that they were at opposite ends of the island. Then, just to redress the balance, after inadvertently revealing her mood to him, she dropped a subtle little bombshell on him. 'But what with the Nymatili leaving so suddenly, I doubt you'll find them in either. They'll be holed up somewhere, bickering about what to do next.'

Nymatili.

Every time he heard it he winced inwardly, and she had known that, the old witch. It was an open sore and he hated anyone touching on it. It was a term of such enormous respect that it was almost sacrilegious to use it out of context. It meant the Chosen, the Exalted, the Adored. Only the gypsies and probably only the oldest among them knew what it meant, what an extraordinary compliment it was, and yet they were the very people who had bestowed it on David and Christina.

It hurt Kelvin. It dug down deep inside him, right into his core. His first reaction, when he dared to think about it, was bitter anger at David and Christina. How dare they presume to usurp such an accolade? Who the hell were they, mere gorgios, to arrogate such a title from the Romanies, to whom it rightfully belonged? It was like a personal affront to Kelvin, outrageous and awful and yet . . .

And yet Kelvin knew with sickening certainty that if they were good enough to have fooled not only the gypsies, but also the numerous broomstick-matrons across Orkney, then they were already way out of the ordinary. At this point Kelvin usually abandoned the train of thought. What came next was an admission which was too painful to be faced.

This time, however, it was irrepressible. As he drove across Orkney from Kirkwall, embarking on what he fully expected to be a frantic and fruitless search for Linnhe and the others, his mind got the better of him.

What if they really were Nymatili?

It was something Meg had said to him earlier on, coupled with Dorothy Thurston's barbed remark, which now pushed him further into the train of thought than he was normally willing to go. 'It's not something quaint and whimsical and fun,' Meg had said. 'Can you not see, Kelvin? It's fire they're playing with and it warps everything around it. Can you not see how dangerous they are?'

Nymatili were dangerous. Kelvin, of all people, knew that. It was his special subject. He could think of half a dozen quotations in which the Romany word for fire, Yog, appeared in the same sentence as Nymatili. He knew how rare they were, even amongst the gypsies. He knew what a Nymatil looked like, how they manifested themselves, what they were capable of doing. He knew that it was all but unheard of for two people, so young, to have that kind of power together. The fact that neither of them was a gypsy, or even anything comparable, was still more unusual. He knew that such a combination was supposed to occur only in the highest form of the phenomenon. To his knowledge the only parallel combination had, to paraphrase Graham Greene, resulted in thirty years of war and bloodshed and the Italian Renaissance.

He also knew that if David and Christina were not what they appeared to be, then they were pulling off an inspired hoax. And the truth was, in the end, that neither of them knew half as much about Romany lore as it would have taken to pretend to be Nymatili. In fact, they seemed confused by the concept and were unwilling to be drawn into it.

That was when the jealousy, hidden in a dark dungeon in Kelvin's heart, began to ooze out; soul-pus poisoning him where it hurt most. It could have been anyone in the world. In fact the chances of it happening at all were minuscule. Through all the convoluted, bizarre twists of fate, destiny had picked out two of the four or five people on earth Kelvin could not ignore. It was as if fate had conspired to undermine him right at the cornerstone of his most treasured beliefs.

The depression, bordering on despair, reared up inside him as he drove across Orkney. He had just walked out on his wife, pleading the call of excitement and pastures new over the coddling certainty of home. But Meg had seen through him, as only she was able to do, pinpointing the monster lurking inside him. Once he had known everything there was to know about David. Now he had to be fucking one of his acolytes just to keep in touch with him. He hadn't even known about their sudden departure. He would have expected to have been the first to know, but in fact he was the last.

It was odd that they had gone, when he thought about it. It was so unexpected that Kelvin was baffled and his hiccough of anguish receded. They never did anything for no reason. Their logic was sometimes a little peculiar, but it was always there. But Kelvin had to admit that he could make no sense of it, not after the events of the previous three weeks.

The Orcadians loved them. David and Christina did not need to go out looking for attention, it just gravitated towards them. They reawakened a long-dormant paganism which, along with a lack of cynicism not shared by the more dour Gallowegians, made them the flavour of the month in Orkney. Everybody was mesmerized by them. They were like the Ring of Brogar in human form; something wonderful and mysterious and immensely powerful. They made more sense in Orkney and to the Orcadians than almost anywhere else Kelvin could think of. They fitted the place like a hand in a glove. It made no sense for them to run away back to Craigairie just when they appeared to have established a power-base up here.

It irked Kelvin that he would have to talk to Rosie Graham for the best chance of finding out why they had gone. Rosie had become their unofficial lieutenant, a position Kelvin considered his own by right. The fact that she obviously had no time for him made his resentment just that little bit more prickly.

The acolytes were not at either Skaill, however. They were not in Stromness, but Kelvin did learn that Linnhe had been in the town earlier, trying to cancel some function David and Christina had been expected to grace with their company. The word was that they had all gone up to Birsay to cancel a much bigger meeting scheduled for eight o'clock that evening. It was six o'clock and Birsay was twenty miles away. Kelvin settled down in a bar.

Three and a half hours later he was just getting into the swing of a bout of hard drinking when they came to him; Linnhe, Rosie, Ed, Em and a phalanx of some twenty people, most of them women. Kelvin was sitting on a barstool, nursing a whisky mac and having a conversation with two fishermen when they came in. He turned, glanced at them, then turned back to his drink. Both of the fishermen climbed off their stools and went over to get a better look. Linnhe broke away from the crush and wound her way through the pub to Kelvin. She sat down on one of the chairs recently vacated by the fishermen.

'What's going on?' Kelvin asked after a moment.

'We've been deciding what to do,' she remarked.

'All by yourselves?' he inquired sardonically. 'Goodness.' She ignored the remark.

'So where've you been?' she asked. He looked around at her for a long moment, then looked away again, shrugging faintly.

'Around,' he said. 'So don't tell me. You've all decided to go south tomorrow?'

'Pretty much,' said Linnhe. 'That's what we've been trying to explain to sixty irate women in Birsay.'

At that point Edward came across and sat down on the other side of Kelvin. He looked down the bar at Linnhe. 'Em was great back there, wasn't she?' he said, waving a tenner at a passing barmaid. Linnhe thought for a moment, opened her mouth to say something, smiled quickly and changed her mind. She nodded.

'What did she do?' Kelvin asked.

'It's a long story,' Edward replied and left it at that. Kelvin was feeling fragile and took offence. Linnhe saw his face and elaborated.

'Well, there was a whole bunch of people who kind of expected to see the Ny . . . David and Christina up in Birsay this evening,' she said.

Kelvin was beginning to notice that everyone who came into contact with David started to speak like him; laconic, deadpan. Linnhe had once had a voice full of lilting poetry and song, but now she delivered her words in a wry monotone. She had also caught Christina's habit of hiding behind her fringe whenever she had something to hide. 'Well, they were all jabbering at once,' she continued, 'you know? All those iron-haired women my aunt hangs out with.' She grinned as she remembered. 'We couldn't get them to shut up. They just wouldn't listen to us. Then Emily climbed up on to a table and screamed . . . and screamed and went on screaming until the whole place was dead silent. Everyone just stopped and stared at her.'

'You should've seen it, Kelv,' Edward said, 'she was an outrage. She told them to stop whingeing and act their ages.'

'So what happened?' Kelvin asked Linnhe, repaying Edward for shutting him out five minutes earlier. Linnhe smiled and shrugged.

'They listened to her. She stood up there and told them that David and Christina had gone and that if they choose to move mysteriously that's their business, and who the hell did these women think they were to assume they had a right to be entertained by the . . . by David and Christina.' Kelvin noticed how she kept coming within an ace of referring to them as the Nymatili, only to remember at the last moment that this was taboo with him. Her tact was almost more depressing than her aunt's lack of it.

'I didn't know she had it in her,' he muttered. At that moment Rosie came up behind them, pointedly ignored Kelvin and led Linnhe away by the arm. Linnhe returned a couple of minutes later and stood behind his left shoulder.

'We have to talk,' she said.

'Orders from the gauleiter?' he asked, without turning around.

'You're pissed,' she said, 'so I'll forgive you for being stupid. Come on.'

He followed her obediently through the bar and out on to the cold, wet harbour front.

'So what's been happening?' Kelvin asked good-naturedly.

'You made a promise,' she said, 'which you didn't keep. You said to David that you were the only person who could keep an eye on the gypsies. Actually it wasn't a promise so much as a boast.'

'There aren't any gypsies here. I mean, what does he expect me to . . .?' The penny dropped.

'Exactly,' Linnhe said. She could be harder than stone, harder than even Meg if she wanted. 'They expect you to know when your Romanies are going ape-shit down in Galloway. In fact it was about the only thing they asked of you. Instead we get this frantic message from Christina's father, saying that the gypsies beat up a couple of health inspectors, then rioted when the police came. Then they put a hex on the local village because the good people therein wouldn't be nice to them. I wouldn't go so far as to say they've blown Craigairie's credibility down there, but they sure haven't endeared themselves to anybody.'

Kelvin stared at her for a minute, then shook his head. 'Naa,' he said. 'They wouldn't do all that stuff; hexing a village and all that.'

'No?' Linnhe inquired. 'Three car accidents in five days, two fires, one of which gutted the village hall, two people hospitalized when a branch of a tree mysteriously fell on them, salmonella found in one egg in the local battery and the whole place shut down indefinitely, the television mast incapacitated by lightning for three days. D'you want me to go on?'

'There's more?' Kelvin asked. He could not help but notice that Linnhe found it funny, behind her stern face. 'That's one serious hex.'

'Not really,' she replied dismissively. 'It's pretty run-of-the-mill, actually. All the gypsies had to do was dump a minor curse on the place and wait for the villagers to do the rest themselves. If they'd really meant it, the place wouldn't exist any more.'

'Sure,' Kelvin said unsurely. What she said carried instant conviction, as if it was a well-known fact. He instinctively wanted to dispute it, although he suspected she was right. Luckily she forestalled him.

'So where've you been while all this was going on?' she asked.

'I was busy,' he said.

'Something important?' she asked. 'Or just busy playing with yourself somewhere quiet?'

'You're pissed off?'

'A mite. I was just getting to know Christina and David and making friends with Em and Ed and Rosie, when suddenly all of you up sticks and leave. I kind of expected you, of all people, to warn me in advance if something untoward was about to happen.'

'There's nothing to stop you from coming down with the rest of us,' Kelvin said.

'Oh sure,' she replied, 'David's really likely to pick a fight with Meg over me.'

'What's Meg got to do with it?'

'She's your wife, remember?' He gazed at her, then shrugged.

'Not any more . . . I just left her.'

There was a very long silence.

'You did *what*?'

'I left Meg this afternoon.' His initial sang-froid was beginning to crumble in the face of her stupefied horror.

'Did she know about me?' she asked quietly. 'Or what?'

'She does now,' Kelvin replied. There was another ominous silence.

'So wait a minute,' Linnhe said, 'let me get this straight. You just walked out on your wife and used me as the reason.'

'I didn't use you. You are the reason.'

'Oh shit, Kelvin,' she groaned. 'That's really sweet, but she's your fucking wife. You can't just walk out on her because of a few fun nights with me.'

'That's what she said,' he replied. 'I thought we had more than that.'

They stared at each other for a while. Linnhe sighed and sagged on her feet.

'What a day,' she said. She shook her head, then took a deep breath, calming herself. 'Listen,' she carried on, 'I've still got stuff I have to do tonight and I really don't have time to discuss this with you. I'll meet you at the Nunnery at midday tomorrow.' She turned and began to walk back to the pub. As she went she continued, over her shoulder, 'Why don't you go and get blasted somewhere and I'll see you in the morning.'

'That's all I'm good for, huh?' he retorted bitterly.

'You said it, honey,' she replied.

6

MORNING

Kelvin did not know he was being backed into a corner until it had already happened. To him, in his inebriation, it had been an apparently avid audience in the Barrhill pub, hanging on his every word. It was easy and excusable, in such a situation, to throw caution to the winds and succumb to a fit of bravado. After all, you didn't have to lie about Craigairie or even embellish – although Kelvin was not above a touch of both, just for effect. All you had to do was tell the truth and the audience was more than satisfied.

There was a group, down at the far end of the bar, who were faintly predatory; watching and waiting. For what, Kelvin did not know or care. They weren't complaining, they were just observing in a rather too unblinking way.

Kelvin forged on, hardly noticing when the predatory group began to join the conversation. He did not notice the fact that they were steering him. They took to asking questions about whether David and Christina knew any of the old cures.

'I mean,' one of them said, 'they dinnae look much like witches.'

'What do witches normally look like?' It was the sort of stock answer he would have reviled, had any of the other acolytes said it in his presence. The questioner was unperturbed.

'Pointy hats, warts, broomsticks, no a wee brammer like yon MacRuarie girl.'

'She's a witch, all right. So's David, for that matter.'

'So they ken a' they gypsy cures?' someone else asked.

'They cured a little girl in Orkney who was epileptic,' Kelvin said. Immediately all eyes were back on him.

'And there was another time when this house had a poltergeist,' he went on, the limelight back on him. 'You know, one of those ghosts that chucks things around.'

'Like your one?'

'Yeah, like Delilah.' His tone was a study of easy nonchalance. 'Anyway, they talked to the little girl who was the daughter of the people who owned the house and the ghost went away; like it was coming from her.'

'Sounds like Annie Moffat,' someone remarked. Alarm bells should have started ringing at this point. Kelvin forged on confidently, regardless.

'Who's Annie Moffat?' he asked easily.

'Tam Moffat's girl. Pretty wee thing.' The man who was speaking now was in the middle of the group of beady-eyed watchers. He was small and wiry, with a weasel face and a sneering expression.

'Who is she?' Kelvin asked. 'What's wrong with her?'

'Naething's wrang with her,' a voice said behind Kelvin. He was looking at the weasel-face and saw a peculiar, mocking look pass behind his eyes. Kelvin began to dislike him violently. The man behind Kelvin continued.

'She went up tae Glesgae, mebbe flirted a wee bit too much for her ain good and got what she's had coming to her for a good while.'

'She was raped?' Kelvin asked, horrified.

'Naebody kens that,' the weasel-faced man said.

'You might no say that if she wasnae your niece.'

'I think she's possessed,' came the startling reply. 'You lot explain everything wi' sex.' There was a surge of scornful noise.

'At least we're no weird, like you didakais.'

'I just mentioned her because of a' this Craigairie stuff. Thocht they micht speak tae her.' He aimed this directly at Kelvin. This was beyond alarm bells; Kelvin had heard David's spiel about not accepting challenges or favours. This was an edict straight from the top but Kelvin was too fired up by this man's air of sceptical disdain. The next thing he said pushed Kelvin into action.

'But they mebbe don't stretch tae people, your witches; just coos and dugs.'

'They stretch to people,' Kelvin replied coldly. 'You just watch them.'

Afterwards there was a good deal of acrimony as to who had been responsible. The consensus was that Kelvin could not be expected to do anything right, and so it was someone else's fault for not keeping an eye on him.

David, who was the first to know, was philosophical. By then Kelvin had done a little groundwork on Annie Moffat and had discovered to his dismay that it was generally accepted as fact in the locality that the girl had been raped in Glasgow. He had therefore landed a seventeen-year-old basket-case on David and Christina. David's only reaction was, 'You got ambushed. It happens.'

'I expected you to murder me,' Kelvin said. David shrugged.

'We'll sort it out.'

'How?' Kelvin asked.

David thought, laughed quickly and shook his head.

'I'm sorry, Davie,' Kelvin said. He could see that David was struggling between conflicting emotions: irritation, frustration and friendship. It took a minute for the last to prevail. He took a deep breath.

'It's cool,' he said. He stepped across and embraced his friend. Kelvin broke away and walked to the door. He put his hand on the handle, then paused.

'You know what they say about you?' he asked, his back to David. 'D'you know what they're calling you?'

'Who? The gypsies.'

Kelvin nodded.

'I'd have to be deaf not to,' David murmured. Kelvin stood by the door, motionless, his hand still on the handle, for a painfully long time.

'Why, David?' There was bitterness and pleading in his voice.

'Why what?' David replied. 'Why me? Why not someone else? Why not a gypsy? Why not you?' He paused and shook his head. Kelvin turned round to look at him. 'I don't know Kelv. I just don't know. It isn't something we asked for. It's not, like, I woke up one morning and said to Iz, "Hey, babe, let's fulfil a Romany prophecy today. That'll really freak Kelvin out."'

'Oh, so you can afford to be flippant about it?' Kelvin retorted.

David sighed tiredly. 'No,' he said. 'No, I can't. Christ, Kelv, I don't even want to think about it. The Romanies may be your people, but they scare the hell out of me. I don't want anything to do with them, or their Nymatili. As far as I'm concerned, it bears no relation to me, or Iz, or to our lives. If you're looking for answers, ask the gypsies, not me. It's their prophecy, not mine.'

'I did ask them,' Kelvin said. David sighed again.

'And what did they tell you?'

'They told me you are what you seem to be,' he replied. David snorted.

'Suitably ambiguous. Never let it be said that a gypsy gives it to you straight when bullshit will suffice.'

'They meant that you are what you are perceived to be.'

'I don't know what that means,' David replied irritably. 'I'm me, Kelv. Look at me. Perceive me. I'm who I always was, it's just circumstances that have changed.'

It seemed, for a moment, that his weary incomprehension had struck home. Kelvin gazed at him, then nodded, turned his back on David and began to pull the door open. He stopped again.

'D'you know what the fate of a Nymatil is?' he asked.

'To live fast and die young,' David replied. 'It's crap, all of it. Life for me isn't preordained. It's high-speed hopscotch. I jump and decide where to land when I'm still in the air.'

Christina found David staring into the fire, his hands on the mantelpiece.

'What d'you think?' he asked as she closed the door. He knew it was her without having to look round.

178

'You were admirably calm,' she remarked, sitting down in an armchair.

'Anger's pointless with Kelv,' he said.

'Even when he drops you in it from a great height?' He looked at her under his arm.

'Is that what you think he's done?'

'What do *you* think?' she replied. 'Personally, I don't even want to contemplate what's wrong with a pretty little cock-teaser who's been wasting away, apparently, since she made an illicit visit to the big city.'

'Neither me,' he admitted. They both went silent for a while.

'We have to see her,' he said finally.

'Why?' she demanded. 'What business is it of ours?' He looked at her again. She tried to stand her ground but soon gave way in the face of those eyes. She sighed, sagging back into her chair. After a brief silence she said, 'Fuck him.' She shook her head. 'Can't he get anything right?' David did not leap to his friend's defence. He just snorted almost imperceptibly and looked back into the fire. After a long silence she admitted reluctantly, 'I guess we could talk to her doctor. At least that way we're not committing ourselves.'

'And how do we know who her doctor is?'

'Find out where she lives and go for the nearest GP,' she replied. David contemplated this.

'Right,' he said finally. He stepped back from the fire. 'Kelvin can find out.'

'Punishment?' she inquired ironically. He shrugged.

'It might keep him out of trouble for a couple of days.'

In the event it was Rosie, not Kelvin, who came up with a doctor. He had havered around for the best part of a week and Rosie lost patience with him, got on the telephone and did it herself. Annie Moffat's own doctor was on holiday, but she managed to speak to his partner, a Dr Grant, who admitted that he knew of the girl only when she made flagrant use of the name of Craigairie.

'I'm up in your part of the world tomorrow,' he said, his curiosity obviously aroused by the prospect of meeting the Craigairie witches. 'I could meet you somewhere.'

Rosie relayed this information to her cousin, who was passing her at that moment. Christina looked faintly amused.

'Tell him to come up here. Remind him about the exclusion zone.'

'Why don't you come up tomorrow?' Rosie said into the receiver. She listened for a moment and laughed quickly, without smiling.

'No, it'll be fine. Just as long as you come alone . . .' She listened again. 'You'll break down two and three-quarter miles outside Barrhill, a feeling of immense torpor will come over you, you'll sit in your car wondering what to do next, then you'll turn around, and before you know what you're doing, you'll be back in Barrhill . . .' She glanced up at Christina. 'I'm not "pretty sure", Dr Grant, I *know*.' She listened, nodded and wrapped up the conversation.

'Easy,' she said, replacing the receiver. 'Why here?'

'By the time he's tried to get a mate through the exclusion zone with him, he'll know better than not to take us seriously,' Christina replied. Rosie frowned at her.

'You're becoming devious in your old age,' she remarked. Christina laughed lightly.

'If you've got 'em by the balls, their hearts and minds will soon follow,' she replied.

The doctor arrived at Craigairie an hour later than he had promised, feeling groggy. He had, as Christina had predicted, taken a passenger on his first attempt to get to Craigairie, just to see what would happen. Predictably they had both ended up drinking stiff whiskies in the pub in Barrhill with the publican discoursing knowledgeably across the bar about 'the stupidity o' some folk', which did little to restore their spirits.

Dr Grant's second attempt to get to Craigairie was made with considerable trepidation, alone. To his amazement he passed the place where he and everyone before him for eight months had broken down. It was a grey, misty afternoon, with a thin westerly breeze which tasted faintly of salt; 'dreech' the Scots would call it. It was eerie, driving through mile upon mile of dark forests knowing that no one had been into this country since August of the previous year; no farmer, no forester, no poacher; no one but the now infamous inhabitants of Craigairie. Dr Grant drove on, trying to ignore the prickling down his spine and trying to remember what his excuse for being there had been.

He had forgotten completely, but he remembered that it had seemed important. He distinctly remembered having ended the telephone call with the woman who had called him in a state of agitated excitement. Then he had done some work, had supper, watched television and gone to bed and had completely forgotten about Craigairie until the middle of the next morning.

He arrived in the farmyard of Craigairie unexpectedly, so engrossed was he in the labyrinth of his mind. It was right on the edge of the woods, amongst a scrawny copse of Scots pines; a white farmhouse with smoke coming out of all four chimneys. There was a painted gypsy caravan, a merry little blob of red, gold and green in an otherwise muddy, winter-stricken yard. He slewed to a stop and had to tiptoe over some ten feet of marsh to get to the peninsula of concrete which came out like a jetty from the back door. He knocked gingerly on the door, then louder when the first knock elicited no response. He waited, then did it again, with the heel of his fist, for added effect. Nothing. He contemplated walking around to the front of the house, then saw the mud and thought better of it.

He scratched his head.

Looking around a little desperately he saw the bumper of a car behind the half-open door of a barn.

'Ah,' he said out loud. He banged on the door again. This, finally, elicited a response; a few seconds later the handle turned and the door opened on a stark naked woman. This, Dr Grant decided at that moment, was going to be every bit as odd as local gossip billed it to be. He could not help noticing that she was a good-looking young woman, with a mane of orientally black hair and an elegant, Pre-Raphaelite look to her. She did not appear remotely perturbed to be standing, nude, in a doorway greeting a total stranger.

'Well, come in then,' she said, forestalling him from making a fool of himself.

He walked inside and found himself in a long room, one end of it an untidy, much-used kitchen, the other end an orderly, dark dining room.

'Nice,' he said out loud.

'' 'Tis, isn't it?' the naked girl replied lightly. She went straight through the room without a second glance.

'Come on through. DAVID, IZZY,' she called ahead. 'Guest.'

A young man with unkempt, shaggy black hair appeared from a door beside the hall. He surveyed the doctor with emerald green eyes from behind his fringe, a lean figure Dr Grant only vaguely remembered as the award-winning journalist. He was like an older brother of the same man; older, wilder, shrewder.

After a couple of moments in which David assessed the doctor, he ushered him into a warm sitting room.

Christina Armstrong-MacRuarie-Graham lay sprawled on a sofa looking completely and utterly ravishing. She was breathtaking, not devastatingly beautiful but surrounded by an almost visible aura of charisma and magnetism.

There was a heady, subtle smell in the room; tuberose, gardenia, something like that.

As they came into the room Christina looked around and sprang to her feet, extending a slender hand to the doctor. He looked at it and took it in his paw.

For the doctor it was as if a spell was broken when she touched him. He had expected close contact to have an effect like an electric eel, but somehow it was quite the opposite; he felt his tongue loosen, strength come back into his limbs and his mind began to move again.

'Why don't you take a seat. Would you like something to drink?' she said smiling.

'A coffee would be nice.'

She thought for a few seconds, then went to the door, opened it and yelled up the staircase.

'Rosie? When you've finished up there could you make Dr Grant a cup of coffee?'

Christina closed the door and returned to the sofa, sitting down with her legs folded beneath her.

'So?' Dr Grant began, more to start them off than to actually start the conversation himself.

'So,' she said, 'to business.'

'Tell me about Annie Moffat.'

For a second it failed to register, then a dam seemed to break in his mind, flooding his consciousness with the memory of the telephone conversation of the previous evening.

'What about Annie Moffat?' he asked a little guardedly.

Christina shrugged. 'Someone recommended us to her parents. Apparently she's not well.'

'You could say that.'

'And as that sort of thing isn't really our line, we thought we'd better talk to someone whose line it is.'

'A doctor,' he nodded sagely. Even as he took a breath to deliver a short lecture on his professional ethics, Christina added, 'So what's up with her?' It was not hurried, but she said it to forestall him.

David felt a slight crackle in the air as she sent out a little exploratory push, just to silence him and to gauge how hard she would have to steer his mind, if necessary.

He looked momentarily puzzled. 'What? Sorry?'

'What d'you think's wrong with her?' she asked. No push this time.

'I'm not sure I'm in a position to discuss one of my colleague's patients,' he replied politely.

'No matter,' Christina replied lightly. 'I just thought, maybe, you might be able to help.' It seemed innocuous enough. In fact to the doctor it seemed a very reasonable and generous reaction; so much so that it occurred to him he could trust these people. There was not much to tell anyway; nothing firm.

To David, whose sensitivity to fluctuations in the ether was constantly at a pitch somewhere close to that of a wild animal, the push she sent out with this apparently innocent remark registered about six on the Richter scale. It wound and twisted its way through the air between her and the doctor like invisible vines, entwining themselves around her intended target.

It was a clever push, aimed to convince his mind rather than to alter it. She had such fine control of this trick that she never had cause to unleash a big, dangerous one. David did not have that kind of control, so he very rarely did it himself; content instead to get information by engaging his prey in mind games, and winning. Trickery rather than telepathy.

'The fact is I haven't really seen her,' Dr Grant replied after a moment. David could see the push working on him and knew that Iz would send out one more relatively small one, just to tip him over. 'None of us has. She refused to see a doctor.'

'But you know about her?' she asked.

David smiled quickly and looked across the room, frowning at a picture on the far wall and counting silently. His lips formed the words of one, two, three, four, five, six, seven, eight, nine, then he pointed at the fire, looking down the barrel of his forefinger. His thumb went down like the hammer of a gun.

The doctor started to talk on cue.

'I'm a wee bit surprised you don't know about her,' he replied. 'She's become a sort of local proverb. Mothers warn their bairns that if they don't behave themselves they'll get like Annie Moffat; sort of peelie-wally, morose, distracted. She can't remember things, she's vague as hell; half the time she behaves like life confuses her and the other half's spent alternately flying off the handle and hiding in her room.' He paused and laughed quickly. 'Two hundred years ago they'd've said the devil had stolen her soul and burned her as a witch. Now they say she's awa' wi' the fairies and give her funny looks in the street. Similar thought, comparable effects.'

'How old's she?' Christina asked.

'Sixteen?' Dr Grant offered. 'Pretty wee thing. She's one of those Lolita-types. Irish mother.' Whether this explained her looks or her temperament was left up to her imagination.

'The symptoms seemed to be severe shock,' he continued, 'but that was at least seven months ago and it hasn't gone away. According to local gossip it began around the time she went to a pop concert in Glasgow, which might explain her state and might not.'

'What d'you mean?' David asked.

Dr Grant shrugged. 'For a lot of people out here Glasgow's a foreign country. A big, noisy, dirty chicken coop full of criminals and weirdos. Just going there carries a possibility of infection.' He paused and smiled slightly. 'So you have to take that kind of rumour with a pinch of salt. On the other hand though . . .'

Christina waited for a few moments and then pushed again.

'Yes?'

The doctor looked at her and shrugged. 'Well, her parents won't listen to us when we tell them their wee girl should be checked over, maybe by a psychiatrist. They take it as a sort of slight against their own sanity. But I'd say, at a guess, that something unpleasant happened to her in Glasgow and it's unhinged her a bit. It happens. People often get partial or total amnesia, maybe a breakdown thrown in as well, after a bad shock.' He winced, as if something unpleasant had occurred to him. 'The thing is we haven't got any real reason to be worried about her. It's not abnormal for a girl that age to be having a bit of a confusing time. There's just something about her that makes me uneasy.'

'What do her parents think?'

'Her mum thinks she's anorectic and her dad thinks she's idle. They both think doctors are fools.' He said it good-humouredly but it obviously frustrated him.

David took a last drag at a cigarette and then threw it across the room into the fire.

'So when someone mentions her name in a pub in the course of a conversation about us, they might not be so much throwing down a gauntlet as spouting a proverb. I mean,' he paused, collecting his thoughts, '. . . if her name's a sort of synonym for incurable oddness they might just have been saying, "You might be weird but you'll never be as weird as Annie Moffat." '

The doctor looked at him for a few moments and then shook his head wonderingly.

'You underestimate yourself, I think,' he said quietly.

'In what way?' David asked.

'I don't think the Moffats are particularly superstitious, but her sister, Abbie Morrison, is married to a gypsy, name of Tam Morrison. It was him your friend talked to in the pub.' He paused and sighed. 'It wouldn't be the first time that someone was unwell and your name came up as an alternative to mine.'

'Really?' they both said together, surprised and rather flattered.

'I don't hold with it,' he added.

'You wouldn't,' David remarked cheerfully.

Dr Grant continued, as if not hearing the interruption.

'Although,' he said, 'it occurs to me that you're not occasionally incapable of some unusual feats.'

They both worked their way through the maze of double negatives and understatement. Christina deciphered it a moment faster than David and was thus the first to discover that it was a compliment; in the Scottish sense of the word.

'Like, for instance?' she inquired innocently.

He shrugged. 'Like last summer, for instance?'

'What about it?'

'Oh come on,' he laughed. 'From the twenty-eighth of June to the eleventh of August it was beautiful every single day and there was either rain or a heavy dew every single night. Forty-six days of unbroken sunshine and more than the average rainfall in that time. The Duisk valley was like Tuscany, only greener. It does tempt comment.'

At that point Rosie came in carrying a mug of coffee in one hand and a three-layered toasted sandwich. As she gave the coffee to Dr Grant, Christina and David leapt in like hungry birds and each took large bites from her sandwich. She waited patiently until they had finished.

'We were talking about the extraordinary weather last summer,' David said, sitting down again.

'The weather was just an example,' Dr Grant said hurriedly, addressing Rosie. He was not going to be sidetracked now that he'd got so far.

'Example of what?' Rosie asked.

'Our magic,' Christina told her. 'Apparently we're not without our admirers.'

The doctor looked at her, then at Rosie. He could not work out what her tone of voice suggested; gentle mockery? Irony? He knew that they had secrets, but he could not find a way of getting them to let him in on them. He could not help being slightly disconcerted by them. They were assured and urbane and attractive; younger than he had expected but so unfazed by him that he felt frustratingly inadequate in their presence. He had expected something much more Shakespearean, more Gothic, hiding in the cocoon of Craigairie. Instead he found them both real and plausible, neither of which he had expected.

'What about the Pinwherry hex, then?' he suggested.

'That was the gypsies,' said David. 'We weren't even here.'

'Besides,' Rosie interjected, tuning herself into David and Christina's wavelength at the first attempt, 'putting together a hex on impressionable country folk ain't no big secret. All you need do is scrawl a few meaningless signs on a couple of dozen doors, mention a curse and there'll be people falling down staircases and crashing their cars in no time.' She glanced at her cousin. She nodded once, smiled and murmured, 'Fifteen–love.'

'And all the miracle cures?' Grant persisted.

'The what?' David and Christina asked in unison. The doctor looked from one to the other. To his amazement they appeared to have no idea what he was talking about.

'Oh, come on,' he said. 'People are attributing miracles to you.'

'Really?' David said. 'I wasn't aware we were poaching your patients.' There was something in his tone, both dismissive and flippant, which stopped Grant short. The last thing he had expected them to say, when he sprang his checkmate move on them, was that they had no knowledge of it.

'Honestly?' he asked.

It was David's turn to look surprised. 'Honestly.'

'Goodness,' the doctor exclaimed, still genuinely amazed. 'I thought you'd know.'

'Know about what?' said Christina.

'Oh, little things,' the doctor said, 'lots of little things. People coming to me claiming to have been cured of verrucas, warts, rashes.' He began to count them off his fingers. 'One case of mumps, a few eczemas, one shingles, a kid who might or might not have had measles; I didn't get to see her till after the event, so I put her down as a maybe . . . Oh, and then there's the gypsies.'

There was a short silence.

'The gypsies?' David asked. 'What about them?'

Again Dr Grant stared at him in consternation.

'Last September?' he suggested, as if trying to jog David's memory.

David shook his head.

'There was an outbreak of chickenpox in the Atchin-tan.' He paused. 'It's what started all this.'

David continued to shake his head. The doctor looked at him for a moment more, then shrugged slightly and went on.

'It was no great surprise to anyone that it happened. The place was . . . is an insanitary, overcrowded shanty-town. I went there and counted twenty-three cases, probably more like forty counting the ones who wouldn't let me in. At that rate I thought it'd probably take out maybe a hundred and fifty kids in ten days. I went back three days later and couldn't find a trace of it. I couldn't believe it; even the kids I'd seen laid up with it were right as rain, not a mark on them.'

'So what happened?' Rose inquired.

'They said they'd been drinking and bathing in the Tarf.'

'What, our river?' Christina asked.

'Your river. At the time everyone laughed, but someone must have put it to the test because the whole of the Duisk got wise to it by November.' He paused and smiled wryly. 'Thereby depriving me of their custom.'

'I wonder why they didn't tell us?' Christina speculated out loud.

'Pride?' Rosie suggested.

Christina nodded. 'Must be.'

At that moment David laughed out loud.

'I can't believe this. These people have been drinking that shite-infested peat water as a curative?'

'You said it,' Dr Grant replied laconically.

'Anyone that lateral deserves to be cured,' Rosie remarked.

David and Christina laughed. The doctor did not.

'I can't believe you don't know about this,' he said, shaking his head. 'I mean, if you had, you might've been pouring tons of aspirin into the river, or something.'

'There's no reason why it shouldn't happen though. If people want to be cured and they really believe the river has magical qualities, then they might well cure themselves psychosomatically. The mind's a very powerful machine, when you trick it into cutting loose a little.'

'So you think it's psychosomatic?'

'Could be,' David replied with a shrug. 'I mean there's no real reason why the river shouldn't have magical powers, but it's less likely.'

Dr Grant stood up and walked over to the fireplace. He was both excited and confused by this conversation and he bitterly regretted not taping it, until he remembered that he did not own a Dictaphone. They were playing with him, letting him continue his questioning and concentrating on what he had to say; attentive, interested, as if they were willing to continue for the sake of an amusing discussion, if nothing else. They parried his questions with contemptuous ease, but they still allowed him to see enough to be curious.

'What if . . .' he began, putting his hands behind his back and his back to the fire. 'What if I asked you what you *really* think? If I gave you the choice between psychosomatic and genuine miracle, which one would you say is causing these cures?'

There was a long silence.

'Archimedes,' Christina said finally.

Dr Grant frowned at her.

'The art of the possible.'

'What? Give me but a lever and a firm place to stand and I can move the world?' David raised his eyebrows in surprise.

'Och, ye cannae spend eight years in a university without absorbing a hell of a lot of useless information.'

He shook his head. 'And I don't see how Archimedes ties up with the miraculous Tarf.'

'Nothing's impossible,' Rosie replied. She had been absorbed in a magazine for some time and her re-entry into the conversation was unexpected. She closed the magazine with a slap and looked across at David.

'You taught . . .' She stopped, her mouth dropping open and a look of horrified amazement scrawling itself across her face.

By luck rather than design Dr Grant had been looking at Christina's reflection in a mirror across the room and had seen the look she gave her cousin the second before she had stopped talking. Her face had hardened momentarily, ice coming into her grey eyes, small muscles had tensed around the corner of her eyes, narrowing them in sharp anger. It was the facial equivalent of a flat-handed slap, and it silenced Rosie instantly.

What was amazing was that Rosie was sitting with her back against the same arm of the sofa Christina was leaning upon. There was no way they could have seen each other's faces. Rosie had to strain her neck around to give Christina a look of pained surprise, like a whipped dog.

Before he knew what he was doing Dr Grant turned to Christina and said, 'How did you do that?'

'Do what?'

'What you just did to her.' He was beginning to regret having asked and was praying that she would let him off the hook. She did, but it was in a way which dumbfounded him. She locked her eyes on to his, rooting him to the spot and derailing his mind. Then a door seemed to open, like an inner ear, deep inside his head. He could still hear with his ears, the sounds of the room, the wind outside, the crackling fire, but he could also hear other things, most notably the ummistakable sound of two people arguing.

'Ignore them,' Christina said, but her lips had not moved and his ears had not heard. It was in stereo.

'As David so rightly pointed out, the human mind is indeed a very powerful machine, when it's tricked into "cutting loose" a little.' All the nuances of her speech; the subtle inflections of faint irony and fainter mischief were there, in his head, in stereo, without her opening her mouth.

It was staggering.

'You see,' she continued normally, out loud, 'the thing is that humanity's undoubtedly Mother Nature's cleverest invention. We are so startled by our own genius that we have to invent gods to account for our existence. We have brains better than computers, hands to make things with, logic and illogic, love and hate. We are the most successful predators ever. Humankind is maybe the most bizarre and certainly the most advanced animal on earth. And yet what does it do? It builds itself concrete prisons and feeds itself on sanitized food full of man-made chemicals, preferably wrapped in a by-product of crude oil. We have distanced ourselves from the world that created us, de-evolving ourselves back to the state of, say, gannets. We both live in colonies, we both care damn-all for anything but our own narrow interests; i.e. eating and bickering with each other. We both produce a lot of guano.' She paused to see if he was with her, then continued.

'Think. This unbelievable evolutionary freak; the most extraordinary creature Mother Earth has ever spawned, reduced to the pitiful condition of hardly being able to move without recourse to a machine. No wonder we think something quite simple, like telepathy, is impossible. What d'you need telepathy for when you've got a telephone?' As she was speaking, heat had gradually crept into her voice, as if she felt strongly about this. The doctor realized that this was as close as he had yet come to finding an underlying philosophy behind Craigairie, which was why he had agreed to go there in the first place. 'There's so much we don't know,' she continued. 'Or we've wilfully forgotten, or we refuse to believe in because it doesn't fit this rational world we've created for ourselves. There's so much that's beautiful and extraordinary and simple in the world, which humanity denies itself because it's somehow below us to admit that there are things we can't explain, which don't need to be explained. Life's very easy, it's a game with surprisingly few ground-rules and a lot of room for manoeuvre. It's us who complicate it by constantly trying to break the rules, not the other way round.' She stopped.

'I get the impression you make a distinction between yourself and the rest of modern man,' Grant remarked.

'They can afford to; they're Nymatili,' Rosie remarked acidly, still smarting from the full impact of what Christina had done to her.

'Ah,' said Grant. 'That word again. I keep hearing it and I'm still not entirely sure what it means.'

'Join the club,' David murmured, but very quietly.

'Is it the reason that they think you can cure Annie Moffat?' Doctor Grant inquired.

'Who's they?' Christina asked, a little nervously. The doctor gazed at her, smiling slightly. 'You don't listen to much of the local gossip, do you?' he said. 'It's all over the Duisk.'

There was an uncomfortable silence.

'They don't really expect us to cure her of whatever it is she has?' David asked at last.

'They certainly expect you to try,' the doctor replied.

Dr Grant sat in his car in the car park of the Black Bull hotel and wondered, among other things, why he was there. The hotel was an old keep situated in a wooded hollow in a bend of the River Stinchar eight miles from Barrhill. It was a compact building, bulky and square, with small, deep-set windows, like sightless eye-sockets, high up in its thick walls. The canopy of interlocking branches surrounding the keep contributed to the dank, somewhat sinister atmosphere which clung to the place, even in daylight. Now, at twilight, it felt damp and cold and slightly spooky; not the ideal place for this meeting between Annie Moffat and the Craigairie witches. But it was near enough the middle point between the Moffat farm, outside the coastal town of Girvan, and Craigairie. It even made sense, in a perverse way, that this business should be conducted in a place which felt like a sort of terrestrial underworld.

He glanced at his watch and wondered for the hundredth time what had possessed him to do this. He had set this meeting up almost single-handedly; making contact with both sides, organizing a mutually accept-able location for their meeting and relaying messages back and forth between them. He did not have a clear idea of why he had gone to all of this trouble, except perhaps that he was curious to see how far David Armstrong and the rest would go before backing down. He was fascinated by them. Everything he had ever taken for granted rebelled against the possibility that there were such things as witches, magic and miracle cures. It went against almost every one of the basic premises upon which he based his existence: his professional scepticism, what remained of his Presbyterian upbringing, his own innate rationalism, his long-standing aversion to superstition. And yet they did not behave like people intent on an elaborate con-trick. On the contrary, there was an honesty and guilessness about them which made them not only difficult to dislike, but also hard to distrust.

They had been candid about their reluctance to be drawn into the Annie Moffat business, admitting to him that their only reason for seeing her was so that no one could accuse them of being frauds, scared of exposure. Even so, it was now past the eleventh hour and Dr Grant was still far from sure whether they would turn up. In a way, he would have been almost relieved if they did not; quite apart from the fact that he would probably have been struck off if word got out that he had encouraged such lunacy, he was growing less and less sure by the minute that he really wanted to know whether the rumours about them were true.

He looked at his watch again.

'Five o'clock,' he said out loud. A light had been turned on at the corner of the hotel and it was now pitch-dark outside. David's promise was that they would be there at five, or when it was dark, whichever came first.

It was both and as yet no one had turned up.

The doctor climbed out of his battered Ford estate, slammed the door shut and caught his breath against the cold. He stood for a moment beside his car and then scrunched off across the frozen slush which covered the car park, towards the trees at the far side. He reached them and cut up through the thirty-yard stretch of woods which separated the car park from the main Girvan–Barrhill road. He was standing in the middle of the road, stamping snow off his feet, when he heard the sound of a car coming from the direction of Girvan. He waited as it drew closer, winding its way along the tortuous, winding road. It seemed to take an interminably long time for the car to get close. Dr Grant moved to the side of the road, just in case the car was not the one he was expecting. To his relief it turned right, into the hotel car park, before it reached him. He trotted back down through the trees.

As he reached level ground the headlights of the incoming car swung across the side of the keep and briefly picked out three figures sitting on a low wall at the far end, just out of the arc of yellow light cast by the lamp on the corner of the hotel. Frowning, Dr Grant changed direction and picked his way across to them. As he neared them they slid to their feet and came to meet him.

'How long have you been here?' he asked.

David looked at his watch. 'Couple of minutes.'

The doctor looked around for their car, although he knew that no car but the Volvo which had just arrived had been close for at least half an hour.

'How d'you get here?' he asked. 'You didn't walk, did you?'

'We came under our own steam,' David replied obscurely. He pointed at the Volvo which was parked next to the doctor's car. 'Is that the Moffats'?'

'It's the Morrisons'.'

'Same difference,' David muttered and stalked away towards it, closely followed by Christina and Rosie. Dr Grant watched their backs for a few seconds and then wandered after them.

When David was about twenty yards from the Volvo all four of its doors opened and three men climbed out, two of them in their twenties, the other one middle aged. They all had the lean, wiry look of gypsies. They ranged themselves in a faintly menacing wall and waited for David and Christina and Rosie to reach them. The latter stopped a couple of yards from the former. There was a short pause.

'Which of you's Tam Morrison?' David asked.

The older one nodded once. ''S me.'

'Where's the girl?'

Tam Morrison nodded over his shoulder towards the car. David inclined his head so he could see the Volvo. There were two people, a woman and a girl, on the back seat.

'Get her.'

One of the men sauntered back to the car and returned a couple of minutes later with both of its occupants. Abbie Morrison was a thin woman with a pinched look, leading a small, obviously nervous girl. They stopped and Rosie heard a faint buzz of communication between David and Christina. She studied Annie Moffat, trying to see what they would be thinking.

She was a pretty little thing, with big, almond-shaped eyes and a mane of dark hair which framed a pale, set face. She did not show any obvious signs of illness, apart from perhaps a shadow of bleakness behind her eyes.

'Hello, Annie,' Christina said softly. 'I'm Christina, this is David, that's Rosie. We have to talk to you. Is that OK with you?' There was no direct push in her voice, but she seemed to emanate calm reassurance. Annie Moffat nodded and stepped forward from her aunt. Abbie Morrison made to follow her but David stopped her with a single shake of his head.

'Alone,' he said.

He turned and gave Rosie a quick look which said 'Hold them'. Rosie nodded and stayed put as David, Christina and the girl walked across to the wall and sat down in clear view, David on the right, Christina on the left.

Left on her own Rosie produced a packet of cigarettes and offered them around in silence. They all took one with muttered thanks and allowed her to light them, hands cupped ostentatiously against the minimal breeze. There was a long silence.

Rosie glanced over her shoulder and saw the three figures deep in conversation on the wall. As she watched, Annie rocked back and a peal of laughter echoed across the courtyard. Rosie frowned, concentrating on the group, listening to vibes. She could hear Annie Moffat; amused, confused, at ease on the surface but in turmoil down below. David and Christina were more interesting, more revealing; they were pouring out positive vibes, but behind that smokescreen of confidence they were not optimistic. They did not think they could do anything for her.

★

Later, after the Moffat–Morrison group had gone, they were sitting inside the pub, talking quietly over large whiskies. David and Christina seemed exhausted, as if they had poured everything they had into Annie Moffat. The doctor and Rosie had been discussing, in oblique terms, the power of local gossip. Rosie had been skilfully guiding the doctor towards the subject of Annie Moffat, so that David and Christina could ask him whatever questions they wanted. It was Christina who finally cut in, speaking for the first time in some minutes.

'Why didn't you tell us she has AIDS?' she asked quietly.

He winced, as if the question stung him physically. He took a sip of whisky.

'I didn't know. Come to that, I still don't.'

'You could guess. You were a student in Edinburgh, AIDS capital of Europe. You must've seen it before.'

There was a short silence before the doctor nodded.

'Aye, I've seen it before and yes, I did guess. Not at first. When she first came to my attention I thought she'd probably got herself raped and was in shock. Then when she didn't seem to be getting any better it began to occur to me that she might've got The Slim.'

'You and half of South Ayrshire,' Rosie muttered.

'*You* must have guessed,' he said accusingly. 'Why did you agree to see her?'

'Because you wouldn't,' David murmured. Christina nodded her agreement.

'What's there to do?' he retorted. 'Get her down to my surgery and tell her that in my considered professional opinion she's going to die?' He paused and sighed. 'I didn't have the heart, so I've been procrastinating.'

'What, then we came along?' David asked.

'What did you tell her?' Rosie asked.

David shrugged. 'That it isn't so bad to die.' He offered her a wry smile.

'So you can't cure her?' Dr Grant asked. He sounded disappointed.

'No, we can't.' David replied. He seemed to stress the word 'we' and Grant picked up on it.

'Can anyone?'

'Lady luck,' Christina said.

'A.k.a. Dé Doveleski,' David murmured.

'She might not have it,' Rosie remarked. 'I mean, she hasn't actually had a blood test yet. Anything's possible.'

'Including a miracle?' Grant asked.

'Don't hold your breath,' David said.

7

NOON

It was said afterwards that they had come in the form of black swans, invisible in the night until they alighted in the snow, graceful and elegant in their magical guise.

It was whispered that they gave her a phial of specially prepared magic potion into which they siphoned so much of their power that it took an entire cycle of the moon to recover.

It was assumed that Annie Moffat had been infected with AIDS before they met her, because her blood was as pure and clean as distilled water afterwards.

Even Dr Alan Grant, who supplied the bones of the article for the Sunday paper which broadcast the story of Annie Moffat to the world, was utterly convinced that they had cured her. His account might not have been quite as wildly sensationalist as those of the locals thereafter, but it was no less sensational.

This should have been the sort of story that no one but the tackier Sunday tabloids was willing to touch, let alone carry with conviction. And yet there it was, on the front of a big, reputable Sunday newspaper not normally given to excitable nonsense such as this. But they took it seriously, therefore many otherwise sensible people took it on trust that there was at least something worthy of interest here.

One night, back in Orkney, Emily and David had been discussing the possibilities for the future and Emily had wondered out loud what it would take 'to convince the world that we're for real'. David had thought about it for a moment and had then replied,

'An accident, I think . . . That, or a martyr.'

At the time, she had taken it as a throwaway line in dubious taste, which was typical of David.

It was only after the whole Annie Moffat thing exploded that she remembered the conversation and realized what he had meant. Nothing, not even a feat of the most stupendous magical prowess could have equalled the combination of half-truths, wish-fulfilment and fabrication that Alan Grant handed on a plate to a public yearning for hope, rather than Australian soap operas and mortgages.

The irony was that they got it wrong.

The magic potion was spring water, the miracle was unintentional and, as Emily pointed out, David and Christina would have travelled as falcons and Rosie could only get the Abra-Melin spell to shape-shift herself into a crow.

And they did not even know they had done it until they read it in the newspaper. To say they were surprised would have been to give a whole new meaning to the concept of understatement. They had spent ten days wondering what to do about Annie Moffat and, to Kelvin's silent relief, invited Linnhe down from Orkney, so that the core of the Mother Coven could be together in this time of worry and uncertainty at Craigairie. After some hasty organization Emily had returned as well.

And so Craigairie was full once more, for the first time since David and Christina had politely but firmly thrown everyone out before Hallowe'en nearly four months earlier. The atmosphere was peculiar; on the surface subdued but underneath volatile, like an active volcano bubbling towards eruption.

They all seemed to be waiting for something and they assumed that this something would come from David and Christina. But they were waiting as well, killing time and hoping for fate or a flash of inspiration to give them a reason to go out into the countryside. It was hard to explain what exactly was wrong, but it was tied up with a sense of failure that they had for the first time in a year run up against a problem they could not solve. It seemed to flaw their entire philosophy, that they could not flick their fingers and unravel the dilemma of Annie Moffat with no more difficulty than they shape-shifted, or read minds.

Rosie, never one to kow-tow to good taste where bluntness would serve, called it a dose of Kelvinitis. It was an accurate description of the restless despondency which pervaded Craigairie. Only Emily remained cheerful throughout; of all the acolytes she had ingested the whole idea of Craigairie most fully, without question or qualification.

It was fitting therefore that Emily was the one who was to break the news to them. She had been running all the errands for them to Barrhill on her own for a fortnight, so it was not surprising that she was the one who picked up the Sunday papers on that wet, blustery February morning.

After she had returned, and after she had washed some pots, pans, plates and mugs, made herself a cup of coffee, stoked the fires and read a tabloid, cover to cover, she picked up a serious newspaper and saw the banner headline on the front page: AIDS GIRL CURED BY CRAIGAIRIE WITCHES (exclusive).

It took about a minute for it to sink in. She stared at it, shook her head, closed her eyes and stared at it again. It was still there. Picking up the paper she looked on the back, then at two randomly picked pages inside, just to make sure it was real and not some elaborate practical joke.

She stood up, her heart pounding. 'JESUS CHRIST.' She turned, upsetting her chair, and ran out of the kitchen, through the hall and up the stairs, an echoing yell of 'DAVID ... IZ ...' preceding her. Without stopping to knock she burst into their bedroom, ran across to the bed and shook David awake. His head emerged from under the covers. He eyed her blearily.

'Em? Wha's 'appening?'

Too excited to speak Emily just stood and snapped the front page of the newspaper taut in front of his face.

'What is it?' he asked sleepily. He took fully twenty seconds to focus, then his eyes slowly widened and his mouth opened until both were theatrically agape. He reached behind him and shook Christina.

She emerged, turned over and squinted over his shoulder. Her face did an action replay of what David's had done a minute before.

'Madre Mia.' She stretched over David and tore the paper out of Emily's hand. Like Emily she turned it over and looked at the back. She turned it back over and goggled at it. A string of expletives poured from her lips. David lay back on his pillow and stared at the ceiling, a huge smile creeping on to his face.

'Thank you, Mother. Thank you, thank you, thank you, thank you.'

If they had expected to cure Annie Moffat they might have been remotely prepared for the scale of the excitement the miracle generated. As it was it caught them completely unawares, detonating in their hands like a home-made bomb, so sudden and shocking that for a while, as the world went berserk around them, they were too dazed to comprehend the vastness of what had happened. Not even David had planned for such an eventuality. He, of all of them, had always been aware of how terrifically media-friendly Craigairie could be, given some luck, some inspired handling and the right circumstances. But both he and Christina had always wildly underestimated the enormous, frightening power which came from knowing something that no one else knew. As far as they were concerned their magic was far too complicated to be shared with anyone but the people who understood it without needing explanations; the gypsies, the Orcadian witches, the covens of Carrick and Galloway, their closest friends. If they had learned anything from the experience of the previous summer it was that when Craigairie was exposed to a wider public, then fabrication, gossip and rumour made just as good copy as the truth. And as neither of them wanted to be the star attraction in a media circus they had gone out of their way to sidestep the attention of anyone who would misrepresent them.

Annie Moffat changed that.

It was one thing to have a reputation amongst a few superstitious teuchtars for magical, healing powers, but it was quite something else to have apparently cured a case of AIDS. This was not measles or chicken pox, but a highly emotive and proverbially incurable sickness – the bubonic plague of the late twentieth century. And Dr Alan Grant was too well qualified a physician and too plausible a person to be ignored out of hand.

Suddenly, unexpectedly and unwittingly, David and Christina found themselves at the centre of a maelstrom of publicity, which made the excitement at the height of the previous summer seem insignificant by comparison. Few people outside the hitherto quiet and still backwater of Galloway, which was at the epicentre of this storm, seriously believed that the girl had been the recipient of a straightforward miracle. Doctors could testify to the impossibility of curing AIDS; historians could trace back a direct lineage for such superstitious nonsense as this, in parts of Scotland, including Galloway and Orkney; clerics could ruefully admit that it was not impossible for someone to encroach upon their territory by tweaking upon some raw nerve of collective Paganism; civilized and urbane intellectuals could marvel at how easy it was to pull off such an inspired hoax, given the undoubted charisma of the Craigairie witches and the remarkable gullibility of some country folk.

If it was a hoax then everyone had to admit that it was a clever and intuitive one. Annie Moffat did not come in isolation, but was just the latest and most newsworthy of a string of bizarre incidents emanating, apparently, from Craigairie over the past year. It was easy to be sceptical and amused by the superstitiousness of the unsophisticated, but once one stopped and looked at what Craigairie had done in Galloway, it was hard not to notice that it had succeeded in awakening something which most informed people assumed had been dead and buried for several hundred years.

The only people, ironically, who fully comprehended the implications and significance of a cult that could be seen to pull off miracles like Annie Moffat were the Christian churches in Scotland; an unlikely coalition of Catholics, Presbyterians, Episcopalians and just about every sub-section in between. They knew that scorn was not a sufficiently powerful weapon to repulse this threat to their own congregations. Craigairie commanded frighteningly widespread sympathy in a great chunk of south-west Scotland and was spreading its influence with every passing day. It simply was not enough to laugh it off as an absurdity which would fade away as suddenly as it had appeared. With this very much in mind the separate branches of the Christian faith in Scotland got their heads together and, in a rare, if not unique, display of ecumenical unity issued a joint statement condemning 'this scourge of pseudo-Paganism'. It was an interesting tract, based upon what little common theological ground its authors could find – from the commandments through to the Epistles of St Paul – which was intended both to see Craigairie off from a purely theological standpoint, as well as to filter its way down to parish level, in diluted form, as a warning to all good Christians.

Inside the cottage there was a general feeling that, whether they liked it or not, David and Christina had reached a watershed. To see them both during that dramatic, exciting fortnight after the news of Annie Moffat broke was to be privileged with the knowledge that they were caught up in an inexorable momentum outside their control. Until now they had been able to maintain at least an illusion of deciding their own fate, of knowing where they were going. But now they could no longer pretend that there was some grand plan which made them able to control and predict the events they themselves generated.

They went out from Craigairie, reluctantly at first, about two and a half weeks after the miracle hit the headlines, by which time the demand for them in the locality had reached fever pitch. It was hard for them, the hardest thing they ever had to do, because they knew what was waiting for them on the outside. They were miracle workers and, as such, they were expected to do it again, and again, and again.

They were the Nymatili.

As the gypsies were wont to remark, in their infuriatingly trite way, it did not matter whether they wanted to be this thing, because it had already chosen them. They could not escape it; the best they could do was resign themselves to it.

So they went out from Craigairie, despite their reservations, and found that it was not so hard to live up to the expectations of those who wanted to believe in them. All they had to do was turn up at a standing stone or cairn in the middle of the night, hang around for a couple of hours dispensing any old cliché they cared to lift from Christianity or Buddhism or the American Indians (David's favourite source) or any other source of enlightenment and the faithful would go home, happy in the assumption that they had just received a chunk of 'Truth'. More often than not someone came away from one of those midnight trysts claiming to have been cured of some ailment or other.

Their reputation grew and grew. Whether, as they themselves were inclined to claim, they were just regurgitating a mish-mash of acquired philosophies tailored to fit in with what little indigenous Paganism there was to work with, or they were indeed as wise as people took them to be, was irrelevant. It became chicken and egg, like the miracles which were attributed to them; they might have claimed that it was quite possible for people to cure themselves psychosomatically, but then if they had not been there to generate such faith, nobody would have been cured of so much as a cough. It was the same with the mutated philosophy they taught; it might well have been derivative and bastardized, but it worked.

As time passed the Mother Coven refined its message and its accompanying activities down to near-perfection. David went out on the nightly forays into the surrounding countryside less and less often, deeming it better if Christina and her attendant witches cultivated their growing following without him around to distract attention from them. At the time it seemed that he had come down with a fit of idleness and it was only in retrospect that anyone realized how shrewd he had been. His greatest asset was in making people listen and think, whereas Christina's strength was her ability to make an audience gaze and wonder. Both of them knew that now was the time to perform, to mesmerize their captive audience, rather than to win people over with clever arguments. Therefore, David remained in the background while Christina danced her moth-dance by the light of a hundred bonfires.

Considering the fact that it was a strategy born from the numbed confusion they had all felt after Annie Moffat, it was enormously effective. The Mother Coven was drawn further and further afield, keeping pace with the growing demand for it in the south-west. The first time Christina crossed the Merrick Hills into Dumfriesshire it was as if Craigairie had edged its way out beyond the safety of its natural base in Galloway, into the uncharted missionary country beyond. But a month later, by the end of the first week of April, she had been sighted as far north as Lanarkshire and eastwards into the Leadhills, Peeblesshire and Ettrick. There was a rumour, one of the many which did the rounds at the tail-end of that winter, that if every coven in the south of Scotland lit a bonfire on the same clear night, there was nowhere south of Glasgow and west of the Cheviot Hills where at least one would not be clearly visible.

Galloway itself was an extraordinary place to be during those months. There was an atmosphere so thoroughly alien to the modern world that it seemed the whole region had reverted to some pre-Christian dark age all of its own; as befitted the cradle of what was coming to be known as New Paganism. On the surface, life went on quite normally, but underneath the place was in ferment. The kirks were empty, the covens were established, there wasn't a standing stone or cairn, however remote, which did not look as if several people were visiting it on a regular basis, leaving little piles of offerings, trampled-down grass and the scorch marks of a recent fire.

There was also a taciturn, closed air which excluded all outsiders. One journalist, after a week of being cold-shouldered up and down the Duisk valley, remarked that he had come across more talkative people in Communist Albania. Unlike Orkney, where witchery and Paganism were flaunted openly, the inhabitants of Galloway were stonily reticent.

Meanwhile the word spread through the hills; from the Merrick, over Nithsdale, Annandale, Eskdale, Ettrick Forest and towards the Borders and Edinburgh. It was almost like watching the progress of a South American revolutionary army, as it gradually advanced upon the centres of population via the untamed highlands, always steering clear of any open confrontations.

From the outside it seemed that Craigairie was waging a carefully planned campaign, deliberately gobbling up Christianity wherever it showed signs of weakness. But from the inside it was just an exhausting couple of months of going out, night after night, to wherever there appeared to be a demand for them. They kept out of the towns and cities because, paradoxically, they felt exposed when they could not slip away into the hills at the slightest sign of trouble, and also because they did not want to be where the media could find them.

It may have appeared that there was a direction and purpose to what Craigairie did during those two months but, if there was, only David was static for long enough to know or care what it was. As far as the others were concerned, the whole thing was a direct and increasingly undesirable result of Annie Moffat. Christina drove them on, apparently compensating for David's lethargy, setting a pace and sticking to it with the air of a person who was always half-expecting a sign which would enable them to stop and take stock of the situation.

As for David, he sat at Craigairie, read books, watched videos, nursed a sick barn owl back to health and spent a lot of time with the gypsies. He sometimes disappeared for days on end, only to return unexpectedly and resume his formless life at the cottage. When Rosie or Emily or even Edward was prompted to question Christina as to what he thought he was up to she replied simply that he was waiting.

When something did finally happen, which turned out to be the sign they were waiting for, it began so quietly that, at first, only David noticed it. In his weeks of inactivity he had tuned his mind so that it would pick up the faintest, most diffuse signals coming from the outside world. He was like the captain of a ship, standing on the bridge, sniffing the wind for the first, barely perceptible hint of an impending tempest.

It began as a tiny news column on the fifth page of the *Daily Telegraph*, which said that the organizers of a pagan festival, due to happen at Glastonbury at the end of April, hoped that they would be able to attract David Armstrong and Christina MacRuarie south, to preside over the proceedings. It was an annual occasion, apparently; a couple of hundred hippies congregating on Walpurgis Night, the night of the Witches' Ball, to do large quantities of hallucinogenic drugs out in the countryside.

It took a couple of weeks for this initial gobbet of information to grow into a full-blown controversy, but the eventual effect of that little news item, whether intentional or not, was a unanimous and utterly disproportionate howl of protest from what could be loosely described as the 'establishment' down south. Until now Craigairie had been a fascinating but distant phenomenon. As long as it had remained in Scotland (the 'where it belongs' was unspoken but implicit), everyone was quite happy to discuss it and analyse it at length; a topic of conversation to enliven the most stultified dinner party. But when they threatened to export their heathenish creed into the heart of rural England they were suddenly much too close to home to be tolerated. There were letters to the big newspapers from the local MP and the Bishop of Bath and Wells among others, making it quite clear that they considered this to be a dangerous, provocative and unthinkable incursion by the Paganism which had been running rampant in Scotland.

The immense and almost laughable overreaction which ensued amounted to a tacit acknowledgement of the power of this new cult. It also made the planned festival on Walpurgis Night into an issue that would never have materialized if there had not been such a fuss. To make a commitment to be there was not just to declare support for 'New Paganism', but also to make a statement about one's freedom of thought and worship and movement. This became even more marked when an MP who had tried to have the blasphemy laws stretched to include 'witchery' the previous summer, shifted his ground to public order and managed to have the festival banned on the grounds of it being a potential riot.

'So will you go?' Kelvin asked David one night. It was just those two and Rosie in the sitting room at Craigairie, late one night in the middle of April. Although the barn-storming campaign they had been waging across the southern uplands had slackened off in the past week, Christina and Emily were out again, somewhere in Kirkcudbrightshire. Kelvin was prostrate on the sofa, his eyes closed. David was slumped in a chair, working a Sabatier knife through the palm of his hand – some kind of illusion – only Rosie was upright, sitting in front of the fire, cross-legged, rolling a joint by the light of a single, black candle.

'To Glastonbury?' David asked distantly. 'No.'

Rosie looked up, slightly surprised by the firmness of his answer.

'Why not?' Kelvin asked. 'Too much hassle?'

'Partly,' David said, still more interested in what he was doing with the knife than he was in the conversation. 'I don't think we're meant to be down there,' he added.

'What d'you mean?' Rosie asked.

'Just a feeling,' he said. 'They don't seem to understand what we're about down there. I mean, they make the right noises, some of them, but to them it's all theory. Up here you don't have to explain Dé Doveleski to people because they live with her the whole time. You get a pretty good idea of your place in the cosmic scheme of things if it's just you, defending your little patch on a moor somewhere, against nature. Down south you get the impression that nature's mostly something faintly twee, or something that happens to other people. When they do have a big storm, or something, everyone behaves as if it was rather poor form, on nature's part. I think, maybe, it's too comfortable down there, too tame. Besides,' he said, even more distractedly than before, 'we weren't there.'

'Sorry?' Kelvin said, muddled by his tenses.

Rosie correctly identified it as a reference to Christina's gift of foresight.

'Iz saw it?' she asked.

'He nodded.

'Why didn't you tell us?' she asked, hurt and annoyed.

'It was just an idea. Iz knew that something important was going to happen at the end of this month, but she didn't know what. So there was basically nothing to tell until we knew for sure what she had "seen".'

'Is that what you've been waiting for?' Kelvin asked the ceiling.

David nodded. 'Yeah,' he said.

'So what's so important about it, if you aren't even going to be there?' Kelvin asked.

David shrugged. 'Who knows? Iz tends not to be very specific. She was aware of the event and she was also aware of the fact that we wouldn't be there. After that it was just a matter of waiting to see what happened.'

'So where will you be?' Rosie asked. 'Here?'

'No, Orkney.'

Kelvin opened his eyes and turned to look at David in the half-darkness.

'You're going back to Orkney?' he asked. 'How long for?'

'Just a couple of days.'

'For Walpurgis Night?' Rosie asked.

He nodded.

'So what's going to happen there?' she persisted.

'Who knows?' he remarked. Realizing that Rosie was far from satisfied by this, he sighed and sat up. 'Listen, it works like this. Before Annie Moffat, even before we went up to Orkney, Iz woke up one morning and said that something important was going to happen at the end of April. She didn't know what, or why; all she knew was that we would be in Orkney when it happened. We basically forgot about it; she has weird dreams roughly three times a week and most of them are either unimportant or irrelevant. Then Annie Moffat happened and we both got the feeling that our fate had suddenly gone into overdrive. We remembered the dream, but we still didn't know what it meant. Then this Glastonbury thing came up and everything sort of slotted into place. The moment I told Iz about it she said that, yes, that was the event she had seen and the reason why we were supposed to be in Orkney was that we weren't supposed to be at Glastonbury. Don't ask me why not. But when I thought about it, it kind of made sense that we should arrange a sort of counterbalance to Glastonbury as far away from it as possible. It's tense enough already down there without thousands of Scots and gypsies getting it into their heads to march down to Somerset like an invading army . . .' He stopped for breath and shrugged. 'But we still don't know what's going to happen down there. We decided to let it run its own course, without interfering, which is why we haven't actually said we've got no intention of being there.' He stopped again and let this sink in, which took a couple of minutes. It was Kelvin who broke the silence first.

'Why?' he asked suddenly. 'I mean, I don't understand why you're doing all this. Is it all working towards something, or are you just stumbling about in the dark?' He paused. Rosie was giving him a surprised, appraising look. Kelvin continued.

'I mean, we've all been watching you both in the last few weeks and I, for one, am beginning to get the shits. It's as if you're trying to change the world in ten easy steps. First you grab everyone's attention, then you build a power-base, then you spread the word, then you consolidate, then you spread it a bit further. It's all very . . . manipulative.'

David thought for a good minute before answering.

'It's not what you think,' he said finally. 'Most of the time we haven't a clue what's going on in our lives; we're just as bemused and freaked out as you are. It's not like we're trying to be messianic.' There was an admission in the way he stressed 'trying'.

'It just works out looking that way, right?' Rosie asked.

'Maybe,' he replied honestly. 'I don't know what it looks like from your side, or to the gypsies, or to everyone else. All I can tell you is that we really tried to fight this thing and it didn't work and it wasn't an awful lot of fun either. So now we're going with the flow. I wish I could tell you where it's all going, I really do; but I don't know and neither does Iz. All we can tell you is that as long as we're caught up in this, for however long that is, everything that happens to us is pre-ordained. We're at Craigairie because we were here. We are what we are because it was always that way.'

'For what?' Rosie asked.

He shrugged but did not answer.

'Don't you ever want to know?' she asked.

'Not much.'

There was a long silence.

'So what else has Iz seen that you haven't told us about?' she inquired.

'Bits and pieces. Nothing important.'

'How d'you know what I consider to be important?'

'I don't. I don't even know if what she has seen is important . . .' He paused, saw that she was unconvinced, and went on.

'Listen, her gift isn't like that, it doesn't work like that. Her visions don't come in any sort of context; they don't set down a neat list of what's going on, when and where. She just gets tiny, fractured glimpses of the future, kind of like *déjà vu* backwards.' He saw Rosie trying to get her head around this explanation, then deciding that it was an unnecessary sidetrack and giving up on it abruptly. The secret of getting the truth out of David was to pin him down to simple facts and not to allow him off on confusing tangents. She was still dissatisfied with his explanation, and he, in turn, was beginning to be exasperated by her incomprehension.

'D'you really want to be told about every half-cocked prediction Iz makes? You think it's like a great gift, right?' He shook his head. 'Believe me, it's not a thing that gives you any peace of mind. It removes any passing hopes you might have had that you're in control of your own destiny without giving you anything more substantial in return than unconnected snippets of the future, all jumbled up in a sort of unchronological mess. You go through the motions of plotting your next moves, but mostly you can flip a coin a hundred times and it makes no difference in the end.' He paused momentarily.

'Haven't you ever noticed how Iz refers to her visions in the past tense? It *did* happen, they were doing such and such, it *has* happened. Your future becomes your past and the only thing you know about it for sure is that you can't change it. Even Iz says she'd prefer to know nothing and get on with life in a state of blissful ignorance, rather than having about an eighth of an idea what's going to happen and spending the entire time wondering when and how.'

Rosie contemplated this for a while, working her way through it until she understood what it was about everything he had been saying that kept setting off alarm bells somewhere deep inside her. It was the same with Christina. Whenever anyone asked either of them about the future they refused to give an answer. Christina evaded it with a sort of airy cheerfulness which implied that it would all work itself out, David gave lengthy and clever explanations of why he refused to talk about it, but neither of them, in the end, would discuss it.

'That wasn't an answer,' she said to David.

Kelvin humphed from the sofa. David sighed.

'I don't trust prophecies,' he said. 'There seems to have been a constant undercurrent of soothsaying behind a lot of what's happened to us and I just don't trust it. I mean, I'm not saying that there isn't a grain of truth in it all, but it doesn't give anything like the whole truth. If you listen to it you end up strung out on all sorts of shit that only means anything if it's in context with all sorts of other shit you don't know about. Like Walpurgis Night, for instance; Iz saw it, but her sight failed to tell her the important bits, or about Annie Moffat, without which Glastonbury wouldn't be happening.' He shook his head dismissively.

'I prefer to deal with the present and forget the bits of the future Iz might have glimpsed. I plan for eventualities, juggle ifs – if this happens, then that might happen and so on. It's not an infallible science, but at least it isn't as nebulous as a prophecy. So I *won't* tell you what Iz sees, or thinks she sees, because it's not something I believe you should lose sleep over; which is about all they ever really do for you . . . OK?'

'Aren't you just scared of admitting that the prophecies are true because if you do, you have to admit you're the Nymatili?' Rosie asked quietly, knowing that she was treading on very thin ice, but determined to pursue the discussion through to the point everyone was always stopping short of.

David snorted and stood up, shaking his head. 'No.'

'Why not?'

'Ask him.' He nodded towards Kelvin, then headed for the door. 'Or the Romanies. It's called an S.E.P.'

'A sep?' Rosie asked as he left the room.

'Somebody Else's Problem,' Kelvin translated.

They heard him go out through the front door, on his way over to the stone, where he would wait in the cold darkness on the silent, wordless hillside where he and Christina both retreated to escape the world the stone had created for them, until Christina returned and joined him there.

For a long time after he had gone Rosie and Kelvin remained in a still, ruminative silence. They both knew that he had not told them anything like the truth, although he had, as always, steered a careful route around any outright lies. Since Annie Moffat any Glasnost there was at Craigairie had been granted sparingly and grudgingly. It was as if they now suspected the truth about themselves and it was too grim a suspicion to be shared. Whatever they had, their extraordinary power and all the priceless gifts it had bestowed upon them, Craigairie, the stone, even their love, drew them inexorably away from even their closest friends.

Rosie realized and understood, with a horrifying certainty, what it was that hurt like heartburn behind everything David had been saying, what it was he was fighting against and denying and evading. He knew when he would die, they both did. They knew where their witching stone was leading them and there was nothing they could do to break free of it, but vainly hope they were wrong. Christina, the eternal optimist, was far further from the abyss of despair into which David was already slipping, but they both knew, in their hearts, that their suspicions were true.

Kelvin began to recite, in Romany:

> 'The flame of knowledge burns short and bright
> A bolt of lightning in the night
> The spark which burns the forest down
> A fierce gleam, then gone.'

' "The song of the Nymatil",' Rosie murmured. She looked up and gazed at David's best friend for a moment, knowing that he knew what she now knew. She ran a tired hand through her thick mane of hair and sighed.

'I don't know whether I have the strength to see this all through to a conclusion,' she said. 'It all seemed so wild and glorious and exciting a year ago, but now it's like we're all following those two to the edge of . . .' She paused, shaking her head. After a moment, she worked herself up to the last handful of words, plucked from the aching core of her anxiety.

'I don't want to wake up one morning and find them gone and me left too far from home to find my way back. It scares me.' She stopped again, staring down at the floor in front of her, shaking her head slowly.

Right up to the last moment David and Christina kept everyone guessing as to where they intended to be on Walpurgis Night. Two days before it was due to take place they were still in the south of Scotland, doing what they had been doing for the previous eight weeks. Kelvin and Linnhe Thurston had gone north a fortnight earlier, taking with them the first of a long, straggling line of gypsies from the Atchin-tan. Emily and Edward had hung around for another ten days.

Rosie was the last to leave, the day after Ed and Em. She would have liked to have been able to stay with David and Christina, but she had agreed to be interviewed by an American magazine in a moment of unguarded euphoria, shortly after Annie Moffat, and could not now extricate herself from it. So she went down to London, leaving David and Christina alone at Craigairie for the first time since February. They remained there, to enjoy the increasingly rare pleasure of being alone together, if only for a few days.

They watched the last few days of the run-up to Glastonbury with some amusement. Thousands of people were converging upon Somerset; some because of the unnecessary banning of the festival, which made it all the more attractive and exciting; some on the off-chance of seeing David and Christina there; some just because it had become the hip place to be on that one weekend of the year. The fact that David and Christina had no intention of making an appearance there and had hitherto made a point of staying north of the border, seemed to be irrelevant.

Meanwhile, David had planned for Orkney meticulously. He had warned the gypsies about it as far back as the beginning of February, knowing that there were at least a dozen kyle-yaks in the Atchin-tan who could foretell the future just as well as Christina; which made it all the more important to warn them about anything important before they made their own plans and disrupted *his* careful planning. He had also been up to Orkney, on his own, back in March and had warned Dorothy Thurston that he and Christina would be there on Walpurgis Night, quite possibly with several thousand 'believers' in tow. He had sent her niece, Linnhe, north with Kelvin, followed by Edward and Emily (who was known as the Little Nymatil in Orkney) just so that everyone up there was absolutely sure that the Mother Coven had made a commitment to be there.

The atmosphere in Orkney, when they arrived, was halfway between that of a very large carnival and a mass pilgrimage. It was a tribute to David's stage-management and Christina's awesome pulling power that in all but media attention, Orkney looked set to wipe the floor with the celebrations at Glastonbury. By the most conservative estimates there were already upwards of thirty-five thousand people on Orkney two days before Walpurgis Night, a number which could easily double in the last forty-eight hours. There was a sprawling temporary encampment along the shore of the Loch of Stenness, half a mile from the Ring of Brogar, in which there were at least eight thousand people, and it was growing by the hour.

With all the endless speculation going on down south about whether the presence of the New Pagans at Glastonbury would spark a riot there was a certain amount of smug satisfaction permeating Orkney that no such thing could even be contemplated there. The weather was beautiful, the crowds were good-humoured, patient and jolly and the locals, unlike the inhabitants of Glastonbury, were proud to be staging such a festival. In Glastonbury town, according to news reports, the shops, pubs, tea-shoppes, guesthouses and hotels had either battened down their hatches in anticipation of the crowds, or were charging exorbitant prices in the knowledge that they had a captive market. There were some fifteen thousand people dossing down in the open; hungry, reviled, sullen and harassed, albeit unwillingly, by a large police presence. To make matters worse still, it was pissing with rain.

In Orkney the general feeling was that if everyone behaved themselves and shared what they had, inhabitants and incomers alike, the whole thing would pass off triumphantly. The will to make it work was reinforced by the widespread belief that this, not Glastonbury, was the real Walpurgis Night festival, the genuine article. With coven witches from all over Scotland, Ireland, northern England and even some from the continent, and gypsies from as far afield as Munster in Ireland, Brittany, some from the south of France and even one or two from the Balkans, there was an authenticity to the proceedings which was notice-ably lacking at Glastonbury, where a motley bunch of middle-class city hoorays calling themselves New Pagans mixed with dubious 'travelling folk', with serious attitude problems, and an embarrassing number of people who only went because they thought there was going to be an impromptu rock concert.

The only thing that was needed to put the final stamp on the Orcadian Festival was the appearance of the Nymatili.

It was only when David and Christina actually showed up that every-one relaxed. They arrived on the Saturday afternoon, the day before the festival was to take place. Instead of going to Dorothy Thurston's house in Kirkwall, where they were most likely to find Emily and the rest, they went straight to Birsay, on the north-western corner of mainland

Orkney, where Kelvin, Emily and Edward had gone for a drink. How they knew where to look was one of those little mysteries which made them both remarkable and remarkably infuriating.

Birsay was a beautiful place to be on a late spring afternoon: a tiny village with a shop, a pub, an old mill which sold home produce to tourists and the elegant ruins of a medieval earl's palace. There was a wedge-shaped island, called the Brough, separated from the land by a causeway, which reared its battered cliffs into the face of the Atlantic. Beyond that there was nothing short of Nova Scotia. Kelvin, Em and Ed had been up on the very top of the cliffs before the tide began to cut them off from the mainland, marvelling at the glassy ocean, so calm and tame that it seemed it could never be so rude as to throw a storm at the tall red cliffs and rolling green hills of Orkney.

Once back on the mainland they sat outside the only pub, drinking beer on the grass, amongst the late narcissi, under the pale blue sky. There were a few other people around, but it was less crowded than most of the rest of Orkney. The last thing they expected, as they drank their beer and absorbed the sun, was to see Christina and David walking along the road from the palace, the former skipping along beside the latter with the peculiar, wonderful dancing walk she performed when she was feeling her most sprite-like. When she saw Emily, her brother and Kelvin she broke into a run, leaving David behind.

She sat down between Edward and Emily, putting her arms around their shoulders, and grinned at Kelvin, who was trying not to stare at her, and failing.

'Good to see us, huh?'

It took an exercise of will for him to tear his eyes away from her. Even after a couple of weeks she was a surprising and remarkable creature; not so much angelic as something created to tempt angels; a potent and subtle mixture of grace, apparent innocence and a remote but distinct air of mischief.

She stretched and yawned. 'Goodness, it's nice here,' she said through her yawn. 'Fuckin' awful down south.'

'Considering the number of witches up here it'd be bloody criminal if it rained,' Kelvin remarked laconically.

'Talking of witches . . .' David said, returning with two pints and handing one to Christina. 'Where's Rose?'

'She called yesterday,' Emily said. 'She was going to call you, but I guess you'd already left. After she'd done her interview she went to Glastonbury, just to see what was going down. She called from there to say that things were looking so rough that she was going to stay. She said something about wanting to ask you if you could send down some of the more reliable young gypsies from the Atchin-tan; the ones who've always taken responsibility for protecting you. She said she needed some "flick-knife diplomacy" down there.' She glanced at Kelvin.

He shrugged. 'We hand-picked fifty good Romanies and sent them down to give Rosie a hand,' Kelvin said. He hunched up one shoulder and leered grotesquely, like Quasimodo. 'Did we do well, masters?'

They both laughed.

That night, after they had seen the Orcadian witches, after they had put Emily on to the last aeroplane out, sending her south to keep Rosie company and to lend some extra clout at Glastonbury, after they had done the rounds of the sprawling encampment on the shore of the Loch of Stenness, showing themselves to their supporters, David and Christina retreated to one of the outlying islands, Papa Westray, on the north-western edge of the archipelago. They sat up on the cliffs under the new moon, huddled together against the cool Atlantic breeze, listening to the waves crashing on the rocks far below.

They had not spoken for hours, but when Christina finally broke their elongated silence it was to snigger quietly.

'What is it?' David asked.

'Emily,' she replied simply.

David laughed. 'She's training on a treat, isn't she?' he said. 'I don't know what we'd do without her and Rosie.'

'All sorts of silly things,' she replied, a smile still in her voice. She giggled again. 'The funny thing about Em is that she's the only one who has any control over Kelv. Everyone else treats him like a lost cause, but Em stuns him with straightforwardness. *Elle est forte, la petite.*'

'I hope they'll be all right down there,' David murmured.

'They'll be fine,' she replied. 'That little, I know.'

'And us?'

She did not answer for a long time, but he could sense a maelstrom of different thoughts whirling around in her mind.

'We'll be OK,' she said at last, with little enthusiasm.

'Just OK?' he asked.

She yawned. 'They've all come to see the Nymatili,' she said. 'And they won't be disappointed. I just wish sometimes we could be us to more people than just each other.'

When Dorothy Thurston arrived at Brogar at eight o'clock on the evening of Walpurgis Night, she was stunned both by the number of people there and by the atmosphere. Even the hour-and-a-half-long traffic jam in the fifteen miles from Kirkwall had not prepared her for the size of the crowds gathering around Brogar and Stenness. On the way, when the traffic had ground to a halt for so long that people left their vehicles and wandered around amongst the cars, exchanging gossip, drink and whatever else they had to offer, with complete strangers, she had been struck by their general good humour. According to police reports on the radio there were upwards of fifty thousand people converging on the centre of Orkney. The majority of them were young and most of them were drinking, but there was not a hint of unpleasantness or danger. There was excitement, anticipation, happiness and enormous patience. It was a joy to behold.

She wandered around in the balmy spring evening, soaking up the atmosphere. The majority of the crowds were down by the Loch of Stenness enjoying an impromptu barbecue a mile long, swimming in the loch and consuming enough marijuana to keep a Third World dictatorship in power for at least a year. Dorothy remained up on the hill of Brogar, where the crowds were much thinner, as if respecting the sanctity of the stones. Looking down on the crowds from above she fell into a musing reverie about the indisputable stars of the evening. She could see them occasionally, moving about down below, always surrounded by a dense swirl of admirers, like a magnetic field eddying around them. She knew better than to claim some personal right to David and Christina, but having known them almost since they met each other she felt justified in being proud of them. They had come a long way since their first visit to Orkney a year earlier.

They had frightened her then. They had even disconcerted her when they were in Orkney at the beginning of the year. There was nothing in their culture, religious backgrounds, class, upbringings, even race, which equipped them to be the recipients of the kind of power they had discovered at Craigairie. It was something no mortal could hope to comprehend in its entirety, in a lifetime, let alone inside a year. If misused, or employed naïvely, or selfishly, or for personal gain, it was the most destructive force on earth. Knowing this, Dorothy Thurston had been as disturbed by Christina's peculiar streak of innocence as by David's lack of it. If the former prevailed, they were likely to underestimate the danger of what they were playing with; if the latter gained the ascendancy, they could well slip into megalomania.

But now that she saw them mingling with their followers she knew, with a great surge of relief, that they had themselves and their staggering power under control. In fact they were not just on top of it; they had it in their hands like a hose-pipe, drenching people with it; like a bell-rope, pulling on it and chiming it out over the crowds. What they were doing, if one stopped to analyse it, was almost too astonishing to comprehend. It was the beguiling simplicity of it which was so awesome. They were generating love. You could feel it in the air and see it on the faces of the people around them.

Finally, after a year of worrying, a knot in Dorothy Thurston's soul relaxed. They had given themselves up to their destiny, allowing it to steer them wherever it chose. That took strength. It took wisdom and courage and an enormous understanding of this power, this magic they had inherited. By all the weird contortions of fate, it had found the right two people. For the first time since she had heard the word, Dorothy understood what Nymatili meant.

They found her, up on the hill of Brogar, at about ten-thirty in the evening, leaving the sprawling, joyous party down by the loch to look after itself. She sized them up for a long moment, then smiled, inclining her head to them.

'Hail, Christina,' she said. 'Blessed art thou amongst women.'

'Careful,' Christina admonished her, grinning.

'And you, Ghostdancer!' Dorothy said, turning to David. 'Your alternative Witches' Ball seems to be coming off with flying colours.'

'We haven't pulled off our *coup de grâce*, yet,' he said.

'There's more?'

They looked at each other and smiled.

For David and Christina the evening was endless, a series of similar conversations with a constant stream of wide-eyed and excited people, a blur of thousands of people who seemed to know them but they had never seen before in their lives. Occasionally there were people they had to recognize, from Orkney, or from Carrick, Galloway and the borders. With these they invariably adopted the same pattern of Christina recognizing the faces and David recalling the names then both of them giving the people a few extra moments of their time. They shook so many hands that their arms ached and kissed so many people that their cheeks were raw. Christina had her hands grabbed and kissed so often that she developed blisters on the back of both.

They did not participate in the wild, joyous party which developed all along the shore of the loch, across the causeway to Stenness and up the shore of the loch on the other side, although they were in the middle of it all evening. They snatched a few, half-charred sausages cooked on one of the many instant barbecues, drank about a bottle of whisky each but did not get remotely drunk, took pulls from several hundred joints but did not get at all stoned and refused enough Ecstasy and acid to send a small army into orbit. When they rested, or settled in one place for more than five minutes, crowds of people gravitated to them and gazed, slack-jawed, at Christina, hanging on every word either of them said and jostling to be in the front row closest to them. If ever the crowds jostled too much their scruffy but efficient gypsy bodyguards cleared a space for them, appearing as if from nowhere and protecting their Nymatili with their own inimitable mixture of quiet menace and brute force.

Finally, at about ten-thirty, David and Christina slipped away from the crowds and climbed the dark hill of Brogar, up to the circle of stones. After they had spoken to Dorothy Thurston and she had gone, they waited. Linnhe and Edward came and found them talking quietly. They greeted each other with high-fives, but understated to the point that they barely brushed each other's palms. Christina lay down flat on her back and David crouched beside her, nursing a bottle of whisky between his legs.

'How are you?' asked Edward, concerned by their obvious exhaustion.

'Knackered,' Christina said from the ground.

'What now?' Linnhe inquired, handing David a lit cigarette.

He thanked her and stood up with an involuntary groan.

'Fire and silence,' he replied cryptically. 'Then more of that.' He pointed down towards the shore of the loch. Somebody was playing the bagpipes down there, the noise muffled by the background hubbub of a very large crowd enjoying itself, heard from half a mile away.

'How many people d'you think are here?'' he asked.

'Over fifty thousand,' Edward said. 'Telephone numbers.'

David snorted and took a swig of whisky.

'D'you think we'll make the news?' he asked.

'You already did,' Linnhe said. 'The Scottish news, at least. I saw it just before I came here.'

'What did they say?' Christina asked.

'That it was a very good-natured crowd,' Linnhe replied. 'And that it was the worst parking nightmare in Scottish history. Apparently they drafted in fuzz from as far south as Aberdeen and Dundee to help park all the cars.'

'Where did you two park?' Christina asked.

Edward laughed. 'Just this side of Finstown. It took an hour and a half to get here from the car.'

'You could send one of the Romanies for it later on,' Christina remarked. 'They're in a helpful mood, after all.'

'Aren't they just,' David agreed ironically. 'You could almost say they're behaving responsibly.'

'Almost,' Christina said. She pushed herself up on to her elbows. 'Talking of which, where's Kelvin?'

'Not behaving responsibly,' Linnhe replied, with the long-suffering tone of voice which afflicted anyone who had the unenviable task of looking after Kelvin. 'He dropped some Ecstasy and was last seen telling a small yew tree that he loved it.'

They all laughed.

'Honey, I don't know why you bother,' David said.

'Because he needs me,' she replied simply.

'Reason enough,' Christina murmured. She sat up straight, then offered a hand to David and he duly pulled her to her feet. She took the whisky bottle from him and took a long swig.

'What's the time?' she asked, when she had recovered her voice.

'Quarter to,' Edward said.

His sister took a deep breath. 'OK. To business.'

They left Edward and Linnhe and walked up to the old tumulus which sat on top of the low hill above the stone circle. When they reached the very top they stopped and turned to look back down. They were the first people to have walked up there all evening, or at least since the dew had settled. They could see the two dark lines of their footsteps cut into the dew, which was glistening a faint silver under the young moon.

'Will fire wake it?' Christina asked quietly.

He shook his head slowly. 'I don't know.'

They stood in silence for a moment.

'D'you want to do the honours?' she asked.

He shook his head again. 'No. You do it. But first I have a little surprise touch.'

'What is it?' she asked, smiling.

He raised one hand into the air.

'Listen,' he said.

'What?'

He did not reply. After about half a minute she began to hear the sound of a bell, right on the edge of hearing. It was a deep, rich, reverberating 'bong' and it grew gradually until it seemed to fill the air. She turned around slowly on the spot, trying to work out where it was coming from. As she did so she was aware of a gathering quietness spreading through the crowds below, as if it had even penetrated the noise of the party. It was not deafening, or even especially loud, but it was resonant and beautiful, accentuating silence rather than breaking it. Christina laughed out loud.

'It's an illusion,' he said, obviously well pleased with himself.

Just before midnight on Walpurgis Night at Brogar, upwards of fifty-three thousand people were silenced by that mysterious and soul-aching chiming of a single bell. It continued for about two minutes, causing the huge crowd to stop whatever they were doing and listen in wonder. Then, with a crack of thunder from a cloudless sky, the tall bonfire in the middle of the stone circle of Brogar erupted into life, firing a blue flame hundreds of feet into the still night air. It burned with such ferocity that it consumed itself almost instantly, throwing clouds of dancing sparks like swarms of red fireflies outwards in a plume which glowed dully on the lochs. Then, as it died down, a vibration shuddered through the ground; like a cold engine starting up, it seemed to splutter and then caught.

It was almost unbearably wonderful. It was as if the whole hill had suddenly come to life; the more one was aware of it, the more bizarre and extraordinary it became. It was such an unnatural thing for a hill to be doing and yet it was enormously reassuring, like hearing the very ground sing for joy. People began to go down on their hands and knees, the better to soak up the continuous vibration, or even spreadeagled themselves, face down, so that it would enter their bodies from head to toes. It was hypnotic, orgasmic. A low murmur of ecstasy rippled over the hill and then a hush descended, so complete that the small, rippling waves on the lochs filled the air, merging with subliminal humming which came from the ground.

Edward opened his eyes after several minutes, slightly surprised to discover that they had been closed. He looked around, slowly emerging from the blissful daze which had held him enthralled since the hill awoke. The fire in the middle of the circle had died down to a small pile of fiercely glowing embers, but there were other fires still burning in a wide circle on all the surrounding hilltops. Around Brogar, all over the hillside, there were hundreds, thousands, tens of thousands of people sprawled all over the ground. Some were wandering through the litter of humanity like somnambulists, occasionally stumbling into each other and hugging silently. It looked like the aftermath of a mass love-in. The only people who looked at all alert and normal were the gypsies, who were standing inside the circle, around the fire, talking quietly. Edward contemplated going down to join them but then thought better of it. He looked for Linnhe and saw her about twenty yards away, clutching on to one of the stones, dead to the world. Finally he remembered Christina and David and went in search of them, up to the burial mound on top of the hill, which was still the only place clear of prostrate humans. He found them sitting in the grass opposite each other, holding hands and staring into one another's eyes.

'Fire and silence, huh?' he said as he neared them.

Christina, who had her back to him, looked over her shoulder and smiled.

'And bells,' she said. 'Don't forget the bells.' She sounded hoarse as if she had been weeping and her brother thought he saw the glistening of tears in her eyes.

'How could I forget the bells?' he said, sitting himself down beside her. She moved, so that she could reach David with one arm whilst encircling Edward's shoulders with the other, drawing them both to her. They remained there in a tight huddle for what seemed like an age and Edward was not aware that Christina was weeping anew until she sniffed and pulled away, shaking her fringe over her eyes. Her cheeks were wet.

'What is it?' he asked.

She shook her head, but did not reply.

Edward turned to David. 'What is it?' he asked again.

'Nothing,' David replied quietly. 'We just realized something we hadn't worked out 'til now.'

'What?' Edward asked.

'Something the gypsies said about us,' Christina murmured.

Edward thought about this for a few moments.

'You mustn't listen to everything the gypsies say,' he said. 'I mean, these're people who seriously think hedgehogs a delicacy.'

There was not a problem in the world, according to Ed, which could not be belittled with a joke. It was a quality that made him invaluable.

*

Six hundred miles away, at Glastonbury, Rosie was feeling much the same way about Emily. She and Em would never be close friends; Em was too instinctive, too exuberant, basically too young, to be the sort of person Rosie chose as a friend. But she would have taken her on a tiger shoot with her, or to a potential riot.

It was not just that Emily had grown into a deceptively powerful witch, and was growing stronger with every passing day. It helped, certainly, that she had Christina's ability and inclination to dazzle and dumbfound with her looks, although not to the same degree. Christina called this trick 'wearing her magic' and Emily, alone of her acolytes, had mastered it. Rosie could induce calm, but it was a slow-working spell and needed Emily's knack of stopping people in their tracks before it could hook into them and take effect.

But there was more to her than just her witchery. She also had a weird and incongruous understanding of the most tricky, difficult, cussed of Craigairie's following. The gypsies loved her, thinking her funny and droll; a tigress in the form of a kitten. She also got on surprisingly well with the hippies and travelling folk who had adopted New Paganism down south. Rosie was too aloof and aristocratic for them and did not bother to hide the fact that she considered them to be more trouble than their support was worth. But Emily treated them with the same cheerful good-humour that she gave to the gypsies and everybody else.

By the time Em arrived, early on Sunday morning, Rosie had managed to defuse some of the tension at Glastonbury. She had seen the Chief Constable in charge of the large police presence – no mean feat in itself – and had managed to convince him to back off from the confrontational tactics he had been obliged to employ by public, political and media pressure. She had also managed to impress upon him the importance of the cold, hungry, miserable crowds being allowed to buy food, drink and other basic necessities, which had not been possible while most of the shops in the area had been boarded up. She had sent out her small contingent of Romanies to exercise their flick-knife diplomacy, giving them her personal permission to use any means, short of murder, to close down the most blatant of the drug-pushers. They did in two days what the police could not have done in two weeks. They scared the shit out of anyone who crossed them and made one or two examples of malcontents, which had a more immediate impact than a thousand gratuitous arrests.

But the situation was still dangerously volatile. The weather was still awful, cold and wet with a blustery west wind blowing up the Severn from the sea; there was still a great deal of bad blood between the locals and the crowds; Glastonbury Tor was still cordoned off and the atmosphere was still dominated by the belief that there would be a riot before the day was out. Added to this there was also considerable bitterness on the part of the New Pagans that David and Christina were not coming, but had instead, in effect, sent a couple of their sidekicks and a private police force in their place. The news that they had turned up in Orkney the previous evening, thus ending weeks of speculation, had cast a noticeable gloom amongst their followers at Glastonbury and had made the task of creating a better atmosphere even more difficult than it had already been.

Emily's appearance, remarkably, put paid to most of these remaining problems. Alone, neither she nor Rosie could achieve what David described, with deceptive simplicity, as weather-bending. It seemed easy, when he or Christina did it, but it took everything that Rosie and Emily could summon up together, just to break the weather system over Glastonbury. Even then the weather did not turn fair from one minute to the next, but the wind dropped and it stopped raining for the first time in a week, although it was still cool and cloudy.

Emily used her charisma to ease tension. It was much easier to influence people when they were talking not of a riot, but of the extraordinary little creature with straw-blonde hair, great big blue eyes and the magic of a whole coven, all encapsulated in five-foot four of raw sex appeal. It was not difficult to see that if one had never met Christina, Emily was pretty much what one might have expected her to be like. She was an invaluable asset to Rosie, and Christina's cousin was neither so pre-occupied, nor so churlish that she did not appreciate her company.

As the day drew on, the talk of a riot decreased and people even began to enjoy themselves. There was never the intensity of emotion that David and Christina could elicit from the faithful in Orkney, but at least there was a more amicable atmosphere – a minor miracle in its own right. The weather got steadily better until, by the early evening, the sun broke through and Glastonbury basked for a couple of hours at the end of the day. Then, the icing on the cake, Rosie managed to convince the Chief Constable to lift the ban on the Tor for an hour either side of midnight. The news of this spread like wildfire, prompting even the most disaffected to admit that they might have been premature in dismissing these two emissaries of Craigairie as mere hangers-on.

Adrenalin kept David and Christina going until after dawn. If they had slept when the need first struck them, they would have done so before midnight, but they could not. So they called up their reserves of second, third, fourth and fifth wind all at once and fired themselves straight through to daylight. By that point they had outlasted all but the die-hards, who were still dancing unsteadily around the remains of the fires down by the lochside, or sitting around talking quietly. The music from a hundred ghetto-blasters which had been drowned by the volume of people during the night, now wafted up on the still morning air from the last remaining four or five, mingling with the twittering of the larks and the insistent piping of the shore birds. The hill of Brogar still hummed faintly, if one stopped and listened, and there were still a couple of hundred people sprawled upon it, too tired and too blissed-out to move. The gypsies were picking through the carnage of litter, piling it into heaps in a desultory way. They acknowledged the Nymatili with the horned salute as they passed, but did not bother to speak, or could not.

David and Christina were too tired to work any more magic, especially not something as demanding as a shape-shift into some form that would get them home. They stood by the road beside the tall stones of Stenness, leaning against each other, and waited for Edward to come and pick them up.

They finally got home to Dorothy Thurston's house in Kirkwall at half-past seven in the morning. They stumbled across the inner courtyard, asleep on their feet, went into the house, through the hall and into the library on the way to their bedroom. It was an odd room, long, narrow and high, with a vaulted ceiling, as befitted the old chapel of the Nunnery.

Dorothy was waiting for them in one of the chairs by the fireplace. As they came in she stood up, waited for them to reach her, glanced at the television and said quietly, 'You'd better come and watch this. There's been a disaster at Glastonbury.'

'What kind of a disaster?' David asked.

'Twenty-one people,' she replied.

It was on every morning news programme. The riot had happened, but not in the way everyone had expected, predicted and perhaps even hoped. It had started in the town, with local youths from Bristol and thereabouts attacking New Pagans with baseball bats, iron bars, knives and various other lethal weapons. As the police were almost all outside the town, watching the Tor, where the revellers were, the trouble had spread unchecked as the frenzied attack swept out towards them. Although most of them were drunk it had been organized in advance, it must have been; there was a vicious method to the way the attackers held together in a phalanx, cutting down anyone in their way. Most of the people who died had been in the town, or on the road out to the Tor. Most, that was, apart from the nine gypsies who were killed and the thirty-six who were injured.

If it had not been for the gypsies the death toll would have been far higher. They saw the trouble coming in time to wade in and slow it down for a few precious minutes, until the bemused police got their act together and came to their aid. Obeying Rosie's instructions to the letter, the gypsies used every force short of murder to stall the mob, aiming to incapacitate their enemies rather than kill them. The number of stab wounds to legs and arms bore eloquent testimony to their restraint. Although they were outnumbered ten to one they fought with a wild abandon which amazed the mob, who had obviously expected a passive target for their vicious neo-Nazi fury.

For about half an hour there was utter mayhem, before the police brought the situation under control with a series of baton charges.

To watch it on television was harrowing, unbearable. There were half a dozen camera crews at Glastonbury, but none of them could capture anything but the chaos. There were people running, shrieking, cannoning into each other. David and Christina saw gypsies they knew being carried out of the fray covered in blood, but they only caught one glimpse of either Rosie or Emily and that was of Rosie right in the middle of the fighting, her face contorted with desperation and fury, trying to wave people back.

In a way, the most graphic images were the scenes of the aftermath that morning. There were ambulances queuing up like a taxi rank, arriving and leaving at a steady rate, ferrying away the walking wounded who were still standing or sitting around in a shocked daze, heads hanging, waiting to be moved. Small huddles of youths were holding on to each other, weeping. The ground was littered with bottles, iron bars, bricks and debris. There were enough bloodstains on the road to satisfy the morbid interest of scores of news crews.

The only glimmer of a silver lining on the terrible cloud that hung over Glastonbury was the general agreement of all who had been there that the New Pagans were not to blame; on the contrary, they were the innocent victims.

David and Christina sat, hugging each other, beside the telephone, until nine o'clock in the morning, praying for Rosie or Emily to ring. They were too tired, too shocked and too remorse-ridden to weep. Christina kept murmuring, 'I should've known,' although there was no way she could have. David, too, blamed himself for not realizing that such a thing might happen. Dorothy Thurston tried to convince them that there was nothing they could have done to stop the festival from going ahead, but it had been their names which had brought so many people to Glastonbury and their creed which had caused such a violent reaction. And if that wasn't bad enough, nine Romanies had died, many more had been injured and neither Rosie nor Emily was yet accounted for.

When the telephone finally rang Christina snatched it off the hook even before the echo of the bell had faded.

'Hi, it's Em.' She sounded almost businesslike.

Christina passed a hand across her brow and sank back against David, letting out a ragged sigh of relief.

'Thank God, thank God,' she said, her voice quavering. 'Rosie?'

'She's OK. A few cuts and bruises, but she's fine. She's gone to bed.'

'I'm sorry,' Christina said. 'I'm so, so sorry.'

'Don't be silly,' Emily said tiredly. 'You can't know everything. It's not your fault if a pack of ignorant savages go berserk.' She let out a quick, mirthless laugh. 'Besides, if it hadn't been for them, we would've

pulled off a bit of a triumph down here. Rosie called them brown-shirts . . .'
There was a short pause. 'But actually they were mostly quite well dressed.'

David saw Christina smile suddenly and shake her head in silent
wonder and gave her a questioning look. She shook her head again. It
was the second time that day she had been jolted out of a gloom by an
unexpected remark.

'But anyway,' Emily went on, 'I heard it all worked out perfectly up
there.'

'Yeah. It was fine.'

'How's Ed?'

'He's well. D'you want me to go and get him?'

'No, don't bother. I ought to go to bed. I was just calling to tell you
we're OK. Tell him I'll call tomorrow sometime.'

'Sure. Thanks for calling, Em. I can't tell you how relieved I am and
how sorry we both are that we put you through that.'

'Don't apologize,' Emily said. 'It wasn't your fault. Oh, Iz, could you
tell David something from me?'

'Yeah?'

'Tell him we've got our martyrs.'

Christina's jaw dropped. 'What?' she asked quietly.

'Well, I once asked him what he thought it would take to make
people sit up and take notice of Craigairie and he said he thought it'd
take a miracle or a martyr. Well, you cured Annie Moffat; now you've
got your martyrs.'

After she hung up Christina sat staring into space for a couple of
minutes.

'Are they all right?' David asked at last.

'What?' Christina asked. 'Oh, yeah, fine. In fact Emily's positively
philosophical.'

Sir James Graham sat at his breakfast table, reading a newspaper over the
top of his spectacles. He was leaning back in his throne-like chair, his
elbows resting on its arms, the paper effectively screening him from the
rest of the room.

He was reading about Christina.

Every morning, almost without exception, since before Christmas, he
had read everything the papers had to say about Craigairie and its
attendant witchery. He had even been sent local Orcadian newspapers
by his niece, Rosie, who had been the only regular contact he had with
the inside of the Mother Coven, ultimately with his daughter.

On the surface it seemed to be a leisurely process; a weighing-up of
conflicting reports and opinions from a detached distance; but he well
knew that interest had long since given way to something akin to an

obsession. In a way he could dodge having to think directly about what Christina was up to by attempting to observe, assimilate; to be a historian rather than a father. He had long realized that Craigairie would be remembered and discussed after he was dead and gone, probably after Christina was around to explain what it had all been about. To that end he had started a file of cuttings, articles and a few of his own comments, for posterity. From this he had been able to discern patterns, both in the behaviour of his daughter and her friends and in the way the press reacted to them. He could see how Craigairie had thrown everything it had into a few months of hectic activity, keeping itself in the fickle spotlight of public interest as if they knew they could not sustain it.

He had also seen how the initial euphoria over Annie Moffat had soon turned sour when the media began to realize what lay behind the miracle. By definition Craigairie posed a threat to a Christian society, and it did not take long before some of the more extreme newspapers, particularly the tabloids, began looking around for excuses to put Annie Moffat on the shelf and to find something dirty with which to tarnish Christina and the rest. They had begun, as is their wont, by digging back into the past of the Mother Coven. David Armstrong's C.V. was unimpeachable, and besides he had a weird knack of not being seen, even when he was centre-stage. Christina, however, was infinitely more visible and was also unfortunate enough to have a chequered history.

They were just getting into the swing of a good, old-fashioned personality annihilation when the news of Walpurgis Night had leaked out; a Pagan festival at Glastonbury, a 'reconsecration of the Pagan Cathedral'. It seemed that Craigairie had handed the self-styled upholders of Christianity and the English way exactly what they most wanted; a controversy.

The why-oh-why brigade had risen to the point of hysteria in the last week of April. Then there had been that one, chaotic night. Then, for Sir James with his piles of newspapers, the most telling reaction of all. Silence. Out of the ten newspapers he had read on the following morning, only two had carried the story, although all of them must have been holding their front pages up to the last moment. Four more put it in tiny 'late news' columns, the other four ignored it completely.

It was such a fascinating phenomenon that Sir James frequently found himself quietly regretting Christina's part in it. It was not that he disapproved of her involvement; even though he could not help but be unnerved by the nature of her beliefs, he was secretly proud of her. It was more that it was nigh on impossible to be objective when his favourite child was being called everything from the most dangerous woman since Pandora, to the co-founder of a new religion, a prophetess.

The only thing that he noticed over and over again was that Craigairie had manipulated the press throughout, with a mastery which was little short of Machiavellian. Whatever they were up to, and not even their most ardent defenders were willing to burn many bridges on that score, they were going about it with a sophistication which owed much more to cunning and nous than to anything more esoteric.

The article he was reading on this particular morning was one of a stock of guardedly effusive pieces this newspaper had been producing. It was called 'The alluring face of New Paganism', which meant it was about Christina and, to a lesser extent, her attendant witches. If it had been called something like 'The mystery of Craigairie' it would have been mostly about David. And if it was 'The wisdom of . . .' it would have been some liberal-minded professor attempting to explain Craigairie without admitting that he or she agreed with it.

This article was more amusing than most in as much as it was so banal that it had to be a sort of dry, journalistic joke. It was a well-written and intelligent fashion article – Christina as the modern face of womanhood – which seemed to be laughing both at itself and at the obsession with Craigairie in general. It had taken Sir James a while to see the joke, but when he did a slow smile grew on his face as suspicion became certainty.

'What's funny?' his wife asked as she passed him on her way in from the door.

His head jerked up in surprise. He usually ceased to acknowledge her comings and goings during his first cup of coffee.

He lowered his newspaper and focused on her as she sat down at the far end of an expanse of mahogany, tilting back his head slightly so that he could see through the half-lenses of his spectacles.

'Sorry?'

'What's funny?' she demanded again.

'Oh, nothing. Something about Christina.'

'I should've guessed.' There was such anger in her voice that Sir James was momentarily taken aback.

'All we ever hear is "about Christina".' She said the last two words as if she intended him to hear them in inverted commas. 'Well, frankly *I* don't want to know.'

'Well, maybe you ought to try,' he replied reasonably. After a fraction of a pause he added, 'darling.'

'I don't see why,' she replied.

He gazed at her for a few moments, then put his newspaper down on the table, as if deliberately relinquishing it in favour of the discussion in hand.

'Shall I suggest a couple of reasons?' he said. 'For instance, our daughter's being credited with the meteoric growth of the first serious threat to Christianity in this country in about eleven hundred years. That's quite apart from being the biggest thing to happen to youth iconography since Che Guevara.' He paused. 'You may or may not like it, darling, but either way I think it deserves a few minutes of leisurely discussion, don't you?'

220

'I don't like it and I certainly don't want to talk about it.'

'You don't want to *think* about it,' he replied. 'Come to that *I* don't particularly want to think about it, but we can't very well go on trying to distance ourselves from it, in our own ways.'

'I don't see why I should be force-fed Christina every damned morning, particularly not by you.'

Sir James seemed momentarily chastened, but it was shortlived. He had climbed on to this bull, now he was going to ride it.

'A startlingly inappropriate name, Christina, now I come to think about it,' he said cheerfully. 'Christ-ina. I should have called her Pandora, or Faustina . . . or Morgana, or . . .' He smiled. 'Lucrezia.'

'Lucrezia,' his wife agreed venomously. 'Selfish little witch. You should've refrained from spoiling her all her life. She runs roughshod over us and all you want to do is discuss it.'

Accustomed as he was to his wife's occasionally lateral logical leaps, Sir James had no immediate reply to this particular line. It caught him by surprise. The idea that his treatment of Christina over the years had caused her present behaviour had simply not occurred to him. He sat and stared at her for a while and she stared defiantly back. Finally he moved one shoulder in a faint shrug and carefully put the tips of his fingers together in front of his face.

'Fair enough,' he said. 'I've always got on with Christina much better than with Georgina or Edward. Edward's much younger and Georgina's very much your daughter. Christina's mine. I think this sort of thing is quite normal in families and I also think that what's happening in our family isn't normal at all. I really don't think my occasional favouring of Christina has any bearing whatsoever on her becoming' – he glanced down at the paper and read – 'the High Priestess of New Paganism.'

She frowned at him in irritated confusion. 'What are you talking about?'

'I'm attempting to discuss something of enormous importance and you're completely missing the point, that's what I'm talking about. My darling, our second daughter, one of the fruits of our marriage, is being seen as' – he looked at the paper again – 'the charismatic and seductive co-founder of a new and revolutionary spiritual creed . . .' He looked up again. 'Whatever that means.' They faced each other for a few seconds.

'I just think maybe we should talk about it.'

'There's nothing to say.'

'There's a great deal to say,' he retorted, beginning to get a little irritable. He gesticulated towards the pile of newspapers. 'These aren't just words. People are seriously attributing miracles to Christina. There have been questions in the House about her. The Anglicans, the Presbyterians *and* the Catholics have all said that she and David are tantamount to being heretics.'

'And you let her leave a perfectly good convent two years early because she wanted to "find herself" in Paris,' his wife cut in. Again he was stopped in his tracks by her sideways leap of illogic.

'Do you really think that makes a difference?' he asked with genuine amazement. 'I mean, do you *believe* that?'

'What else am I supposed to believe?' she retorted heatedly. 'That she got all this tosh from a standing stone? The truth that you can't seem to see is that she is shacked-up with a junkie conman and she's drugged up to the eyeballs. All this rubbish about peace and harmony is drug talk. The least you could do is to try and talk some sense into her. Instead you sit there reading your damned newspapers and making tasteless quips about her name.'

'How could I possibly talk sense into Christina when I can't even make sense of what has happened to her?' he retorted angrily. 'You seem to think this is all some elaborate plot Christina has hatched to embarrass you.' He paused and shook his head. 'I tell you, I wouldn't be the only person in the world who would be profoundly relieved if you were right. Sadly, it's not that simple. We've got to try to understand this.'

'There's nothing to understand,' she said, standing up. 'Frankly I don't give a damn what Christina's up to. She can hold a black mass in Hyde Park for all I care, but she's not coming into this house again.' She finished the sentence as she passed him on her way to the door.

'And that's final,' she added before sweeping out of the room, slamming the door behind her.

Sir James sat for a few minutes in contemplative silence. He was exactly halfway between his wife and his daughter, torn between the sense of the former's anger and disgust and the extraordinary attraction of Craigairie. It had an ephemeral quality which he found irresistible, even if he disapproved of it. It was everything he had ever adored in Christina refined down to near-perfection.

And yet there was something hidden inside it which made him terribly uneasy. It was nothing he could put his finger on and it was not a religious qualm. There was something not quite right in David and Christina's attitude, and to a lesser extent in Rosie as well. It was as if they knew something, or suspected something which they were not divulging. Every time he had seen them, from the moment they had cured Annie Moffat, there had been something different in their behaviour. Sometimes they appeared to be as joyous as ever, perhaps a little wilder than before. At others, however, they had seemed tired and sad.

Unfortunately, Sir James's need to talk to Christina was unrequited. She had been everywhere but Craigairie in the weeks after Annie Moffat. Then came Walpurgis Night and, one way and another, it had not been either possible or opportune to interfere until ten days after they came home from Orkney.

If anyone had needed final, clinching proof of the weird, symbiotic relationship between Craigairie, the Romany Atchin-tan and the inhabitants of the Duisk valley, that homecoming left no more room for doubt. Wherever it exported itself and whatever happened to it in the outside world, this phenomenon belonged to Carrick. It had begun there, had grown there, consolidated itself there and it was to the safety of those wild, open moors and hidden green valleys that it ran when something awful happened to it. Facile phrases such as 'New Paganism' meant nothing there, because Craigairie had always been where it was, tucked away in the darkest corner of the bleak hills, where not even time had been able to reach it. And the empty opinions of the outside world meant less than nothing; Craigairie and its habitants could be praised or criticized by the people of the Duisk, because it was theirs to praise and criticize if and when it deserved it. But when they came limping home to lick the wounds they had received on the outside, Carrick closed ranks around them so fast that a shrew could not have sneaked through to them unbidden or unchallenged. Far from eroding the popular appeal of Craigairie in Galloway, Glastonbury had finally made people realize that this was theirs and they could be proud of it.

The return of the nine dead gypsies from the south was a peculiarly moving affair. Thousands of locals lined the road to pay their silent respects as the coffins were carried from the station to a little valley behind the Atchin-tan, two miles away, where they were to be buried. The entire Mother Coven was there; Emily, the Graham cousins bedecked in tartan and David Armstrong, grim as stone, speaking a few words by the gravesides, and reducing everyone to tears.

Sir James was there, but he could not bring himself to approach Christina, so he left it for a couple of days, then called Craigairie and agreed to meet her the following evening, at an extraordinary meeting of local folk in the Barrhill kirk.

When he arrived there he climbed up into the organ gallery and watched the proceedings down below while he waited for his daughter. The irony of four hundred people crushed into a consecrated kirk in order to discuss how best to show solidarity and support for a Pagan cult was not lost on him. Craigairie had not just supplanted Christianity here, its supporters were even using Christ's house as their debating chamber.

He sat up in the darkness of the organ gallery and gazed down at normal people, farmers and housewives, shopkeepers, smallholders and most of the local masonic lodge, suddenly aroused to vehement fury over suggestions in English newspapers that they were harbouring a band of dangerous lunatics. These were not naïve youths, or career subversives cashing in on a volatile situation. They were real people.

He was so engrossed in it all that he did not notice Rosie come up the stairs, with a six-man, four-woman Romany escort. They remained at the back of the gallery while she went down and slid on to the pew beside her uncle.

'Christina couldn't make it, I'm afraid,' she said. 'Unavoidably detained in the Atchin-tan.'

'Someone die?' he asked facetiously, faintly irked to have been stood up by his daughter.

'Actually, yes,' Rosie replied. 'One of the kids from Glastonbury. Just nineteen.'

'I'm sorry,' Sir James said, genuinely abashed.

'Don't be,' Rosie replied. 'He could never have been in life what he is in death.'

'I don't know why, but that sounds oddly brutal,' Sir James muttered.

She shrugged. 'I realize you wanted to speak to Iz, but if I can help, I'd be glad.'

He looked at her for a moment, nodded slowly and turned his attention back to the proceedings down below. The minister had appeared and was standing in the pulpit, trying to make his voice heard over his wayward flock, who were ignoring him. Sir James watched with a peculiar half-frown, torn between feeling rather sorry for the man and wondering why he was bothering. He obviously thought that he still had a congregation, not able to understand that he had long since lost them and was now deep in missionary country.

Sir James watched for a while, then seemed to come to a decision.

'What does Nymatili mean?' he asked.

Rosie began to give him the usual spiel about 'the Chosen', 'the Favoured', but he cut her off in mid-flow.

'No, what does it *mean*? What does it entail to be one of these things? Or to be around one of them, for that matter?'

'Two,' Rosie corrected him, after a moment's contemplation. 'One Nymatil, two Nymatili. That's unusual, for a start.'

'Why?'

'Because they don't normally pair up. They normally come one at a time.'

'How normal is normally?' he asked, surprised that he was even getting this far and hoping that it would last. 'How often do these . . . Nymatili occur?'

'Not very,' she replied, more guardedly, '. . . often.'

'What? Every decade? Every millennium?'

'In between. They're not regular. They just pop up.'

'What? A couple a century?' he persisted.

'Ish,' she replied. 'I mean, sometimes you get two close on each other, sometimes you can wait two or three hundred years. Also, sometimes, they're no more exciting than a particularly sussed-out shaman, a teacher, but at other times they're *BIG*.'

'What d'you mean by BIG?'

'Earth-moving,' she said. '. . . What I'm trying to say is that they're not *so* abnormal. I mean, it's weird but it isn't unique. The gypsies claim

to have had dozens in the past thousand years, but only little ones ...'
She paused, then added, 'For all the good it's done them.' She paused
again, collecting her thoughts. 'In which time the gorgios had fifteen,
maybe sixteen, that they're aware of, not counting Davie and Iz. But I
suspect they – the gypsies, I mean – only count the really important
non-gypsy ones. Sort of professional jealousy.'

'And are David and Christina "really important"?' he asked. Are they
"BIG"?'

'According to the gypsies?' she asked.

He nodded.

'Oh yes,' she said.

'And do you know who the other non-gypsy ones were?' he inquired.

She smiled slightly and shrugged. It was an expressive gesture of
refusal. He thought for a few seconds.

'You said it's unusual to have two Nymatili together. How unusual? I
mean, how big a coincidence is it?'

'There's no such thing as coincidence,' Rosie replied. It was almost an
automatic response for her, so often did she say it, or think it. 'Not how
you mean it, anyway. There's synchronicity; meaningful coincidence,
but not blind chance.'

'What does this one *mean*, then?'

'It's not a coincidence, it's a phenomenon. That's why the gypsies
have a name for it.'

'A name?'

'Nymatili. That's why they know what to call two Nymatils.'

'Or three?'

'Never more than two.'

'Never?'

'Never, ever.' She looked down at the crowd below and grimaced
involuntarily. Since Glastonbury she had been unable to look at a crowd
without feeling a sharp pang of cold fear.

'Listen,' she said, turning back to Sir James. 'I think I know what
you're asking me. You want to know whether you should take this
Nymatili thing seriously, or if it's just superstitious mumbo-jumbo?'

'And?' he asked.

She thought for a couple of seconds. 'If you were an educated man
living in Judea at the time of Christ, would you have believed he was
God, in all honesty?'

He had to think for a moment.

'I'd like to think I would have,' he replied.

'Because of his personal charisma?' she asked. 'Or because of the
miracles he was reputed to have performed? Or because he fulfilled the
scriptures? Or just because you wanted to believe he was what he
appeared to be?'

'Because he rose from the dead,' he replied.

'No, before that,' she said. 'When he was still alive.'

'A bit of all of those, I suppose,' he said. 'But . . .'

'So, in effect,' she continued before he could object, 'you'd be willing to believe that a man was God incarnate because he fitted the bill? Because all the available evidence pointed to him being the messiah?' She paused. Again she continued before he could answer. 'It's not so different with Iz and David. The gypsies would tell you that they are Nymatili because there's a point when an accumulation of apparent coincidences becomes irrefutable proof. They fit the bill.'

'So you think they are?' he asked.

'It's not important what I think,' she said. 'Or at least it isn't important to anyone but me. Nymatili, like beauty, are in the eye of the beholder. It's not a name they give themselves; in fact they hate it. It's a name other people give to them because of what they seem to be; because of their charisma, their miracles, because they fulfil the prophecy and because people want to believe it.' She paused, frowning at him. 'Am I making sense?' she asked.

'I'm not sure if you're telling me that they categorically are, or categorically are not, this . . . thing,' he replied.

'Neither,' she said. 'They *are* extraordinary, though, and part of what makes them extraordinary is that they're surrounded by a sort of web of synchronicity. As David once said to me, they can flick a coin a hundred times and it makes no difference, because it invariably comes out in their favour.' She stopped, patting her pockets for her cigarettes. She located them, removed one and was about to put it in her mouth when she remembered where she was and put it away again. Sir James was surprised and oddly reassured to see that she still had some vestige of respect for the church.

'Which, incidentally,' she continued, 'is one of the requirements of the Nymatili. It's one of the reasons why the gypsies are so excited, one of the many reasons. As far as they're concerned this is the first pair of gorgio, non-gypsy, Nymatili in about five hundred years and the last ones were responsible for the Renaiss . . .' She stopped. 'The point is that David and Iz are the first for a very long time, if they are at all. They fit the bill. Don't make the mistake of thinking that the gypsies are superstitious fools; they don't pin this sort of hope on anyone. On the other hand . . .' She paused and yawned. 'It goes in endless circles.'

'What d'you mean?' he asked.

'Just that there are catch-22s built into every faith. Faith itself is the biggest of all . . . "I'm God," says God. "Believe in me." "Why should I believe in you if you don't do anything to deserve it?" asks man. "Because I'm God," he replies. Q.E.D. . . . This stuff isn't any different. It's constructed so that it can claim its successes and disassociate itself from its failures. As a Christian you believe Christ was God because he fulfilled the scriptures and because of the word of his followers that he rose from the dead; a bunch of Galilean peasants who'd just seen their messiah nailed to a cross alongside a couple of thieves – not the most reliable witnesses. So, in effect, you believe he was God because you're both able and inclined to make that leap of faith on his behalf. The scriptures were there to be fulfilled by anyone plausible enough, clever enough, sharp enough and powerful enough to do it. The difference between a mortal with extraordinary powers and God incarnate is circumstantial evidence, plus your faith.'

'Along with half the world,' Sir James remarked.

'Not the Jews,' she replied. 'And he was fulfilling their prophecies, after all. But anyway, I'm not trying to do down Christianity. All I'm saying is that prophecies are made to be realized. It's another catch-22; you set down a list of rules by which you're able to recognize your messiah, when he comes, and sooner or later someone will appear who's powerful enough to fit the requirements. And wherever that rare super-person turns up, there will always be a set of local requirements for messiah-dom waiting to be realized. That's what Nymatil means; the super-person who's sometimes mistaken for God.' She stopped to let him digest this. He thought for a while, then rubbed his eyes and shook his head, as if trying to dislodge something inside.

'It's simpler than I've made it sound,' she said. 'It's a question of faith. If you believe there's such a thing as Nymatili, then Iz and David are, if you don't then it doesn't matter and they aren't. Ask David about it, or Kelvin. They know it all much better than I do.'

'Do you believe they are?' he asked quietly, adding, 'Just out of interest,' before she could embark on another lengthy sidetrack.

'Does it matter what I think?' she asked.

'Yes,' he replied. 'It matters to me.'

She looked extremely reluctant to commit herself and she had to think before she answered.

'No,' she said finally, sounding less than certain. 'I don't know.'

'Which one?' he asked.

She thought again, biting her lip. She sighed. 'Maybe,' she said. 'I just don't know.' It was the first straight answer she had given him and it hit home harder than he would have dared admit, even to himself.

'I ought to go,' she said, beginning to stand up. She peered over the balcony, at the meeting which was starting to break up down below. During their conversation it had risen in a crescendo, with a lot of people shouting and arguing, punctuated by spells of relative quiet with only two or three of them talking and the rest listening. It had been tailing off, however, over the past ten or fifteen minutes. The crowd was thinning out, emptying like water from a bath through the door directly beneath the balcony. Only a few remained. Rosie recognized the Rutherfords, Tam Morrison – Annie Moffat's weasel-faced uncle – and a few others she knew. If a conclusion had been reached she and Sir James had been far too engrossed to know about it.

He had wanted to know whether it was all nonsense. If he had talked to Christina she would have told him not to worry; that it *was* nonsense, and he would have gone home with a reassuring half-truth, so that he could sleep sound at night. Instead he had talked to Rosie and she had presented him with the basic dilemma of the nature of faith; a tug of war between unquestioning belief in an idea and an objective scepticism which dismissed the same idea as absurd superstition. And, like a true Devil's advocate, she had used his own faith in Christianity to underscore her point. Far from reassuring him she had contrived to send him home with an infinitely more complicated dilemma than the one he had brought with him. Either he believed the weight of circumstantial evidence, or he dismissed it and in doing so admitted that he had one standard for his God and another for his daughter.

And so he sat in his chair, in his dining room, with the debris of his breakfast and his piles of newspapers around him and, for a moment, faced the despair he had been avoiding so studiously over the past few months. However hard he tried, he could not convince himself, in the end, that he was not terrified for Christina. Even if the odds on her being this phenomenon that only the gypsies had hitherto known about were a thousand to one, that one chance in a thousand was one too many.

He sighed, stood up, picked up his pile of newspapers and trudged off to his study.

8

EVENING

It had been a bleak, grey day, with fitful squalls of rain riding in from the sea in dark, ragged curtains. But as evening came, just about as Christina's father was leaving Craigairie after a two-hour visit, the weather made an effort to behave in a way more befitting the season. The wind dropped, the clouds lifted and dispersed and suddenly it was one of those early summer evenings when everything is calm and soft and placid. Rabbits hopped around behind the lengthening shadows cast by the yellow-flecked gorse bushes, moving out into the last rays of the red sun to comb their ears and play-fight with each other. The piercing whistles of nesting curlews studded the evening air, mingling with the high-pitched mewing of four buzzards, two young, two old, which were caught in a thermal high over the valley.

After Sir James had driven away David and Christina wandered out on to the hill, their arms around each other. They walked down to the river in silence, breathing the resinous smell of pine trees a few hundred yards upwind. They reached the river, removed their shoes, rolled up their trousers, still in silence, and waded through the reeds to the nearest rock. The Tarf was high and dirty after the rains and they had to hop from rock to rock; David first, helping Christina across. They were about halfway over to the far side when there was a splash upstream. Christina stopped, on the verge of joining David on his rock, and stared up river. David followed her gaze. There was nothing to look at for a minute, but they waited, still as stone, as if they could have remained in the same positions all day if necessary. Their patience was rewarded. A small head popped up in the middle of the glittering, silver pool, sending a small ripple of about ten perfect circles towards the dark, shadowy rushes. It looked at them for a moment and then ducked under the water again, its smooth, sleek back snaking through the surface as it drove down into the murky depths.

'I didn't know we had otters,' Christina whispered above the murmuring of the river.

David slapped his neck, where a small army of midges was dancing, awaiting their chance to get a clear shot at the exposed skin.

'Ten more years and it'll be Craigairie National Park,' he replied.

Christina humphed mirthlessly, with a little more feeling than his innocuous remark deserved. He gazed at her for a moment from his rock and she looked back, avoiding his eyes. For about half a minute her eyes danced around, slowly locking into his steady gaze. Finally she breathed out a short laugh, shrugged slightly, put her hands on her hips and met his gaze. They looked at each other for a few moments. David stretched out his hand to her.

'Are we walking the policies or are we fucking around in rivers?' he asked quietly.

Christina held her gaze on him for a second more, then smiled quickly, looking away. She gave him her hand.

Once clear of the marsh and into the bracken on the side of the hill they struck straight up, towards the stone. About halfway through the thick, tall bracken they stopped and turned, holding hands. Craigairie was in the spotlight of the dying sun. The Scots pines were tipped with crimson, as if smouldering against the clear sky behind. Craigairie stood in amongst their dark stems, a well-proportioned little lump of white and black with its attendant huddle of outbuildings flanking it.

They could feel each other's thoughts like a small, grey cloud around them. After a minute or two David let out an impatient little noise and pulled Christina behind him, on up the hill. She came reluctantly at first, as if immersed in a deep reverie, but did not resist for long. The pull the stone had on them was still immense. Not even a lingering look at the cottage could hold her attention for long within two hundred and fifty feet of it. Every trick of natural magic they had ever performed had been accompanied by an image of that leaning granite phallus. It had formed a backdrop to so much of their dreams, as well as their consciousness, that no part of their minds could now avoid it. Christina had terrifying nightmares for a fortnight after the curing of Annie Moffat, recurring night after night after night. They were all the same, horrible images of rape by that cold, coarse rock, brutal and animalistic. They had faded, but she remembered them daily, and nightly.

The stone was the third right-angle in the weird triangle which constituted the very heart of Craigairie. It demanded more and more of them because only they were able to keep pace with it and to nurse its power out of it. Only they could walk up to it and stand in the hollow, at its base, and touch it. It had become wild and arbitrary, lashing out at anyone foolish enough to go near it, as a half-wild pony kicks out at strangers. Not even Rosie or Emily could get nearer to it now than the bottom of the hill, below the bracken. Sometimes it was possible to make it up the hill without meeting unbearable resistance, but that was usually just to lull the unwary into a false sense of security, before letting rip with a psychic stun-blast at close range.

It was tame with David and Christina, like a kitten purring under their gentle stroking. Here they could hear the song, the unbroken chord of life, better than anywhere else they had visited. Each stone had a different degree of clarity, depending on the amount of human interference to which it had been subjected; it was slightly fuzzy in Orkney, muffled in Glastonbury, near-pure but very distant at Avebury. But here, in Craigairie, it was loud and crystal-clear, pitched exactly to Christina's and David's inner ears. They could, and often did, stand and listen to it for hours. But the sun had sunk and the long, slow evening was setting in, so they left the stone and walked through the damp heather up the valley. They headed towards the knoll above the long, easy bend in the Tarf a mile upstream from Craigairie. It was called the Witches Hill, because of the five, hunched, gnarled rowans on its summit, the closest point to Craigairie which could be seen from outside the exclusion zone.

It was a steep climb, necessitating some tacking around peat hags to take the sting out of the hill. They had not spoken since the river an hour earlier, but they still held hands, David in front pulling Christina behind him. As they climbed an early owl began to hoot behind them, way down the valley, its call carrying for miles on the still evening air. They reached the top and the Galloway Hills undulated along the horizon in front. There were still patches of white high up on the shoulders of Merrick, the highest of the chain. Above them, about a foot above the horizon, a big, white moon stared down on the darkening landscape.

They walked through the small coven of trees, both of them unconsciously pointing the horns at the ground as they passed over the centre of the circle, acknowledging the old ones with unthinking deference. On the far side they settled down on the remains of a drystone dyke and gazed northwards, up the valley, towards Barrhill. A fire had already been lit, one of the score of beacons around the perimeter which were lit every night by the faithful, out there in the world.

For a long time neither of them spoke. It was Christina who finally broke the noisy silence of their contemplation.

'I don't want to die, Davie,' she said matter-of-factly. 'I want to see more places, do more things . . . have babies; *your* babies. I've got too much still to do to give in to the whim of some damned prophecy.' She paused. Heat had crept into her voice and it took her a moment to regain the tone she had started with.

'I don't want to die,' she said again.

There was a short silence.

'Neither do I,' David said simply. When it became clear that he was stopping there, she turned to look at him.

'Just that?' she asked.

He twitched one shoulder in a faint shrug. 'I don't see the point in tearing out my hair and gnashing my teeth. If it happens, it happens.'

'And if not?'

He snorted. '*Then* we settle down somewhere remote and make babies.'

It seemed to calm her for a while, but she was flattering to deceive. Thoughts had been washing around behind her impassive expression, like water in a bucket. It wasn't long before something else spilled.

'You know Kelvin's doing junk?' she said.

He nodded. 'I know.'

'How long', she asked, 'have you known?'

'Not long enough, I fear,' he replied quietly. They lapsed into another short silence.

'Why does he do it to himself?' Christina asked. She sounded genuinely bemused.

David glanced at her, smiled quickly and looked away.

'Because he hears but he doesn't listen,' he said. 'He thinks all the wrong things are special and he continues to ignore all the good things. Junk doesn't bring spiritual ease, but it does a good enough impression of it to fool Kelv, and it's a lot easier to come by. Besides, Kelv always thought that the fact that you were ingesting your karma through a ten pound note somehow dignified the process.' He paused and laughed dryly. 'A natural drug addict.'

'So what did you do? Did you talk to him?'

He nodded but did not reply.

'So what happened? Do you want to tell me?'

'Not particularly. It was ugly for me and it would be equally ugly for you.'

They lapsed into silence, watching the moon edging up into the clear, starry sky. After a few minutes Christina raised her left hand, pointing her hand at the moon, her outside fingers extended in the horns. The heavy, ancient ring on her finger gleamed dully in the moonlight, the ruby like a drop of dark blood on the thick gold band.

'So how did this Kelvin thing end?' she asked absently.

He shrugged. 'I told him not to kill himself,' he replied. 'It lacked conviction, under the circumstances.'

'Does he know?' Christina asked. 'Stupid question,' she added before he could answer.

He let out a breath of laughter. She turned and gave him a wry smile over her shoulder.

'And so Linnhe knows, so Dorothy knows, and, of course, Rosie knows,' he remarked.

'Emily?'

'Emily thinks we're immortal,' he replied dryly. He stood up, stretched, yawned, shivered and looked back down the valley. Lights were on in the cottage, throwing little pools of yellow on to the lawn. Behind the cottage, the beacon fires gleamed along the horizon on the dark hummocks of the higher hills overlooking the perimeter of Craigairie. Each one marked the gathering place for people who had come from hundreds of miles to hang around Craigairie, waiting for something to happen.

Craigairie was putting the Duisk valley on the map and the continual rumours of new miracles had not let up with the influx of outsiders. For better or worse, people believed in David and Christina. As Rosie had remarked after one visit to the town, 'You get the impression that if Davie and Iz announced they were going to ride into Barrhill tomorrow morning, on donkeys, they'd be waiting, waving palm fronds and chanting "Hosannah".'

Each of those fierce little glimmers on the horizon was like a link in the chain which surrounded Craigairie. From the inside it was like a siege which had reached deadlock. They could get in and out with practised ease, turning up miles away without anyone seeing them leave. But when they were inside, it was no longer possible to stand here, on the Witches Hill, or on Glenkitten Fell or Eldrig Fell, and see just emptiness and space. There were people out there now.

David stared down the valley for a while, his jaw set, his thoughts making no imprint on his face.

'I'm tired,' he said at last. Although he said it flatly there was something indefinable about the remark which gave it more significance than it might otherwise have had. It was an altogether bigger fatigue than could be cured merely by sleep. He let out a long breath.

'I used to tempt death for a living,' he said.

She looked up at him, now a featureless silhouette standing in front of her and a yard to her left. His profile was chiselled; the mane of hair, the beak of a nose, the firm line of his jaw. He looked more like one of his hawks every time she looked at him.

'I used to do it for fun,' she replied. She saw David nod and heard his small laugh. A dog fox barked somewhere out on the moors. Christina pulled herself to her feet and he moved to envelop her in his arms. She allowed herself to be embraced.

'At which point did we lose control?' she said into his collarbone.

'At the risk of being cloying, I think it was at the point we fell in love.'

'Ah,' she said. 'A long time back.'

'A lifetime,' David replied. He thought he heard a breath of laughter but it was a long time before she was ready to explain it to him. They stood, embracing each other as the last light of day faded into the blue twilight of the summer night.

Kelvin glanced at his watch, frowned and murmured something to himself under his breath. He walked over to the window of the room he was in and looked out.

Below him, a couple of hundred feet below, the bottom end of Princes Street curved around the St James's Centre, came to a big roundabout and left it at the top of Leith Walk. From his vantage point on Calton Hill Kelvin could look out over Leith, its grey roofs bathed in evening sunlight. Once, not so long back, there had been a couple of miles of green fields between Edinburgh and Leith, but the former had crept out and swallowed up the latter, like a slow mud-slide creeping irrevocably down the hill, towards the Firth of Forth.

Beyond, in the distance, Fife rose in a long, hazy line, peaking in the aptly named Paps of Fife and then sliding away out into the North Sea.

Kelvin took all this in with one, long, wistful gaze. Then his eyes strayed down to the darkness below the flat, where the kids met to sniff glue from plastic bags, and then to stumble over four lanes of traffic in order to hang about by the closed entrances of the St James's Centre. Even for Kelvin, who had never claimed to be a puritan where drugs were concerned, the sight of them was sickening.

But, like the kids down there in the shadows, he bombed out and pumped any shit he could lay his hands on into his arms, up his nose, into his mouth and even up his bum, just for that delicious surge of release. He still sometimes had flashes of memories of those first spliffs he had sneaked with David in the woods behind school. He still got a kick out of a well-rolled joint or out of lining up two little tramlines of coke on a polished mirror, or out of the shuddering rush of an Ecstasy hit.

Admittedly the shit he had been pumping into himself had been grade 'A' of late. The pickings of Craigairie were of goldmine proportions; if you were not shackled by some ridiculously holy moral obligation not to screw the public. People sent money to Craigairie; usually cheques but often cash, enough to pay for a man's drug habit without worry of detection. Rosie and Em sometimes pocketed cash as well, but only when they were flat broke and there were things that needed to be bought. David and Christina paid no attention to it, remaining aloof even when they were sitting around a table with four or five other people, all of whom were sifting through a pile of money and cheques, picking out 'the pinkies', the Scottish fifty pound notes. It was a fair system, because there weren't many pinkies, but there were enough of them to supplement everyone's meagre purses. The rest – and there was a lot – went to the bank account of Friends of the Earth in Glasgow. They were nothing if not 'right on'.

Kelvin was less magnanimous when he was left on his own with the pile. He was usually delegated to drive it to Glasgow every couple of weeks, and the fortnightly burrow through the bag of money had become a relished ritual. He did not just take 'pinkies'. He took blue ones, purple ones, red ones, as many notes as he thought he could take without anyone noticing.

As far as Kelvin was concerned, if people were stupid enough to part with their money for people who then sent it straight to Friends of the Earth, and broadcast the fact at every opportunity, then they deserved to be ripped off. It didn't hurt anyone, the charity got the majority of the money, neither Craigairie nor the people who originally sent it appeared to want it or need it.

Kelvin, however, did need it.

He had had some friends around the night before and five of them had consumed about four hundred quid's worth of his coke. Good coke, too. The effects still formed a soft cushion underneath his consciousness, shielding him from the more unpleasant thoughts caught in his mind.

He had meant never to do another of the Mother Coven's gigs again. He was too old to be treated like a retard by his friends and peers. They never quite knew whether to patronize him, reason with him or allocate incomparably dull but time-consuming chores to him, as if to keep him out of trouble.

None of these worked on him any more. It was them, not him, who had gone off on some private trip, leaving him to stumble along behind, asking them what it was like. He had decided enough was enough; he wouldn't do their dull menial chores for them any more, he wouldn't listen to Linnhe's gentle murmurings any more and most of all he wouldn't be held responsible for the Romanies.

But then he had spoken to David and David had not patronized him, or reasoned with him or allocated him a task; at least immediately. He sat in silence and listened, trying to understand, not an ogre, but a friend.

Kelvin thought about it as he stared out of the window and it sent a kick of shame and self-contempt through the pit of his stomach. When he was away from David he could quickly construct a perverse, spiky edifice of bitterness and contempt. He could imagine himself telling David to fuck off with his pathetic hippy crap. He pictured himself sweeping out of the sitting room at Craigairie, leaving David goggle-eyed and slack-jawed behind him.

Instead he had been so sweet, so naturally true to his beliefs that Kelvin had been first dumbstruck, then reduced to tears, then finally to clinging to David, weeping uncontrollably.

They would not pity him, or get angry with him, or waste a lot of breath over him, but they would be worried and anxious.

It had made him feel so fucking small.

It had also made him agree to do another chore for David. He would keep the gypsies in line one more time, basing his plea on the fact that Kelvin and himself were the only two people who knew them well enough to do it; which was true.

Kelvin had been here, in this flat in Edinburgh, before he realized how completely he had caved in.

'Pathetic,' he spat out to the empty flat.

It was a stoater of a flat, though. Roomy, light, with three bedrooms, a bathroom and a sort of studio-sitting room upstairs, comfortably furnished, covering the whole of the upstairs floor. It belonged to some art dealer who got his rocks off telling people that he had lent his flat on Calton Hill to 'those Craigairie people'.

Effete bastard.

He knew better than to come here now. The last time he had been, Kelvin double-locked the door so he couldn't get in.

Nice flat though.

Kelvin glanced at his watch again and stamped his feet irritably.

'Jacko, where are ye, ya bam-pot. Ye said ye'd be here at seven.'

There were four Ecstasy tablets burning a hole in his pocket and with only four hours until he was supposed to be on Arthur's Seat he was beginning to get jittery.

He stalked around the big room, sighed noisily, went over to the drink tray and cracked open a beer, then he put on a record, turned up the volume and fell into a sofa. The first continuous organ note of U2's 'Joshua Tree' swelled in the room, then the guitar began to fade in, then finally the bass, the drums and the song. Kelvin stood up again, digging his right hand into his trouser pocket. He produced a matchbox and opened it. Four little pills lay on a cotton-wool bed, just the same as when he had last looked at them. He closed the box and put it in his pocket again. Then, a moment later he had a change of heart and pulled the box out again, opened it again and spilled the pills on to the low coffee table. He sat down again.

'One can't do any harm. Jacko and the others will be here any minute. They won't miss a thing.' He reached out and picked up one of the pills. He inspected it, turning it over in the palm of his hand, sorely tempted but nevertheless still slightly guilty.

'Ah, what the hell,' he murmured and popped the pill into his mouth, taking a swig of beer to wash it down.

For a long time nothing happened. The song ended.

Then the next one, then the side was finished. Kelvin got up and turned over the tape. He remained on his feet, dancing slowly across the room to turn the fire on.

He felt all right, but he was mildly panicked that he felt no different from before he took the pill, thirty-five minutes into the trip. He stood with his back to the fire, pulling heavily on a cigarette, trying to detect the first hint of that glorious, soft, silken taste of smoke which Ecstasy induced.

He had been staring at the three pills on the table two yards in front of him for five minutes before he realized what he was thinking. He glanced at his watch.

'Ten minutes,' he said out loud. 'I'll give them ten minutes more.' He said it as if the idea of him taking another pill on the point of lift-off was a sort of threat to Jacko and the rest, rather than rank insanity on his part. He knew that Ecstasy always worked; sometimes a trip wasn't so sweet, but otherwise it was a reliable drug.

He also knew that two pills would blow him through the roof well into the night, which wouldn't be popular.

He chose to ignore the first problem and scorn the second one.

He looked at his watch again.

His legs were shivering violently and he was dancing about on the spot, half-absorbed by the music and half-distracted by a blind panic that was rising up inside him. He observed the inexorable onslaught of paranoia coming at him like a freight train in a tunnel. He let it get close to him, right in so that he could see its red eyes and feel its clawing talons on his skin, then he lurched across the room, grabbed another of the pills and swallowed it. For a moment, a matter of a few seconds, he stood beside the tracks and watched as the freight train rattled and clattered past.

Then it was gone.

In the space of those five or ten seconds Kelvin had taken another of the pills, just to be sure.

Emily did not know where Kelvin was and, specifically, she didn't care. He was not where she was, which was the beginning and end of the matter as far as Emily was concerned. When she finally realized that even if Kelvin did turn up, it would be too late to rein in the gypsies anyway, she confined her opinion on this state of affairs to two words.

'Bloody typical,' she said.

This was her first open meeting in a city and, so far, the vibes had not been good. She had curried up a fair amount of interest in the university a couple of months earlier, but that had been covert, well away from the jaundiced gaze of the media and the general public. In a perfect world she would not have agreed to grace this gathering with her presence, but when it became clear that it would go ahead with or without Craigairie's blessing, it had become imperative for one of them to be there. Ever since Glastonbury they had been understandably jumpy about potential flash-points, and Edinburgh fell squarely into this category. Cities were always a problem for Craigairie.

Em had been feeling uneasy and on edge since she had got there and it had grown in the next couple of days. It was as if a warning bell was ringing in her mind. She had thought that getting out above the city, on to Arthur's Seat, would dispel her inexplicable agitation. Instead it grew, becoming even more urgent when she had driven past Holyrood Palace at around eight that evening, on to the road up Arthur's Seat.

That had been over three and a half hours ago. She had sent Edward off to look for Kelvin at ten-thirty, but he had not yet returned.

He would, she knew.

Edward was reliable, if occasionally dopey.

She smiled quickly, thinking of Ed, then she glanced at her watch and the smile faded again.

'Where are you?' she said out loud, although there was no one within earshot of her. She was on the summit of the northernmost of the double peaks of the hill. Below her, in the saddle, a quarter of a mile down in the thin darkness, people were moving around between small bonfires; red puddles of light congealing into a lake.. There were a lot of people down there; there had been a steady stream of them coming up the hill from the city since the middle of the evening and there had been upwards of two thousand when she climbed away from them an hour earlier.

There had been an odd, not altogether pleasant atmosphere down there. The gypsies sensed it, although few of them recognized it for what it was. They too were on edge but they were not able to identify it as a big red light of danger.

There were, for instance, Bible-thumpers down there. Not the faintly whimsical clerics she had grown up with, nor even the outraged Christians Emily was conscious of attracting. These were big men, with bellowing voices, who used antiquated biblical phraseology to express their fear and hatred of what they saw as devil-worship. Christina called them the 'mullahs', which was an accurate description. Catholics Emily could cope with and the Anglicans were a walk-over; other religions she let be, unless they came to her. But the mullahs, the Scottish Presbys, or worse the Northern Irish ones, or worse still the Wee Frees, always scared her.

But there was something else about this gathering which wasn't right. It was not so much to do with the bad atmosphere, although that had a lot to do with it. It was inside Emily; a wrenching knot in her stomach which seemed to be telling her to get the hell out of there.

She took a deep breath, thrusting this sense of foreboding back into her subconscious, and began to walk down the hill, sliding on the wet turf. She had gone about ten yards when she saw a figure toiling up the steep incline below her. She called out 'Hello?' and quickened her pace. The figure stopped and straightened.

'Em?'

'Ed?' She bounded down the hill to him and skidded to a halt.

'D'you find him?' she asked. Edward was bending over trying to catch his breath.

'Find who?' he asked without looking up.

'Kelvin, of course.'

'Oh, right. He wasn't at the flat. He's been there recently because the kettle was still warm. Also one of the downstairs bedroom windows had been jemmied open, but I searched the place with a fine tooth comb and nothing seemed to be missing.'

'I hope not,' said Emily. She bent down to kiss him on his ear. 'Sherlock.'

He looked around, into her eyes, began to smile but then frowned worriedly.

'Listen, Em. I talked to David when I was in the flat. It was just luck that I was there when he called, but it's damned lucky someone was.'

'Why, what's happened?'

'Nothing's happened. Yet. Tina had one of her premonitions this afternoon. It was a baddie, David said, the worst she's ever had. She went into a sort of trance and got delirious, apparently, and kept repeating "Blood on the Seat".' He paused and twitched one shoulder with a shrug.

'I know it sounds silly, but, as Davie said, it's equally silly to ignore it.'

'No,' Emily said. 'He's right. Besides, it doesn't sound that silly; I've been getting the heebies all day . . .' She stopped, thinking hard. 'Is she OK? Iz?'

'She was in bed,' Ed replied. Emily looked at him quickly. 'No,' he said, shaking his head. 'She's OK. She's fine. They exhaust her, those visions, but she wakes up the next morning bright and beautiful.'

Emily thought for a couple of minutes more.

'So what did he suggest? Davie?'

Edward gave her a funny look. 'He thought we should call tonight off.' His tone suggested that he had meant to add 'of course' even if he didn't actually say it. Emily reacted by going through a spectrum of emotions in a matter of a few short seconds.

'What?' Anger and ridicule. She glanced at her watch. 'Jesus, it's supposed to start in ten minutes.' She bit her lip, sighed, shook her head, gazed down at the milling crowd around the bonfires and, after a moment, shrugged tiredly and sighed again.

'Well, let's do it,' she said.

'How?' Edward asked, turning and trotting to keep up with her.

'God only knows.'

They went down the hill in silence, walking at first, but quickening their pace when they began to identify the noise the crowd was making below them. It was not loud, but it was threatening. It somehow conveyed the confusion and menace of a large body of people about to fly off the handle. They began to pass people standing on the hillside, above the main body of the crowd. The noise was now rising, gathering momentum. There were knots of people in the crowd, shouting and chanting and others shouting back.

They reached level ground and slowed up as their way began to be blocked by the crowd. They all seemed to be looking away from the outside of the crowd, straining to see towards the centre.

There were at least four camera crews in sight.

At this rate it would have taken Em and Ed half an hour to reach the centre of the crowd. She stopped and asked Edward out loud the question that had been repeating in her mind like a stuck record for the past ten minutes.

'What would Dave and Iz do?' she asked.

'Divert their attention.'

'How?'

'However they could.'

Emily ran her hands through her hair.

'How can I?' she asked, panic registering in her voice. 'What have I got?'

Edward was thinking calmly. He was standing with his hands in his pockets, looking like he was wondering which bus to catch.

'Your voice,' he said. 'You've got your voice.'

'In this noise?' she asked. The hubbub was now accompanied by movements shifting through the crowd like ripples in quicksand.

Edward looked at Emily and saw her gather her breath and then, without warning, let out a piercing scream.

People began to turn around to see her, giving way so that she stood in a clearing of her own, still letting out this amazing noise. It went on and on, not a continuous note but a very distracting one. People began to go silent around her, then further away, then people began to turn to see what was happening, only hearing the scream when they fell silent and listened.

Edward reckoned that it lasted about thirty or forty seconds, which said a lot for her lung power. Her breath finally ran out and the scream tailed off into nothing, leaving Emily gasping for breath. Edward took her arm.

'Let us through,' he called, pushing past a BBC Scotland camera crew into the crowd. Emily straightened, drew her breath again and used the 'voice' – a knack hitherto unique to Christina and, to a lesser degree, David.

'Get out of here,' she ordered. She unleashed all the power of an amateur, with no restraint or direction. It just burst out of her and punched its way on to the nearest people.

Watching on television the next morning, Linnhe, David and Christina could not hear the power she unleashed, because it was not picked up by microphones. All they could see were the effects on the people around her. They put their hands up to their ears, but it was not a thing of hearing. The crowd began to part in front of her, many of them looking dazed and confused, like people who have just woken up and found themselves darning a pair of old socks.

Edward saw a gypsy he knew and nodded him over. He was one of the survivors of Glastonbury, a twenty-five-year-old called 'Nebbie' Jackson, because of his rudder-like nose.

'I cannae stop it,' he said as he came up to them, giving Emily a gaunt look before turning back to Edward.

'Have you tried?' Emily asked. It was toneless, but there was a sharp rebuke in there. She pushed her way onwards and people stepped out of

240

her way. There were people yelling up in front, often many at once but occasionally dropping to two or three.

The core of the problem constituted about eighty people in a defensive circle surrounded by twice as many Romanies.

'Get them to let me through,' Emily said to Nebbie. He stood and looked at her for a moment too long.

'Do it,' she ordered.

He did as he was told. With his help the three of them forced a way through the ranks of the gypsies. Emily saw the silver glints of knives at waist level, unsheathed, ready for use. As they turned to see what was disrupting their tight ring they saw Emily, then a couple of cameras still following her progress. They hid their blades.

Emily reached the couple of yards of no-man's-land between the gypsies and their intended prey. She stopped and faced the mad Bible-bashers.

'*Whore,*' someone yelled out somewhere in front of her. Other voices rose in support. 'Spawn of Satan.' 'Devil-worshipper.' '. . . And the triple-headed whore of Babylon shall arise . . .' The rest was lost in the gathering roar of abuse. Emily waited, hands on her hips, for three minutes before they, like her earlier, ran out of breath. She had lost her temper once already and had used the voice, a power she hadn't known she had until five minutes before. She was almost more scared of what she might do if it happened again than she was of these fanatics.

She waited until they tailed off into a sullen silence.

'I have no fight with you,' she said, loud but not shouted. 'This is a free country and we have the right to our beliefs.'

'Not if they're *blas*phemous,' someone yelled.

'Leave,' she replied viciously. She felt the voice curl around the word, like the long echo of a single gunshot in a silent, still glen. She took a sharp breath, trying to rein in the beast she was unleashing. It took a moment; it was a wild and beautiful monster, this power, more attractive in ratio to the more it was out of her control.

Emily turned to the gypsies behind her. 'Go on, leave,' she said.

They stared at her, or past her, their hands on their belts.

After a moment, miraculously they began to fall back.

She turned back to the fanatics.

'They're going away,' she said. 'They're going home. Why don't you do the same?'

Silence.

'Listen, you may not like me, or trust me, but I've just saved you from being torn apart by people who eat hedgehogs.' The joke fell on deaf ears, although it made a couple of reporters still in the vicinity grin.

'Give me a break,' she said, keeping her voice and her temperament level. 'Go home, write to your MP, demonstrate in front of Westminster, hate us all you like, but please don't get yourselves killed over a difference of opinion. Don't you have families to think about?' She stopped, cast a look over her shoulder to where a wider ring had formed, thirty yards back from the line of the first one.

'Go home,' she concluded.

There was a long silence then, slowly, movement in front of her, one or two began to break ranks, pushing through from behind and walking out, past her. They gave her and Edward looks of undisguised hatred as they passed. One spat at her feet but she did not step back, or even react. She turned away from the man, back towards where a file of people were beginning to follow the first.

'Are they letting them through?' Emily asked without moving her lips.

Edward nodded, then answered. 'Looks like it.' He heard a long, quiet breath beside him and could feel her sagging with exhaustion and relief, although they were a foot apart. He stepped closer to her, beginning to put his arm around her shoulders. What happened next was so quick that there was no time to do anything but react instinctively. And yet to both Edward and Emily it seemed to happen in slow motion, with a ponderous certainty which picked out every minuscule detail.

The movement directly in front of Emily was sudden and immediately threatening. The man was wearing a blue anorak, black trousers, black wellies and a dark cap. As he grabbed under his anorak Emily saw the muscles of his biceps and forearms tighten. His hand pulled back, out of his jacket, revealing a skene-dhu, unsheathed, its short lethal blade glittering red in the firelight. He brought it back in a pendulum motion, pointed out, towards Emily. It was at that point that Edward's initial movement of affection and concern became one of protection. The arm around her shoulder caught her and swung her backwards even as he turned side on in the path of the oncoming blade, trying to turn his back on it. His right hand went down, grabbing towards the wrist behind the hilt of the dagger.

Then the blade was into his side, punching coldly into the soft flesh and muscle at the bottom of his ribcage. It was curiously painless; just icy cold, like an icicle inside him.

The attacker had meant to get Emily and was pulling the blade out almost before it was into Edward. Ed felt it slide out, followed by a warm rush of blood. He staggered sideways, to his knees, clutching his side with blood pouring between his fingers. He heard someone yell 'MURDER'.

Emily had been partially off-balanced by the force of Edward's attempt to get her out of the way, but she was quick to recover. As Ed stumbled aside, leaving the way clear for the wild-eyed lunatic and his bloodied dagger, she fell down on one knee, her hair swinging around over her face. But as he came on she slowly stood up and flicked her hair back. She could feel her anger like a volcano inside her; inevitable, unstoppable.

She flicked her hair away from her face and the man stopped dead, his mouth falling open.

She could see Edward writhing to one side, and the white faces behind the attacker, some shocked, others baffled, others exultant. She could hear a journalist's camera clicking somewhere to her left. A small part of her was saying that it was too like a bad film to be really happening, but the rest was too preoccupied with hatred of the man who had hurt Edward and now had the gall to think he could hurt her.

She raised her hands, fists clenched, beside her and brought them slowly up to her temples. She pressed the heels of her hands into her temples, pushing harder and harder until the pressure made her forearms and head shake. She drew in a snarling breath.

'Now do it to yourself,' she said quietly.

He staggered back, naked terror in his eyes, shaking his head. Her voice was all over his mind, like snakes in a snake-pit, entwining itself around his reason and choking it off.

'Do you want to die?' she asked, her fists still clamped to the sides of her head. 'Or are you scared that the Pearly Gates *aren't* waiting for you on the other side?' She had achieved in twenty minutes, in anger, something that had taken Christina six months to attain, in cold blood. She had refined the voice to trick, rather than to bulldoze.

It was infinitely more effective.

A sort of insane gleam came into his eyes and his lips curled into a contemptuous sneer.

'I'm scared of nothing,' he spat out. As he said the last word his left hand came up and joined his right hand on the hilt of his dagger. He looked at her, straight into the pale blue irises of her eyes and, arching his back, he drove the knife down into his stomach.

It slid through the material of his clothing and Emily found herself wondering at the sharpness of the blade. He must have honed the edges until they were razor sharp. She watched with fascinated horror as the dagger went up to the hilt in his guts. He wrenched it free, gasping but otherwise silent. His eyes were still locked on hers; triumphant, jubilant. He drove the knife back down into his stomach.

Once would have been bad enough.

Twice, or three times would have constituted a frenzied attack on himself.

Nine times was way over the top.

The shutters of the cameras clicked and the faces of the onlookers turned from shock to gathering disgust. After the first few he began to stagger around drunkenly, but he went on doing it. Even when he was doubled up and his arms were threshing back and forwards like some horrible, suicidal pistons, his head was back and his eyes were still locked on hers.

For Emily it was more horrible than anything she had ever imagined as she stood, transfixed, and watched this self-destruction. Everything was in perfect detail; the involuntary punch of rapidly exhaled air as the knife drove into his midriff; the spurts of blood emitting from different holes as his stomach contracted under the weight of the blows; the tattered, bloodied fragments of clothing and flesh around the hole in the middle of his stomach, big enough to put a fist through and to let some of his steaming intestines fall out.

He sank to his knees, his arms still going, his eyes still on hers, a look of entreaty and pleading in them, and of agony. He wanted to stop. He wanted Emily to break the spell, but she could only stare back, not knowing how to stop him, or herself. She knew it was coming from her, but she had no idea how, or from where. This man was massacring himself in front of her eyes and would continue to do so until death or Emily broke the spell.

But he could not break the eye contact, whereas she could. The moment she took her eyes off him, just as he completed his ninth stab, he stopped, his eyes staring, dead, and fell over on to his side on the muddy ground, half-rolling on to his back. His hands were still clenched, white-knuckled but liberally spattered with blood, around the black hilt of his dagger.

The moment Emily broke the spell a black dizziness rushed up through her body into her head, forcing upwards as the second, third and fourth waves swept up behind the first. She staggered back, her hands unclenching from her temples to splay across her face like an elaborate, skin-tight mask. Her legs buckled, then folded and with a groan she fainted.

All of this was on film. Both BBC Scotland and a Channel Seven crew were within fifteen feet of Emily when it began, their cameras trained on her. One shot the scene from the right of Emily, and slightly back, the other from the other side, roughly halfway between them. A couple more ordinary cameras caught it in one second lapses.

Watching it on television at Craigairie, the scene was agonizingly clear. When Emily had first translated her fury into real power a shiver ran around the room.

They had cheered up when they saw and heard her speaking to the fanatics, but Christina's unease settled into bleak dread when she saw the file of people passing Ed and Em. She had seen that before, in the chaos of her delirium the previous afternoon. She stood up and quietly left the room.

In the eye of the camera the movement which sent Edward staggering to the ground and Emily reeling back, was a flash, a split second. David and Rosie watched in silence as Emily righted herself and the attacker fixed his sights on her. Then she flicked her hair away from her eyes, revealing a vicious glare of murderous hatred. David drew in a sharp breath. Rosie ducked her eyes away, covering them with her hand.

The film stopped and the newscaster returned to the screen. 'What happened yesterday has renewed widespread objection to the so-called 'Craigairie Mother Coven' and criticism of the government for not making a stand against it earlier.

'The Moderator of the Church of Scotland today accused the Scottish Office of "dragging its feet" over the Craigairie situation.'

'Fuck off,' Rosie said, pressing the off button. There was a short silence, then the door opened and Christina came back in.

'I got through,' she said simply.

David and Rosie swung around.

'I got one of Emily's minions,' she said. 'Ed's in intensive care, but he's supposed to be "stable". Seems like a contradiction in terms, if you ask me.'

'And Em?' Rosie asked.

'She disappeared from the flat sometime last night; flew the coop. My guess is she'll go home to Orkney or Callanish. She'll have to cross water if she's going to break it.'

'Before it breaks her,' David added dryly. 'Christ, what a mess.'

The first thing Emily thought when she awoke was 'where the hell am I?' Even in the dark this high, narrow bed was unfamiliar, and the shape of the room, low and long, was strange. So too were the only two sounds she could hear. The first was in the room; a clock almost directly in front of her, on a mantelpiece she did not know with the red embers of an old fire glowing dully in the grate below.

Emily tried to move, but had a peculiar feeling that her body was only awake from the neck up. The rest was heavy as lead, but not unfeeling or dead.

She began to notice the second sound again. It was an easy sound to grow accustomed to; a faint, lulling hushing on the edge of hearing. The sea.

Orkney?

She was not in Kirkwall, that was for sure. Someone would be clattering about downstairs and the carriage lamp in the courtyard would glow yellow through her curtains.

She slept again, returning to the turbulent roller-coaster ride of her dreams.

Later, it was still dark, but then Emily was not sure if she was awake or not, so it could have been broad daylight for all she knew. She had a short conversation with Ed. He stood at the end of the bed in a peculiar, hunched position, as if he had an attack of stomach cramp, and gazed down at her. When he saw that her eyes were open he gave her one of his sweet, open smiles.

He looked at her for a while in silence.

'Did you ever wonder what's so great about the "To be or not to be" bit in *Hamlet?*' he asked suddenly. His eyes spoke, but otherwise his face was still.

For a moment a fleeting glimpse of memory scuttled past the end of some long corridor in her mind. Something about eyes . . .

'Don't think about it,' Edward said. 'It's gone, it's happened.'

'What d'you mean?' she asked confused.

'To be or not to be, that is the question,' he replied. 'It's in fact the *only* question as far as Craigairie's concerned.'

He gazed at her for another couple of minutes and she lay underneath his gaze, waiting for him to speak. When he did it was to look at his watch and say,

'Shit, I have to go.'

'Where?' she asked. 'Why? Don't go.'

'Give me a reason not to,' he said slyly.

'What reason d'you want?' she asked. 'Because I want you to stay. Because I like your company. Because, despite the fact I sometimes treat you like you don't have any feelings, I love you.'

'Really?' He brightened up visibly.

Then she was asleep again.

Meg, who was sitting next to the bed, with the reading light beside her on the bedside table pointed discreetly at the book resting on her thighs, stopped reading when Emily began to speak. It was a weird, uncanny, one-sided conversation. It gave Meg the shivers, but it fascinated her as well. As far as she knew Emily had not said one word since she had been found on the harbourfront of St Mary's five days earlier, naked, exhausted and dead to the world. Doctors had been and gone and had shed no light on her condition.

In a perfect world Meg would never have had anything to do with Craigairie again, but it had a nasty way of landing on one's doorstep unexpectedly, as it were.

She thought of Emily as a victim, rather than a protagonist of Craigairie. She had been exposed to David and Christina when she was too young to understand them, or to fear them. She was their Frankenstein's monster and perhaps their downfall. What she had done, or had seemed to do, on Arthur's Seat defied description, explanation and belief, yet it had happened, on film.

For the first time Craigairie, or part of it, had bared its fangs in public, showing its cruel, instinctive side. It took the filming of Emily on Arthur's Seat to show people how terrifying the power behind Craigairie could be.

For the first two days, after Meg found Emily, the morning after Arthur's Seat, she seemed to have no will to live. Her heartbeats had gone down to almost nothing, her breathing had hardly been enough to show on a silver spoon held close over her mouth.

Then, after two days she steadied into a deep sleep. You could pinch her and she would not feel it, but she murmured and mumbled a great deal.

This was the first time Meg had heard her say anything lucid. She was obviously thinking of Edward, who had been on and off the critical list since that awful night. He had haemorrhaged badly and it was a nasty wound, deep and wide, which appeared to be unwilling to heal itself.

The reactions to what happened on 'the Seat' had been confused. Everybody who saw the incident swore that, in their opinion, Emily had somehow killed the man, or made him kill himself. The cameras seemed to back this claim, but also clearly showed that whatever she did or did not do, she was unarmed, off-balance, facing a maniac with a knife who had just stabbed her lover.

However, the incident gave considerable impetus to a sizeable body of powerful people who thought that Craigairie was unacceptable, whatever its plus or minus points were. The newspapers had gone down on their knees and thanked the gods that such a deliverance had fallen into their laps. Leader-writers had condemned the Mother Coven and all of its network of affiliates, urging the government to extend the blasphemy laws to include Craigairie and all that went with it.

As yet no one knew where Emily had gone. So she was safe for the moment. Meg had taken her in after she had been found like a fallen sea-bird on the jetty in St Mary's. It had not been a thing of pity, and had certainly not been through any sense of duty or obligation. It had almost been out of admiration. She knew the Mother Coven well enough to know their occasionally bizarre modes of travel. When Emily turned up 'with her arms all splayed out like a bird' – according to the man who found her – Meg did not have to speculate as to how she got there.

In a perverse way it amused her that little Em had been the only one of the acolytes to have put together a display of magic, or whatever they called it, worthy of David and Christina.

It must also have taken immense strength and will-power to get herself back to the safety of Orkney after that night in Edinburgh. She did not go to Craigairie, a third of the distance away, but fled back to Fortress Orkney instead.

Meg sighed and stood up, upsetting her book on to the floor. She swore quietly, picked it up and stretched, yawning. She began to move towards the door, but as she reached it the doorbell rang downstairs. She looked at her watch.

'Nearly midnight,' she said. 'Christ.'

She walked downstairs slowly, in which time the doorbell rang again. She pulled the door open and stopped, her mouth slightly open, her eyes wide.

'Hi, Meg,' Christina said.

247

She was dressed in a fisherman's jumper and a long black skirt, with her hair the colour of white gold in the harsh glare of the porch light, and her oval face so lovely that it made Meg's heart lurch momentarily.

'Can I come in?' she asked.

Meg stood aside and allowed her in. She walked past her, stopping politely in the hallway, waiting for Meg to lead her wherever she wished.

'We'll go to the kitchen,' Meg said quietly as she closed the door again. 'The Aga's on.'

'You've done some painting,' Christina remarked. Everything seemed clean and ordered. The whole atmosphere of the house had changed. It was warmer, lighter, incomparably tidier.

'I started to do some cleaning up last autumn and I'm still doing it now.'

She led Christina through into the kitchen. A stock pan simmered on the Aga, strings of onions and bunches of herbs hung from old hooks in the ceiling, a collie lay sprawled on a grey rug in front of the Aga. It had become a real kitchen. As Christina sat down she noticed the wall beside the door she had just come through. It was papered from floor to ceiling, with only a foot or two in the far corner not yet covered, with newspaper cuttings. Right in the middle, the only one in colour, was a twelve-by-nine-inch photograph of the standing stone.

Christina stood up and walked across to the wall, fascinated and amazed by the sheer volume of words Craigairie had generated and surprised that Meg, of all people, should have put together such an extensive collage.

'Where's Emily?' she asked after a while, still with most of her mind on the wall.

'Upstairs,' Meg replied. 'How did you know?'

Christina shrugged, her back still to Meg. Meg had been bracing herself for an attack. They would have been quite justified in being furious with her for taking Emily in without telling them. After a while she relaxed, feeling mildly deflated.

'Aren't you angry with me?' she asked.

'No,' Christina said. She looked over her shoulder at Meg. Her mouth was hidden but her eyes were smiling.

'You're angry with us, remember?'

She looked back at the wall.

'I was,' Meg admitted.

Christina turned her back on the wall, pulled a chair away from the kitchen table and sat down. Meg noticed that she had dark circles under her eyes and her beautiful, translucent skin had a pallor to it she had never seen before. Then, finally, she gave up trying to be cool with Christina. She took a bottle of whisky off a shelf, picked up two glasses and placed them in the middle of the table. They looked at each other for a few minutes, then Meg walked around the table. Christina stood up and they hugged each other. Meg pulled away first and went back around to her chair. She sat down.

'Is he OK? Edward?' she asked.

Christina made a movement which could have been the faintest tired shrug.

'He'll live,' she said. 'How's Emily?'

'Alive,' Meg replied. 'She was exhausted when they found her. She's been in a kind of semi-coma; I mean she's been out cold for the past three days, but she's been dreaming all the time.'

'Figures,' Christina muttered.

'Will she be all right?' Meg asked after a moment. Christina thought for a few seconds, then bit her lip, laughed quickly and shook her head.

'Emily used the power to kill a man. You can't do that kind of thing without a part of you dying at the same time. The question isn't whether she'll recover, but what she'll be like when she does recover.' She stopped, shook her head again and sighed, rubbing her eyes. 'Another casualty.'

'You always knew there'd be casualties,' Meg said. 'Long before I did.'

'Much consolation,' Christina murmured. There was a long silence. Meg was just about to speak again when Christina began to recite quietly, 'For art thou not the fairest of all his creations? Is thy hair not like a flag of golden thread, and thy skin not like the finest Cathay silk, and thy beauty not like a sickle moon on a velvet black night, or the morning star glittering above the dawn? Thou art the last blizzard of winter, the first crocus of spring. Thou art a distant beacon fire in the night.' She paused, took a deep breath and concluded this weird eulogy in the same quiet, dreamy voice. 'Thou art flame from the hand of God; fierce and pure and brief. All thou touchest burns with thy fire and is consumed.' She fell silent, staring at her hands on the table in front of her.

'What's that?' Meg asked. As Christina had recited it, an icy little chill had tingled down Meg's spine. If it was, as it seemed, about Christina, then it was beautiful and true, and yet somehow cold.

'It was written for one of the last gorgio Nymatili to come in a pair,' Christina said.

'Who?' Meg asked. Christina levelled her grey eyes on Meg and smiled faintly.

'Would you believe me if I told you that it was Lucrezia Borgia?'

There was a short, uneasy silence.

'I thought you didn't believe in that stuff,' Meg said.

'I don't,' Christina replied. 'What's there to believe in someone else's prophecy? I do, however, believe that there's no such thing as an accident; nothing's original, everything's related to something else and to the whole. Everything has a reason and a counterbalance. In its simplest terms, if you light a fire with a word of command at Craigairie, then in all probability you're causing another fire somewhere else in the world to go out. There's no such thing as coincidence; not at least if you take coincidence to mean unrelated but identical occurrences. There's no such thing as asymmetry.'

'I don't think I get it,' Meg said. Christina gave her a tired but affectionate smile, as if to say 'you never did'. She pushed back her chair and stood up wearily.

'I have to go,' she said.

'I thought you'd stay here.'

'D'you want me to?' Christina asked.

Meg thought, then nodded. 'Yes. Yes, I do. You can have your old room.' She saw that Christina seemed to sag with relief. 'But before you go, you have to tell me what you were talking about just then.'

'Of course,' she said. She stood for a second, then spoke. 'There was something Kelvin once said to Davie. "Did they make the prophecy?" he asked. "Or did the prophecy make them?"' She paused. 'The answer's both, and neither. Nothing's unique, everything has a precedent and a reason and an equilibrium. There have been people before Davie and me who were like us; who were what the gypsies call Nymatili. they weren't necessarily conscious of being Nymatili, although they probably knew they weren't quite like other people. The name is a Romany thing, but the concept is possible in any human. Look through history or religions and you'll find Nymatili popping up every now and again, under different names; shaking up the status quo, disrupting people's complacent ideas about how the world works. The gypsies believe they're put there deliberately by Dé Doveleski so as to kind of drag humankind back on the tracks. She gives them knowledge, which is often synonymous with power. And in turn, power is generally thought to be a dangerous, destructive thing, even when it's used correctly.'

'The flame from the hand of God?' Meg asked. The phrase had stuck in her mind. Christina nodded.

'Fierce and pure and *brief*; all thou touchest burns with thy fire and is consumed.' She paused and smiled ruefully. 'We never wanted to be this thing; partly I s'pose, because it seemed like outrageous arrogance even to contemplate the possibility, but mostly because, one way or another, Nymatili tend to follow the same patterns and conform to the same rules as each other.'

'Which are?'

Christina gazed at her. 'You still don't see, do you?' she said, gentle and sad. 'David and I have to die, not because we're Nymatili and the prophecy says so, but because to have the knowledge, and the power to be what we are, we necessarily have too much knowledge and power for two people alone. It's a fierce flame, therefore it's brief. It couldn't possibly keep burning for three score years and ten; it couldn't sustain itself that long.'

Meg stared at her for a long, long while. She could not believe what she was hearing. Part of her wanted to yell at Christina, 'This is the twentieth century, woman, snap out of this shit,' and yet she knew that Christina believed it to be true. The only thing Meg had ever known for sure about Craigairie was that one had to resist the temptation to dismiss it as absurd nonsense. It was invariably as unreal as it seemed.

She took Christina to her room in silence, gave her a hot-water bottle and fussed around for a couple of minutes. Christina slumped into an armchair and watched her dully.

'Are you sure about this?' Meg asked, avoiding Christina's eyes.

'Yes,' Christina replied simply. It was the brevity of this answer which caught Meg and elicited a hot rush of compassion in her.

'How long?' she asked.

'From this week, every day that passes is a day too many. We'll try to stay until everything's sorted out, but these things have a way of making themselves happen, if you hang around too long.'

David, Christina and Rosie arrived in Edinburgh the evening after the fiasco on Arthur's Seat and immediately parted company. David went off on his own, muttering something about having to 'sort some things out', leaving Christina and Rosie to join the rest of Christina's family at the hospital where Edward was still comatose. It was not a pleasant meeting. Edward's critical condition and the circumstances which had caused it were the last straw as far as Christina's mother was concerned. Her bitterness and anger with her younger daughter had transcended mere acrimony and now bordered on hatred. She refused to speak to Christina, or even to acknowledge her presence and scorned Sir James's efforts to mediate. Despite this Christina refused to be cold-shouldered from Edward's bedside and stayed there, without moving, sleeping or eating for two long days, until she was satisfied that he would not die. Then she kissed her father goodbye, gave him a letter she had written to her mother and went to Orkney, in search of Emily. Sir James watched his beloved daughter go and knew that he would not see her again. It was a miserable parting.

Rosie had already left the hospital by then, and went to the flat on Calton Hill, where she found no trace of David. There were some journalists hanging around outside, but not as many as there might have been. A rumour had got around that David and Christina had called a meeting of witches at Callanish, in the Outer Hebrides, thus tempting a large number of news-hungry paparazzi on a long wild-goose chase.

David's movements during that week were typically inscrutable. He did return to the flat two or three times, always when Rosie was either asleep or out, and left tantalizing clues as to what he had been doing. For instance, she found a sheaf of hand-written notes on a sofa, scrawled hurriedly on headed letter paper from a firm of solicitors. They were obviously copied down from expert advice he had taken on behalf of Emily and said, basically, that there was no way anyone would try to prosecute her for what she had done.

The notes concluded by saying that the only possibility was a civil suit for damages, brought against Em by the family or friends of the dead man. But this option, too, seemed unlikely as, in David's words, 'It would be extremely hard to prove she did it and anyway it would inevitably end up being a show trial with Craigairie, not Em, in the dock. It won't happen – not at the moment, at least . . . too sensitive.'

The second time he returned to the flat he deigned to leave a note for Rosie, if only a very short one. It said:

'Dear Rosie, still haven't found Kelv, still looking. If C. calls tell her I'm on the "Angus Petrie Interview" this Sunday, 9.00 p.m. and we should hit the road after that. Love D.'

As messages go, it wasn't the most informative. The only part which meant anything to Rosie was the bit about getting himself on to the Angus Petrie show, a one on one, live, Freeman-style interview on Scottish television, which had a reputation for making important people look small, and had sizeable viewing figures to show for it. On the surface, therefore, it seemed like an odd decision on David's part to choose this as the place where he would at last come out of the shadows and present himself to the world.

As for the comment about 'hitting the road' after the interview, Rosie had heard no mention of them going anywhere, until now, and it both perplexed and slightly unnerved her. Invariably, when David and Christina hatched a plan between themselves and didn't tell anybody about it, it was because there was something they didn't want to admit.

But Sunday was still a long way off. Rosie stayed put in the flat, watched the television, read the papers, listened to music and waited for David or Kelvin to turn up. And she read Kelvin's book.

She found the lever-arch file Kelvin always carried around with him, lying on a coffee table in the flat, when she arrived there. It had immediately struck her as odd that he had not taken it with him to wherever he had gone; as long as Rosie had known him that file went wherever he did. It was his chronicle of Craigairie, which he had been writing ever since David first wrote to him describing Delilah the poltergeist. She swore to herself that she would only take a quick look, just at the last few pages.

The last few pages, it turned out, had been written only a week earlier and described, in vivid detail, an emotional conversation between David and Kelvin at Craigairie.

She read more. Then, all of a sudden, she found herself slumped in a sofa early one morning, having read the whole thing. It was a very remarkable piece of writing, for all sorts of reasons. For a start it was astonishingly lucid, considering how confused and fucked-up Kelvin always appeared in his day-to-day behaviour. It was also a very complete account, describing incidents and moments in the past year Rosie had not hitherto known about, or had forgotten about, or had not thought about, or had not considered important until she saw them in an overall context, as they were in Kelvin's manuscript. It was not written as a diary, in that the entries were irregular and it often wandered off into pages of prose or conversations he recorded verbatim, or snippets of poetry, prophecies and quotations relevant to the script. But it was as clear, complete and objective an account of the phenomenal rise of Craigairie as anything Rosie had ever seen, or imagined.

It was also honest in a way Rosie had never hitherto thought Kelvin capable of being. There was something almost schizophrenic between this and his habitual sour cynicism, as if he could happily let his personal self-respect slip away to the point of self-destructiveness, but his writing was sacrosanct, pure, unblemished. It was almost as if Kelvin had channelled everything he had into writing it all down as calmly as he could and in doing so had driven himself into the pit of despair.

As she read the manuscript Rosie began to understand Kelvin and, slowly, began to feel a new sympathy for him. It was no wonder that he was such an emotional mess; the only wonder was that he had not gone AWOL months ago. Poor Kelvin, she found herself thinking; he had, she now realized, guessed what was happening even before David and Christina had come to understand the full implications of Craigairie; but he had been unable to do anything about it but be their unofficial chronicler as they unwittingly stole his culture from him. It was like the ultimate curse of the artist, to observe others living one's dreams, without being able to participate oneself.

And with this new-found compassion came an increasing unease and concern, which grew on Rosie the more she read. She knew enough about drug culture to know that Kelvin had a serious problem.

He had a dealer in the Atchin-tan, another in Glasgow and one called Jacko who lived somewhere in Edinburgh. The last time he had been in the city, back in March, he and Jacko had 'played with Charlie' for three days on the trot, which meant that one of them was able to supply enough coke to sustain a seventy-two-hour binge. Although there was no mention of Jacko prior to this visit, Rosie would have laid a large bet that, whoever or wherever he was, he could shed some light on to Kelvin's whereabouts. Someone who did hard drugs as often as Kelvin appeared to wouldn't have wasted much time between hitting the city and contacting his local pusher.

After she finished the book, early on the Friday morning, five days after Kelvin had disappeared, Rosie sat for a long time, worrying about him. She understood completely if he never wanted to see David and the rest of them again, in fact it made a great deal of sense. But if he had been blowing out with a dealer since Sunday, he needed to be found, extricated and got to somewhere safe; to Orkney, preferably, where Meg could look after him. The mood he had been in when he wrote the last hundred or so pages of his chronicle, going back about six weeks, was frighteningly fatalistic, as if he had given up on himself and was only holding on to see Craigairie through to the last act. It was no mood to be in if he had easy access to heroin.

She was still thinking about it several hours later, in the middle of the afternoon, when David walked in, looking unshaven and haggard with exhaustion. He came into the studio on the top floor where Rosie was lying in front of the television, threw his jacket on to a chair and poured himself half a tumbler of whisky.

'Did you find Kelvin?' she asked, trying not to sound too concerned. She did not know how she was going to admit to him that she had read the manuscript and found the name of 'Jacko'. She was more relieved than she cared to admit when he nodded, turning away again.

'Yeah, I found him. He's staying with a guy I used to know.'

'Called Jacko?' she asked.

He continued to stare out of the window for a few moments, then turned and looked at her with a peculiar half-smile.

'I thought you'd read it,' he remarked. He looked away again.

She was glad he could not see her blush.

'Yeah, he's with Jacko,' he said.

He went in search of Kelvin that evening. Rosie went with him, driving him out of the city to Dalkeith, just south of Edinburgh. They went to a squat, grey tenement on the outskirts of the town, which had broken and boarded windows and a dark, dank interior with layers of graffiti on the walls, syringes on the floors and an overpowering, all-pervasive smell of urine, acrid and bitter, which caught in Rosie's throat.

They reached the second floor, went through a fire door and along a dark passage to a door at the end, on the left. It was made of steel, with rivets around the edges and a peephole at face height, the sort more normally used in prisons to keep the inmates in, rather than the outside world out.

'Is this it?' Rosie asked nervously, glancing over her shoulder down the passageway.

David nodded.

He hammered on the door with the heel of his hand, the dull, echoing boom reverberating along the corridor. After a couple of minutes the peephole slid open.

'Who is it?' a muffled voice asked from the inside.

'It's me, David.'

'Oh, right.' A bolt clunked back, high up on the inside of the door, then another in the middle, then another close to the floor. A latch turned. The door swung open, revealing a short passageway and a tall, rangy man with greying dark hair and a beard to match, aged about forty, Rosie guessed. He was wearing torn jeans and a black tee-shirt and there were tracks on the insides of his arms, but his eyes were sober.

'Hi, Jacko,' David said.

The man smiled a surprisingly sweet smile. He looked like a kind man.

They hugged each other like old friends.

'I'd like you to meet a friend of mine,' David said. 'Rosie Graham, Jacko, Jacko, Rosie.'

They shook hands.

'I've heard about you,' Jacko said to her.

'Nothing bad, I hope,' she said, for want of something else to say.

He laughed quickly and shook his head. She got the impression he knew all there was to know about her. He eased past them and led them along the short corridor into a sort of living room. It was furnished sparsely, with a sofa, an armchair, a couple of stools and an upturned tea-chest for a table. There was an unmade bed in one corner with a small, black and white television on the floor beside it. There was a battered 'Clash – London Calling' poster on one wall and, above the false fireplace, a five by three foot, black and white poster of David and Christina by the standing stone, enlarged from a photograph Kelvin had taken at the golden height of the previous summer. David, with a buzzard on his shoulder, was watching with quiet amusement as Christina threw back her head in laughter. Both David and Rosie stopped dead and stared at it, not having seen the picture for ages and never in the form of a poster. For both of them it unleashed a sudden, unexpected flood of poignant memory. At the time they had all thought they would never forget that timeless happiness and yet now, less than a year later, it was as if it had been an aeon ago.

'Where is he?' David asked, still gazing at the poster.

'Sulking,' Jacko said. 'He's been in his room since you rang last nicht.'

'I'd better go and see him,' David murmured.

'First door on the right,' Jacko said.

David wandered out, leaving Rosie and Jacko still admiring the poster.

It was easy to think, in retrospect, that the sudden anguished howl of 'NO-O-O' which came from the next room, happened almost immediately after David went through. But in fact Rosie had time to exchange some pleasantries with Jacko and sit herself down on the sofa while he went to make her a cup of coffee, before it happened.

She had never heard a human being make a noise like that. It came straight from the soul; a hoarse, raw, elemental cry of bitter, powerless rage and grief. The moment Rosie heard it she knew what it meant and ran to the bedroom, a step ahead of Jacko, knowing what she would find.

The room was a chaos of discarded clothes and papers and smelled overpoweringly of sweat and vomit. In one corner, underneath a dirty window through which the red light of the dying sun filtered into the dank, cheerless room, David was hunched on a narrow bed, hugging Kelvin's head against his chest, his face buried in the unkempt, tousled hair of his friend, rocking back and forth in silence. One of Kelvin's arms dangled limply over the edge of the bed, a rudimentary tourniquet still knotted above the elbow. As Rosie watched from the doorway, it slipped down his arm and caught on his hand.

'Oh Christ,' she said quietly. She took a step into the room then stopped again. David did not look up, or let go of his friend for a moment. He just crouched there, clutching Kelvin's cold, inert, lifeless form, lost in the vacuum of grief which had yawned into his soul. Rosie and Jacko stood for an age, spectators on this last, pathetic embrace, unable to do anything but watch, until Rosie mustered up the courage to cross the room. She put a hand on David's shoulder and lingered there for a couple of eternal minutes, then saw the note lying on the bed where David had discarded it.

'Dear Davie,' it said.

'I never found greater love than I have for you, or more unbearable pain. You are the only person who ever really made me want to live and you're the only person who could make me glad to die.' Two sentences were assiduously scrubbed out. Then, 'I can't remember ever having been to a place you had not reached ahead of me – I think maybe this will be the first and last time.' Then some more scoring out, then finally, 'Don't blame yourself. We're all victims in this. I'm just trail-blazing for you and Christina. If you have time, tell Meg I love her and I'm sorry. Farewell. See you anon. Kelv.'

It took a long time before Rosie could move him. She stood for two hours at the foot of Kelvin's bed while David silently mourned. Should she leave him there, hugging his dead friend until he came to? Finally, he kissed Kelvin's cold forehead, laid him carefully back on the pillow, and stood up, with tears pouring down from his cheeks.

'OK,' he said, 'let's go home.'

Emily awoke the morning after Christina arrived in St Mary's. She came down to breakfast, looking bright and breezy and sat down between Christina and Meg, who had been having a quiet conversation and were both gobsmacked by Emily's appearance.

'Where's Ed?' Em asked. She looked at Meg, then at Christina. 'Why're you staring at me like that?'

She remembered nothing. As far as she was concerned the previous five weeks, since she had last been in Orkney, had not happened. She seemed dazed and confused, compensating for the gargantuan gap in her memory by merging the reality she vaguely remembered with the distorted dreams she had been having for the past few days. When she discovered that Ed was not there she reacted with mild disappointment and the inexplicable remark that he had said he would stay.

Meg remembered the uncanny one-sided conversation she had listened to just before Christina arrived late the previous evening. She did not find out until a long time afterwards that for three minutes, just before midnight on the same night, Edward had slipped into a serious relapse and had been clinically dead. His heart stopped and frantic attempts to resuscitate him had appeared to be failing until, to the amazement of the doctors, his heart kicked into life again all on its own.

David rang up very late on Friday night and spoke to Christina for about five minutes. She had been talking to Meg and Em in the kitchen before the call, but she flew out of the house the moment she put the receiver down, not returning until early the next morning. She was silent when she came back and Meg thought she had caught a chill; she kept succumbing to violent fits of shivering and she looked grey, wan. She seemed crushed, as if the life had been squeezed out of her. Once or twice Meg thought she caught Christina giving her worried, almost pleading looks.

Then, just after lunch, David called again. He talked to Meg for half an hour, in which time Christina, sitting in the next room, heard her side of the conversation undulate unevenly between rage, fury, misery and despair. She came off the telephone shattered, too shocked to be capable of anything but disbelief. In her heart she had dreaded this moment for such a long time that it had almost seemed it would never actually happen. For years she had tried to ride the wild horse of Kelvin's deathwish and tried to tame it and, although she had never succeeded, some demon of optimism inside her had led her to believe that blind luck would see him through, where her own gentle minister-ings failed.

But Kelvin had never been lucky, and now he was dead. In her anguish, Meg railed against Craigairie as a whole, David in particular. She stormed and yelled and wept and stormed again and Christina took it all, all the bitterness and fury and blame Meg could hurl at her, until they were both so exhausted that there was nothing left for them to do but hold on to each other, weeping uncontrollably. Then, finally, when Meg sobbed herself to sleep, Christina sat by her bed and held her hand, pouring all the strength she could still muster into Meg's tormented dreams.

In the middle of the following morning Christina went downstairs to the kitchen, where she found Emily reading a Sunday newspaper. Christina sat for half an hour, chain-smoking, and then seemed to come to a decision.

'Em, I have to talk to you,' she said.

Emily placed her newspaper on the table and looked at Christina. 'Fire away,' she said bravely.

'Not here,' Christina replied. 'Come for a walk with me.'

Emily glanced out of the window. It was not an ideal morning for a walk. A strong west wind was blundering around the house, bringing with it an incessant, misty drizzle. Low, grey clouds had caught upon the bulk of Hoy, obscuring most of the island. Emily grimaced.

They borrowed the car and drove to Kirkwall, then out, towards Brogar on the Stromness road. Just out of Finstown, five miles short of Brogar, Christina took a right turn on to the road up to the north of the island. They drove for a few minutes, then Emily plucked up her courage and asked, 'Where're we going?' It was the first time either of them had spoken since leaving St Mary's.

'Birsay,' Christina said. 'I need to be on an island.'

They drove for another couple of miles, through the rainswept interior of Orkney, before Emily plucked up her courage again.

'We're on an island, aren't we?' she said.

'It's too big.'

At this point Emily gave up. She fell to thinking back through the confused muddle in her mind. The last thing she remembered with any clarity, coincidentally, was being at Birsay on a hot, sunny afternoon, with Christina, David, Edward and Kelvin. It had been the day before Walpurgis Night, but for some reason she had no recollection at all of Brogar.

'Goodbye and farewell from David,' Christina murmured, out of the blue.

'Sorry?'

'Nothing. Just something Davie asked me to do.' She took a deep breath. 'We're going to Birsay because I need to be somewhere where I'm the only power.'

This made a little sense to Emily; not a great deal, but enough to satisfy her.

They did not speak again until they reached the small hamlet of Birsay, dominated by the early medieval earl's palace; an impressive skeleton left over from the last of the great Viking earls. Beyond it, over a short causeway, the island of Birsay rose in a steep wedge, its blunt end facing the grey vastness of the Atlantic Ocean. The tide was out just far enough to allow them over the causeway, on to the island; although they had to wade through a foot of cold sea-water, Emily quietly congratulating herself that she had elected to wear Wellingtons.

Once across, Christina led Emily up the steep slope to the crest of the wedge. Until they reached the top they were sheltered from the worst of the wind and the rain, but when they arrived at the point where the island fell suddenly away vertically down to the sea the elements blasted them with renewed force. The rumbling, crashing waves raged two hundred feet below them, throwing thin, glittering spray high over their heads, where the wind caught it and whipped it inland. The rain bit and stung Emily's face and she huddled deep inside her thick coat, her hands plunged into its pockets, with the wind buffeting clumsily around her.

They stood side by side on the very edge of the world and stared out over the vast, cruel desert of the ocean. Emily knew, or thought she knew, why Christina had brought her there. No one who was conscious of Dé Doveleski, of the living earth as a thing of beauty and power, perpetual and incalculably ancient, could look out from where they stood and not be impressed, awed even. Beside this the minuscule doings of humankind were a shout in a gale.

As they stood, Emily felt Christina's presence swelling around her and the familiar odour of gardenia began to intoxicate her senses, as if it was carried on the gale all the way from Newfoundland. The wind began to die down and the clouds above the small island cracked open, allowing a shaft of golden light through the murk. Emily glanced over her shoulder and saw that the beam of light lay only on the long crest of Birsay. Behind them swathes of rain still swept over the mainland, and in front the sea was still flecked white with the curling manes of thunderous waves.

On Birsay it was calm.

'Look upon my works, ye mighty, and despair,' Emily murmured.

Christina turned to her, raising her eyebrows.

Emily had been looking out to sea, but she turned now. A cloud passed behind her eyes and she winced suddenly, drawing in a sharp gasp as if a spasm of pain had momentarily gripped her.

'Something terrible happened,' she said quietly. She frowned, trying to remember. 'I did something terrible . . . I can't remember.' She shook her head.

Emily looked up and met Christina's eyes, sinking into those pale, blue-grey irises, the colour of thunder clouds. Memory flooded over the younger girl; a look of horror, then of panic filling her face. She stared, her hands coming involuntarily to her face. Christina reached out and took them.

'It's OK,' she said. 'It's OK. You'll forget again. I'm sorry; I had to make you remember.'

'What did I do?' Emily murmured. A sob heaved up through her body and broke from her. 'What've I done?'

'You made someone look into the eyes of the dragon,' Christina said.

'It mustn't happen again. You can't afford anger. You have the power to unleash it, but if it happens again you won't have the power to control it like you did last time. It knows you; it knows where your weaknesses are and it'll use them against you. If it can it will destroy you.'

'Never,' Emily replied, still shivering with horror. 'Never again.'

'Don't ever say never. Don't stand in the present and think you have control over your future, because of how you feel now, here. Things happen which no one . . .' – she smiled quickly – 'not even Nymatili, can plan for. You have to meet them as they come at you. You have to remember this, always. Never relax, never become complacent, always stay alert. David and me aren't going to be around any more to pick you up when you fall over. You're on your own from here on out.'

'So it's true?' Emily asked.

Christina smiled, nodding slowly. 'It's true.' She let go of Emily's hands and they flopped limply to her sides. Christina raised her right hand and waved it in a circular motion over her head, as if swinging an invisible lasso. Emily staggered back as the clouds closed in and the wind and rain returned, sweeping back over the island as it had before, when they first climbed to the top. She recovered ten yards down the hill and stumbled back to the forehead of the wedge, where Christina was still standing, her hair streaming out behind her.

She took the younger girl in her arms and hugged her. Emily began to cry in great, heaving spasms, her tears pouring on to Christina's shoulder. They held like that for an age before Christina finally pulled away.

'Now go,' she said softly. She slipped the big, heavy Roman ring from her finger, placed it in Emily's hand and folded down Emily's fingers, enclosing it.

'I can't take that from you.'

'Give it to your daughter,' Christina said. She took Em's elbow and guided her on to the causeway, albeit reluctantly.

'Farewell,' she said with a slight smile. She turned and walked back up the incline, murmuring beneath her breath, '*Eloi, Eloi, lama sabachthani?*'

Emily did not look back and, when she reached the mainland, she could not remember why there were tears pouring down her cheeks.

It took enormous strength for David to return to that flat the next day and make the necessary arrangements to get Kelvin's body home to Orkney as quickly as was humanly possible. He never thought it would be easy, without getting Jacko into trouble, without the circumstances of the death becoming an issue and without drawing the attention of the press, who had been hanging around all week waiting for a juicy carcass to get their claws into. But after two days of unseemly and, in his view, unnecessary wrangling with officialdom, in various of its guises, it seemed that it might have been easier to have raised Kelvin from the dead like Lazarus, than get him home to Orkney with a modicum of dignity.

Rosie stayed with him throughout, from the moment he left the Calton Hill flat on Saturday morning to the moment they returned there late on Sunday evening, having taken Kelvin's coffin to Edinburgh airport, ready to fly north the next morning. She saw how he dealt with the police, the red tape, the press, the organization and with Meg on the telephone. She had always rather prided herself on her efficiency in a crisis, but what David did that weekend was unimaginable, awesome.

She had always found him faintly disturbing, ever since she had first set eyes on him at Craigairie. It was not that he was in any way evil or malevolent, but he had a hidden strength as hard and cold as steel; the fact that he only ever used it as a shield to protect himself was scant reassurance to Rosie, considering the nature and hugeness of the power he could muster. But now she realized for the first time that what was really frightening about him was not his potential for megalomania, but the self-control which kept that potential in check. There was something inhuman about it, as if he had taught himself to turn to stone whenever there was the slightest danger of him letting any emotion fly. It was to Christina's eternal credit that she had found how to extract blood from that stone.

Even so Rosie did not think for a moment that he would do the Angus Petrie interview; not until they got back to the flat on Sunday evening and he went to his room, returning half an hour later wearing a black suit and a black polo-neck sweater. He had bathed and shaved and looked almost refreshed, quite apart from this being the first time Rosie had ever seen him in a suit. But his eyes still burned with the uncanny inner fire she had been trying to ignore since Friday night.

'You're not going to do it?' she said, stunned.

'Why not?' he said.

'You know why not,' she retorted. 'For Christ's sake, David, save a little pity for yourself.'

'If there was time for self-pity, believe me I'd be wallowing in it,' he replied quietly.

When the interviewer opened the discussion with a sly commiseration, expecting to unseat David at the outset, his reply was devastatingly simple.

'It's a shock,' he said. 'He was my greatest friend. I loved him like a brother.' Kelvin was not mentioned again after that.

Christina had arrived, exhausted and silent, just as David was about to go on air. She had been ushered into the small, sparsely lit studio even as he was sitting down, with people fussing around him, dabbing at his face with last-minute touches of make-up. He had been sizing up the

261

camera which would be on him over the interviewer's shoulder throughout, but he knew Christina was in the room the moment she came through the door. He peered into the gloom beyond the studio lights until she came into view, then he greeted her with his eyes. She looked back at him for a moment, then raised the horns with her left hand. A flicker of a smile crossed his lips and he inclined his head to her, then looked away. Christina retreated to where Rosie was standing. They acknowledged each other without speaking, Rosie's hand going out to Christina's, to receive as well as to give support.

The lights went down, the hurried activity dispersed and David was out there, on his own with an interviewer well known for punching low. He looked calm and a bit grim.

Holding Christina's hand for half an hour was about the closest Rosie could have come to gauging what emotions were going through that composed, tranquil mind. When nothing else betrayed her, muscles would flicker in Christina's hand. When she was concerned on David's behalf, her pulse, which was normally unusually slow, would pick up for a couple of seconds before calming down again.

She needn't have worried. He did not put a foot wrong in the entire interview. He was rational, persuasive and in control from start to finish. He had a knowledge and an understanding of cameras, of having people around him, which began to unsettle his interviewer quite early on and grew steadily throughout the half hour. It was somewhat like watching a brilliant raconteur telling stories to a particular person, but holding an entire room enthralled while he spoke. Whenever he looked like being close to uneasiness he exerted a little bit more authority on the conversation, just to re-assert his control. He not only had the ability to enrapture with his voice, and to disarm all opposition with his intelligence, but he also knew exactly how good he was at it. He met each new question, however difficult, with the same ease, turning what could have been an inquisition into what amounted to an audience.

Rosie never realized quite how plausible David could be when he could be bothered to try. He trusted himself to be right instantly, without having to weigh up alternatives between any given question and his reply. This formidable capacity for instantaneous reaction gave him the time he needed to control his voice, so that it would never betray him.

Impressively, to the casual observer he sounded languid and conversational; whatever was happening beneath the surface was entirely his own affair. He also looked good on camera: the sharp shadows of his face were eased by the flat perspective, leaving his fiercely green eyes to control attention. He was hypnotic throughout, answering each question succinctly and unambiguously. Towards the middle of the interview he managed to articulate the core of Craigairie in something less than five minutes.

It began with the question, 'How does your magic work?'

'It gets coincidence to work for you,' David replied. He watched the interviewer grapple with this concept and then give up. He was ready for the next question when it came.

'What does that mean?' Angus Petrie asked.

'It means that if there's a possibility that something can happen, however remote, then there's a probability that it can be made to happen. There's a law of coincidence or synchronicity, just as there's a law of gravity or relativity. If you know how it works, then you can make it work for you.'

'How?'

David smiled. 'What does $E = MC^2$ mean?' he replied. 'I mean, even if we had the time to explain it, people still wouldn't have the faintest idea what we were talking about.'

'So it's like a mathematical equation?'

'It's a law of nature. In fact it's an integral law of nature. There wouldn't be life without it.'

'Surely that's straying into theological territory?'

'Of course it is,' David replied. 'A large part of any religion is to do with explaining the inexplicable, or at least attributing to it a greater power than humanity. The moment you start to find physical laws for the mysteries of the universe, you find yourself treading on the toes of religion. Remember Galileo, or Darwin.'

'So does this all constitute a science, or a separate philosophy or' – he paused theatrically – 'or is it just a new form of apostasy?'

'A very old form of apostasy indeed,' David replied acidly.

'So it is a distinct creed?'

'If you like.'

'So what, would you say, is *your* creed?'

The camera remained on David. He ran his tongue over his lower lip, his eyes narrowing momentarily as he thought. Then he made a slight shrugging motion with the corners of his mouth and began.

'I believe in Mother Earth,' he said. 'I believe that humankind is a product of the earth – Dé Doveleski to the gypsies – and not that the earth was created to accommodate mankind. I can't, I'm afraid, put my faith in any god which places mankind above the rest of creation. We're a bizarre freak of nature – an animal capable of rational thought and of having emotions – but that doesn't set us aside from nature, it just makes us a peculiar part of it.' He paused for a second.

'Also,' he went on, 'the god I believe in isn't sentient; she doesn't have the capacity to get up one morning and say, "Oh, I think I'll create a new animal today." She just *is*. She's completely arbitrary, as responsible for fluffy kittens as she is for a volcano erupting. You can't pray to her; it'd be like praying to the wind, or the sea; and the idea of having faith in her is meaningless, because you don't need to have faith in the planet

263

you're standing on.' He paused for breath again, this time giving himself a little more time for his mind to catch up, before continuing.

'What I believe,' he said, 'is that the moment humankind got to the point when it was able to destroy the entire planet, nothing else was as important as the enormous responsibility we suddenly shouldered not to do so. Conflicting politics, or opinions, or even religious beliefs became utterly irrelevant at that point, because if we screw up the planet now, there won't *be* any politics or religion left. If we go on as we are going now the last thing we'll know before we cease to exist will be that whether we were Christians or Hindus, capitalists or communists, men or women, creation died with us. We have to learn to live with each other and to cooperate, or sooner or later we'll find a way of destroying ourselves and everything else with us.

'Think of that,' he said, 'it'd be like a single ice-cube freezing an entire ocean, or a lone ant conquering all of civilization. It's preposterous to think we even have the right to fight with each other, when we're teetering on the brink of Armageddon. And yet here we are, looking into the most uncertain future in the history of this planet, bickering about trivialities and sending polite little delegations to the Amazon so that they can come home and write deliberately equivocal reports for uninterested governments.'

The entire atmosphere in the studio altered after that. What had been a verbal duel now became a proper discussion. Both Rosie and Christina felt each other relax and turned to each other, smiling with quiet relief.

It became so chummy, in fact, by the end that the interviewer inveigled Christina across for the last five minutes, and she transfixed everyone while David sat back and watched, his eyes smiling.

When it was over everyone in the studio clapped, and clustered around them to congratulate them. Rosie held back and observed the adoring male faces fastened on Christina. They were all so mesmerized by her that they hardly noticed the real star of the last half-hour breaking free of them and walking across to Rosie. They hugged each other and she felt the fatigue shuddering inside him.

'You did great,' she said.

'Will it stand as a suitable epitaph?' he asked.

Rosie could not answer.

They wormed their way out of some reception, or dinner, after the interview and sneaked away, just the three of them. Christina was in a peculiar mood, enthusiastic and lively in a somewhat forced way, as if trying to pull David up with her own last precious droplets of adrenalin. She made it a fun evening, but there was an air of finality about it.

Christina had made a passionate speech on behalf of chicken korma, poppadoms and nan bread, so they hunted out an Indian restaurant on the Lothian Road and had the closest thing to a normal evening any of them had had in the last six months. Constantly buoyed up by Christina's infectious determination not to be depressed they had a long, pleasant and slightly drunken dinner, then moved on to a pub where they sat, drinking and talking, deep into the night.

They staggered home to the flat at three o'clock in the morning, singing snatches of nationalist songs in strong Edinburgh accents, hooting with laughter, then shushing each other noisily. When they got home Rosie solemnly handed out some Valium she had found in Kelvin's bedroom, where she was forced to sleep now that David and Christina had appropriated the double bed. Then they all went to bed. Ten minutes later, Rosie moved upstairs, dragging her duvet behind her, and crashed out on the sofa. Nothing could exorcise the memory of Kelvin from that bedroom.

9

NIGHT

And at the end it was simple again.

Long before the responsibilities and the prophecies and the tragedies reared their gorgon heads, Craigairie had been a thing of peace; an idyll David and Christina had built for themselves around the stone. Somewhere along the line they had lost control of their destinies and had been left to ride the tornado of events which swept into their lives, as best they could. But before that, before fate uprooted them and hurled them into their brief, extraordinary ministry; before layers of responsibility encroached into their lives, they had been just the waterbabies; brown and sleek and in love in their little private paradise.

As they headed for home that final time they shed their worries one by one, and it was as if a great weight had been lifted off them. Some of the old joyousness returned as they consciously played out their last scene with each other. There had always been something knowing, almost theatrical, in their behaviour. Latterly it had become a weapon for them, a way of getting people to notice them and to keep noticing them. It was more pointed after Orkney and Annie Moffat, but it had been a part of their lives since they first met.

When Rose first came across them, a year back, she had written in her diary 'in a great romance, each person plays the part that the other most wants to see – D and C have it down to a fine art.' They didn't need an audience. They were so enraptured by each other that spectators were not necessary – although they enjoyed showing each other off every now and again.

Now they were free again, for a short time. Kelvin was dead, all the others but Rosie had dispersed and the Nymatili had done what they were meant to do, or what they thought they were meant to do. They had no more obligations or responsibilities and, without those shackles, they regained some of their old wild fire.

Their progress west from Edinburgh to Craigairie was slow and erratic. They went down to the Borders first, because the weather was beautiful and David wanted to stand on Scott's View, above a bend in the Tweed, and look out towards the Eildon Hills one last time. It was worth the diversion.

Standing up there on a warm summer evening, with larks twittering incessantly all around them, looking out over that majestic view, like a living oil-painting stretched out in front of them – was like coming to an oasis after months in the desert. The thick silver gash of the river Tweed curved gracefully around them, with cool, dark pine forests massed in its elegant loops. Beyond them, three or four miles away, the triple-headed Eildons rose high out of the lush green countryside; blue-green against the azure sky. It was a view unlike any other in Scotland; not bleak and jagged like the Highlands, nor half-tamed moors like the south-west, but equally impressive in its still, silent grandeur.

They sat up on Scott's View until long after the sun had set, drinking beer, smoking the last of Kelvin's hash and occasionally, on David's insistence, playing foolish but amusing games on the steep hillside. They seemed to have put their past behind them and, for one wonderful evening, Rosie allowed herself to believe that this was perhaps the beginning of a new future. They had slept off the exhaustion of the previous night and had left all their worries behind in Edinburgh and were now almost carefree. It was the sort of evening one remembers for ever, not because it was their last, or because anything particularly memorable went on, but because it was a moment of peace and beauty in an otherwise harrowing time.

After they left Scott's View they went down off the hill to Dryburgh Abbey; a solitary, still place on the banks of the Tweed in which the handsome ruins of a medieval monastery stand amongst the green fields and old, wide trees. It is a timeless place where history stopped when the monks dispersed, leaving only their ghosts behind; not evil or frightening, just there, in their rightful place. David said that he could not even distinguish the ruins which remained from the images he was seeing through his mind's eye. He stood in what had been the nave of the church and described the heavy oaken ceiling, and the stone altar with a large, rough-hewn cross hanging behind it. To him it was just as it had once been, but to Rosie the altar was a rectangle of rock, like a flagstone, in the grass and the roof was nothing but the black boughs of trees and the star-flecked sky.

They made a fire on the bank of the river, with the water sliding softly past them, and spent the short night under the stars. When Rosie awoke they were not there, which sent her into an immediate panic. She woke up in a couple of seconds and leapt up, scouring the riverbank. Then she climbed up the bank and looked up the field towards the abbey. A thick white mist lay like dry ice on the ground in the muted light before dawn.

There was a deep, profound hush, accentuated rather than broken by the low murmur of fast-flowing water. Nothing was moving, nothing disturbed the serenity of the beautiful, silent scene. It was only after a couple of minutes, when her eyes had become accustomed to the light, that Rosie saw two figures moving slowly through the ruins of the abbey a quarter of a mile away. As she watched they stopped and came together, their two small forms merging into one.

She watched for a few minutes before she noticed a feeling akin to shame creeping up on her.

She turned away from them and walked back down to the riverbank. Passing the last orange embers of their fire she continued until she was right at the water's edge. She gazed at the river for a minute, then slowly stripped naked, contemplating the inky water all the while. Then she waded in, until the current washed up over her right hip-bone, splashing icy droplets across her breasts. She stood for a moment, holding her arms over her head until the bottom half of her body began to mistake the clean, regular wash of cold around her for warmth. Then, with an elegant, flipping dive she launched herself into the dark depths, relaxing so that the river could take her where it wished. She could think of no good reason for struggling or trying to fight against the inexorable current, so she just drifted steadily downstream until the currents deposited her in a thicket of brittle-spined bulrushes. She waded out and walked a mile and a half back to Dryburgh, with the mist slowly evaporating in the first rays of the morning sun. At first she could not see her feet beneath it, but soon it was only wisps around her ankles, then it was gone. Beneath it a delicate carpet of minutely interwoven cobwebs began to reveal itself. It stretched in all directions, woven between every adjacent blade of grass for acres all around her, beaded with millions of tiny, pearl-like droplets of dew. Rosie knew that it doubtless had sinister intent, but it seemed to her that the countless spiders which had woven it had gone out of their way to make it aesthetically pleasing. She waded through the grass, leaving two straight, dark lines behind her.

The dawn smelled wonderful as well. It was a subtle smell, clean and pure but hardly registering on her sinuses. It was the smell of a meadow waking; dew-wet grass, damp earth, a hint of distant pine trees. It poured into her sinuses and seemed to leak back into her brain swamping all of the dust and cobwebs inside, washing it clean. There was not a hint of pollution, of mankind; it was not something that could be bottled, and yet it was as clear and refreshing as anything Rosie had ever smelled.

By the time she reached the spot from which she had started her mini-odyssey she felt ready for anything. She did not realize, as she was swimming or walking, that she was not worrying about David, Christina, Kelvin, Meg, Emily, Craigairie; the lot. But when she returned and found David and Christina chatting beside the re-awoken fire, it struck her and her heart leapt in her chest, rejoicing to have been allowed such a release, if only for a couple of hours.

They greeted this naked, Pre-Raphaelite apparition coming up to them through the meadow with quiet smiles, then continued their conversation as she dressed again.

They, too, had caught the magic of the morning. They had, it seemed, had a glorious time freaking out an insomniac guest from the hotel close to the abbey, who was taking a dawn walk in the park. He had been treated to the amazing and no doubt disturbing sight of what appeared to be two full-grown wolves copulating on the lawn of the hotel. Later in his walk a small dollop of mist had risen up from the ground and coagulated into a little cloud which followed him around, drizzling on him. Finally he had walked into a six-hundred-year-old matins in the abbey, complete with monks, incense, harmonic singing and an intact monastery where yesterday there had been a ruin.

Their sense of mischief was only equalled by their limitless power and imagination in putting it into action. The raincloud over the poor man's head was very much one of Christina's tricks. It was silly and surreal, much less overtly disturbing than David's phantom matins.

A little later they set off westwards, following the silver line of the Tweed up out of the Merse into the empty hills of Ettrick. The warm sun rose behind them as they fled west, high over the tortuous valleys and the worn stumps of old mountains. For Rosie, who had never before travelled half this distance under the influence of the Abra-Melin spell, the experience of being a bird was unnerving, exhausting and fantastically exhilarating, at the same time. Over short distances it was possible to do it without being conscious of what it was like. The sensations were so utterly alien that it took some time before one could begin to comprehend what it felt like to be a bird, to fly.

Over the longer distances, however, the initial discomfort of the shape-shift; of being a human mind trying to accept imprisonment in the body of a bird, receded as instinct took over. It was, first and foremost, a feeling of glorious lightness and freedom to stretch one's wings and take to the air. It took a while to come to terms with the immense speed and sensual magnification of bird-dom. To fly as a big hawk or falcon was to be living life at an astonishing pace; the sort of pace and instantaneous judgement which allows a falcon to fly flat out through a wood without ever worrying about colliding with a tree. Everything was enormously magnified; sound and sight particularly. You could see for miles, picking out minute details at a distance no human eye could even contemplate.

David led them west and south following the Tweed valley almost to its source and then detouring south into Liddesdale, some of the bleakest, most desolate hills in Scotland. He brought them, finally, to an open space deep in the hills which managed to feel evil and gloomy even in the warm sunlight of a summer afternoon. Unspeakable violence had happened here; murder and rape and fire in the night. The fear lingered like a bitter smell, centred on the squatting bulk of one of the most brutally functional fortresses either Christina or Rosie had ever seen.

'The Hermitage,' David explained. 'My reiver ancestors used to do their stuff from here.'

'Must've been a merry bunch,' Christina muttered. She looked around her with amused distaste. 'So this is the place you chose?' she said. 'Has anyone ever told you you're perverse?'

'You have,' he replied blithely. 'Frequently. Don't you like my choice? I thought it was suitably . . .' He searched for the right word. 'Gothic?'

'For what?' Rosie demanded. 'What is all this stuff about choices?'

'Date, honey,' Christina replied.

Rosie thought for a minute. Realization dawned in her face.

'Midsummer's Eve,' she said.

'The summer solstice,' David murmured distantly, gazing at the fortress. 'I think it needs some thunder and lightning, don't you?' he asked Christina. 'Sort of sharpen things up.'

Christina looked back at him, smiling slightly. 'You're way over the top, my darling,' she said. 'But yes, if you're thinking melodrama, a bit of noise and light wouldn't go amiss. It'd amuse the gypsies, no doubt.'

'The gypsies?' Rosie inquired.

'Didn't we tell you?' David replied casually, looking at the castle. 'We're having a farewell party.'

Rosie had somehow been able to sideline the knowledge that they were going to die during the last few traumatic weeks. There had been so much else to think about and she had convinced herself that she would face that problem when she came to it, or it came to her. There had never been a doubt that it would happen and the savage suddenness of Kelvin's death had served as a brutal reminder that when David or Christina made a concrete prediction, they were not just talking for the hell of it. But there had always been an element of open-endedness to the prediction, as if they would go when they chose and not before.

And if Rosie had needed further reminders of their imminent demise their behaviour in the past couple of days should have provided more than enough proof. There had been a wistful poignancy behind everything they did, as if they suddenly realized how little time they had left to enjoy life.

It was not until that afternoon at the Hermitage, however, that she read the signs and knew that they were staging their swan-song, that they did not expect to see another day after this one. It was hard to explain quite what it was about their behaviour which betrayed them. They were still smiling and laughing and in good spirits, as they had been in the morning, but there was something exaggerated about them, almost as if they were doing everything in slow motion.

The day seemed endless, not dragging by tediously, but passing with a sort of serene, stately slowness, like a royal procession. David and

Christina behaved as if every minute was precious, concentrating all of their remaining energy into appreciating and loving the minutest details of the world around them. David spent much of the afternoon getting stoned with a bunch of young gypsies from the Barrhill Atchin-tan, making them laugh and putting them in a mood in which they could do the same for him. They talked about the 'old times', the little things which had passed unnoticed in the shadow of much bigger events; the Pinwherry hex; the riot when health inspectors threatened to close the Atchin-tan; the time when the Barrhill minister had stumbled upon a midnight tryst at a standing stone out by Colmonell and had tried to break it up, thus bringing upon himself the mischievous side of Craigairie and the anger of his parishioners, most of whom had been at the stone that night.

Christina, meanwhile, spent over an hour wandering back and forth through a field of thick, ankle-deep clover; meandering around dreamily, occasionally stooping to pick out a bog reed to chew, or a knife-blade of grass on which she blew long, raw whistles, like the cry of distress of some weird, prehistoric bird.

Rosie watched for a while, enraptured by her, and slowly it dawned on her that every movement, however abstract, seemed to have been calculated and finely judged for a maximum effect, almost as if they had been choreographed. She was creating a slow, mesmerizing dance, a sort of living hymn of thanks to the earth; graceful and ethereal and dream-like. She was loving every moment of it, every cool, damp barefoot step which bruised down the soft clover. Nothing could have distracted her from her total enjoyment, nothing could have broken her flow.

But all the time she knew that people would watch, were watching and that they were more likely to remember her as she was that day, that afternoon, than any other. Today the Nymatili were to belong to their closest, most ardent followers and were dedicating their memory specifically to them alone.

Rosie had suspected that something odd was up when she heard mention of the gypsies, but she was not remotely prepared for the scale and composition of the crowd which gathered throughout the afternoon. It was not that it was a particularly enormous congregation of people by Craigairie's standards; somewhere between twelve and fifteen thousand people was well within their range. But it was unlike any of the many, big and small, Rosie had ever seen. The Romany kyle-yaks, the wise-women and elders, were there, as were the younger gypsies who had always assumed responsibility for the physical well-being of the Mother Coven. But the mass of Craigairie's gypsy following had not come.

The real bulk of the crowd consisted of the massed covens of South Ayrshire, Galloway, Dumfriesshire, Ettrick, the Borders and Northern England. It had always been rumoured that five hundred covens had come out of the woodwork to pay homage to the new Nymatili at

Craigairie on the night of Hallowe'en. Personally, Rosie had doubted it, but she considerably underestimated just how deep Craigairie had cut into the fractured society which surrounded it. Every parish from Eyemouth to Withorn, Lindisfarne to the outskirts of Glasgow, seemed to have sent at least a representative of an established coven. Many of the covens, particularly the ones from the south-west, where Craigairie had always been strongest, came en masse.

There were a staggering number of them. Rosie was awed by the totality of Craigairie's effect; it transcended social barriers; comprising old and young, men and women, doctors, schoolteachers, gentry, farmers, smallholders, housewives, Catholics, Protestants, everyone. There was something almost masonic in the way it had infiltrated every corner of society. These, Rosie knew, were the fifth column, the secret army the Nymatili had mustered and would leave to carry the word after they had gone.

Then, finally, she knew it was over.

The thunderstorm, when it came, added to the unavoidable tension considerably. For most of the afternoon and early evening it had been clear and beautiful, but as night drew gradually in the distance, echoing thunder began to grumble across the still, silent hills, grinding its way inland from the Solway valley by valley. By the middle of the evening silver flashes were flickering in the distance, behind Arnton and Saughtree Fells, the thunder following on behind thirty or forty seconds later. A thick, heavy thunderclap mushroomed miles up into the evening sky, creeping across the stars like a vast inkblot. It became very dark and murky, the air thickening and beginning to sweat as the stifling lid closed in on the landscape. The bonfires the gypsies had built and lit, hitherto great roaring infernos of heat and light, now seemed to die down sullenly, cowed by the heavy, thick air.

Words fell dead from one's lip, conversations faltered and dried up, movement became an effort and even breathing became difficult and uncomfortable, like trying to force porridge through a sieve. The crowds waited, sitting around the base of the castle, each coven hardly aware of all the others as they awaited their last chance to meet the Nymatili.

Until it began to get dark David and Christina had been with Rosie, wandering around outside the castle. But when the storm closed in, they retreated into the interior of the fortress, on the unspoken understanding that they did not mind meeting representatives of each coven in small, manageable groups, but they could not cope with all fifteen thousand of the waiting people. As the only entrance into the shelled-out interior of the castle was through a low postern door, a sort of order was imposed on those who were elected to represent each coven and Romany family. With several young gypsies acting as bouncers on the door a long queue formed which was let inside in groups of between five and ten. Once inside, they had five or ten minutes with the Nymatili, like final consultations, before coming out again.

The implication on David and Christina's part seemed to be that they were trying to do this as efficiently as possible. They had no more time to waste on enchanting a mass of people with the sort of seductive glamour they had splashed around at Brogar on Walpurgis Night, nor indeed for the coy teasing which had characterized their relationship with the public as a whole. This was the last business they had to clear up before they finally let go.

It was, in an odd way, the first time Rosie had ever seen them unquestioningly accept their status. They were not David Armstrong and Christina MacRuarie, with normal needs and longings and distinct personalities; they were the Nymatili, here to meet the subtle jihad they had unleashed, one last time, before they left it to run its own course.

Rosie did not know what was being said to the slow filter of people going in and out of that small door, but she saw the looks on their faces as they came out, and knew that David and Christina were working their magic to the last. The faithful went in apprehensive and blunted by the oppressive atmosphere and emerged thoughtful and calm, some of them even smiling to themselves as they hurried back to their covens. When asked by clusters of people who gravitated towards them what had been said, most of them just shook their heads and shrugged. Some, however, paused for long enough to attempt an explanation. None said anything Rosie had not heard a hundred times before, until she was sick of the sound of it.

She did not want to know. She felt, suddenly, bitter and angry and miserable. It expanded in her chest like a pall, until she could hardly breathe without the first of many sobs using the opportunity to bubble up and break free. She did not want to hear their spiel to these people. She wanted them to be there, with her, telling her what the hell she was supposed to do with her life after they had gone. One way or another everything she had to give had been given to them. She had allowed them to sap away her strength and resilience until there was nothing but a dribble left, with precious little in return but their love. She had held on through thick and thin. Through Orkney and Glastonbury, to the disaster on Arthur's Seat and Kelvin's subsequent death. And she was still there, when all the others had faded away, with them to the bitter end.

And they were giving pep talks to hick witches and to the gypsies who had caused most of their problems.

It hurt deep inside Rosie. She felt both used and betrayed and she hated herself for feeling that way. She was disgusted with herself for being jealous and possessive enough to think that she deserved them more than anyone else, but nothing could make her stop thinking it. They had never wanted to be this double-headed messiah, it had been thrust upon them when all they wanted was to be left alone with each other. And here they were, accepting a responsibility for which they had never asked when they had all the justification in the world to be eking out their last few hours together, in private.

She resented them for it. She hated them for leaving her, for ever drawing her to Craigairie, for telling her what and how their end was to be, for making her trust them. The prospect of adjusting to life without them was so horrifically bleak that it made her mind reel just to think of it.

All the time this despair was building inside her the storm was rumbling closer. Now, when the bruised clouds spat white fire down at the earth it came in jagged prongs of lightning, caressing the hilltops with skeletal fingers, followed by long booms of thunder. It was pitch dark and the searing light leapt across the brooding landscape like the flash of a camera in a dark room, for a split second illuminating everything in negative, all shining silver and monstrous shadow, before darkness gulped it away again.

Rosie had been wandering around in a private storm of bitter despair until this point, but the nearness of the real storm shook her free of it at about eleven o'clock. She realized that, whatever David and Christina intended to do, the thunderstorm looked destined to hit a peak around midnight; another of David's touches. And if that was the case, tying into the endless, intricate little knots of imagery with which the Nymatili were wont to surround themselves, it suggested a sort of finale when the storm hit base. They would not hang around after that.

With a sudden panic which swallowed up her fury she began to hurry through the sullen crowds towards the black lump of the castle. She went the entire way around the base before realizing that she had missed the small door. She had expected the queue to be protruding from the side of the castle, indicating the way in, but it was no longer there. At this point Rosie began to lose control of herself, her composure finally cracking up after the immense pressure of the long day. She sprinted back around the castle, weeping as she ran, until she found the door, still guarded by four or five gypsies. She ran up to them in a terrible state and sobbed, 'Are they still in there?' When they nodded she rushed on, ducking through the door into the dark interior.

She stopped.

Inside the black shell of the castle it was like a huge, stone cauldron, densely hot, the air evaporating under the leaden lid of the clouds above. Rosie could not see a foot in front of her face and was gripped by a sudden, irrational terror which sang up and down her spine. She began, very slowly, to pick her way over the rubble-strewn ground and called out, 'Izzy?' It did not echo at all, it hardly even had the power to fill the air around her. At that moment a flash of lightning filled the castle with light, illuminating the ruined interior like a set from a horror movie, only a lot more frightening. Rosie was recovering from this when a figure loomed up right beside her, causing her to shriek and retreat rapidly.

'It's all right,' David's voice said. 'It's me.' He went over and took her hand, squeezing it to calm her uncontrollable shivering.

'Where're we going?' she asked as he began to lead her to one side of the castle. 'Where's Christina?'

'On top,' he replied.

It was a long way from the ground to the battlements and it twice entailed having to scale ladders lashed to scaffolding on the inside of the building. Rosie was unashamedly glad that it was too dark to see what, if anything, was beneath her. Even this slight reassurance was abruptly denied her by another flash of lightning, which revealed that there was something to break her fall if she slipped, but it was a hell of a long way down.

Finally they reached the top, where the air was marginally clearer and less murky, and walked along a narrow catwalk which ran along the inside of the battlements to the front of the castle. Christina was sitting in a crenellation, gazing out over the crowds, westwards towards the hills. As they arrived, a three-pronged fork of lightning stabbed down on to the summit of Saughtree Fell, only a couple of miles away. The thunder which immediately followed it began with a crackling roar, notably louder than anything before it, then tailed off in a long, uneasy rumble, fading then growing, then fading again.

The three of them waited until it died away, then for a while longer before Rosie said,

'This is it, isn't it?'

They both nodded. She looked from one to the other, then hung her head. Christina stood up and went to her, enveloping her in a tight hug. After a couple of minutes Rosie broke away, sniffed wetly and shook her head.

'What am I going to do without you?' she asked, her voice cracking.

'Live for me,' Christina replied. 'Remember us. Don't mourn for us, we went willingly.'

'Is that what you told them?' Rosie demanded, jabbing her finger towards the people down below.

'We told them what they had to hear,' David said distantly.

'So what do I get?' Rosie inquired miserably. 'What's going to console me? I'm going to wake up tomorrow morning without you. Don't you know what that means?'

'It means we're dead and you're still alive,' David said. 'I can't tell you it's any easier than that.'

Christina was about to add to this but a thunderclap interrupted her. She waited, but when it began to fade away it was David who spoke first.

'This is all we have left.' He waved his arm vaguely towards the hills. 'One thunderstorm and a few more drops of adrenalin. We're done here, we're tired out; it's over. We were never going to live for ever, we accept that. We always have accepted it. It's our fate.'

'You *never* accepted it,' Rosie retorted bitterly. 'You always said it was an antiquated fucking prophecy which had nothing whatsoever to do with you. How can you tell me you accept your fate as Nymatili when you've always denied it has anything to do with you?'

'Because it's true, I'm afraid,' David said.

'Impending death gives one such a marvellously uncluttered perspective,' Christina added. She sighed and settled back on to the battlement. 'Almost everyone who remembers us after tonight will remember a myth of us, not the real people behind it. To them we're the Nymatili and after we go the myth will be all there is of us. It'll grow until there's nothing left of us in it but our names. Your curse was that you were the only friend we had at the very end; you get to remember two small people behind a sort of legend. I'm sorry, Rosie my darling, but it had to be this way. It was.'

Rosie stared at her and shook her head. She turned to David.

'What about you, ice-man?' she demanded bitterly. 'I never thought I'd see you give up so meekly.'

'Who's meek?' David said. 'I'm the brutal realist, remember. I'm just being brutally realistic.'

For some reason it was David's unwavering irony, more than anything else, that broke Rosie's self-pity. They were teetering on the brink of oblivion and still they were who they always had been. They had to say goodbye to her, which must have been dreadful for them, especially for Christina, but they were doing it with such calm dignity that she had spent her misery on them, when all they must have wanted was her love. She relented and stepped over to Christina, pulling her cousin to her feet and hugging her, then pulling David in as well. They remained like that for some time, the three of them on top of the old fortress, with the storm flashing and roaring all around them. Then Rosie stepped back, let out a long sigh and smiled wanly.

'So what now?' she asked. 'Will I see you again? Where do Nymatili go when they die? I mean, should I say *au revoir* or farewell?'

'*Ciao*,' David said laconically. 'I just hope the Christians aren't right. We're going to look fucking silly explaining all this to St Peter.'

Rosie smiled, but there were tears welling up in her eyes. She retreated a step and looked at her cousin.

'We'll meet again, my love,' Christina murmured. '*Après moi le déluge*, I'll be waiting for you.'

She went to Rosie and kissed her. Rosie stepped back, tears pouring down her cheeks.

'Will you come down?' she asked. She laughed quickly. 'I mean, you might get struck by lightning up here, or something.'

They both smiled.

'We'll be done up here in a minute,' David said. For a split second it occurred to Rosie that this was not an answer to the question she had asked. She looked at them for a moment then, with a quick nod, turned and began to walk away. She had gone about ten yards when Christina's voice followed her.

'Rosie?'

She stopped and half turned. 'Yeah?'

There was a short pause.

'Remember me to the dawn.'

When they did not follow her she assumed that they intended to stage their curtain call up there, on the battlements. The storm was grinding ever closer and Rosie was not the only person to be expecting a climax of some sort at the stroke of midnight. It fitted into David's relentless melodramatic imagery – the nearing storm, the expectation of something frightening and dangerous.

It seemed to take hours for the last few minutes before midnight to pass. The noise was deafening, the jagged shards of light were caressing the trees just down the valley, then the cottage only a hundred yards from the castle. The atmosphere was crushing.

Then it exploded; a shattering roar of thunder, an avalanche of sound accompanied by three different branches of lightning, all converging on one single conductor, high up over the battlements.

At that point the skies opened.

It rained.

Spontaneous, torrential, drumming rain. It drenched everything instantly, turned the ground into a slippery mire in a matter of minutes and glutted the small stream. Rosie had never seen rain like this outside India. She stood, arms outstretched, and let it pour on her. It was so deliciously refreshing that she stood there for almost ten minutes, forgetting everything, allowing it to massage her head and face and shoulders.

The thought that shook her out of it came from nowhere, unannounced. She said it out loud as it entered her mind. 'They weren't there,' she said. 'Shit, you stupid bitch, they weren't there.' What with the crescendo of the storm and the explosion of rain she had somehow contrived to miss the fact that Christina and David had not featured in the climax of the storm.

'Craigairie,' she said, her heart sinking with realization.

Of course they would return to Craigairie at the end, not to some godforsaken haunted castle in the middle of nowhere.

They had gone home to Craigairie and they had a fifteen minute start on her. They were also a lot quicker.

Rosie had been racing against the impending dawn, trying to reach Craigairie before the sun cleared the hills.

She lost the race by minutes.

Their clothes were by the river, which got her momentarily excited. She picked her way through the reed-beds, with the delicious smells of the world wakening after a storm singing in her head. She fully expected them to be in the deep pool, playing amongst the water-lilies, the eternal youths.

They were not there.

Rosie waded across the Tarf and walked slowly up to the stone. They were not there either, but a fire had filled the bowl around the stone recently, charring the grass down to the dark earth. Some tufts of peat still smouldered dimly. Rosie remembered a dim red glow on the horizon in front of her some time before the sun had risen. At the time she had thought it was a trick of the light.

She walked back across the valley, to the cottage. As she climbed the wall into the garden Shuduch the fox got up from the front doorstep and slunk away around the corner of the house, his tail fastened along the ridge of his belly. Rosie went through the open door, glanced into the sitting room and went up the stairs.

Their bedroom was empty. Rosie stood by the window for a while, and stared out over her past, her face blank, expressionless.

Then she went through to her room, opened the curtains and found the notes on her bed. She sat down slowly and opened them. The first was from David.

'Do you want me to finish Kelvin's story for you?' it said.

> And at the end it went full circle, back to the point where it had just been them, the stone and Craigairie. They only had a short time, but they lived another lifetime before the sun rose on the twenty-second of June.
>
> Thou art flame from the hand of god; fierce and pure and brief. All thou touchest burns with thy fire and is consumed.
> We burn tonight
> Yours in perpetual melodrama,
> With all the love and thanks I have left,
> David

Underneath, Christina had written, in her beautiful, calligraphic hand:

> Farewell, Rosie my love.
> Sorry it had to be so abrupt. Be strong. Some day you might learn to remember the good bits.
> Two thoughts to cogitate upon, which might or might not help.

> 'What is life? It is the flash of a firefly in the night, the breath of a buffalo in winter. It is the little shadow which runs across the prairie and is lost in the sunset.' – Crowfoot, Chief of the Blackfoot Indians
> 'To die will be an awfully big adventure.' – Peter Pan

The Goddess be with you always.

I love you,
Christina
P.S. The picture's my last and best, though I say it myself.

It was.

It came with the note, on the back of a sheet of Dryburgh Arms letter paper. Although she had used only a pencil she had managed to create a delicate masterpiece of the ruined abbey as seen from the river, across the park, on that last dawn. Two figures were walking out of the picture, hand in hand, only half an inch high but ummistakably David and Christina.

With shades of black and grey she had managed to convey all the fresh, open expectancy of that new day. She had captured it for ever.

Rosie gazed at it for an age, then hugged it over her heart, rocking back and forth in silence.

She had nothing left to give. She sat, staring emptily in front of her, out through the window to the new summer morning outside, clutching the last remnants of David and Christina to her chest. After a long, long time she succeeded in articulating the words which had risen from a lone cry deep in her subconscious to a massive shout, like a hundred thousand voices, filling her mind to bursting point and drowning all else.

'They've gone,' she said.